Sometimes trust is th

Sophie Shaw is days away from signing a contract that will fulfill her dream of owning a vineyard. For her, it's a chance to restart her life and put past tragedies to rest. But Duncan Jamieson's counter offer blows hers out to sea.

Duncan still finds Sophie as appealing as he had during boyhood vacations to the lake. Older and wiser now, he has his own reasons for wanting the land. His offer, however, hinges on a zoning change approval.

Bribery rumors threaten the deal and make Sophie wary of Duncan, yet she cannot deny his appeal. When her journalistic research uncovers a Jamieson family secret, trust becomes the hardest lesson for them both.

Books by Sharon Struth

Blue Moon Lake Series
Share the Moon
Harvest Moon
Twelve Nights
Bella Luna

Published by Kensington Publishing Corporation

Share the Moon

A Blue Moon Lake Novel

Sharon Struth

LYRICAL PRESS
Kensington Publishing Corp.
www.kensingtonbooks.com

Dec. 2015
Dear Judy,
Let the moon be
your guide...
merry christmas!
Sharon

Lyrical Press books are published by
Kensington Publishing Corp. 119 West 40th Street New York, NY 10018

First Electronic Edition: August 2014
eISBN-13: 978-1-61650-563-9
eISBN-10: 1-61650-563-X

First Print Edition: August 2014
ISBN-13: 978-1-61650-588-2
ISBN-10: 1-61650-588-5

Printed in the United States of America

Dedicated to my mother, Joyce Shafer, for your support, enthusiasm, and love.

Acknowledgements

I once read a quote that stated, "gratitude is the best attitude," and my writer's journey is filled with appreciation to so many people. First, thank you to my agent, Dawn Dowdle of the Blue Ridge Literary Agency, who has made my writing dreams come true. These dreams didn't even exist until Linda Chiara started me on a writer's journey with her encouragement and teachings. For that, and Linda's input to Share the Moon, I offer my eternal thanks. None of this would be possible without the support and love of my sweet husband, Bill, who I thank for everything…including his insights about fly-fishing to aid in research for this book.

Special thanks to Lyrical Press (Kensington) and Renee Rocco for believing in my book, and my fabulous editor, Paige Christian, who put the finishing shine on my work. A special shout of appreciation to my friend Lisa Buccino for test reading early drafts of this story and to Matthew Knickerbocker, Bethel, CT's First Selectman for helping me understand the public hearing process used in this story.

Last—but definitely not least—I want to thank the members of my local RWA Chapter (CoLoNY) for their support and friendship. Writing is a lonely job, but with them I never feel alone.

Chapter 1

New Moon: When the moon, positioned between the earth and sun, nearly disappears, leaving only darkness.

November

The sabotaged kayaks beckoned. Sophie Shaw trod a thin layer of ice pellets on the lawn as she headed to the lake's edge, where eight boats waited to be returned to the storage rack. The fickle New England weather had offered sleet-dropping clouds an hour earlier. Now, a wink from the sun reflected against Blue Moon Lake.

She dragged the first boat up a small incline, annoyed some bored teenagers had considered destruction of property entertainment. Growing up she and her friends had respected the local businesses.

A UPS truck screeched to a stop in front of a row of shops on Main Street. The driver hopped out and ran into Annabelle's Antiques with a box tucked under his arm. Sophie glanced both ways along the road for signs of Matt, whose new driver's license and clunker car played to every mother's fears. Fifteen minutes earlier, she'd texted him for help with the boat mess. He'd replied "k."

Sophie's flats glided along the slick lawn. She gripped the cord of a bright orange sea kayak and, using two hands, struggled backward up the slope. Her foot skidded. The heel of her shoe wobbled for security but instead, her toes lifted off the ground and flashed toward the clear sky. The burning skid of the cord ripped across her palms just as her other foot lifted and launched her airborne. *Thud!*

Air whooshed from her lungs. Pain coursed through her shoulder blades, neck, and spine. The ground's chilly dampness seeped into her cotton khaki pants, raising goose bumps on her skin. Seconds passed without breath before she managed to swallow a gulp.

Lying flat on her back, she stared at the cornflower blue sky and spotted a chalky slice of the moon. The night Henry died, a similar crescent had hung from the heavens, barely visible nestled among the glittering stars. She prepared for the scrape that threatened to tear the gouge of her scarred heart. Seven years. Seven painful years. She closed her eyes and after a few seconds, the weight of sadness lifted off her chest.

Tears gathered along her lower lashes. She pushed a strand of unruly long hair from her face. Footsteps crunched on the ice pellets and headed her way.

"Matthew Shaw…" Fury pooled in her jaw as she resisted the urge to yell at her son. "You'd better have a good excuse for taking so long."

A man with cinnamon hair, short on the sides with gentle waves on top, knelt at her side. She studied the strong outline of his cheeks and the slight bump on the bridge of his angular nose that gave him a rugged touch, but he wasn't familiar.

"Are you okay?" He searched her face.

The stranger hovered above. Tall treetops, clinging to the last of their earth-toned foliage, served as a backdrop to her view. A vertical crease separated his sandy brows. She couldn't pry herself from his vivid blue eyes, in part stunned from the fall, but also by her first responder.

For several long seconds she stared, and then mumbled, "I think so. Just a little shocked."

A whiff of his musk cologne revived her with the subtle charm of a southern preacher casting his congregation under his spell.

He frowned. "Does it hurt to move anything?"

"Sometimes it did before I fell."

The stranger's face softened and his lips curved upward. "A sense of humor, huh? That's a good sign."

"I suppose." His deep voice relaxed her like a cup of chamomile tea, the balanced and certain tone of his words easing her wounded spirit. Maybe this guy was a sign her rotten luck might change. "So, where's your white horse?"

"In the stable. Today I came in the white Camry." He motioned with a wave of his hand to a corner of the parking lot.

She pushed up on her elbow to look and a sharp pain jabbed her neck. "Ow!"

"Careful." His smile disappeared. "I was on my way over to help when you fell. You hit pretty hard."

The heat of embarrassment skittered up her cheeks. Not only had he witnessed her spastic aerobics, but she never played the distressed-damsel-on-the-dirty-ground card. A woman proficient at fly-fishing, who learned how to drive in a pickup truck and who, in her job as a journalist, had uncovered a corrupt politician, should be up and running by now.

"Go slow." His request suggested doling out orders came easy. "May I help?"

She nodded. He slipped a gentle hand into hers. The chill coating her skin melted against his warm touch. His well-groomed nails and thick fingers suggested he didn't work outdoors, rather the clean hands of a man who spent his days in an office. No wedding band either. He helped her sit and studied her as if a question perched on the edge of his thoughts.

"Can I call someone?" He blinked. "Your husband?"

"Oh, I'm not married." She caught the slight twitch of his mouth. "My son's supposed to be on his way to restack the boats."

Since her divorce from Mike, she'd concluded the available men in Northbridge were as predictable as the assortment at the dollar rental video store, filled with decade-old hits she'd seen so many times they held little interest. This man was a refreshing change.

"Ready to try to stand?" He took her by the elbow and she nodded.

Once on her feet, their hands remained together.

He glanced at them and let his drop. "You'll probably think this is crazy but—"

"Sophie?" The owner of Griswold's Café stood across the street and wiped his hands on a stained white apron. He'd placed the call to her father to alert them about the vandalism at Dad's boat shed. "You okay?"

"I'm fine." She waved. "Thanks."

She returned to the newcomer's gaze, as blue as the deep Caribbean Sea and as shiny as a starburst.

He raised his dirt-stained hands. "You might want to check yours."

Sure enough, her palms carried the same smudges from the impact of her fall. "Hold on. I have something to clean us off."

She trotted to her car, hoping the backside of her blazer covered any mess on the back of her pants.

After finding a package of wipes in the center console, she cleaned herself spotless and peeked in the rearview mirror. Her dark chocolate curls scattered with the freewill of a reckless perm. She neatened them with her fingertips then grabbed her cell and tried to call Matt but landed in his voice mail. The second she hung up, the phone rang. Bernadette's name showed on the display.

"Hey."

"Is your speech ready for tonight? You're our star speaker."

Bernadette always latched onto a crusade. The first was in third grade, a petition over the slaughter of baby seals for their skins. For tonight's public hearing, Bernadette had promised everyone the fight of her life. Her special interest group's concern about the large-scale development on Blue Moon Lake proposed by Resort Group International was a sore topic for many local residents, especially Sophie.

"Better find a new star speaker. There's a change of plans." Sophie readied herself for a negative reaction. "I'm covering the story for the paper now."

"You? Has Cliff lost his mind?"

"No. The other reporter can't do the assignment. Her father had a stroke earlier today. Cliff wanted to take the story himself, but I insisted he stick to his job as editor and let me do mine. I even made a five dollar bet I'd get a headline-worthy, bias-free quote from the company president."

"Do you think you can? I mean, RGI stole that land right out from under your nose. What was it…three days before signing the contract?"

Those were almost Cliff's exact words, along with some mumbling about how the paper's cheap new owner had cut his staff and he saw no other choice. "Two days."

"Honey, why would you want this story?"

"I have my reasons. This won't be the first time one of us needed to report on something close to us."

"Yeah, but wouldn't some public chastising against the corporate giant be good for your soul?"

"In a way." Sophie hesitated then decided to tell her best friend the truth. "Look, this is a chance to redeem myself. Prove to Cliff I really *can* stick to my journalist's creed after…well, you know, what happened with Ryan Malarkey."

"Mmm, forgot about him. He makes all us lawyers look bad." A long pause filled the air. "Guess that's a valid reason."

Sophie still harbored guilt from the last time a story got personal and she'd been fooled into violating her hallowed reporter vows. "Hey, on a lighter note, it's raining men over here at the lake."

Bernadette laughed. "What?"

"Some kids vandalized Dad's kayak shed. He asked for my help and this handsome guy appeared out of nowhere to help me. Fill you in later. He's waiting."

On her way back to the stranger, she studied his profile. Men this desirable didn't drop out of the sky around here. Why was he in town? Visitors to Northbridge weren't unusual in the summer, but not late fall.

He faced the water, looking in the direction of the rolling hillside of Tate Farm, the property under discussion at tonight's controversial public hearing.

She neared the visitor and he turned around.

"Are you the owner of this place?" He pointed to the wood-sided shed with a sign reading "Bullhead Boat Rentals."

"No. My father runs it with my brother. Dad's too old to be walking around in this icy mess and my brother is gone for the day." She handed him a wipe. "They also operate the local tackle shop and Two Rivers Guided Tours, guided fly-fishing trips."

"I remember the tackle shop." He cleaned his hands and tucked the dirty wipe in his jacket pocket. "My family came here for a couple of summers. Close to thirty years ago."

Sophie studied him again. Summer vacationers passed through here with the blur of a relay race.

He brushed a dead leaf off the knee of his faded, well-pressed jeans. "Such a great little town." He scanned the main street, unhurried and relaxed, then took a deep breath, as if to savor a nostalgic moment. "Quintessential New England."

Although she'd lived all her forty-four years in Northbridge, she looked around with him. A few cars parked on the road near a long row of pre-WWI buildings, now housing retailers who had serviced the town's residents for countless decades, such as Handyman Hardware and Walker's Drugs. The retail stretch was sandwiched between her favorite place to eat, Sunny Side Up, a metal-sided, trolley car-shaped diner and the weathered façade of Griswold's Café. The popular hangout for waterfront meals had a karaoke night the locals rarely missed.

She examined his profile again. Surely she hadn't forgotten someone with such a sexy full lower lip and strong chin?

"I can't imagine anybody being unhappy here," he said, his tone quiet.

She held in the urge to retort with a cynical remark. Every time she stuck a foot out of town, circumstances jerked her back. "Too bad you picked today to return. Most of our visitors enjoy the warmer weather."

"I'm house hunting."

"Oh. Well, we have a lot of summer residents."

"I want a year-round place."

The absent wedding ring held renewed interest. "Where are you from?"

"Manhattan."

She adjusted her crooked scarf. "Living here will be a big change."

"I know. I've always loved this place, though." He reached out and tenderly brushed a leaf off Sophie's shoulder. His gaze flowed down her body like a slow trickle of water.

An unexpected burn raced up her cheeks.

He lifted his brows. "Hey, I never knew the lake went by another name. The town website said the original name came from an old Native American word."

She nodded. "Puttacawmaumschuckmaug Lake." The long name rolled off her tongue with ease, the pronunciation a rite of passage for anyone born and raised around the body of water. "It either means 'at the large fishing place near the rock' or 'huge rock on the border.'"

"What?" He chuckled. "Puttamaum…"

She shook her head and repeated the difficult word.

"Puttacawsch—"

"Nope. It's a toughie. That's why a reporter who visited here at the turn of the century suggested in his column we change the name. He said the water's beauty was as rare as a blue moon, and the phrase stuck."

He grinned, easy and confident. "My kids will love this place."

Kids? Sophie buried her disappointment. "Are you and your wife looking at the other towns bordering the water?"

"No. I like Northbridge. Oh, and I'm not married," he said matter-of-factly. His gaze arm-twisted her for a response.

She wanted to fan her hot cheeks but instead regrouped while pointing across the lake. "If you have a spare few hundred thousand and want to help the town out, take a look at Tate Farm. A developer wants to buy it to put up a large resort. Maybe you can outbid the guy."

"Oh?"

"Uh-huh. There's a public hearing tonight."

The hearing would be her first chance to meet the corporate vipers from Resort Group International face-to-face and she couldn't wait to hammer firm president, Duncan Jamieson, with some tough questions. With any luck the zoning board would vote down their request so the offer she'd made, along with her dad and brother, would be back in play.

The stranger's brows furrowed and he stroked his chin.

"Don't worry. I'm confident our zoning board will vote no on their proposal and keep the nasty developer away. By the way, I'm Sophie."

He dropped his gaze to the ground for a millisecond then looked back up. "I'm Carter."

If Nana were still alive, she'd have said in her thick Scottish brogue, "Verra good sign, Sophie. Carter comes from the word cart: someone who moves things." Nana held great stock in the art of name meanings.

He'd certainly moved Sophie.

Matt's rusty sedan whipped into the lot, ending the lusty thoughts. Her son hurried over, unease covering every corner of his face. "Sorry I'm late."

"What took you so long?"

"Grandpa called to make sure I helped you." He dragged his hand through his messy dirty-blond hair. "We were talkin'."

She had her suspicions about the topic but rather than ask, she introduced him to Carter.

He turned to Matt. "What do you say we let your mom take it easy and we'll finish this job?"

Matt nodded and trotted to the boats.

At her car, Carter opened the driver's door. "Better hop in." His tone lowered. "Your hands were cold before."

Sophie's knees softened and she tried to speak, but no sound came out. Turmoil reigned inside her body as he jogged away from her and caught up with Matt.

She tried to shake off the lost control caused by this stranger. This little incident had stolen some of her strength and lately every morsel was necessary to stay afloat. On the roller coaster of life, she had been taking a wild ride. First due to a chance to own the vineyards, giving her a helping hand from her inner grief and fulfilling a life-long dream. Then two weeks ago, RGI had barged into town and yanked her offer from the table.

Carter pointed to a kayak and said something. Matt laughed. The scene made her miss having a man in their household. Her heart softened, awed by the way this knight who'd arrived in a shiny white Camry galloped in and took charge...and how she'd simply let him. Was something good finally stepping into her life?

Disappointment skimmed her chest. Who was she kidding? Nothing would come of this.

Her cynical nature hadn't developed overnight. Rather, she had soured over time. Lost opportunities, gone due to circumstances beyond her control: Mom's cancer, Sophie's unplanned pregnancy, her subsequent marriage to Mike, even her lost bid on the land RGI now wanted.

Time to forget this guy and concentrate on her job. She'd have to work harder than ever to stick to her journalistic creed, but any teeny, albeit truthful, crumb of negative news about RGI or its president, Duncan Jamieson, could sway the scale on the zoning board vote. Then the greedy developer would disappear from Northbridge forever.

Her family wanted that land. Land their ancestors were the first to settle back in 1789. Land where the winery plans of their dreams could come to life. The most important reason, though, was protecting the sacred place where her firstborn son, Henry, had died.

Chapter 2

A long line of cars pulled into the well-lit high school parking lot, higher than usual volume for a public hearing. Sophie grabbed her bag and hurried toward the entrance, hoping she could still get a seat up front.

As she neared the large regional high school, she passed a noisy group standing in a circle at the front of the building, chanting the plea "Save our Lake." Their signs bore the acronym "S.O.L.E." stacked on the left and the words, "Save Our Lake's Environment" extending from each corresponding letter. Protestors weren't the norm at these types of events and their presence added a thick cloud of tension to the cool night air.

Bernadette marched with the vocal group. Nana had liked to remind everyone how Bernadette was living proof her name theory worked. "I canna think of a better name for that lassie. She's named to 'be brave like a bear' and sure acts the part." There were times Sophie found *any* explanation about people's behavior to offer a measure of peace. After all, a wise person took heed in all the messages around her and her name meant "wisdom."

She waved to Bernadette, who yelled with more exuberance than any other protestor. A rosy glow highlighted her full cheeks and her large green eyes burst with equal excitement. She shook a defiant fist in the air.

"Nice boots," Sophie yelled over their noise. Bernadette had tucked her jeans into new boots, with razor thin heels and pointy toes, which crossed the border into sexy. Opposite of the sensible heeled style Sophie wore. "You're Northbridge's own *Che Guevera* in her Jimmy Choo's."

"You'd better start reading *Vogue.* These are from Target." Bernadette pushed aside her sable brown bangs, which always seemed due for a trim. "Grab a sign."

"I'm working. Remember?" Any public appearance of bias while covering a story could get back to her editor.

"Yeah, yeah. Same old excuse." Bernadette punched a follow-up fist of solidarity at the sky and resumed her chant.

The details about Carter would have to wait until after the hearing. Since Sophie's chance meeting with the handsome visitor, she couldn't shake her craving to learn more about him, a sensation that left her liberated and scared at the same time. Talking to the stranger was easy and comfortable, the way sliding into a pair of well-worn slippers let her know she was home, safe and exactly where she belonged.

She turned toward the entrance and slammed into a stiff body, making her stumble back a step.

"'Scuz me." Otis Tate dipped his bushy eyebrows in annoyance, his Adam's apple jutting out just beneath the scruffy edge of his white beard. As usual, his younger brother, Elmer, lagged several steps behind, shoulders stooped and taking away the extra few inches of height he held over the senior of the two septuagenarians.

"Sorry. I didn't see you." A cold breeze sent a chill through Sophie's wool skirt and tights, numbing her immediate reaction to scream "traitor." The mere sight of them made her blood boil. After they'd accepted Resort Group International's offer, they didn't even have the decency to give her a phone call. Bernadette had learned about the deal at her law office and called Sophie, adding to her humiliation. They probably hadn't given any consideration to the deep ties she held to the land. With no wives or children, their only goal was to sell to the highest bidder and retire near some friends in Florida, a consideration no self-respecting New Englander would utter aloud.

Otis cleared his throat. "Listen, we want you to know this isn't personal."

"I'd suggest you look up what personal means."

Both his brows arched. "Listen Sophie, we hadn't signed anything with you yet. Business is business. You'll find another spot for your winery." He elbowed Elmer.

Elmer flinched but didn't respond. Instead, he stared at the protestors, his downturned mouth giving away his sadness.

Otis leaned close enough for her to catch the warmth of his breath. "I heard Cliff gave you this story last minute. I assume you'll give it fair coverage."

The comment struck Sophie as hard as a kidney jab.

Her tone downshifted to a harsh whisper. "Nana was a friend of your dad's. She told me his name meant honorable. I wonder what she'd say about his sons."

Otis' face turned beet red and Elmer's froze like ice, as if her words cast a voodoo hex, Nana-style.

She raised her voice. "You don't have to fret over my coverage. I'll report on this with the unbiased dedication of an attorney defending a murderer." She turned to walk away then stopped and glared at both men. "Correction. Alleged murderer."

Elmer dropped his chin to his chest and it touched the ends of his flannel shirt collar. Sophie didn't care if she'd shamed the nicer of the two brothers. He, of all people, understood why she didn't want the land in the hands of strangers.

Two weeks after her son died, Elmer had paid Sophie a visit. Several people in town wished to set up a memorial garden for Henry, right on the spot where he'd passed away on the Tates' land. Elmer had requested her permission, admitting he wanted the memorial too. Henry had worked their farm every summer since turning fifteen and had grown close to Elmer, often calling the gentle old man his surrogate granddad. She'd agreed to the garden.

Now the place was hallowed ground. She visited there every year on the anniversary of Henry's death, his birthday or any other time she needed a tangible reminder of his life.

"If you'll excuse me, I have to get inside." The thick lump settled in her throat and tears burned in the back of her eyes.

Once inside the auditorium, she managed to get one of the last seats in the front row. On stage, members of the Northbridge Zoning Board had already taken their places behind a dais of two old rectangular fold-up tables with several microphones spaced along the tops.

She took a breath to relax. Attitude accounted for ninety-nine percent of any situation and regret over her backlash at the Tate brothers moments ago hit hard and fast. The wall clock showed three minutes before seven, so she used the time to scribble more questions for RGI on her notepad. A minute later, the group of protestors noisily filled the empty row behind her, where they'd left a few belongings to save their seats.

"How'd we sound out there?" Bernadette craned her neck to examine the crowded auditorium and slipped off her coat to reveal a white tee shirt with green letters spelling out S.O.L.E. printed across the bust line.

"Menacing. Only a fool would face you guys."

Bernadette pointed with her chin to the back of the auditorium. "Speaking of fools, here they are now."

A group of five men in suits had entered. Amongst town officials, she recognized the lawyer from Hartford representing RGI, who dressed fancier than the locals in his expensive-looking suit. She studied the two men to the attorney's side and stifled a gasp. The pitter-patter of her heart picked up speed.

Bernadette tapped Sophie's arm. "There's the head fool himself. Duncan Jamieson, president of RGI."

"Which one?"

"The hot tamale on the end, with wavy hair and wearing a navy suit."

"Are you sure?"

A puzzled expression flitted across Bernadette's face. "Absolutely. He came into the office two days ago to schmooze with one of the senior partners."

Sophie's mouth went as dry as dust. Bernadette had just identified Duncan Jamieson, head of RGI, as none other than Carter.

His presence begged for attention and separated him from the other men. Besides the expensive shine to his suit, assuredness permeated from every pore. He surveyed the crowd then leaned close and said something to his attorney, who nodded.

The group of men walked toward the stage. As he neared Sophie's section, his gaze met hers then dropped to the press badge dangling from her neck. He looked at her again and blinked. She held her breath, as much afraid he'd remember her as he'd forgotten her. After a negligible pause, his lip curled into a smile of clear delight. Before she could react, he winked and sealed the acknowledgement.

Sophie's pulse pounded in her ears as she neared code red. His cozy wink not only told others they'd met but dredged forth the lusty awareness of him which had consumed her body earlier. A sharp poke jabbed her back.

"What the hell was that?" Bernadette whispered. "Do you know him?"

"In a manner of speaking." She refused to turn around.

Carter, a.k.a. Duncan Jamieson, took the steps up to the stage and sat behind the long table with the other men. That guy had played Sophie more smoothly than a winning hand of poker, but she wasn't about to take his lies in silence.

Chapter 3

"Welcome to tonight's public hearing. For those who don't know me, I'm Northbridge First Selectman, Buzz Harris." Buzz spoke close into the microphone and his rough voice made the speakers screech. "Since this is a zoning matter, our moderator tonight will be...."

Sophie's anger drowned out his chatter. She clamped her jaw vise tight as she watched the man she *now* knew as Duncan Jamieson whispering into his lawyer's ear.

She flinched when both men stopped talking and stared right at her. She glanced stage left to the dark curtains as her neck and ears went impossibly hot. Wait. She wasn't the liar. She snapped her head in their direction, but they'd turned their attention on Buzz.

The second-term selectman gripped the sides of the podium, his brown suit jacket tightening around his stocky arms. He continued his opening statement in support of the resort project, the lines on his square face pulled more taut than usual. A sweep of his fingers through the thick gray hair near his temples, a habit of his whenever controversy was present, confirmed his discomfort.

Buzz continued his opening address. In his role as a full-fledged member of the local old boy's network, he manipulated the boards under his reign with ease. Sophie kept a careful watch on politicians like him, just waiting for them to cross the fine line into genuine corruption. What kind of pull did he have with zoning on this matter?

As she scribbled down one of Buzz's statements, she remembered her five dollar bet with Cliff. Would he consider "Reporter Wooed by Nemesis" an adequate win?

Buzz introduced Duncan Jamieson. The handsome executive strode to the podium with the self-assurance of a king. He leaned with his elbows on the walnut top, fingers steepled together while he surveyed the crowd.

His gaze lingered over her longer than the others. This time, she didn't look away and tried out her best death glare.

He cleared his throat and scanned the room. "First, I'm happy the hearing is so well attended. One thing is clear. The residents of this community care about its well-being." His arms opened wide, a gesture that would've made Dale Carnegie proud. "The vision RGI holds is for our resort to become a part of the lake's history and to honor the people who live here by our contribution to the area."

The confidence Duncan had exhibited when taking over Sophie's boat problem was magnified in his formal presentation. He addressed Board members with familiarity, as if he'd known them forever, and discussed the town with the authority of a newly anointed mayor.

Bernadette's dated auditorium chair squeaked. Her breath gushed next to Sophie's ear. "Jeesh, you'd think this guy was the new grand pooh-bah."

Sophie turned sideways. "Confidence isn't one of his problems."

Bernadette raised a questioning brow.

"Later."

"RGI is committed to working collaboratively with all parties." Duncan put on a contemplative frown. "Especially those who have concerns. We hope to have a partnership with S.O.L.E. because my firm cares about the environment as much as the rest of you."

Bernadette exhaled, so loud Duncan's head jerked in their direction. Her seat squeaked again and she whispered in Sophie's ear. "I'll bet he thinks he'll finish and waltz out of here tonight without a single question. Guess he doesn't know how things work in Northbridge."

Sophie nodded. Their small New England form of government was called a town meeting format. The residents were seasoned pros at public forums, where local decisions were often made. Public hearings were their idea of a fun night out. Bernadette liked to brag she could recite *Robert's Rules of Order* with the same ease she could list the ice cream flavors at the Dairy Inn.

"Most important, RGI wants full disclosure of all information." His gaze drifted to Sophie, causing the same jolt she'd received the first time they met. "I hope to work closely with the local press to ensure everyone is informed."

She attempted no outward reaction. Inside, though, her emotional needle swung back and forth between desire and rage.

Bernadette surfaced again with the persistence of a pesky gnat. "Hmm. I'll bet he does."

Sophie narrowed her gaze at Bernadette, who leaned back in the seat, her lips pressed into a thin smirk.

How could she interview this guy afterward? His flirty wink suggested he hadn't thought twice about the sham he'd tried to pull on her.

He finished to applause mixed with low boos. The moderator and zoning board chairman, Adli Zimmerman, went to the podium and opened the floor for public comments.

Bernadette popped from her seat, in perfect position to win the relay race to the microphone. Several others lined up behind her. Adli ran an anxious hand across his bald scalp, centered between trim white mounds melting into sideburns.

She grabbed the microphone fast and tight. "Bernadette Felton. Twenty-four Appletree Drive."

Buzz hurried from his seat and went to Duncan, his forehead crumpled with deep lines of worry. He whispered in Duncan's ear. The executive nodded, but the slight wilt of his shoulders suggested the secret stole some of his confidence.

Sophie's nerves twitched. One question circulating around town about this project was founded in pure gossip. Nobody had the nerve to ask this in a public venue. Nobody except Bernadette.

* * * *

Three hours later, the line at the microphone had dwindled to one person. Sophie's bottom ached from sitting so long and she wanted to run to the restroom yet didn't want to miss something good. This would go down as the longest public hearing on record and she hoped this speaker was the last.

The speaker finished in less than a minute. Bernadette hooked her hands over the back of Sophie's chair. "My first trip to the mic was a warm-up. Watch this." She bolted for the metal stand, her zeal as she grabbed it holding the promise of a hullabaloo.

Buzz's jaw unhinged and pure fear settled on his face, as if the ghost of Elvis just entered the building. "Excuse me, Adli." The speakers screeched. "Only those who haven't spoken should come forward. Many of us want to get home."

A low boo rumbled from the crowd.

From behind the podium, Adli adjusted his wire-framed glasses. "I understand your concerns, Buzz. However, the first time Bernadette spoke, she represented her special interest group. In fairness, we should give her an opportunity to speak once on her own behalf." He peered over the tops of his spectacles at Bernadette. "If that's what she intends to do."

Bernadette tucked one side of her layered hair behind an ear and tilted her head. "Yes, it is. Thank you, Adli." Her sweet tone oozed charm. "My question is for our First Selectman."

Buzz clenched his jaw tight, so tight it seemed seconds away from snapping.

"Mr. Selectman." She adjusted the microphone to her height. "There's a great deal of talk around town suggesting some of our elected officials might personally gain from changes in the current zoning. Can you assure the public a fair and democratic process will take place on the board and members won't be...well, let's just say I hope they won't be tainted by outside financial influences." She paused and stared straight at RGI's president. "Such as bribes."

Duncan Jamieson had appeared to listen to the last hour's worth of speakers with neutral interest. Bernadette's comment, however, made the color drain from his face. His worried gaze traveled to Buzz, whose profile resembled stone, his anger so tight she half expected his cheeks to crack and crumble.

"Rumors are *not* statements of fact, Mrs. Felton!" Buzz's roar shook the room. "I'm a patriotic man and take our democratic process quite seriously. I resent your implication that I, or anybody else in my administration, would do what you're suggesting."

Voices filled the air like the low roll of thunder. Buzz pushed his microphone back and threw an angry glare in Adli's direction. Adli nodded.

"All right, everybody. Calm down. This has been a long night. Most of you have spoken. I am calling an end to this meeting at ten forty-five. Do I hear a second for this motion?"

Someone seconded it and Adli shouted above the noise, "Thank you all for coming."

Sophie stood, opened her bag, and stored her notepad and pen. Bernadette returned and picked up her jacket from the seat behind Sophie, her satisfied grin suggesting great pleasure over tonight's outcome. "Guess I raised a few eyebrows, huh?"

Sophie slipped a wool scarf around her neck then zipped her bag closed. "You sure did, my friend. Any idea where the rumor started? It's just the kind of lead to help me find some legitimate dirt on RGI."

"No idea." Bernadette leaned close and whispered, "Sooo...what's going on with the sandy-haired hottie?" She fanned herself with her fingertips. "Lawdy, lawdy. If his wink didn't tell all."

"I'll discuss it later. I need to interview him now."

Bernadette twisted her lips and shook her head. "Be careful. You blushed when he winked."

"I was angry."

She shrugged. "If you say so, but from where I sat, the last time a guy made you blush, you know what happened."

Sophie threw a warranted glare at her friend. "Yes, I remember." She leaned close to Bernadette and whispered, "Listen, this is my chance to prove to Cliff my personal feelings won't interfere with a story ever again."

Ryan Malarkey's arrival in town three years ago would forever fill Sophie with embarrassment. She'd met him around the time she emerged from the dark hole of her divorce and losing a child. Ryan was the defense attorney for a well-known writer living on the lake who'd been accused of murdering his wife.

Ryan's wavy brown hair and rich chestnut eyes would score an eight on the appearance scale, but what had ruptured Sophie's better senses was his suave manner and focused attention on her. Each time he begged her to go on a date, she'd refused. After all, she hadn't completely forgotten about her integrity as a journalist. However, his extra doses of attentiveness soothed her aching soul, empty and untouched for so many years. Thus, when he'd tossed some story leads her way, all favorable to his client, she'd chased them like they were nuggets of gold. They'd run a story based on those leads, leads eventually revealed as false. After reality hit, Cliff just shook his head and mumbled, "Seems your lawyer friend actually is full of malarkey. Now we look like fools." He'd forgiven Sophie in no time, yet she still hadn't forgiven herself.

Bernadette touched Sophie's forearm. "Honey, I'm not sure what's already gone on between you and *El Presidente*, but be careful this time. I know how much you got hurt when Ryan took advantage of you. Okay?"

"Trust me, Bern. I'll never forget how stupid I felt."

She turned her attention to the stage. Duncan Jamieson schmoozed with two zoning board members, the three of them all smiles.

"Your mention of the rumor definitely ruffled a few feathers up there, starting with RGI's president. In fact, he just gave me my first lead."

* * * *

Duncan hurried to the parking lot. After the hearing he'd been pulled aside into a private meeting with the board members and had missed his chance to catch up with Sophie.

He'd wandered to the different pockets of residents huddled in groups talking, searching for her face. Several people cast dirty glances in his direction as he scrutinized them in the dim light. When he entered the auditorium earlier, he'd been elated to spot her amongst the crowd. Her scorching glare, a few seconds after the shock of seeing him passed, reminded him of his misleading introduction.

He turned to the sound of footsteps. Sophie rushed to her car, her blazer tails flapping with a gentle breeze.

Duncan trotted toward her. "Hi. I wondered if I'd run into you tonight." Puffs of condensation exploded with each word.

"Oh. Hello, Mr. Jamieson. Yes. I work for the local newspaper." Her relaxed tone from earlier now sounded stiff and formal. "I've been looking for you, too."

The tall parking lot lights glinted off her press badge. "*Blue Moon Gazette*, huh? I wouldn't have recognized you from the picture."

In the photograph, Sophie wore her dark brown hair shorter and her pretty eyes seemed void of life. Different than the long, soft curls she had today, or the smoky quartz sparkle of her gaze that blew him away when he'd helped with the boats.

She wrapped her arms across her chest and covered the photo. "It's old. I'm the paper's staff reporter." She straightened her posture. "As long as you're here, may I ask you some questions?"

"Sure."

She removed a pad and pen from her bag, all while her unmistakable glare scorched his skin.

"I'd be happy to answer any questions, but first—"

She flipped open the pad. "What specific steps will your firm take to address environmental concerns—"

"Wait." He held up a hand. "I'm concerned you might be wondering why I'd tell you my name is Carter."

"Tell me the specifics about what you plan to do."

"I plan on having an environmental group perform a study. Sophie, earlier I didn't—"

"Plans with the scope of RGI's development are unheard of on this lake. Would you consider modifying them to a smaller scale project if the results show significant damage to—"

"Did I do damage by telling you—"

"That your name is Carter and you're here to buy a house for your family? You sure did." She shoved the pad back into her bag. "Neglecting to mention you're the president of RGI and *you're* the one buying the land. That's what tipped the scale."

"Sophie, my middle name is Carter. It's used in—"

"In Northbridge, Mr. Jamieson, a person's reputation and word go a long way. Actions are never forgotten…both good and bad."

Duncan counted to ten in his head so he didn't blow his stack. This frustrating woman had unraveled the calm cool exterior he wore at all times, especially when conducting business. If he yelled at her the way he wanted to right now, God knows what would end up in the newspaper. He couldn't recall anybody ever having talked to him this way. He drew a breath and then slowly exhaled. "Based on your anger, I'd say I've done something so unforgivable neither you nor your newspaper will give fair coverage to my resort story."

"Fair coverage?" She squeaked. "Is that all you care about?"

A couple walked by and said hello to Sophie. She nodded and forced a weak smile in their direction. When they passed, she looked at him and lowered her voice. "Is your appearance at the kayaks today even a coincidence?"

"What?" Her directness threatened to loosen the bolts of his rusty confidence.

"Look, people have done far crazier things than flirt with someone to manipulate the press."

"You thought I was flirting with you?" Maybe he wasn't so rusty. He tried to put on a some-day-we'll-look-back-on-this-and-laugh grin, hoping she'd find humor in what had happened.

"Whatever!" She waved her hand in the air. "Look, I don't know what your game is. I'm sure you think you're very clever." She stepped to the car door.

"I wasn't trying to be clever, and I—"

"I think you've answered all my questions, Mr. Jamie—"

"Stop being so formal!" A blast of heat rushed up his cheeks. Damn her! The final cord of control belonged to him and he refused to let her end this conversation. "Call me Duncan…or Carter. You're not even listening to—"

"My work is done here." She pulled open the door. "Thank you for your time."

Sophie scooted into the driver's seat and slammed the door. The car started and her window rolled down. For a half second, he hoped she'd reconsidered leaving.

She glared at him, yet sadness smoldered in the very depths of her dark-brown eyes. "This lake means something to me you'd never understand. Before you go changing things, think about those of us who live here."

She threw the car into drive and peeled out of the lot. Her taillights disappeared down the road, leaving Duncan's ego as flattened as if she'd run him over on her way out.

What the hell had just happened?

Regret over the white lie he'd told when they first met doused any remaining confidence. He pulled off his leather glove, reached into his pocket, and removed a hard butterscotch candy. His fingers fumbled as he removed the crinkly cellophane, then he popped it into his mouth. The smooth, sugary treat pacified his nerves like a Glenlivet on the rocks. The day he'd spotted the buttery candies in a drug store, just like the ones he used to enjoy when he visited his grandmother's simple home, he'd located a satisfying replacement for his Marlboros.

The sound of footsteps made him turn around.

"Sophie's bark is worse than her bite." Buzz's smug smirk hinted he'd heard some of their conversation.

"What?"

"She seemed mad."

The selectman's coat hung open over his suit. Duncan's winter wool overcoat was buttoned to his neck with a scarf and he still had a chill. "We had a little miscommunication."

"Because you trumped her on the deal with the Tates?"

"She was the other buyer?" He rolled the candy over his tongue and digested the new information. He bit down and it shattered.

"Yeah. Her brother and father wanted in on the purchase too. A big stretch financially for them, though." Buzz raised a dismissive hand. "They wanted to restore the vineyard, produce wine there like the Tates did years ago. The finances got complicated. Otis and Elmer were pretty happy when you came along."

He'd heard another buyer had been close to signing. Duncan never dreamed it was Sophie. He swallowed the candy remains. "When you told me about the land, I wish you had mentioned I'd outbid *her*."

"Why?" The cracked age lines in Buzz's skin furrowed with a frown. "Would you have changed your mind?"

Would he? "I'm a businessman. I like all the facts."

"Okay, okay. Not a biggie. Besides, you oughta be able to handle Sophie. With your charm, I'm sure she'll find her way to your side. Remember, if we can get the local paper to push the favorable points of this project, it'll make things easier for zoning to vote for the changes."

Over the years, Duncan had acquired a carefully balanced appreciation for politicians like Buzz. He didn't care for them. Still, they were a necessary part of dealing with the types of projects his firm handled.

"Buzz, I want the press on my side, but only if we do things properly. Tactfully." Duncan paused and replayed his little fib to Sophie. "And with the truth…as much as possible."

"Uh-huh. Don't go fretting over that tree-hugger study, either." He shoved his hands into his overcoat pockets, as if he wished to instead stuff away his earlier aggravation toward the special interest group spokesperson. "Bernadette Felton's always on the opposite side of the fence from me. I swear to God, if I opposed your proposal, she'd support it!"

The mention of the S.O.L.E. activist and her bribery accusation brought a return of the sick pit in the hollow of his gut. "Any idea where those bribery rumors started?"

The selectman's face tightened. "No idea. One person speculates in this town and suddenly the theory spreads like wildfire. Like I said, don't lose sleep over her."

"She's not what I'm worried about. It's…never mind. I want the local *Gazette* to have good things to say about my firm. An environmental study might be the thing."

"I guess." Buzz pressed his lips tight.

"What's Sophie's story?"

"Hometown gal. Got divorced a while back." Buzz cocked his head. "That should work in your favor."

Duncan ignored the implication. "She'd probably love to see my project fail."

Buzz's throaty grunt showed agreement.

"Anything else I should know about Sophie? I mean, if I'm to get her to come around to our side."

Buzz hesitated a second too long. "Nope. Do yourself a favor. Don't try to figure her out. Or any other woman, for that matter."

Duncan forced a smile but only to hide an unexpected wave of sadness sweeping over him. If he'd been able to figure out his wife, maybe their marriage would've been happier. "The voice of experience, huh?"

"Married almost forty-five years." Buzz turned to walk toward his car and Duncan followed. Buzz chuckled. "I met my wife back in tenth grade, when the fellas bet me that if I asked a pretty senior named Marion Price to the prom, she'd say no."

The tender tone in Buzz's voice surprised Duncan, who'd only seen the political side of him until now. "So she said yes and the rest was history?"

"Nope. Lost the bet and had to shave my head. As the bristles grew in, they started to call me Buzz." He shrugged. "Name stuck. After college, I tried again and this time got Marion."

Duncan chuckled. Buzz had just proven he didn't give up easily, a quality Duncan respected in others.

After several seconds of silence, Buzz looked at Duncan. "There's another reporter at the paper. Cliff had assigned her this job. Not sure why Sophie showed up. Want me to talk to the editor?"

"No." He liked seeing Sophie again after so many years. She hadn't remembered him, but he'd changed a great deal from the pre-pubescent boy who hung out at the tackle shop. "I can handle her."

Chapter 4

Sophie tapped the keyboard of her office computer with tired fingers as she replied to an e-mail. The church bells at nearby St. Mary's tolled, most likely the start of a funeral she'd seen on her way into the office, but the sound made her mind wander to the story her mother often shared of the magical moment she met Sophie's dad.

Mom had arrived on duty for her shift in the ER. She'd pushed aside a curtain to deal with her first patient, a tall blond man wearing a fishing vest with his ankle propped on a pillow. Sophie imagined her mother with creamy peach skin and thick dark hair twirled into a bun and tucked under a nursing cap, like her college graduation photo. A picture that showed the resemblance she bore to her mom. Mom's eyes always glowed when she'd shared the next part. "The next second, I swear the church bells in town chimed. I'd met the one."

Sophie had always believed the bells were made up. After the encounter with Duncan Jamieson, she wasn't so sure. The instant desire her mother described had only happened to Sophie once in her forty-four years: yesterday morning, when she stared at the blue sky and the handsome developer peered back. An insane admission since her non-libido-related thoughts screamed reminders about his lie. And she couldn't forget the bribery rumors. Alone, the rumors meant nothing. Coupled with his reaction to Bernadette's accusation, they were a lead.

Sophie yawned and stopped typing to cover her mouth right as her desk phone rang.

"Blue Moon Gazette. Sophie Shaw speaking."

"Hey, it's Marcus. I tried to catch up with you at the hearing last night. Want some dirt?"

"You were there?" Since she'd met Marcus six years earlier, his gig as the *Hartford Courant*'s suburb reporter only brought him to Northbridge when one of the governing boards took a vote on something big. "Why? This RGI zoning request is pretty much of local interest right now."

"My editor's thoughts exactly. Then he got a call from the paper's owner. Seems the head of RGI called him. They have mutual friends. Suddenly, I'm told I *have* to drive here and cast some positive light on the resort plans."

She snorted. "I'm not surprised, considering the bribery rumor. You've given me another reason to dig for more. That firm president can't be trusted."

"Watch yourself. He's not only connected, he's sitting on some big bucks. So is his family."

"Interesting. Well, I just got this assignment. Gabby had to be removed because of a family problem."

"Yeah, I was surprised to see you there in reporter mode. I figured they wouldn't want you to cover this one."

Marcus had offered a sympathetic ear during her recovery from the Ryan Malarkey incident, although somehow she suspected he'd never let his heart guide a story as she'd done. "What else did you find out about Jamieson?"

"He grew up in Bronxville, right outside of Manhattan. Town's so rich, the flowers smell like the inside of a bank vault. His father started a huge law firm in New York City, with offices overseas. My brother-in-law is a lawyer in Manhattan. I asked about the senior Jamieson and he said he's a guy used to getting his way. Hold on." Sophie heard a voice in the background then Marcus said, "Gotta run. Let's catch up later."

"Okay. Thanks for the info."

Another black mark against the Jamieson name, a jab that pleased her reporter side. The single woman side, however, tried to ignore the disappointment welling inside her chest.

Too much had happened in the past twenty-four hours. She'd give anything to travel back in time and take a do-over on the parking lot interview. The level of her rudeness broke boundaries, exactly the opposite of how she should treat someone whose cooperation she needed to perform her job.

She recalled her flirting accusation and died a little inside. His amused grin proved seducing her hadn't even crossed his mind. It would take a glacier to reduce the swollen bruise to her ego.

None of it mattered anyway. Gabby, who should've reported on this to begin with, hoped to get a helping hand from her brother with her dad's health issues. Sophie would be thrilled to pass the baton of the story. It wouldn't prevent her from following up on the bribery, though, merely allow her to do so without compromising her duties at the paper.

She looked up to the ceiling as a low thunderous sound came from Cliff's second floor office, most likely the rolling of his chair. Fifteen minutes earlier, he'd walked off with a fresh cup of coffee to read her article on last night's hearing. The story wouldn't win any awards. A crumpled five dollar bill was stuffed in the pocket of her khakis, the bet she'd made with him a sure loss. The proposed headline, "Goliath RGI Defends Project" had merit, yet her tough editor sniffed through details the way a bloodhound tracked a scent.

She propped an elbow on the cluttered desktop and read another e-mail. Cliff's footsteps tapped the wooden staircase of the turn of the century colonial and seconds later, he entered the main office area. He stopped alongside her desk.

She looked up. Beyond his bulbous nose, he watched her, his full gray brows squished together and her story clasped in his hand.

"What's wrong?"

"Nothing's wrong." Cliff handed her the paper.

Several red-inked question marks spotted the margins. "You're missing quotes from a key player." The worry lines across his forehead were more pronounced than usual.

Ever since the takeover of the newspaper two years earlier by CNMedia—aka Community News Media—Cliff had metamorphosed from relaxed man approaching retirement to stressed guy trying to please his new boss.

Sophie twirled in her chair to face him and spotted a stain at the bottom of her long-sleeved pull over. Now she knew where the coffee she'd dripped earlier went. "Whose quotes are missing?"

"Jamieson. RGI's president."

The sales manager, who sat at his desk, peeked over the top of the paper in his hands, probably since Cliff rarely criticized Sophie's work.

"So, the piece is no good?"

"It's good but…" He slipped his hand behind his neck, inside the collar of his blue flannel shirt, and rubbed. "Was Jamieson unresponsive?"

The idea of blaming this on Duncan held great appeal. Deceit however, according to Bernadette, registered on Sophie's face like the "cha-ching" of a cash register drawer popping open. "No. It wasn't him. Guess I rushed our interview. Do you want me to contact his office for more details?"

"Only if you're interested in doing a thorough piece." Quite matter-of-fact, he turned to walk away, but she couldn't miss the corner of his lip wrestling a grin. "Last chance before you owe me five bucks."

The dig settled under Sophie's perfectionist-laden skin. She hunted down the phone number to RGI's Hartford headquarters. Duncan's secretary transferred her to company spokesperson, Carl Hansen. Mr. Hansen addressed Sophie with formality, as if reading from a well-crafted press release. After he answered her questions, she thanked him.

"Any time, Ms. Shaw. In the future, though, Mr. Jamieson suggests you direct all your questions to me."

Ouch. Seemed her flippant remarks in the parking lot caused a roadblock on the bridge leading to Duncan Jamieson, not her smartest professional move.

Sophie updated her piece with Carl Hansen's comments and printed off a final draft for Cliff's review. While waiting, she Googled "Duncan Jamieson." Under the results, the middle initial "C" appeared in several sites. One displayed his full name, Duncan Carter Jamieson. An uncomfortable weight settled in her stomach, the kind that comes the second you admit you might have been wrong.

She clicked on the images button. Photos popped up on her monitor of the well-off company president dressed in casual attire, as well as suits. One photo, taken at a New York City hospital fund-raiser, showed him in a tuxedo. Very GQ. Centered among a group of administrators, Duncan stood out from the others. His handsome face, rich blue eyes, and faded bronze curls made her breath stall.

She replayed the events at the kayak cleanup. At the part where she'd pointed at the Tates' land then begged him to save her from the nasty developer, she froze the frame. Bingo. A confession at that moment would've saved her from a great deal of humiliation.

Nope. Duncan Jamieson would get no apology from her.

* * * *

Sophie trotted up the lit walkway leading to Meg McNeil's raised ranch. The once-a-month Friday girls' night would provide the needed respite after the public hearing two nights earlier. The deep bark of a dog at the house next door broke the silence of the quiet cul-de-sac, shared by five houses of the same design.

She couldn't wait to talk to Meg, who worked for the only real estate agent in Northbridge. If Duncan Jamieson planned to move here, Meg would have all the details.

Sophie balanced a ceramic platter on one hand and tapped on the door. Nobody replied so she went in. Laughter rose above the aroma of Meg's famous homemade *focaccia*, the number one reason they'd decided on "Italian Night" for their gathering theme. The number two reason—they'd all agreed—was an excuse to watch "Under the Tuscan Sun" again. Heading down a hallway lined with soft pink and mint striped wallpaper, she went straight to the combined dining and kitchen area.

Sophie once called Meg's décor "A Hallmark store gone wild." Bric-a-brac covered every free space: fragranced candles, teeny picture frames with cute sayings, little statues of angels and figurines for any occasion, lace doilies, frilly curtains. If she added a card rack and cash register, the chain might let her operate as one of their retail outlets.

"Sorry I'm late." Sophie pushed aside a plate of mini pizzas and a tortellini salad to make room for her platter on the oak table.

Bernadette and Veronica sat around the table, which was decorated with pastel pink placemats and matching floral napkins. They were dressed in the only allowable attire for this event—jeans or sweatpants and a comfortable top. Anybody who gussied up would be sent home to change. Sophie had sufficiently under-dressed in black yoga pants and an oversized sweatshirt reading CAPE COD in bold letters across her chest.

Bernadette cased the food like a starving dog. "We've been waiting for this." She tugged up the cuffs of a long-sleeved Red Sox T-shirt and removed the plastic wrap from the platter. "Your antipasto is the best."

"The one thing we agree on." As director of the town's library, Veronica approached everything with the logical order of the card catalog, not with the outspoken passion Bernadette often unleashed. She playfully batted her dark lush lashes at Bernadette and grinned.

"True. I think we also agreed that Hugh Jackman is the hottest man alive."

Veronica laughed and looked at Sophie. "Haven't seen you in a while." She looped a finger through her signature pearls. The group allowed the dressy indulgence, certain nobody ever asked Barbara Bush to remove hers no matter what the occasion. "Things okay?"

"Yeah." Sophie nodded. "Just busy. Nice haircut, by the way. Edgy. A little Pat Benatar."

Veronica dropped the pearls and they disappeared inside the opened collar of her fleece pullover. "It wasn't what I asked for, but I'll live. I have a blind date this weekend." She crinkled her nose and the teeny turned-up end lifted. She raised a hand. "Don't ask."

Bernadette clanged a fork on her glass. "Ladies, Meg has some scoop to report. Probably on your new friend, Sophie."

"He's not my friend."

"I'll bet he thinks you are." She winked.

Veronica giggled.

"I think you mistook his nervous tic for something flirtatious. In fact, I'm starting to think you're developing a tic."

Footsteps pounded the basement stairs. Meg hurried in carrying a bottle of wine and scrutinized the table filled with food. "Damn. I'm never going to be able to stick to my diet."

"Weight Watchers again?" Sophie had joined with her this time last year in order to shed fifteen pounds added from stress eating after Mike moved out. The pounds slid off Sophie like wet soap while poor Meg had looked on with envy.

"Yeah. I've got those rules down pat, could probably run the meetings. Too bad I can't stick to the plan." Meg's rosebud lips pouted. "Roy made a not so subtle remark the other day about the size of my wedding gown compared to my size now. I'll show him."

Sophie had never liked Roy, a jerk even when they were teenagers. "You worry too much. Nobody had more boys after her in our younger days than you."

Meg uncorked the Chianti. "You're exaggerating."

Meg's extra childhood pounds now molded into nicely shaped curves, a voluptuousness Sophie had admired in those early years of developing. Topped off with her beautiful round face, shiny auburn hair, and positive outlook, most boys in high school had found her quite approachable.

"Hurry up and sit, Meg. We want your scoop." Bernadette patted the empty chair to her side.

Meg put the wine in the center of the table and did as commanded. "Well, we have a very wealthy, very single man who's about to call Northbridge home." Her emerald eyes widened.

Bernadette smirked. "Sophie already knows him."

"Is it Duncan Jamieson?" Sophie lifted the napkin over a basket of *focaccia* and inhaled.

Meg frowned. "You knew?"

"Kind of. So he really does want to buy a house here?"

She nodded and her mid-neck blunt cut shook. "I took him out Tuesday afternoon, right before the hearing. Boy, oh, boy, was I glad when he offered to drive while I showed him places. I couldn't have concentrated on the road with him sitting nearby. He sure made me want to drink a large glass of water."

"Were you thirsty?" Bernadette's sarcastic lilt filled her voice. "Because if you're trying to say he's a handsome man, the expression is 'he's a tall glass of water.'"

Sophie recalled the day in tenth grade English class when Meg anointed herself the queen of idioms. For the most part, their group of friends overlooked her incessant misuse of the clichéd quotes, Bernadette the one exception.

"Whatever." Meg narrowed her glance at Bernadette. "You knew what I meant."

"He's wealthy?" The white Camry he'd been driving—the one he'd pointed out seconds before wrapping his warm hands around hers—certainly didn't fit into her image of wealth. "Why would a rich guy be driving a Toyota?"

"It's a rental." Meg bobbed her head. "He travels a lot. He flew into Bradley Airport, rented a car, and then drove here. How'd you know what he drove?"

Sophie revealed all the details about their first meeting. "When I realized he owns RGI, I thought he lied to me about moving here."

Veronica paused with a forkful of eggplant just outside her slender lips. "Is that why you were arguing with him by your car after the hearing?"

"Jeez, are there hidden cameras all over town?"

"Guess again. I ran into Viv Taylor. She had coffee with your neighbor, Sue, who claims to have passed you and Mr. McMoneybags in the parking lot after the meeting. She's quoted as saying 'Sophie snapped at the nice-looking resort guy so badly I thought she'd take his head off.'" Veronica chuckled softly. "True or pure fiction?"

"A slight exaggeration, but he got an earful." She turned to Meg. "Did he find a place to live?"

"Yup. We checked out six places, but he fell in love with the old Burnham estate. Said he loved its Craftsman style and seclusion. Plus, it's empty. He wants to move in ASAP. Before Christmas. We signed the papers yesterday."

"That's fast." Veronica speared a chunk of Italian sausage. "Where's he from?"

"New York City. His wife died three years ago." Meg's usual cheery optimism melted. "Poor guy. He has a daughter who just started college and a son in high school."

"Are you sure he wants to stay here year-round?" Bernadette opened her palms and wavered like an antique balance scale. "Manhattan or Petticoat Junction." Her right hand plopped on the tabletop. "Manhattan wins."

"I'm positive. He wants a simpler lifestyle. His family visited here when he was younger. Said everything is still quaint." She poked Bernadette's arm. "I heard about your aggressive posturing toward our First Selectman at the hearing. Thank God you didn't scare my client off."

"Meg, not everyone believes the masses should stay silent and the government will run fine on its own." Bernadette flipped her head and her bangs shifted, revealing her thin brows. "Dissention is part of the process."

Veronica pushed around a piece of eggplant with her fork. "Didn't a Jamieson own a summer house here years ago?" Her voice mimicked a snobby tone. "I believe they lived on 'the upper east-side.'"

Sophie grew up on the other side of town from the high-priced, private community. Her father told her it had come to life in the early 1900s when the lake gained fame and the new name, thanks to Harry Langstrom's column in the *Hartford Courant*. Local folks began to refer to this enclave of the rich using the same name as the affluent NYC neighborhood. Most estates were only occupied in the summer.

Veronica didn't wait for an answer. "I think they lived here around the time we started high school. I remember my parents whispering about something gone haywire with that family, like they were selling the house because of something the son did."

Sophie didn't remember any such gossip. "I wonder what he's really up to by returning here. Even the resort seems far-fetched. Who'd want to vacation in Northbridge?"

"We're forgetting the most obvious way to size up this guy." Bernadette twisted her mouth into an eager grin directed at Sophie. "What would Nana have said about him?"

Sophie laughed. "I'm ashamed to admit this. I Googled the meaning." She popped a pitted, oily olive into her mouth.

"And..." the ladies chimed in unison.

She licked the salty remnants from her lips. "Duncan means 'dark prince.'"

"Ha!" Bernadette's palm slapped the tabletop. "Prince Duncan. How fitting.... He pranced into town like he already owns the place."

Meg shook her head. "He's a prince, all right, but not the way you're seeing him. Mr. Jamieson's been a delight to work with. If I were single… well, I'd be all over him like an egg noodle."

Bernadette's mouth dropped open with a ready blast. Sophie kicked her under the table.

"Ow." Bernadette scowled at Sophie but clamped her lips tight.

They all understood Meg meant wet noodle. Besides, when Duncan helped Sophie with the boats, she'd walked away with the same opinion.

* * * *

Duncan pulled into the driveway of his parent's whitewashed brick colonial. The lamppost cast a spotlight on an arrangement of various-sized pumpkins and wilting mums near the walkway leading to the entrance. The charming houses in the quaint town of Bronxville sold for far more than they were worth anywhere else in the country, a fact he'd never realized growing up.

His gut swirled as if a herd of butterflies had come to life inside. He parked behind his dad's Mercedes sedan and took a second to calm down. Only his parents could cause this much unease. Not true. Sophie's speech in the parking lot left him uneasy, too, with all the awkwardness he'd possessed as a teenage boy. Giving her the brush-off when she called the next day and directing her to Carl for future questions might have soothed his beaten ego, but days later, the act seemed petty. He blew out a breath. Stop thinking about her and focus on tonight's hurdle.

He stepped out of the car. After a quick knock on the front door, he wandered in, never quite sure of the formalities in his former home, a place where attachment had never come easy.

"Mom? Dad?"

His mother's disembodied voice traveled from upstairs. "Be right down."

Duncan shrugged off his jacket and tossed it over an antique chair in the marble-floored foyer. The kitchen door at the end of the hallway popped open.

Dad walked out nibbling on a julienned carrot stick. "I'm glad you're finally here. I'm starving." He furrowed his dark brows, threaded with strands of gray, into an annoyed pose as he held up the carrot. "Your mother has me on a diet. All she'll let me have before dinner are these damn things."

"You look great, Dad. Not sure why she's worried."

As a child, Duncan thought his father slept in his three-piece suits. The fast-growing international law firm of Jamieson, McDonald & O'Reilly rarely allowed him time at home. Today he wore a heavy cardigan, filled out in the midsection, and casual slacks. His once-dark hair had turned mostly white and seemed more disheveled than usual.

His dad offered a hand to Duncan. The greeting somehow evolved into an awkward, back-patting hug. Duncan's height and sturdy build had always been much like his dad's. Today, however, Duncan towered over him and he took more care as he embraced the frail shell of his father's once firm frame.

Duncan handed off a bottle of wine. "Sorry I'm late. You know how Friday night traffic is on the Saw Mill Parkway."

Footsteps tapped on the wooden spiral staircase. His mother came down, each step carrying the sophisticated gait of an actress from a 1940s movie. Graying bronze hair touched her shoulders and bounced as she stepped down the last steps to the foyer, her willowy frame always graceful.

"Hello, dear." She placed a distant peck on Duncan's cheek and headed to the kitchen. "I'll tell Annabelle we're ready to eat."

The next half hour dragged. They sat at the end of a formal mahogany table large enough to sit sixteen comfortably. The vacant chairs reminded Duncan how lonely he'd often felt in this spacious house. So many times during his childhood, he and his brother had stayed with the live-in help while his dad traveled for work and his mother was off on a philanthropic cause. Everybody in town knew if Norma Jamieson got involved in any charitable effort, it would get attention.

Between bites and casual conversation, his gaze drifted to the étagère. A family photo sat at eye-level, taken when he was in ninth grade and Trent a sophomore. His mother wore a chiffon gown and stood close to Trent, near the fountain in the lavish hotel where his cousin had thrown her wedding. Mom's arm draped Trent's shoulder. Duncan stood on her other side, leaning close but not quite touching. Both the gap and his posture summed up their relationship. His father stood on the other side of Trent, glancing to the side, barely engaged with the foursome. The snapshot might represent any day in their lives.

When their utensils scraping the plates filled the void in conversation, he lowered his fork. "I have some news."

They both peered up with mild curiosity.

The pulse in his throat quickened. "I'm going to try to cut down on my work hours. Spend more time with the kids, enjoy life for a change. Between my executive assistant and Trent, I've got two strong hands to help at the firm."

Dad grunted. "Good luck with your brother."

His mother cast a silent reprimand in her husband's direction, always Trent's advocate, even though he was now a grown man.

Duncan sipped his merlot. Why hadn't he simply slipped a note under the door to announce his move? He'd never get their approval. Never had. Since losing his wife, he'd vowed to treasure the things in life that really mattered. Family mattered. All the love he had for his children flooded his heart, somehow making his mother's negative attitude less important.

He cleared his throat. "I've also decided to move out of Manhattan. To someplace quieter."

His mother's face brightened. "Oh? There's a lovely house for sale about three streets away. We'd see more of Patrick and Casey."

A jealous twinge nipped at Duncan's heels. His mother had spent the better part of his childhood barely noticing him but now found time for her grandchildren. He swallowed the comment. "I meant quieter than Bronxville too. I'm moving my headquarters out of the city to Connecticut. Hartford, actually. I've also purchased a house in Northbridge to live in year-round, on Blue Moon Lake."

Dad chewed slowly, but looked up from his plate. His cold gaze pierced Duncan, the age lines surrounding his eyes not wilting their power. He returned his attention to the food and cut another piece of roast beef.

Duncan met his mother's judgmental gaze and raised his brows. "Hey, you're the one who sent me there in the first place to buy the land for Trent."

She stared at her plate, pushing the green beans around the fine china, but didn't come to his defense.

Dad brought the loaded fork close to his mouth then stopped. "Move to Northbridge? I don't even understand why you agreed with Trent's idea to turn the land into a resort." He cut an irritated glance to his wife. "Or your idea, Norma, to buy that land for Trent."

"I told you, Frank. Trent's therapist believes his substance abuse ties into feeling inadequate over being adopted into this family. Buying the land of his birth father is a perfect way to hand him a little piece of his past." A dark flash crossed her face. "The purchase of Tate Farm doesn't involve you because you wanted nothing to do with it."

She always jumped to Trent's rescue. Heck, so did Duncan. The only one who didn't was his father. When Mom requested Dad look at the property for Trent, he'd immediately said no. She'd come straight to Duncan. She'd never asked him for help with anything so he said yes, with hopes they'd grow closer. He swept aside the past and his appetite went with it. His gesture for her praise hadn't changed a thing.

Dad's voice rose. "Still, why on earth would you move there, Duncan?" He popped the meat into his mouth and chewed.

Duncan's soul cringed with each bite and, rather than answer, he stayed silent.

His father swallowed. "You have a beautiful townhouse in the city. A life. Friends."

Mom nodded. "The business investment is one thing, but moving there?" Judgment covered every corner of her face. "I mean, with all due respect."

The condescending phrase showed anything but respect and crawled under Duncan's skin like a squirmy bug. He clamped his jaw tight.

"It's a lovely place to visit." Mom dabbed her mouth with a napkin. "Will Patrick be happy living there?"

"He's excited." Duncan tried to sound upbeat, but their opinions, like raindrops on fresh snow, deteriorated his enthusiasm.

His father's fork clanged as he dropped it on his plate. "In my opinion, it's a huge mistake."

Duncan's forearms tensed. He'd heard these words from his dad before. When he'd announced attending law school was off the table and how the law firm his father founded didn't suit his career path. Then again, on the night he'd taken them to dinner to share his plans to start his own property development firm.

"What would Elizabeth say?" His father's glare demanded an answer. "She loved New York, the culture, the opportunities."

Duncan's gaze landed on the lace tablecloth. He lifted the fine stemware then took a slow sip of his wine. His last conversation with his wife, Elizabeth, was one of a few honest moments in their relationship. A comment of hers played in his head daily, like a ticker tape of life's lessons, *Start to appreciate the life around you, Duncan. Some day you might be sorry. I know you have a heart. Start to use it.*

Those words had changed him.

Duncan put down his wineglass and stared at his dad. "I think she'd tell me to trust my heart." He waited a long beat then turned to his mother. "Mom, would you pass me the bread?"

She glanced at her husband but did as requested. They resumed eating. After a long silence, she started to chat about the latest gossip at their country club involving a longstanding member of her tennis group who'd come out of the closet. While Duncan buttered his roll, he looked across the table. The old man watched him, his square jaw set in firm dissatisfaction. As a kid, Duncan would've cowered. This time he didn't blink until his father finally looked away.

Chapter 5

Sophie glanced at the display on her ringing cell phone and pulled off Lake Shore Road near an empty field, where morning frost glistened from the sun. "Hi, Dad. Everything okay?"

She'd taken him to brunch over the weekend since he'd missed the hearing and insisted upon a face-to-face discussion about every last detail. This Monday morning call was out of character.

"All this technology sure takes the mystery out of life."

"It sure does. Anything wrong?"

"No, nothing's wrong." His annoyance carried through the phone. "Why?"

Ever since that horrible morning a year ago, when he'd called her at five AM saying he felt dizzy, cold, and clammy, unexpected calls from him were always met with an overreaction. Everyone in town knew Alan Moore as a sturdy, barrel-chested seventy-five year old who had never been sick a day in his life, at least until that day. She'd told him to call 9-1-1 and, thank God, he'd listened. The doctors found the blockage causing the problem and installed a stent.

She sighed. "You know why. Can't a daughter worry about her father?"

"Yes, but I'm fine now, honey. I forgot to ask you on Saturday if Matt could help out at the shop on weekends during the holiday season. You know how traffic picks up between Thanksgiving and Christmas. Jay decided it would be a good time to have a sale on our kayak inventory."

Dad talked in detail about her brother's plans for the boat sale but she stopped listening. From where she'd pulled over, she viewed the hillside where Tate Farms grew their grapes. The leafy green vines of the summer were gone. Instead, the trellis system, made of strong wooden end posts connected by a wired line in each row, sat vacant amidst scraggly, dried vines. Across the road, the cold waters of Blue Moon Lake shivered with a gentle breeze.

Her dad's silence made her return to the conversation. "Sure, Dad. I'll have Matt call you later today. Listen, I'm running late for work. Can I call you later tonight? From home?"

"Sure, sure. Bye."

She tossed the phone into her purse but didn't drive off right away. To the far right of the hilly fields, sat the old farmhouse where the Tates lived. In her childhood, they'd come here early June each year to pick strawberries in the produce fields on the flat land behind one of the property's three barns. Far beyond the barn near the woods stood the cemetery of her ancestors, with tombstones dating back to the seventeen and eighteen hundreds.

Back in the late seventies, word got out that Ehren Tate, father to the current owners, might start wine production on his land. The governor had just lifted the ban on commercial wine production in the state, established during Prohibition. Up until then, the Tates sold their grapes to other wine producers out of state. That first summer, the new winemaker hired Sophie's brother to work the fields. Jay loved the job and talked about nothing else. A few years later, the summer she'd graduated from high school, she got a job in their newly opened tasting room. Being an insider to the nuances and secrets of each bottled creation made her feel like a part of something bigger than their small town. Several years after Ehren died, wine production had ceased but they still grew and sold grapes to other winemakers.

Sophie's gaze drifted across the street to where the Tates' land extended to the water's edge. A gentle ache rolled against her chest as she examined the memorial garden planted for her son, the summer flowers gone but evergreens still giving some color. Over the years, her trips to the garden had brought her a strange measure of peace. Sometimes she pruned the flowers or weeded the area, a way to still care for Henry. Many times, she simply sat nearby on Putticaw Rock, a local landmark named after a shortened version of the lake's original Indian name. What would happen to the only thing left of her son if RGI's bid went through? Would they destroy this garden?

She swallowed the hard lump in her throat, threw the car into drive, and her tires spun on the roadside dirt as she pulled away. Nope. She wasn't done with this land and it wasn't done with her, either.

* * * *

"Morning, Gabby." Thirty minutes later, after a quick stop to get breakfast to go, Sophie pulled the drawer open on her old steel desk and dropped her purse inside.

"Hey there, Soph." Gabby beamed bright. Her short pixie-cut, petite height, and need to bring homemade cookies to the office at least once a week had earned her a nickname as their honorary Keebler elf.

Sophie threw a pod of French vanilla into the coffeemaker. "I'm so sorry to hear about your dad's stroke. How is he?"

Her chin buckled with a frown. "We've got him in a nursing home. Time will tell."

"Cliff thought you'd be out until Wednesday. I'm surprised to see you here today."

"I needed a break from the nursing home. My brother flew up from Florida and said he'd stay a week or two."

"If you need help with anything, let me know. When you're ready, I'll fill you in on what happened at the hearing. Boy, you sure missed a good one. It's your story whenever you want to take it back."

"Sounds like a plan." Gabby smiled, more gently than usual.

Sophie started her computer and opened the foil wrap of a warm breakfast sandwich she'd picked up at Sunny Side Up. The computer's motor whirled to life and she went to her e-mail, opening one marked "urgent" sent from Cliff an hour earlier.

Will Steiner wants us to interview Duncan Jamieson. Let's talk asap.

Will Steiner? Her shoulders tensed. There wasn't an ounce of love lost when it came to the man who ran their parent company.

Sophie blew out a breath and her tenseness relaxed. What was she doing? A few short days ago, she'd begged Cliff to give her the story. Even though he'd think she was fickle, the time had come to tell Cliff what had happened at the kayaks. It might be in the best interest of all parties for her to step aside. She couldn't recall the last time she'd just given up on anything, though. The idea gnawed at her, carrying the sour aftertaste of losing a well-played game.

She gulped a swig of coffee and stood. "This should be good."

"It can't be that bad."

Sophie snorted. "Guess again. The powers from above are dictating what we report on."

"Above meaning God or good ol' Willy-boy?" Gabby chuckled. "May as well make the best of it. I think he's here to stay."

"Who? God?"

"Him too." Gabby grinned. Sophie marveled at how her coworker stayed so positive, even with the stress in her personal life.

Sophie marched up the stairs. At Cliff's office, she leaned on the doorjamb and crossed her arms. "Got your e-mail."

He sat at his desk editing a document squared in front of him. With one swift movement, he dropped the pen and tipped his glasses to the top of his head. "Good. You're here. Have a seat."

She plunked into the chair across from him and pushed up the sleeves of her cardigan, staring at an autographed Larry Bird poster from the early years and a framed Super Bowl XXXI program on the wall behind Cliff. Besides sports, fishing was the only thing to draw him away from his desk.

"I can't stand editing these reader submissions for *Eye Around Town.*" Cliff's face reddened, matching the fire engine color in his plaid shirt. "They get worse and worse. How can we let the public give us news? Half this stuff probably isn't even true. Why doesn't a smart guy like Will realize you get what you pay for?"

"Because he knows anybody who has two index fingers and a computer can give us free content." She grabbed a lone paper clip off the edge of the desk and unbent the curved metal. "That dumb column is right up his penny-pinching alley. If he gets enough free material from them, I'm the one who'll be out of a job, not you."

Cliff frowned. "You're supposed to calm me down, not get me madder."

"That's Gabby's job." She tossed the ruined clip into a nearby can. "Why is Will in a big hurry to get a story about Jamieson?"

"Because Jamieson's a rich guy moving to a small town. A town where he's making a huge financial investment. I hate to say this, but it's not a bad idea."

"Don't you think a busy guy like Will calling on such a trivial matter is odd?"

"Normally I'd say yes, but he's friends with Jamieson."

Sophie slapped a palm on the desk. "Did you know RGI is pulling strings at the *Courant* too?"

Cliff shrugged. "There's politics everywhere."

Annoyed by the way Cliff had returned to his levelheaded self, she stifled the rest of her rant.

He picked up the pen. "Oh yeah. Will said to give the developer some good press. I told him we'd do our best."

Sophie bit the inside of her cheek. A quiet rebellion raised havoc inside her. Had journalism changed since she attended college? Who? What? When? Where? Why? How? So What? Keep it simple. Ensure the story remained fair and balanced. These days, everywhere she turned the lines between journalism and opinion blurred.

"You might have explained to Will the difference between reporting and editorializing."

"Uh-huh. Well, I'd like to keep my job until retirement." The bags under Cliff's lower lids suggested a tough night's sleep and he didn't appear in the mood to have this conversation. "Approach this the way you do every other interview. See how it falls out. Who knows?" He smirked. "Maybe you'll end up loving the guy."

Will's demands sapped her energy. Maybe it was a sign she should give this up before she compromised her journalist ethics in a whole other way, to suit the needs of someone above her.

Besides, a whole sidebar of issues prevailed. The way she peeled out of the parking lot after telling Duncan off was rude and ladies' night conversation had confirmed the indictments she'd thrown in his face were untrue. Worse than anything, her imaginary flirting accusation still left her with the embarrassment of an escaped burp.

She could just tell Cliff the truth; that she'd been lying to him for the past week.

Instead, she slipped on her best overwhelmed-but-willing face, hoping it didn't look like she was in pain. "What about my conflict of interest? Maybe now that Gabby's back, she should take the story. From what Will's saying, this sounds urgent. I mean, I've got the Bellantoni's Market hours change to work on." Cliff stared back, clearly unimpressed. "Oh, and this week I'm scheduled to interview the head of Public Works about the left turn signal at the school park."

"Thought I'd be dead before they addressed that stupid traffic light."

"Me too." Even back when Sophie had attended school, the signal at the main intersection of their educational park didn't have a left turn arrow on the traffic light. Oncoming traffic was delayed by a good thirty seconds once the light turned green, however, during busy hours the precarious moment right before the oncoming light switched to green became a game of chance. "So, you'll put Gabby on the zoning story?"

"Can't." Cliff rubbed the tip of his long chin. "Will said Jamieson specifically asked for you to do the interview, but I'll call them and tell them no if you think you can't handle—"

"Are you sure he wants me?"

"You two met at the hearing, right?"

She nodded.

"Then you're the Sophie Shaw he's asking for." Cliff lifted a yellow Post-it, held it out at arm's length, and squinted, apparently forgetting about the glasses on his head. "He said to arrange it through Carl, um…."

"Carl Hansen?"

His vision shifted over the top of the note. "You know him?"

"Oh, yeah. Carl and I go way, way back." Sophie stood and left. The worn wood staircase creaked as she headed to the first floor.

When she hit the last step, Cliff yelled, "They'd like the story in by this Friday too."

"Of course they would," she mumbled but yelled back, "Okay."

Sophie phoned Carl, who slotted her in with Duncan on Wednesday afternoon. She had two days to figure out how to mend her mistakes. She'd called Duncan a liar, speculated he'd flirted with her to gain professional favor, and then spat out the last word and sped from the parking lot. Two days? She'd need two weeks to find the right words to fix this mess.

Chapter 6

Waxing Crescent: Varying amounts of the lunar surface are illuminated offering the appearance of growth.

A trip to the West Farms Mall put Sophie ten minutes behind schedule for her appointment at RGI's Hartford office. She pushed the accelerator and violated the posted speed limit on I-84. No point in giving the almighty Duncan Jamieson one more thing to add to her list of infractions. As she'd tried to sleep last night, she instead flipped from side to side, riddled with anxiety over how to handle today's interview. By three AM she'd reached a conclusion: the first thing she needed to do was apologize. She wasn't too happy about it, though.

As she neared the exit for RGI, the unpalatable taste of crow lingered in her mouth. By the time she pulled into the parking garage, she'd accepted the bitter tang.

A glance at the dashboard clock showed she now ran twelve minutes late, thanks to a few traffic lights. Sophie grabbed her bag and hurried along the concrete floor of the garage toward the elevators. The clickity-clack of pointy Jones New York pumps Bernadette had insisted Sophie buy from the clearance rack at TJ Maxx echoed against the concrete walls. Up until now, they'd only seen the light of day on Easter Sunday. She'd dressed professionally in her black pencil skirt and a white silk shell covered by a tweed, cropped jacket. As a finishing touch, she'd twirled her hair into a fisted bun. Dressed as professionally as a reporter from the *New York Times*, she'd force Duncan to ignore the mistakes of her last interview and erase the image of her as some local gal working for a teeny small town paper who couldn't control her rage.

She bopped the button for the eighth floor and, in mere seconds, stepped out into Resort Group International's tropical lobby. The same interior designer must've also done the Waikiki Hilton. She turned to the sound of water, where a miniature waterfall cascaded into a lily pad laden pool.

At the welcome desk, she snickered and grinned at the receptionist. "Do you serve mai tais here?"

The receptionist, whose wrinkled face defied her platinum blond hair, looked up but offered no smile. "Can I help you?"

"Um, yes. I'm Sophie Shaw. I have an appointment with Duncan Jamieson."

"Sign in here." She pushed a guest book across the desk.

Under "Reason for visit," she scribbled *Appointment D. Jamieson*. Three lines above where she signed, she spotted the name Joseph Dougherty, a member of the Northbridge Zoning Board.

Sophie's finger followed to the line for reason he visited.

The receptionist tugged the book away. "Please have a seat. I'll let Mr. Jamieson know you've arrived." Her wrinkles creased further with a "gotcha" smirk.

Sophie waited on a sleek contemporary sofa. Mural-sized photographs of locations where RGI had built resorts draped the walls. From the sunny beaches of California, to snow-capped mountains in the Alps, to the flaxen hills of Tuscany, RGI's modern luxuries awaited the weary traveler. Joe's visit nagged at her subconscious, but the issue could easily be resolved by asking Duncan why the zoning board member had been here. Years of reporting proved one thing: never discount anything. A single question might change the course of a story.

"Sophie?" A fit man with tidy brown hair approached her with an extended hand. His smile showcased his perfect pearly teeth but lacked sincerity. "I'm Carl Hansen."

She recognized him from the public hearing. "Sorry I'm a little late."

"No problem."

The tenseness in her jaw relaxed.

"Although, Duncan can be a stickler for punctuality."

Her stomach tugged into a hard knot.

Carl's dark suit and striped tie made her glad she'd dressed up. He led her down a long hallway, with office doors spaced evenly on both sides and a name plaque on the wall near each doorway. Cardboard boxes sat on the floor outside some of the offices.

"Please excuse the mess. We're still transitioning while we close the New York office."

They entered a large suite. The sleek corporate atmosphere of the hallways disappeared, replaced by paintings of nature, a mission-styled sofa, and tiffany lamps. Meg had mentioned Duncan's purchase of the Burnham estate, a home known for its Craftsman design. A slender woman, with shoulder-length hair almost the same color as her taupe suit jacket sat at a desk, furiously typing.

"I guess this where Frank Lloyd Wright sits," Sophie said then chuckled. Surely, with this décor, Duncan's staff would know about the architect who embraced the Prairie School of Design, the Craftsman qualities similar to the home he'd purchased in Northbridge.

Carl blinked and just looked at her for a second. Strike two on the joking around with staff. "Karen. This is Sophie Shaw. Duncan's appointment."

Her catlike eyes lifted with a smile, perhaps a pity offering for the joke. "He's finishing a call but said to send Ms. Shaw right in."

Carl tapped on the half-opened door, stood aside, and waved her inside. The door clicked shut. He hadn't joined them.

Duncan sat behind his large mahogany desk with his phone's handset wedged between his shoulder and his ear while he leaned back and studied a sheet in his hand. "Uh-huh. What'll it end up costing us?"

He glanced at her over the top of dark-rimmed, half-framed glasses. A force seared Sophie, like a momentary zap of electricity. His gaze shifted to a digital clock positioned in the corner of his desk and he frowned. Carl's hint that Duncan was the punctuality police made her belly squirm with butterflies. Why hadn't she left the mall sooner? Besides the added calories, she'd pay for the last stop at Aunt Annie's Pretzels in more ways than one.

Duncan motioned with his chin to a seating area then lifted a second sheet of paper from a military-neat pile. "Wow. Great price. Including labor?" He chuckled. "No. I'm not asking to pay more."

Sure, she needed to apologize. In no way did she have to jump to his rude chin tip command to sit, though. She roamed to the wall not far from where he sat and studied a collage of ten or so photographs. All showed a blue and white hulled sailboat, tipped on an angle with a wind-filled jib and mainsail steering the vessel through choppy waters. When they'd first married, she and Mike had a small sixteen foot sailboat, a midget compared to these. Similar large boats sailed in the background, perhaps a race. A close-up from behind revealed one boat's name read "True Love." Another photo showed Duncan standing in a group of men dressed in shorts and matching T-shirts, which read "You Can't Beat True Love." His curls ruffled from a breeze and his pale skin glowed pink from a day in the sun.

She glanced toward his desk, where he remained wrapped up in his phone call. The top button of his crisp white shirt was undone, visible beneath a loosened red power tie. Cuffed sleeves, folded neatly to below his elbow, revealed strong forearms. He lifted his gaze over the rims of his glasses. She froze.

"Hold on, Kevin." He covered the mouthpiece. "Please. Have a seat."

"Sorry." Duncan returned to his call. "We'll have to wrap this up. My appointment arrived. Anything else we need to discuss?"

He'd requested her for this interview but didn't seem happy she actually showed up. Did he have another reason, like to retaliate for the parking lot outburst?

She approached an expensive-looking leather sofa and removed a tape recorder, pad, and pen to a teak coffee table but, on principle, refused to sit. Jay often remarked how he hated her passive-aggressive behavior. The reality of his observation came to full light with this situation.

An end table held a picture of Duncan with a pretty, dark-haired woman huddled close to two children, the backdrop some European city. Meg had said his wife passed away. Had she suffered a long illness like Sophie's mother or was her death sudden?

"Not again?" Duncan sounded annoyed. "You're right. Okay. I'll send Carl this time."

She lifted the photograph. The teenage girl appeared in her early teens and had the cute nose of the woman and her dark hair. The young boy had Duncan's features, with brighter cinnamon hair and freckles around his nose.

The room's silence suddenly screamed. Sophie glanced over, afraid Duncan's angry scowl would have returned. Instead, he studied her with a softened stare. His thoughtful gaze appraised her legs, paused midway then inched the remainder of her torso with a smooth caress. He stopped at her face and those damn crystal eyes pinned hers in place. Sophie's breath hitched.

Pink rushed his cheeks and he twirled his chair to the back credenza and acted as if he were searching for something. "I'm sorry, Kevin. How much did you say?"

Sophie strolled to the large windows overlooking Hartford. Heavy traffic on the street below seemed oblivious to the lovely crisp autumn day or the fall foliage beyond the city limits.

He cleared his throat, but she didn't turn. Ignoring his request still gave her the upper hand, something she clung to with strange desperation at this moment.

"Good. Fax me the price quote. We'll take it from there. Anything else?"

She sensed his stare through his pause in conversation.

"Thanks, Kevin. Then we'll talk in the morning." He hung up. "Hello, Ms. Shaw. Give me another second to refill my coffee. Would you like some?"

Ms. Shaw? She turned around. "No thank you."

He nodded and lifted a mug printed with a simple blue and white image of a sailboat, confirming her guess sailing was one of his hobbies.

Even during her rant in the parking lot, he'd called her Sophie. She blew out a breath and leaned closer to the window, noting how high up they were. Did this higher altitude change his attitude toward her?

A traffic jam blocked the intersection below. A driver attempted to make a left-hand turn from the far right lane. Right now, her emotions were in the dead center of an internal jam, confused by the unexpected turns of Duncan Jamieson. She wished Gabby were here instead of her.

Awareness of his presence from behind fell over her, followed by the waft of his familiar cologne.

"Gorgeous view, huh?" His softer, less businesslike voice landed near her ear.

"Lovely." Her peripheral vision caught him close enough to touch yet far enough away to be appropriate.

"Especially over there." He pointed at the horizon and his arm brushed her shoulder.

She followed his finger and noted a space in the distance, where dots of evergreen added color to leafless treetops. His arm returned to his side, but an invisible impression where he'd grazed her shoulder remained.

His tone dipped, quiet enough to be a thought he didn't intend to say out loud. "Reminds me that my new home in Northbridge isn't far away."

The motives for his closeness left her suspicious. "Well, Connecticut's the third smallest state in the nation." She took a step to the side and faced him. "You can pretty much see everything if you stand dead center."

He provided a pity grin to her stupid remark.

She vowed not to say one more sarcastic thing for the rest of this meeting.

He offered his hand. "Good to see you again."

His handshake meant business, but was appropriately tempered for a female grip. The warmth reminded her of the moment he'd taken her cold hand right after she slipped.

"Sorry I'm late." She gently pulled away and dropped her gaze to the floor for a second, where she concentrated on his shiny black wingtips. A path of distrust with this interviewee was prudent.

"No problem. Let's sit." He motioned to the seating area. "You know what they say, though?"

She settled on the sofa. "About what?"

"Punctuality." He lowered himself into a chair across from her. In the bright daylight, slivers of gray threaded in the sandy-colored curls near his temple stood out. "It's the soul of business." The handsome company president tilted his head, as if his little quote taught her a valuable lesson.

"Oh? I've heard punctuality is the virtue of the bored." Her close-lipped smile felt starched, not normal. "And please, call me Sophie."

His mouth crumpled and he nodded. "Thanks for meeting with me on such short notice."

"When the paper's owner sends a direct request, we oblige."

His cheek muscle twitched. Cliff would give her a "tsk-tsk" over the bitchy dig. Why couldn't she simply have said, "You're welcome"?

"Let's clear up any misconception about this meeting." He folded his hands in his lap and crossed an ankle on his knee. "After our last conversation, I didn't expect to hear from your paper again. That's why I contacted Will Steiner. He's been a friend of the family for years."

Heat brushed Sophie's cheeks, but she grabbed the opening. "I understand. Look, about what happened, I'd like to apologize for my reaction after the hearing."

He raised his light brows. "Oh?"

"Learning your real identity surprised me."

The slight movements of amusement played at the corners of his mouth. "Does being surprised always make you angry?"

"No. Being lied to does." The angry snipe escaped without warning. "Anyway, I hope you'll forgive me."

His face melted into a pensive stare. "Thank you, but I must confess something. I planned to apologize to you today. The first time we met, I wasn't truthful with you."

A sarcastic sound seeped from Sophie's throat.

"I had a reason."

"So that made deceiving me okay?"

He held up a hand. "May I finish?"

She crossed her arms over her chest.

"Buzz told me the town was split on the resort plans. I didn't plan to mislead you. At the kayaks, after the way you spoke about how much you hated RGI...." He paused for several drawn-out seconds then his deep voice shifted, softer and more personal. "You hated me, too, for bidding on the land. I scrounged for any manner to stay in your good graces." He dipped his chin and stared into his mug. "It's tough to be the bad guy." He looked up. "Especially when meeting a beautiful woman."

The hard finish of her prior opinion cracked. She hadn't expect this, especially because he'd laughed at her flirting remark after the hearing. Her folded arms slipped apart.

He stared. "Are we okay?"

"Yes, of course." Sophie tried to sound sincere but still didn't trust him and had a job to do. "How about we start this interview?" Before he could answer, Sophie tipped her chin toward the tape recorder. "Mind if I record? You seem busy so this would be the fastest way to get through this."

"Um, sure. Go ahead." His forehead wrinkled, some hesitation obvious.

She pushed forward with questions about his background; how he got into the resort business. She wanted to get this over with since everything about this guy unwrapped her like a gift at Christmas. He discussed college at Stanford and how, a year before graduation, the idea for RGI developed with his college roommate and current partner, Ross Manson, during a semester abroad in Spain.

"Why develop on Blue Moon Lake?"

"Ross lives in Westport and fishes around there. One day we were discussing untouched and more remote places to build. He mentioned Northbridge. Kind of surprised me since my father's family owned a home near the covered bridge. We only visited a few times, but those were memorable summers."

"Does your family still own the house?"

"No. After our last summer there, Dad sold the place."

Veronica's comments at ladies' night took on some possibility. "Why? Sounds like your family enjoyed the location."

Duncan did a double-take on the question and frowned. "I don't know."

Sophie scribbled, *Dad sold a year after last summer in NB,* then scanned her questions to give him a second with his thoughts. His uncomfortable reaction corroborated Veronica's speculation that their son had something to do with them selling their lake home.

He shifted in his seat. "There's a reason I wanted you to do the interview today."

"Oh?" She lifted her head.

He kept a steady gaze on her, yet his usual confidence seemed to have a slight tear. "We met back then. At the tackle shop."

"We did?" She searched through her memories of the summers she worked there. So many new faces but few really remembered. "Are you sure it was me?"

His lips wavered and didn't quite reach a smile. "Positive. My dad liked to fly fish, so we went there for our supplies. You have an older brother, right? Looks a bit like your dad?"

"I do."

"One time we were shopping and you were having a big debate with him over the best dry fly to use in the spring. The discussion got heated and your father stopped talking to my dad and stared at the two of you. After about thirty seconds, you both caught on to the silence and settled right down."

She chuckled. "Dad's stares have more power than most modern day weapons."

"You left quite an impression on me. Coming from the city, I couldn't believe a girl knew so much about fishing. The girls from my school were focused on clothes and makeup, but you wore cut-off jeans and sneakers."

"I was a bit of a tomboy in those days."

He appraised her with a swift brush of his gaze. "Not anymore."

Either she blushed or someone set the heat to scorching. Sophie reached for her collar to loosen it, only to realize she wore an open-necked blouse.

"Um, let's see…" She eyed the pad and willed her body to cool down. "When you made the offer to the Tates, didn't you think zoning would be an issue?"

"Sure. Sometimes we have to rethink our plans."

"Or pursue zoning changes?

"That too."

"Has your firm ever been accused of bribing officials on past projects?"
He flinched. "What?"

"The rumor at the hearing suggested possible bribes offered to zoning board officials." She waited a few long seconds. "Has RGI had any other accusations of this nature?"

He pressed his lips tight. "No."

While scribbling *No bribery charges in the past—acted weird,* she tried to think of a casual way to slip in a question about why Joe Dougherty might have been at the office.

He stood and walked over to a credenza, returning with something in his hand. He extended his open palm. "Candy?"

"No thank you."

He pocketed one but kept the other folded in his palm, watching her carefully as he took his seat. "You know, Sophie. I'm an honest man. I'd never bribe anybody."

"I didn't mean to question your integrity, Mr. Jamie—"

"Duncan."

"Okay. Look, I've been reporting in Northbridge for many years. When rumors surface, there's often a reason." His stiff jaw cautioned her to use care with her next words. "I'm sure you're honest. You do have a lot of people working for you, though. Could one of them be involved?"

His gaze darkened. "I hope not."

* * * *

Duncan rubbed his temple while Sophie scratched some notes. This interview was going worse than the time he went on a roller coaster with Patrick at Six Flags, a bonding moment he hadn't really thought through. At least with the crazy ride he could anticipate a wild curve or when he'd be thrown down a steep ramp. Had Sophie uncovered blemishes he'd hoped were erased on his firm's history?"

Her arrival created a double-whammy of effects. In the course of discussing the business nature of their meeting, he'd caught himself flirting with her, as he would with any woman who captured his interest. Her responses, however, were more unreadable than fine print.

Sophie's full lips parted as she read something on the pad. What'd she put down? He fiddled with the candy wrapper ends, twisting the twirled cellophane ends even tighter.

She looked up. "Why do you want to move to Blue Moon Lake?"

"I took my son there this past summer. We both agreed we needed a change of scenery. Besides, I need to be in one place. I've spent too many years traveling, too many years away from my kids." All his wife's complaints, yet repeating them aloud left a rock hard pit of remorse in his gut. He fled the disabling sensation by concentrating on Sophie's chestnut eyes. "Sometimes, we all need an escape."

"But if you love the area, why didn't you purchase only a single residence? Why the resort too?"

For half a second he considered telling her the real reason the land mattered to his brother, but he didn't want to violate any confidences. "I have my reasons."

"Did you ever stop to consider how some of the things you love about the lake could be lost by your business proposition?"

"I don't think they will."

"Perhaps you're not seeing the big picture."

"I'll address the environmental impact. I don't want to hurt the lake, but this will boost the Northbridge economy and create jobs."

"The area may suffer too. If Zoning passes those changes, they'll lead to additional development along the shoreline."

He shrugged. "I can't control everything."

"No. You can control what you do now, though."

"Communities are often resistant to change." Duncan tried to sound convincing but felt weakened by her demanding gaze. "Things seem to work out."

She cocked a confident brow, like someone about to yell the word checkmate. "Won't this be the first time you've stuck around long enough to find out?"

"I visit my sites."

Sophie twisted her mouth, not even bothering to hide her skepticism. Idealistic. Yes, that described her. This woman preached high standards for everyone, including herself. Duncan considered her perseverance as appealing as it was annoying.

She lowered the pad to her lap. "Living there is different. I'd go so far to say you're..." She pressed her lips together. "Never mind."

"What?"

"Listen, I don't wish to end up apologizing twice in one day."

He opened his arms to each side. "Come on. Hit me with your best shot."

She gave him a you-might-be-sorry grin. "Well, Jamieson is Scottish, right?"

He nodded.

"My Nana was born in Scotland. She once told me a story about a Scotsman who was asked to express an opinion about the pyramids who replied, 'A lot of masonry work and no rent coming in.'"

He snorted. "Then you think I only care about money?"

"No, but you're approaching this purely from a practical, business-like viewpoint. Stop. Think about why you love the lake." Her potent gaze settled on him, saying more than her words. "I'll bet one thing is the simplicity."

Her honesty was unexpected and refreshing, so unlike his wife's. "Any other problems with my plan?"

She studied the sofa arm, where her index finger made imaginary circles in the soft leather. "The land you're thinking of buying has better uses." She lifted her chin and met his eyes. "Did you know for over thirty years the property operated as a farm? Besides regular produce, they had sizable grape crops and for about twenty years produced wine."

"Is that why you're interested in the land?"

Her creamy cheeks turned crimson. "You knew?"

For the first time since the interview began, Duncan regained control of the reins. "I did. Well?"

"Does it really matter now?"

"Maybe. Will it compromise this story?"

She laughed. The kind of laugh where you couldn't believe anybody would say something so ridiculous. Duncan wished he hadn't asked the question.

"I treat reporting the old-fashioned way. I only got your story in the first place because—"

He raised his palm. "My accusation wasn't fair. Listen, I'm sorry to have outbid you on the land so close to the closing date. A pure business decision and not personal."

"I never thought it was. Besides, the land isn't yours yet." Her brows arched.

"Point taken."

"For the record, though, I write news. Not opinion pieces. I want to clear up any misconceptions since Mr. Steiner requested we put together a favorable piece."

"I didn't request special treatment." He squirmed in his seat. "Write the story as you see fit."

"Trust me. I will."

Once again, she'd left him as winded as if he'd hit the bottom of a huge crest on a roller coaster. Her stare burned through him.

"May I switch gears?" Duncan ached to reclaim control.

"Sure." She crossed her shapely legs.

"The other night, in the parking lot, you told me I'd never understand why you wanted the area to remain unchanged. It's understandable you'd be unhappy about my bid. Is there something else I need to know?"

Her dark gaze averted to the tip of her jiggling foot and she blinked, making her long lashes flutter. He wanted to look, too, but didn't want to appear as if he were checking her out again. His earlier trip past her pleasing calves and nicely rounded bottom had given him the urge to unpin her knotted hair and do something that would earn him a slap across the face. Instead, he watched her expression, now more sad than angry.

Her hand lifted to her slender neck, where her fingers slowly massaged beneath her chin. "No. Just the vineyards." She met his gaze, but a story rested in the pain behind her empty stare.

Sophie switched topics, but the need to understand her overwhelmed him in the most unsettling way.

Chapter 7

From the window of his room at the downtown Marriot, Duncan admired the sparkling lights of the city while he spoke to Patrick. "How was school today?"

"Boring." His son always had the same answer. "Got a B on a Bio test. The teacher said I got the highest grade in the class."

"Sounds like a tough one. Congratulations." He stepped away from the view and picked up the drink he'd left on the hotel room desk. "I'll be home right after the closing tomorrow, probably by lunchtime. Let Helen know they've changed the location to my lawyer's office in Hartford. After that, the house in Northbridge will be all ours."

"Oh yeah. Helen said to tell you the movers called to confirm things. She told them you'd call back."

Thank God for Helen. When Elizabeth got sick, a search through the grapevine at the office yielded the seventy-two-year-old grandmother of three. She'd stayed on to help with the kids after his wife died, making life as a single father easier.

He sipped his drink and the ice clinked. "Two weeks until we move, buddy. Are you psyched?"

"Yeah. A little nervous, but kinda feel like this is our adventure."

Patrick's optimism made him happy. "Life's too short not to enjoy a good adventure. See you tomorrow. Love you."

"Love you too."

Duncan tossed the phone on the bed and returned to the window, slowly sipping his drink. He wished his daughter would warm up to his efforts to be a better father. Since starting college three months ago, she'd grown more distant. Only time would tell.

An airplane light blinked in the sky. Against the cityscape, the aircraft reminded him of that horrible day when the World Trade Center crumbled to the ground in the same city he worked and lived. Profound sadness welled in his chest as it always did when he remembered the horrors that unfolded. That day also marked the one time in his adult life he thought about what really mattered. He'd lost many friends, but luckily his family had remained safe. For a couple months he'd made more effort to be with them yet, as life returned to normal, so had he. Only years later, when the doctor gave his wife's cancer diagnosis, had he regretted the return of his old ways.

He shut his eyes and rubbed the bridge of his nose. Yes, life could change any day without warning. Sophie's re-entry into his life had changed him, especially after today's interview. She'd pried off layers of control he'd fine-tuned over a lifetime. He tipped back the bourbon and got lost in the slow blaze igniting his throat and warming his entire body, a reminder of her closeness today and how it had made him stir.

The day he'd gone to look at houses in Northbridge, running into her at the kayaks had really blown his mind. Good thing he hadn't told her the truth about their early encounters years ago. She'd have doubled over in laughter learning she'd been his first boyhood crush. Jesus, she didn't even remember him.

An image of the first time he saw Sophie crystalized in his mind, clear as if it were yesterday, not the summer when Duncan had turned thirteen. His mother had insisted the family forego their usual July vacation to Newport and head to their long-forgotten lake home. Dad always offered his granddad's lakefront home to friends, leaving the maintenance to a property firm.

The first morning there, his father dragged Duncan and Trent out of bed at dawn to go fishing. After a trip to Bullhead Bait n' Tackle, they'd left with fly rods, hand-crafted flies, and a map of the best spots along the Housatonic River.

The event marked one of the few moments his father engaged in any type of activity with both of his sons. Duncan hated the early hour and wasn't sure about the fishing, but he'd found treasured gold in the camaraderie with his workaholic father.

Duncan's attitude toward fishing had changed with the first tug on his line. "Dad! Come here. Hurry. I've got something."

His father had waded through the water, shouting excited instructions. Duncan followed every word, walking backward and cranking the reel.

"Let the fish struggle." He'd never heard his father so excited. "Tire him out."

Duncan had played with the fish. When his first shimmering trout emerged, dangling at the end of his line, Duncan—like the fish—became hooked on the sport.

Later they'd returned to the tackle shop for a cold soda. A pretty girl his age stood in the back loading Coke bottles into an old boxy refrigerator. Her flowing hair had caressed her shoulders, almost like the wild branches lining the trail they'd taken that morning to reach their fishing spot on the river. Cut-off denim shorts and a black, fitted Led Zeppelin T-shirt had disclosed the start of her womanly curves, a far cry from the outfits worn by the girls at the private school he'd attended. Duncan had peeked from behind a rack of fishing vests, rendered as debilitated as a stunned fish.

The shop owner, Mr. Moore, had yelled, "Sophie, bring three Colas up front, please."

She'd appeared a minute later and dumped the bottles on the counter.

An unforeseen force, one he'd never experienced in his life, generated a magnetic pull, leading him to the back of the store. He'd loitered around a display of rods and feigned interest but covertly observed her every move.

Sophie had bent down and lifted a bottle from the case. Instead of stacking it with the others, she'd twisted around and smiled at him. "Hi. First summer here?"

His mouth had gone dry. He'd nodded.

"How was fishing?"

"Good," he'd mumbled, dumbstruck by his own desires.

"Yesterday morning I caught a bunch of small-mouth bass below the dam. A little past the bridge. They're pretty good fighters."

He'd nodded again.

Sophie's eyes had swum with playful brightness. "You might want to give 'em a try if you go out tomorrow. That is, if you think you can handle them." Her voice had teased with the sweetness of honeysuckle.

Desire had snared his hormone-laden body, leaving it vacant of words.

He'd obsessed about her the entire visit, learned they were the same age. Over the four weeks of their stay, he attempted to recover from the first awkward conversation. He'd tested the waters, carefully dipping in a toe every time he visited the family shop. He'd possessed all the desire to deal with her but none of the skills and had returned to New York with dry feet.

The Jamiesons had returned the next summer, when Duncan was about to enter high school. Like many boys his age, he hadn't quite sprouted. She'd shown no signs of remembering him from the year before. Her attention had focused on an older boy with a dirt bike who hung around the shop.

Their visit in Northbridge had ended abruptly, two weeks earlier than planned. He woke one morning and his father said they planned to leave right away due to a problem at work. The next spring, his father had sold the home. Much like the photographs they'd taken of their visits to the lake were subsequently stored in a closet to collect dust, his thoughts of Sophie were forgotten, too.

Her question during today's interview had thrown him. Why would his dad's old family house sale in Northbridge matter now? He vaguely recalled some tension between his parents the last summer they had come here. So what? They didn't have a perfect marriage. The house sale a year later had surprised Duncan, though.

His cell phone vibrated. He answered and told his old college friend he'd be right down to meet him for dinner, gulped the rest of his drink, and tossed on his suit jacket.

The elevator whisked him to the lobby while his mind raced with images of Sophie. Compared to the sophisticated, ivy-league educated women he'd been with over the years, she was more granola, less dolled-up than her urban counterparts. Her full lips and creamy skin could compete with the best of them, and he longed to run his hands through her untamed hair.

Aroused by thoughts of her, one thing remained clear: he wanted a second chance to win her over, this time as the confident grown man he'd become. His adolescent feelings for her had never disappeared. Maturity had made them deeper, filled with the craving found within the folds of one's heart. A place he'd shut off years ago.

A wary sensation roiled in his stomach. The kind you got before taking the biggest risk of your life.

* * * *

Sophie pretended to focus on scrubbing a metal pan while she eavesdropped on Tia, who sat curled on the sofa with the phone pressed to her ear.

"Really, Dad? Florida? When?"

Sophie stilled and listened more closely. Mike was a model father. His insensitive side was reserved for her, evident once again with the e-mail he'd sent two days ago.

His offer to take the kids to Florida in January wasn't a big issue. That he'd choose the anniversary date Henry would have turned twenty-five for the getaway, which left her sitting home alone wallowing in the sadness of the day, irked the hell out of her. She wrote back, requesting he consider a different date. So far, he hadn't responded.

Their son's birthday should be just another day. On matters of Henry, though, common sense vanished. Anniversary dates knocked down barriers that kept her functioning the rest of the year. Matt and Tia also had a way of keeping her grounded in reality.

Since their divorce, Mike's approach toward Sophie bordered on bitter cold. Not a surprise given the attitude he'd carried the day he asked for the divorce, a moment from five years ago that shaped their current relationship.

The problems had started in the morning, when she'd stumbled upon a nest of dead baby robins. The adult robins had skittered in the tree near the fallen nest, their nervous chirps asking why. Sophie had run inside sobbing and stowed away in bed with her head buried in a pillow to muffle her tears. Like the robins, Sophie had been left confused as to why her nest had been turned upside down and damaged, left to live with a smothering ache that reminded her she'd been cheated out of graduations, first jobs, and grandchildren.

Later that night, Mike had quietly appeared at the bathroom door while she'd patted dry her freshly washed face.

"Listen, Soph. Nothing can change what's happened in our lives, but I've been trying to move forward."

She'd lowered the towel.

His shoulders had sagged. He'd scrubbed the late day shadow on his chin with his palm and stared at the white tiled floor.

"What are you trying to say?"

"You're holding me back." He'd looked up and his eyes had glistened with tears. "I can't live like this anymore."

"Are you asking for a divorce?"

He'd nodded. "Something's missing." She'd never forget Mike's hollow stare, a stark realization their love had completely dissolved. "Something besides Henry."

The numb layer formed over her skin for two years had cracked. Mike's words had cut like a sharp stab of the truth. Henry had been the adhesive bonding them in forced matrimony. With his death, they'd come unglued.

The confrontation had forced her to give better care to her two living children and seek professional help. It took some time, but last year her therapist said she'd reached the final stages of grief. Yet, Mike's current disregard for the twenty-fifth anniversary of Henry's birth stirred up old anger.

She honed in on Tia's excited chatter. "I get out of two days of school too! Cool."

Giving the dishwasher start button a tap, Sophie yawned, suddenly exhausted after the long drive to Hartford and the interview with Duncan. After close to an hour with him, she only had more questions to his vague responses. All the way home, she couldn't forget how his nearness as they'd looked out the office window traveled straight to her core. Or how his "you don't look like a tomboy anymore" remark made her nearly melt in her seat. There was always a chance he'd made the remark to throw her off-kilter, a reminder to approach him at all times with caution.

Tia giggled and Sophie's irritation with Mike returned. Maybe this double-dose of set-backs—losing the land and now the kids being gone on such a tough day—warranted a call to Dr. Keller, the therapist she'd seen right after Mike left. A rational, guiding hand couldn't hurt.

Bella, their wheat-colored terrier mix scoured the kitchen for leftover scraps. She crouched and stroked the dog's strange blend of soft, wiry fur. "At least you won't leave me that weekend, huh?" The dog's tail swayed, but behind rich brown eyes, she begged for a handout. Sophie got her a treat.

Tia galloped into the kitchen, long dark hair flapping with the breeze. She stopped her colt-like frame within inches of Sophie. "Dad's going to take us to Disney World in January!"

"Great." Sophie faked an upbeat posture. "Did he give you the dates?"

"Here." Tia slapped a Post-it note on the front of the refrigerator. "Wait'll Matt gets home and finds out." She skipped down the hallway, sounding more like an elephant than a slender teenager.

Same dates. What a coward. Couldn't even tell her in person.

She ripped off the sticky note, went to the desk in the living room, and slammed the Post-it on the cover of her planner. Next to the trip dates were the notes from her meeting with Duncan. Sophie's anger veered in a new direction. If her vineyard plans were still in the works and he hadn't taken Tate Farm from her, she'd bet her focus wouldn't be on Henry's birthday. *Damn you, Duncan Jamieson!*

She clenched her hand into a fist, so tight her nails dug into her palm. Fury searched in all directions for another victim when it hit her...who was she really mad at? She had no idea.

Chapter 8

"Fourteen, fifteen...five more."

Sophie raised her shoulders for the grueling stomach crunch and tightened her abdomen beneath an oversized T-shirt. The militant exercise instructor at her Tuesday strength class continued the count, momentarily drowned out when a floor mat and a set of five pound weights landed with a loud thud on the tired gym floor to Sophie's right.

Bernadette plopped on top of the matt and whispered, "The other lawyers in my office loved your fluff piece on Duncan."

"It wasn't a fluff piece." She inhaled and continued with the count.

"Oh, please. I'll bet his Mommy taped the article to her fridge."

Sophie rolled her head to the side, where Bernadette stretched her long legs, covered in tight black yoga pants. Sophie poked her arm. "The piece was fair. We'll talk afterward."

She tried to concentrate on the class, but Bernadette's criticism badgered her. Writing the RGI article had pulled her in more directions than a wad of saltwater taffy. Her journalist's ethics worked in overdrive, swerving from any possible bias.

They exercised hard for the next thirty minutes and finally finished.

"Jeesh, Bern." Sophie stood and picked up her mat. "You'd already told me you weren't thrilled with the story on Saturday. Are you done?"

"Sorry. Dan Sawyer nudged me all day yesterday at work. You should have heard him." She deepened her voice. "You couldn't even get your best friend to write anything bad? I think you're wrong about this project." Her voice returned to normal. "God, I can't stand him."

"He's bugged you since ninth grade." Meg lifted her mat and weights from the floor. "Let it go."

"She's right." Sophie grabbed her weights. "Besides, the facts were pretty clear and didn't lead to anything negative."

"You could have pushed him about those bribes."

"I asked. He said no. Jeesh, did you want me to use torture?"

Bernadette raised her brows. "You'd do that for me?"

Sophie chuckled, but Meg just shook her head. They put away their equipment and headed to their cars in the back parking lot.

Sophie zipped her sweatshirt and pulled her ponytail out from beneath the hood. She stopped near Meg's slightly rusted Jeep. "There was something a bit odd, something I didn't put in the paper."

Several ladies from class hurried past so Sophie lowered her voice. "Remember at our girl's night Veronica said a Jamieson had lived on the lake way back when? She thought they had a problem son?"

They nodded in unison.

"During the interview, Duncan mentioned they spent a couple of summers here when he was in middle school. He said we met at the tackle shop back then, but I don't remember him."

Meg stopped searching through her oversized bag for her keys. "Really? How could you forget a hottie like him?"

"He was around thirteen. I'm sure he looked different."

Bernadette's thumb and index finger swirled the tip of her layered brown locks. She stared off into the distance, blinking. Her gaze drifted to meet Sophie's. "Do you think Duncan caused the trouble Veronica heard her parents discussing?"

"My Internet research shows he has a brother. I figured someone older than us might remember something."

"Ladies." Meg's round face brightened. "I think this is a case for the Northbridge Nancys."

Sophie warmed at memories of how one summer the close-knit gaggle of girls kicked off their Nancy Drew Marathon. Their over-active imaginations had stretched everyday situations into a mystery—the neighbor's missing cat, an absent neighbor, or a newcomer around town all led to endless speculation. They'd baptized their group the Northbridge Nancys.

Sophie laughed. "I could use some help."

"You know what they say." Meg paused, like a comic waiting to deliver a punch line. "Great minds think alike."

Bernadette beamed, always proud when Meg got a saying correct. "How about some of your contacts, Meg? Like Mr. Wilson."

"That's what I'm thinking. He'll love the added attention." She started to search her bag again then stopped. "I swear, ever since he retired two years ago, he still spends half his week visiting the office. He needs to find friends at the senior center or something. Our receptionist looked ready to kill him the other day when he sat around reminiscing about old times while she tried to work."

Sophie glanced at her watch; she was falling behind schedule. "Guys, I've gotta run, but please keep this between us."

Meg's fingers touched her mouth in a turnkey motion. "Mum's a word."

Bernadette hesitated and Sophie waited for the correction. Instead, Bernadette made the same motion. "Yup. Mum's a word."

* * * *

Sophie trotted to the *Gazette's* front entrance ten minutes late. She wrapped her corduroy blazer tight, the brisk air seeming colder than the forty degree temperature reported on the thermometer outside her kitchen window, not chilly enough for a real coat by her standards. The day her fingertips turned ice white marked the official start of winter.

An old metal mailbox hung on the siding next to the front door of the old colonial. Sophie opened the rusted lid and removed a manila envelope. Large block letters spelled out "S. Shaw," with no address or return information.

She went inside and tossed the envelope on her desk, going straight to their single-cup coffeemaker in the kitchen. Popping in a pod of pumpkin-spice roast, she grabbed a thick ceramic mug from the cabinet, set it down on the small coffee tray, and pushed the button.

"Morning, Sophie." Cliff hollered a few seconds later from his upstairs office.

"How'd you know it was me?" She yelled back, waiting for the cup to fill.

He didn't answer so she prepared her coffee then took it upstairs to Cliff's office.

Cliff held up the newspaper, folded to the sports page. He looked over the rims of his reading glasses. "I knew it was you because an old newsman like me notices the details." He flipped his dark frames to his head and lowered the paper. "When Gabby arrives, she starts her computer before doing anything else."

"Remind me never to underestimate you." She sat across from him. "Anything happening today?"

"Nope. Just the way I like my job during Thanksgiving week. What are you working on?"

"The elementary school has their annual Indian-Pilgrim show." She sipped the fresh brew, breathing in the spicy autumn scent. "Bart's joining me to take photos."

He crinkled his nose. "I hate those flavored coffees."

"I know."

"By the way, I got an early morning call from Duncan Jamieson. He liked your piece. Good work. We had a nice chat." He picked up his newspaper and lifted a hand to the rims of his glasses.

"Really. What'd you chat about?"

Cliff stopped and left the glasses on his head. "Well, he hoped to work with you more." He stared at her, blinked a few times then pressed his lips tight.

"That's a chat?" Cliff was a man of fewer words than most men. Gabby always said the task of pulling details from him required more dragging than her rake got during foliage season. Sophie rolled her hand several times for him to continue.

He sighed, lowering the paper to the desk. "We discussed his move to Northbridge."

"And…"

"We said we'd do lunch one day to discuss some ad revenue from the resort. Overall, he seems like a decent guy."

Sophie snorted. "Seems like an optimistic guy. They haven't approved the zoning changes yet."

"Oh, and Duncan asked for you to call him. Wants to thank you personally. Said you have his number."

She stood. "You betcha. I've got his number all right."

Cliff grinned. "Let's hope he's got yours."

On the way to her desk, she had second thoughts about her strong defense of Duncan with Bernadette earlier. Somehow, both Sophie's professional and personal feelings on this assignment had been dumped into the same pot then stirred into an inseparable mix. Did this issue influence her ability to report without a bias? Especially since her instincts warned that Duncan's intentions in Northbridge came with a secondary agenda. She'd need to up her guard around him.

Confident or corrupt, which was he?

Sophie went to her Rolodex for the business card Duncan had given her with his direct line. At least she no longer had to be channeled through Carl Hansen.

She dialed. The phone rang while she tore open the thin manila envelope left in the mailbox. Sophie removed two sheets of paper.

The phone clicked into a recording of Duncan's familiar voice. She compiled a response while glancing at the words on the paper, but the written message made her freeze and she hung up.

* * * *

Sophie's adrenaline worked overtime as she sat inside her car and waited for the Northbridge Library to open. The mother lode of leads had been dumped right at the newspaper's front door. By whom or their reason why was unclear. Again she studied the contents of the envelope left at the *Gazette* offices.

The first of two sheets contained cut-out letters from magazines and newspaper clippings that spelled out a warning:

The Jamiesons are corrupt. Both now and in the past. Question the gunshot.

She flipped to the second sheet, a printout from the July 1981 edition of the *Blue Moon Gazette*. Yellow highlighter marked a story under the police blotter section with the lead-in, "Shots Fired at House." She reread each word.

On July 26 at 8:05 PM police were called out to the house of Daniel "Buzz" Harris, 32 Lakeview Circle, after neighbors reported hearing gunshots coming from inside the home. When police arrived, Mr. Harris said he'd inadvertently pulled the trigger on his gun, believing the safety was on, while he cleaned it.

Several markings on the bottom of the printout proved the story came from the Northbridge library microfiche and showed the date it was printed. She hoped Veronica, who'd been director here for the past ten years, arrived early and had time to help her find out who unlocked the microfiche cabinet the day this paper printed. Then she might know who wanted her to have this information.

Before she'd left the paper, Cliff called a buddy who worked in the Land Department to confirm when the Jamiesons sold their house. The 1982 sale date confirmed they'd owned it at the time of the gunshot. Whether or not they were physically here was another matter.

The pieces of a trail were beginning to fall into place. This note gave some credibility to the rumor Bernadette made public at the hearing. It didn't have to do with the current land deal, but it suggested the Jamieson brood had a history of corruptness.

Some of the control Sophie had lost over her future when RGI barged in and flashed their money at the Tates now seemed within her grasp. A little digging might uncover just enough of the truth to make RGI uncomfortable hanging out in town. Maybe they'd pull their offer. Otis and Elmer would be at her door begging for her family's offer to resurface. She could even renegotiate a lower price to make up for all her troubles.

The front door to the hundred-and-fifty-year-old white clapboard house-turned-library finally opened. Sophie hurried straight to Veronica's corner office. "Surprise!"

Veronica glanced up from her computer screen, looking classy in a black cashmere sweater, a scarlet polished finger wrapped around pearls. "Hey. Didn't expect to see you today. What's going on?"

"Take a look at this. At the bottom." She handed Veronica the printout of the gunshot story. "This came off the fiche machine here, right?"

Veronica nodded. "Indeed it did. Five days ago, at two-o-seven in the afternoon, from printer number two. Why?"

"Any idea who manned the back desk that day? I'd like to find out who requested the old *Gazette* microfiche."

Veronica clicked a few keys on the computer. "Mrs. Payne. She's there now. Go and ask. A word of warning. She can recall the name of every single student over her forty year career but forgets things that happened five minutes earlier."

Sophie headed to the rear of the library where the eighty-seven-year-old former elementary teacher stretched on her tiptoes trying to shelve a book. Her arched back appeared to make the act quite difficult.

Sophie hurried over. "Hi, Mrs. Payne. Let me do that."

The older woman smiled and a smudged spot of ruby lipstick showed on her teeth. "Hi, Sophie. Thank you for the help."

The brown curls she'd worn years ago had made way for white, thinned waves showing glimpses of her pink scalp.

"You're welcome. I'm wondering if you can help me. I have a microfiche printout and hoped you might remember who asked for the *Gazette* fiche for nineteen eighty-one last week." She offered the paper and pointed to the date.

Mrs. Payne studied the print off and blinked. "Yes." Her head bobbed. "Oh, what's her name?" She folded her hands in front of her bright red sweater, the same way she used to do in class. "Oh my. I can't remember."

Sophie considered offering a quick dose of ginkgo biloba to jar the volunteer's memory. Heck, she was almost half her old teacher's age and there were days when her recollection was challenged.

"Heavens. I can picture her. Round face. Glasses."

Sophie waited, the description too generic to even take a guess.

"Fiddlesticks, the name just escapes me."

Sophie patted her shoulder. "Thanks anyway. If you remember after I leave, can you tell Veronica?"

"Certainly, dear."

Sophie returned to Veronica's office "I asked her to let you know if the name comes back to her."

"Let me see that article again." Veronica held out her hand. Sophie stood quietly while she reread it. "That gunshot at Buzz's is news to me. Do you remember this?"

"No. Perhaps a visit to the selectman's office is in order." Sophie returned the papers to her bag. "How exactly do I ask Buzz if he knew the Jamiesons back then?"

"Carefully." Veronica's mouth pinched. "Remember his temper at this year's town budget meeting when I went to the microphone to complain over cut library funds."

"Yeah. He needs anger management classes." The large clock on the wall told her she had an hour before picking up Tia at the high school band practice. The town's municipal offices were only a short walk from here. Maybe she could catch him before town offices closed for the Thanksgiving holiday. "Zoning might pass RGI's request any day now. If there's dirt on the Jamieson clan, I plan to find it. Let's hope Buzz is available."

Veronica flashed the thumbs-up sign. "Godspeed, my friend."

Chapter 9

December

"Hope to see you around town." Duncan hung up and tried not to let his dissatisfaction drag him down. He turned the page of the environmental report on his desk, but the words blurred.

After a week of phone tag with Sophie due to the Thanksgiving holiday, they'd finally caught up. He complimented her piece on their interview, a ruse for the actual reason behind his call. When he mentioned he'd become an official Northbridge resident this past Saturday, she replied, "Yes. Meg told me."

His real motive behind the call, to ask her out on a date, disappeared with the lukewarm response. Even though they'd parted at his office on what he thought a warmer note, maybe he'd read her wrong.

Given their history, he wasn't shocked. At the kayaks, he'd broken the seal of trust. He wished he'd never lied about his name. She'd probably still hate his firm for outbidding on the land, but he'd have a fighting chance on the personal front.

He picked up the environmental impact study and reached for his reading glasses. The door creaked open.

Carl stuck his upper body inside. "Ready?"

Duncan closed the report. "Come on in."

Carl entered carrying a large stainless steel travel mug. Duncan had hired his executive assistant not knowing both men were early risers. They often found themselves in the quiet office before normal business hours to plan the day ahead.

"How'd the move to Northbridge go this weekend?" Carl settled into the chair opposite him, suit jacket still on.

Suit jackets were always too stiff and formal for Duncan's tastes. The second he arrived at the office each day, Duncan removed his jacket, unbuttoned his sleeves, and folded them to his elbows. An employee once said he looked like he'd rather be sailing. A true statement.

"A few minor bumps. I'm not sure why I thought doing it over this holiday weekend was a good idea."

"Because when you set your sights on something, you aim straight for the goal and shift into fifth gear before the rest of us hit second." Carl tossed out a perfected smile, an asset in dealing with clients. "One of the reasons I like working for you."

Duncan recalled his wife saying something similar about his drive, although not with the tone of admiration found in Carl's statement. Disdain laced her comment, one suggesting his strong-willed attitude and certainty had overpowered their marriage.

He forced aside the past. "I'm getting too old for fifth gear these days."

"You old? You keep this place humming."

"Have you read this yet?" Duncan motioned to the thick packet he'd just put down.

"Cover to cover." Carl rested his mug on the edge of the desk and slung his bent arm over the chair back.

"What'd you think?"

"Unfortunately, the report makes a better case for those who oppose the project. Let's get a second opinion. Expert testimony can vary, depending on who you ask."

"Exactly what I thought."

Five years ago, Duncan met Carl at a trade conference. Carl had impressed the hell out of him with his knowledge in the field. After their chance conversation and dinner that same night, Duncan stole the eager thirty-three year old employee from one of his major competitors, a real corporate touchdown.

Duncan stroked his chin. "I figured with the slope of the property, runoff on the lake could pose some problems, but not nearly to the extent this study suggests."

"Me, too. Has Trent seen this?" Carl cocked a judgment-filled brow.

"I asked him to take a look. He hasn't gotten back to me." He'd sent his brother out of town on some site visits. "Can you follow-up with him? He returns from a site visit later today."

"Sure. I have a contact from my old job that does these studies. Want me to give him a call and explain what we need? He'll rush the report through if I ask him."

Sophie's pyramid comment replayed in his mind, like a subtle public service warning reminding you of the risks of secondhand smoke. Damn her! He wanted to tell Carl yes, but the way Sophie's beautiful gaze clung to him during that short moment still unraveled him, nearly as much as her clever observation. She was right. He'd been drawn to the lake's simple beauty, in the same way he'd been drawn to hers.

Carl waited, forehead furrowed and most likely wondering why Duncan didn't say yes, as he normally would.

"Make the call, but with one caveat. Tell the Northbridge officials we're doing this. I don't want news to surface later we completed multiple studies and only handed over the one with the most desirable results."

"Wouldn't be the first time."

"This is different." The statement annoyed Duncan, but he couldn't pinpoint why. "Shoot off a copy of this report to Adli Zimmerman on the Northbridge Zoning Board."

"Will do." Carl stood. "I'll ask him to keep the information under wraps until we can meet so we're consistent in how we spin this. By the way, nice article from the local paper. I worried about the reporter. One of the guys I talked to in Northbridge told me she's the one we outbid. At the hearing, she kept talking to that S.O.L.E. spokesperson."

He shrugged a shoulder. "She's harmless and seems fair. It's more important to me we don't appear to be hiding anything."

Carl covered two more items then left. Duncan lifted his newest Monte Blanc fountain pen and started a to-do list.

He tried to ignore an internal tug shifting his confidence askew, instead noting the pen's smooth cylinder in his fingertips. High-end pens had interested him ever since his Uncle Stan gave him one as a graduation gift. Whenever he tested the feel of one to purchase, he knew in an instant if it possessed the ideal combination of nib and barrel size for his needs. The selection of properties came from an intuitive place inside him too. When he stood on a site, the land's potential spoke to him. He'd never purchased the wrong fountain pen or the wrong property.

The idea to buy Tate Farm, though, stemmed from an altogether different place. Otis Tate had called Duncan's mother in late October to report their property was for sale. He'd shared that he knew his brother Elmer was on record as being Trent Jamieson's birth father, before the Jamiesons adopted him. While Trent wasn't a legal heir, he was the closest either of the elderly brothers had come to having an offspring. Otis had offered her a chance to bid on the property. A way to keep the land with relatives, at least as far as bloodlines went.

Duncan recalled the glee in his mother's voice at the prospect of acquiring this land for her favorite son. When Frank Jamieson had refused to get involved, she'd asked for Duncan's help and he jumped on board, ashamed right afterward that he'd only helped her in the hopes she might show him a little appreciation.

The unusual motivation behind this purchase had made him uneasy from the start, however, he'd ignored his gut for the sake of family. What choice did he have? Much like a fly stuck in a spider's web, Duncan could only wait and watch the purchase play out.

* * * *

Not now, please. Sophie pushed away a tear then shut off the car. Sitting in the dark school parking lot, she took several deep breaths. An image of Tia's excitement while getting ready for tonight's band concert, wearing her new black pleated skirt and starched white shirt, caused more tears to spill.

She retrieved a tissue from her purse and wiped her nose. Tonight the similarities between Henry and Tia reared their ugly head in the most unsettling ways. Their personalities were alike. They looked similar, with Sophie's dark hair and fair skin. They shared a love of music.

Tonight, thanks to Tia's first high school concert, she'd be in the same room with Henry's music teacher for the first time since her son's funeral. A dark day where she had gone through the motions of greeting those who came to pay their respects, her body present but her soul lifeless. Responses to condolences had been robotic, very few of the conversations remembered. In the long line of guests, though, Mr. Fisher, the music teacher, had stood out. The aging hippy had stood before her, red-eyed and sniffling as he took Sophie's hands in his. He'd quietly offered how her son was one of his brightest students, how his selection into a county-wide regional performance the prior December had filled him with pride. Sophie had burst with pride over his accomplishments, too. On the drive home from Henry's last concert, he'd announced to her and Mike his plans to major in music in college.

What would his life have been like if he'd lived?

She closed her eyes and tipped her head onto the headrest. Her stomach flipped, weightless, as if she'd been pushed off a cliff. Instead of hitting bottom where her misery would end, she hovered in space surrounded by the silent horror of waiting to slam to the ground. Exactly the way she'd felt for so long after Henry died. More tears escaped down her cheek. If only the appointment with her old therapist were tomorrow instead of next week.

Sophie inhaled deeply, counted to ten, and opened her moist eyes. With no choice but to follow her daughter's path in life, she wiped the wetness off her face, stepped out, and marched inside with her chin held high.

Inside the auditorium, she stayed in back and scanned the room. The stage held rows of chairs formed into a semi-circle with the band teacher's metal stand in the open center. She spotted her ex-husband up front, leaning over an empty seat, talking to an old high school buddy. Besides her fury with Mike over the date for the Florida trip, sitting with him tonight would be too much like old times. She'd find a seat and watch this alone.

Noisy band members clamored down the side aisle toward the stage so she plopped in the nearest seat, happily hidden in the back from the thick crowd of parents up front. Across the aisle from Mike, Ken Hollingsworth stared in her direction while he flagged down his wife, who'd entered right behind her. He caught Sophie's eye and waved.

The Dick Clark look-alike and her producer at the local cable program *Northbridge in Focus* had called her yesterday about next month's show, where she'd served as co-host for the past three years. He wanted their next topic to focus on RGI's offer and the proposed zoning changes.

The topic created a surge in her investigative pulse and an increased sense of urgency to the cryptic finger-pointing note about the Jamiesons and their corruption. When she'd been alone in Duncan's office during their interview, the executive's nearness threatened to sway her better senses. On a live TV program, he'd be forced to keep a respectable distance from her, where she could concentrate on the real issues at hand.

Chairs scraped on the wooden stage floor followed by a stray toot from a clarinet. She snapped out of her thoughts and she searched for Tia in the crowd of kids.

"Is this seat taken?"

Sophie looked up. Duncan watched her with a closed-lip smile, one that made his eyes soften and shine with hope. Empty seats surrounded her and after several seconds, she realized he wanted to join her.

"No. No. Please join me." She took her purse off the seat, but her mind raced. When he told her on the phone he'd moved in, she never dreamed she'd run into him so soon. She casually smoothed her gauze skirt and brushed a hand against her tear-swollen cheeks. "What brings you here? Taking in the cultural highlights of Northbridge?"

He chuckled. "You might say that. My son plays the trumpet." He motioned to the stage on the right. "I think I see him over there."

"Same here. Clarinet section. My daughter."

"Mr. Fisher is a good guy." He removed his wool coat and tossed it over her onto an empty seat. "He sent Patrick the music two weeks ago, so he could practice and participate tonight."

The memory of Henry's funeral once again threatened her composure and she worked hard not to flinch. "Yes. Mr. Fisher is a good man."

Duncan was dressed in his work clothes, the tie loosened, top button undone, and suit jacket probably shed in the car. He settled in next to her and their arms brushed on the armrest. She shifted in her seat.

After a second, she dared to peek his way. "So, everything unpacked from your move?"

"Getting there." He moved his large frame and their shoulders bumped. He turned his head, studied her face as if he'd never seen her before, the power of his gaze easing back the rusty hinges of her heart. "We have some projects to be done. I may need advice on a handyman or carpenter." The loud chatter in the auditorium died down as the band teacher walked on stage. Duncan tipped his head closer to her. "Maybe we can talk later?"

She nodded, catching a whiff of the cologne she'd admired during his kayak rescue. She focused on the stage, but an invisible impression of his closeness left her skin warm, about a hundred times more intense than that lowlife lawyer, Ryan Malarkey had ever made her feel. Caution would be prudent. What did Duncan really want from her? Good press, most likely. Guilt pinged against her chest, like radar offering a beep of warning over her lie of omission to Cliff over her first encounter with Duncan.

The sensation eased as the band launched into their first number, Rossini's "William Tell Overture," also known as the theme to the *Lone Ranger*. Yup, the race was on, but which way should she run, toward this man or away?

* * * *

The second Sophie got home from the concert, Matt ran into the kitchen and almost slammed into her. "Okay, Mom. This is your last chance to say yes."

"Yes." She went the refrigerator and got out two water bottles, handing one to Tia.

"Not funny." He frowned.

"I thought so." She chuckled and twisted the cap. Tia grinned too.

"Seriously. Connor Johnson said his older brother can drive us to the concert. He's twenty-five and Connor's parents said it's cool. He'd even stay with us in our hotel room."

"That's supposed to make this better?" She started to leave the kitchen. "Come on. Drop this, Matt."

"You're neurotic!" Matt spoke louder than she'd normally accept, but she didn't yell back. "Even Grandpa said so."

"Grandpa? When did you talk to him?"

Matt ran a hand through his blond hair, his gaze scooting to the floor. "He called me the day you went to pick up the kayaks...to make sure I'd go help you. I figured as long as he was on the phone, I'd get another opinion."

His admission that he'd tried to gain his grandfather's support raised the bar of her irritation. There were moments she hated single parenthood. At least Dad possessed the good sense not to try to persuade her to have sympathy for Matt's side. Last time he caved to Matt's manipulations, she'd had a rare fight with her father.

"I doubt Grandpa would call me neurotic. You'd better stop running to him when I say no to something. Trust me, as a father, he was tougher than me."

Matt's fair skin turned pink. "You're so unfair!"

"Stop it." Tia's soft voice squeaked from the other side of the room. "Mom's fair. If she says no, she has her reasons."

"Thank you, honey, but this is between your brother and me." Sophie gave her a slight nod of thanks and recognized a bit of herself in her sensible daughter. She turned to Matt. "Moms are allowed to be cautious."

"You're just afraid." Matt's voice escalated further. "You think something bad will happen. Like what happened to Henry."

The blow struck like an unexpected slap across the cheek, leaving her too stunned to reply. He'd never spoken to her that way before.

"Dad even thinks I should go." Matt raised his chin, satisfied, as if he'd one upped her. The expression reeked of his father. "He said you're being unreasonable. He thinks you're afraid too."

This second strike to the same raw wound flipped her switch. She coiled like an angry snake. "I don't really care what Daddy thinks." She jabbed a finger in his face. "He left this family. Remember?"

Matt jerked his head back. A red hue coated his cheeks and his jaw flexed tight.

Tia's eyes watered and she ran from the room.

Sophie covered her mouth with her hand. What had she done? She'd never spoken that way to Matt before. Self-loathing sunk deep. She hated herself right now for saying those words, but the person she hated the most was her ex-husband for manipulating their son.

She slowly lowered her hand. "Matt, no matter why you believe I made the decision, it's the one I'm sticking with. Please don't ask again."

His glare seared her skin. He rushed from the room and, seconds later, slammed his bedroom door.

Matt's nasty comment echoed in her head. Pure hatred toward her ex burned through her veins. Mike had slammed her with similar logic the night Henry died. She'd wanted to say no to her son's outing with his friends, but Mike insisted they let him go, accused her of babying him. So, Henry had gone out but never came home. Her granted permission could never be taken back. The outcome could never change.

She buried her face in her hands and tears spilled. Grief sunk deep into her chest when a notion suddenly hit. The suffering didn't only belong to her. Both her children had lost a sibling, too. She cried harder.

After she got the tears out of her system, the pain subsided. She slowly headed up the stairs to give both kids the hugs they deserved instead of this sadness.

Chapter 10

The bells on the tackle shop door chimed as Sophie pushed it open. Jay stuck his head out of a curtained doorway leading to the store's office. "Hey, Sis. Didn't expect to see you today." He stepped out and gave her the once over. "Why all gussied up?"

"I'm not gussied-up." The dressy black slacks, starched blouse, and herringbone patterned blazer were a switch from her usual casual style, though. "I have an official appointment with Buzz. Couldn't even just pop in like usual. According to his secretary, he's been busier than the governor this week. Where's Dad?" She plopped her leather bag on top of the case.

"Home. I told him to take a day off. Mid-week is quiet. Of course, he fought me. He's a pain in the ass sometimes."

"Oh, yeah. It's not like you'd ever do that."

He grinned and his bowl-round chin changed shape. She'd inherited her dad's calm, levelheaded way of thinking, tempered by occasional female outrage. Jay had Dad's knowing eyes and his blondish hair, also starting to turn the same soft silver. He'd also been blessed with the Moore stubborn gene,

"So, why the visit to Buzz?" Jay flipped open the box top and pulled out some Ross fly reels. "Is he your new best friend too?"

"Too?"

"I heard you and the Resort Group guy are chummy." He narrowed his eyes and rested the reels on the glass counter.

"What are you talking about?"

"Bart and I went out for a beer the other night at Griswold's. He said the firm's president winked at you during the hearing. What gives?" Jay shook his head. "The guy is our arch-rival."

"Once again, you two knuckleheads have proven how the volume of beer consumed is commensurate with the exaggeration of any given story."

"Huh?"

"This isn't the first time you and Bart have drank at Griswold's and spun a tale worthy of a woman's sewing clutch." Relief settled over her, glad he hadn't learned she'd been sitting with Duncan at the concert two nights earlier. "Maybe you'd like the real facts."

He grunted and reached his arms up to tighten the band on his short ponytail. "So, what really happened?"

She explained about the kayak clean-up, offering a modified version of Duncan's fib. Jay didn't need any more gasoline thrown on his steady stream of scorn for the developer. The lines of Jay's face stiffened while he listened.

When she finished, he swatted his hand through the air. "Whatever. Speaking of him, I read your nice story in the *Gazette*." Jay's mouth pinched. He brushed past her and picked up a stack of mail by the cash register, flipping the envelopes with force. "Jesus, Sophie. Jamieson ruined our plans. Aren't you angry?"

"I am, but you know I couldn't show that in my piece." His nonchalant shrug annoyed her. "I'm here for a reason. Two reasons, actually. Something's been bothering me."

He looked up from the mail.

"When we were about to sign the contract for the land, did you ever worry about the money?"

"Why would I?"

"It's a big step. Selling both your house and Dad's to make it work. Taking a loan. The stress of your family and Dad all living under one roof. I mean, Dad is pretty set in his ways. Then there's the risk of a start-up venture."

"What?" Jay's pale eyes went a shade darker. "You don't want the land now?"

"I didn't say that. I worry. What if the vineyard isn't profitable or what if—"

"Stop being so damn logical, Sophie! For once in your life, go with your heart. RGI railroaded us, but I plan on getting back on track. You'd better too."

"I'm voicing a concern." She was in no mood to fight with Jay. "If we're going to run a business together, you'd better learn to be ok with me speaking up. And you need to be honest with me. The money doesn't scare you a little?"

He dropped the mail on the glass top and rubbed the back of his neck. "I don't know. We were finally getting a chance to do something special. Go for a dream we'd given up on. It was worth some risk."

Jay stared past her. "Guess ever since I left the restaurant to come home and help Dad, I'd hoped someday to find an opportunity here to make up for what I lost. My chef training has gone to waste at the shop." Jay's eyes met hers. The down-curved U of his lip showed all the sadness he hid inside.

"Our dreams aren't over." She spoke quietly, without her usual conviction.

"The Tates' land is perfect, though." He crossed his arms.

"There could be a location, a better one that we haven't considered."

Jay studied her face intently. She didn't dare bring up the things they couldn't replace, like Dad's hope to recoup his family's land and, of course, her son's memorial garden.

He forced a weak smile that didn't reach his eyes, the way he always did when admitting he'd taken his angst a step too far. "So what else did you want to talk about?"

Sophie dug into her bag. "I come bearing a possible reason for RGI to remove their bid and I need some help. Set your brain back to the early eighties, when you used to listen to Michael Jackson."

He snorted. "I never listened to Michael Jackson. Is this some kind of trivia thing?"

"Sort of." She unfolded the newspaper story reporting the gunshot incident at Buzz and Marion's. "Read this. Tell me if you remember anything."

He took the paper and wiggled his fingers in his flannel shirt pocket. "Damn it. I can never find those glasses." He stretched his arm out as far as it would go and squinted.

Sophie retrieved his dollar store pair from the far counter and handed them over. "Sucks getting old, huh?"

"I wouldn't be so smug." He grinned then started to read. After a minute, he looked up. "Sure. I remember this. My buddy Andy Murray had started working at the station right around the time this happened."

"Andy from your baseball team?"

"Uh-huh. At Griswold's one night, Andy went on about how the station kept something quiet that happened at the Harris household. All of a sudden, he clammed up. Wouldn't say any more."

"Now read this." She handed off the warning note.

"The Jamiesons are corrupt. Both now and in the past. Question the gunshot." Jay looked over the rim of his glasses. "How are these connected, besides that both mention a gunshot?"

"Both were left for me by an anonymous donor at my office. Do you ever hear from Andy? Maybe he'd talk now."

"Last time we spoke, he'd started a job near Hartford. I don't have his number. I can do a little digging."

"Thanks." She picked up her purse and threw the strap on her shoulder. "It's so weird. I don't even remember this gunshot at Buzz's. Thanks for your help. Don't forget to ask."

"Sis, if there's a chance this could get our land back, you have my word."

* * * *

After a quick stop in the office, Sophie entered the municipal building and went straight into Buzz's reception area.

"Have a seat, hon." Wanda tucked the corner of her curly mop behind her ear, further exposing heavy gold hoops dragging down large earlobes. "He'll be a few minutes."

Sophie plopped into the chair across from his door and crossed her legs, taking inventory of the dated gray carpet and hotel liquidation artwork. Certain areas in the town facility were in serious need of a makeover, starting with their First Selectman's reception area.

Wanda swiveled her head between the computer and a document stand, her long neck like a giraffe's. Voices behind Buzz's office door rose and an argumentative tone seeped through the cracks, barely tempered by the wood.

Wanda cleared her throat, not missing a beat on the keyboard. "So, how was your Thanksgiving?"

Wanda possessed the loyalty of a Labrador when it came to her job. As someone who tried to stay neutral when reporting, Sophie admired how this woman maintained her position through multiple administrations of both political affiliations. Nobody knew if Wanda registered Democrat, Republican or Tory Party member.

"Thanksgiving was good. We went to Jay's. Can't go wrong with his cooking. How about yours?"

"Same as always." She stopped typing and gave her full attention to Sophie. "I slave over a hot stove for twenty people and go to bed exhausted."

An obvious hush settled in Buzz's office.

Wanda resumed her typing. "Anyway, one more crazy holiday month ahead. I can't wait for January second."

Sophie nodded her agreement. She pretended to study a nearby bulletin board, her ears trained to the low voices in Buzz's office, much calmer than a minute ago.

Seconds later, his door clicked open. Sophie's stomach clenched, knowing his mood after an argument could range from mild to spicy. He stepped out with Adli Zimmerman behind him. Both men nodded at her without even a pressed-on phony smile. Buzz turned to Adli. "I'll speak to you before the meeting. Sophie. Come on in."

She gathered her bag, took two steps, but stopped short when Duncan stepped outside of Buzz's door.

They stood close, so close she could see dark flecks in his rich blue irises.

"Sophie." His eyes softened. "Good to see you again."

Her heart pounded loudly against her ribs. Neither moved for what seemed like an eternity but probably amounted to three seconds. He wore an open-necked white dress shirt tucked into his khakis, making the pink hue that rushed his neck more obvious.

"You too." The swift patter of her heart sounded in her ears.

His attitude shifted, suddenly business-like and he stuck out his hand in Buzz's direction. "Buzz. I appreciate the time today." He offered the same gesture to Adli and returned his gaze to her when finished. "Thanks for the names you gave me the other night. The carpenter is coming over tonight to talk."

"Good. Glad to have helped."

Adli, Buzz, and Wanda looked on while a burn seared her cheeks. She hoped the redness wasn't obvious to their small audience.

Duncan's expression shifted. "Well, then. Uh, men, thanks for your time. Sophie, guess I'll see you around."

He walked out. Adli walked by her, too, holding a thick, bound document with the word "Environmental" in bold letters on the cover.

"Hey, Adli?"

He turned around and glanced over the half-rimmed glasses positioned near the tip of his nose. "Yes?"

"Anything new going on with the lakefront zoning changes?"

"As a matter of fact, we're looking carefully at two environmental studies Duncan had completed." He nodded to the thick package in his hands. "We may delay the board's vote. No sense rushing things."

A delayed vote brought relief. More time to research RGI and possibly find something to sway the zoning board vote against them. A little resuscitation for her family's bid.

Buzz scowled from his doorway, but Sophie ignored him. "When will you decide if you're going to delay things?"

Buzz grunted and disappeared into the office.

Adli's jaw flexed. He turned to her. "Next Tuesday night. At the regular meeting."

"Okay. Thanks." Sophie scooted inside the selectman's office. "Do you want the door shut or open?"

"Depends on what you're here to discuss."

She shut the door. Buzz flinched.

She sat opposite him at the large oak desk. "I'm not here about zoning issues. Even if I was, I'm not Bernadette."

"Yes. I know." His shoulders relaxed. "Things have been pretty tense lately. I can't help that my back is up. People don't understand how I'm trying to do what's right by this town."

"I'm sure you are."

"What can I do for you today?" His polite, businesslike tone didn't hide the edgy stiffness of his expression.

Sophie removed the article and slid it across his desk, keeping the block-lettered warning note to herself for now. "I wanted your take on this."

Buzz took the paper. Deep lines creased his forehead as he scanned the page. The muscles of his face twitched like a horse's hide. The wall clock ticked loud, the only sound in the room.

Finally he drew in a deep breath. "Yes, of course I remember the day this happened." Buzz appeared to reread the words while his fingers drummed along his chin. He chuckled, an uncomfortable little snort, and met her stare. "Very embarrassing. The neighbors called the police when they heard the gunshot. Why do you have this?"

The nervous pulse in her throat throbbed, as it always did right before she raised a controversial issue. "Oh, let's say something led me to it."

He shrugged, as if in doing so the item would slither off his shoulders and go away. "It's nothing more than the article says."

"Then it doesn't involve the Jamieson family?"

Boom! His jaw tumbled, followed by a bright hue splaying across his face. "It has nothing to do with them. Why would you say that?"

"I heard they owned a house here when it happened."

"So?" In his attempt to regroup, the cogs in his mind were nearly visible. He frowned. "So. What's your point? A lot of people owned houses here back then."

She leaned forward, breath now steadied, thanks to confidence in her conclusions. "You're telling me this police report has no connection to their family?"

"It most certainly does not."

Sophie scribbled on her pad but still saw him fidget in his seat and chew a cuticle. She jotted *uneasy* along the margin.

"Did someone say otherwise?" Nervous curiosity laced his tone.

"No. The Jamiesons' arrival is the only unusual thing happening right now. I'm grasping at straws."

He tilted a suspicious brow. "Where'd you find this story, anyway?"

"At the library. If you say there's nothing to it, then I'm barking up the wrong tree."

He avoided her eyes as he handed back the paper.

"Thanks for seeing me." She tucked the story back into her bag. Sometimes she needed Buzz and smoothing over the bed she'd ruffled was prudent. "Hey, how's the statue of Dewty coming along?"

Buzz's face brightened like a five-year-old being offered candy. Exactly the reaction she'd hoped for. "Do you want to see the artist's sketches?"

"Sure."

Buzz went to his filing cabinet, took a folder off the top, and flipped through the contents.

Every school kid in town had learned about Northbridge's most famous resident, Dewty Flynn. He'd earned fame in the early 1900s for his vaudeville productions, later joining forces with Harold Sullivan and traveling the country performing under "The Family Theater of Flynn and Sullivan." To mark the showman's 150th birthday celebration next spring, Buzz had made a shrewd political move to commission a bronze statue to display in front of the museum, one of his better ideas.

"Here are three sketches." Buzz's tone lightened. "Which do you like?"

Sophie gushed over the choices, picked the pose where Dewty tipped his derby hat in greeting and even suggested she interview the artist. Buzz glowed. She'd played him as smoothly as freshly Zambonied ice, same as he often did with her.

Five minutes later, despite his earlier assurances, she left with the belief the article and incident had *everything* to do with the Jamieson clan. Exactly why, though, remained as clear as frosted glass.

Out on the municipal building's front steps, the first snow flurries of the season greeted her. She tightened her scarf and tucked the ends into her buttoned blazer. Something made Sophie glance over her shoulder. Buzz stood in the window watching, his stare as icy as the air surrounding her. He turned away.

Feathery flakes danced in the air as she rushed to the car and just as she reached the door, a frigid wind gust slammed into her, sending a shiver to her core. Time to take out the winter coat.

Chapter 11

Duncan tooted the car horn. What the heck was taking Patrick so long? While waiting, he studied the front of his new home, his chest swelling with pride. He noted each arched peak and unique architectural detail, especially the custom-made stained glass installed in a few key windows. The day Elizabeth had remarked money couldn't by him happiness popped into his head, a moment he'd regrettably treated in his usual detached manner. She was right. Money couldn't buy him happiness, but his earnings bought this place and a chance to start a new life with his children.

She'd made the comment a month away from their fifth wedding anniversary. He'd opened her early gift to him, a beautiful shaker gift box containing an itinerary for three weeks of European travel. "I appreciate the idea, Liz, but I can't be away from work this long."

After some discussion, she'd stormed from the room mumbling the clichéd saying.

At the time, he hadn't understood how she failed to realize why work commitments mattered and forced him to say no. Early in their relationship, he'd explained how badly he needed to prove himself as a success apart from his father's reputation and wealth. Upon her death, he'd remembered the incident and squirmed with embarrassment over his actions, like he did right now.

Was he trying to buy happiness?

Patrick flung open the door and jumped into the SUV's passenger seat, still tugging on his Northface jacket. "Sorry. Couldn't find my coat."

"If you hung things up like Helen suggested, you'd find it next time."

"Yeah, yeah." Patrick rolled his eyes and Duncan suppressed a grin. "How far away is this fishing store?"

"They call them bait and tackle shops." Duncan threw the car into reverse. "About ten minutes."

They drove in comfortable silence along Lake Shore Road. Yesterday's inch of snowfall left a thin layer of bright white outlining the naked branches. Though pretty, they also seemed empty and cold.

Just like his marriage. Losing his wife had made him address the dark place in his heart, a place he'd clung to most of his life. A few years of dating since then, he'd come to one conclusion—love wasn't worth the trouble and he made a horrible husband. Yet, running into Sophie upon his return to Northbridge had shaken his invisible barrier and made him reconsider an emotion he'd become convinced didn't fit into his life.

"Bet Casey likes it here." Patrick stared out the passenger window.

"I hope so."

Duncan wished his daughter could enjoy their new home, but she'd returned to college the day after Thanksgiving. Casey's final words were, "I'll see the house at Christmas." Her tone had roared with negativity, his daughter never one to hide her real feelings. Gaining lost ground with her after years of neglect as a parent seemed insurmountable. They were alike. Both driven toward what they wanted and both difficult to stop when headed down a path. Neither paid any attention to how their stubbornness impacted others.

How many times had he done the same thing to his wife, ruining her chances for a life of happiness? A stone lump formed in his throat. He swallowed hard, but the sadness didn't dislodge. The firm hand of regret pressed to his chest and he rode out the guilt.

"Do you miss your sister?"

Patrick shrugged. "Yes and no. Our guy time is fun."

"I think so too." At least one kid didn't hate him.

The trip continued in silence until Duncan turned into a parking lot. Gravel crunched beneath the car's tires. He'd hoped to find Sophie's Subaru there but only saw a truck and Ford Taurus with a rusty fender. Still, she could be here. The adolescent anxiousness that had seized him so long ago returned. The confident aloofness he'd fine-tuned for years, one that attracted many women, was lost in her presence.

They stepped out of the car and Duncan studied the red-clapboard building. "Pretty much the same as it was years ago."

The exterior of the multi-room shop had weathered slightly over the years with only two obvious additions: A sign plastered on the side of the building reading "Parking for Bullshead Bait n' Tackle Patrons Only. Violators will be towed," and a large storage shed at the end of the lot.

Duncan opened a screen door then pushed open a solid wood one, triggering the tinkle of a bell. A slight musty odor rushed at him, knocking him back to his teenage years, kicking off a remembrance of all the times he'd entered this place.

A voice behind a curtained doorway yelled, "Be right with you."

"Thanks."

So much had changed, yet so much remained the same. He and his son wandered the front room, still housing regular fishing gear. Pictures of customers with their catches from the lake were nailed in every possible spot, many taken decades ago. A large, square, glass-encased counter in the store's center space held pricey equipment.

Patrick pointed up. "Can I get one of those?" The planked ceiling rafters held a line-up of poles.

"They're for spin fishing." Duncan motioned to a wide doorway leading to a second room. "Let's look in there, the fly fishing area, where we'll find most of what we're looking for."

They entered the area. Old pine paneling against the far wall had been replaced since Duncan last saw it with stark white walls holding shelves stacked with boxes of waders.

He went to a floor display of fly rods, pointed upward at attention like soldiers in a small army. "Here. This is what we want."

In the far corner, a new Aquafina and Coke machine replaced the old white soda refrigerator where he'd first seen Sophie. An unexpected gust of disappointment swept by him, the newer refrigeration having stolen a piece of his past.

"Good afternoon." Mr. Moore headed toward them, older but still recognizable. He still had a full head of hair, now silvery-white and neatly brushed back on the sides. "Can I help you folks?"

"Yes. We're here to get my son outfitted for fly fishing this spring."

A teenage boy Duncan recognized followed behind the older man. In a split second, he realized they'd met when he helped Sophie with the vandalized boats.

The teenager studied Patrick. "Hey. Aren't you the new kid in my pre-calculus class?"

"Yeah. I'm Patrick."

"Cool. I'm Matt." He pointed a finger at Duncan. "I know you. You're the guy who helped me and my mom with our kayaks."

"I did. Any more problems with them?"

"Nah. Mom thinks some kids were messing around." His attention returned to Patrick. "Are you the one Coach Saunders said was joining the basketball team?"

"Guess so. I'll be at practice tomorrow."

"Cool." Matt bobbed his head and shoved his hands in the pockets of his worn jeans. "You fish?"

"My dad wants to teach me."

"Come on." Matt motioned with a hand wave. "Come see the rod and reel I use. It's in the office." The boys headed off.

"Mr. Moore, I'm Duncan Jamieson." He extended a hand. "My father and I used to visit your shop a long time ago. Around nineteen eighty. My dad's family owned a house on the lake."

"Welcome back. Call me Alan."

Duncan noted the difference between the shop owner's faded red plaid flannel shirt as compared to the fleece pullover Duncan wore from the Orvis catalog, one he'd hoped would make him blend with the locals.

"Is Sophie here?" Duncan tried not to sound eager.

"Not today. She only helps every so often during peak season." Alan picked up a reel someone had left out and motioned for Duncan to follow him toward the glass case.

Duncan hid his disappointment but saw an opportunity too. Right after the public hearing, Sophie remarked how he'd never understand why the land meant something to her. She'd avoided his question when he asked her in his office too.

"The day I helped your daughter with the kayaks, I was quite surprised to run into her. I remembered her from our visits years ago. She even interviewed me for the paper. When the idea for a development in this area popped into my head, I never dreamed I'd open up such a can of worms—no fishing pun intended."

Alan formed a noncommittal smile. "Change is hard for people. Some of us enjoy the area as is."

"Then you don't support the development either?"

The barrel-chested man stroked the fleshy area underneath his chin. "It's not that simple."

"I understand Sophie and her brother have an interest in the property."

"We all have ties. My family used to own the land."

"Really? I thought the Tates had always been there."

"Nope. My great-granddad first settled that land. Used to raise cattle. The title transferred to Ehren Tate when my great-uncle Levi lost the land to him in a poker bet."

"A poker bet? Must've been a great hand."

"Story goes he held a full house—three aces and two kings. After pushing what little cash he had left on the table, he—quite literally—bet the ranch. Unfortunately for my family, Ehren held a royal flush.

My uncle will be forever known in the Moore family history as Levi the Loser." Alan grinned behind tired eyes then shifted to a serious tone. "Land's pretty special to us, though. There's a small cemetery there where many of my ancestors are buried."

Regret pounded, unexpected and hard. A winery could sprout anywhere. The land of this family's forefathers was another matter. "Guess I can see why you'd want it back."

Alan shrugged. "Can't change the past."

"Guess those family ties explain why Sophie wants this land so badly."

The older man's gaze dropped to the floor but, before it did, a deeper pain flashed. The bell over the door sounded and they both looked over. "Hey, Jay." Alan seemed eager to end the topic.

A younger, thinner version of Alan Moore scuffed toward them and gave Duncan an evil-eyed onceover. Duncan recognized Jay's friend, who had a full round face and closely shaved scalp—the polar opposite of Jay—as the videographer filming the public hearing.

"This is Bart Sweeny and my son, Jay. Boys, meet Duncan Jamieson." Alan motioned with his hand.

Bart reached out and politely shook hands, but Jay stared with a hard glare. "Yup. Recognize him from the paper."

Duncan offered a firm hand to Jay, who shook with a grip stiff as a tree limb. "Glad to finally meet you. I've heard you were interested in the Tate property too." Big game hunter, aiming straight for the elephant in the room should work with this guy.

Jay shifted his shoulders and his broad chest seemed to expand as he jerked back his hand. "I still am. If I recall, zoning hasn't passed the changes you requested yet."

Mr. Moore threw a calm-down glance at his son, who ignored him and studied Duncan, poised for a challenge.

"The zoning board's exploration is something I support." Duncan chose his words with care. "My company wouldn't want to do anything to destroy the beauty around here. Were you at the hearing?"

Jay wet his lower lip. "I was out of town."

"When we made the offer, we knew others were interested but we were told nothing had been signed. I didn't know it was your family. Sometimes this happens in our business."

Jay's jaw stiffened. "Knowing you didn't intentionally shaft me doesn't help. Anyway, may the best man win." He glanced at his dad. "We'll be in back working."

Jay nodded at Duncan, but a thickness heavier than a humid Mississippi day still lingered between them.

Aim, shoot, miss. Was Duncan losing his touch?

The two men left, disappearing through a doorway against the back wall.

Alan Moore rubbed the side of his neck. "Sorry. The purchase meant a lot to him." He frowned and averted his stare to a spot on the old hardwood floors.

A hard reality smacked Duncan in the forehead. He'd never once thought about those who he'd outbid in his dealings or the people opposed to his projects, not on a personal level, anyway.

"No, Alan. I'm sorry."

How many other times had he stolen someone's dream and plowed ahead oblivious?

Chapter 12

On her way out of the church's kitchen, Sophie smiled as she passed a poster hanging off the door. Beneath a landscape of fresh fallen snow set against a cloudless, sapphire sky, it read, "A snowflake is one of God's most fragile creations, but look what they can do when they stick together."

The sentiment summed up her love for those in her community. Especially the special folks who attended the Northbridge Methodist Church, the place she'd been baptized and had worshiped her entire life.

She returned to the large gathering room and dumped a few more pine branches on top of the table where Bernadette stood cutting wire. "I'll bet we can get two swags out of this."

Since childhood, Sophie had loved the church's annual Christmas ritual called "Hanging of the Greens." Rooted in the English tradition of decorating homes for the Christmas season, their normally austere Protestant church came to life with a little help from Mother Nature.

Sophie grabbed a branch and inhaled the resinous aroma, certain it ranked amongst life's most precious scents.

Bernadette twisted wire around two branches. "I made turkey chili for the potluck supper. What'd you bring?"

She looked up and before she could answer, her heart stalled. A lean teenage boy with dark hair strolled into the room with a girl his age who attended the church. It took a mere micro-second for her brain to register he was the boyfriend of the teen, not Henry. The look-alike moment, which happened on occasion, crushed her between wishes and reality.

"Baked macaroni and cheese." She dared to take a closer look at the boy, whose similarities ended with the basics.

She shook off the sad moment by concentrating on a lineup of pastoral photos on the wall next to them. The pictures started with the Reverend Daniel Dobbins in 1886 and ended with their current pastor, Reverend

Felton, better known to Sophie as Bernadette's husband Dave, who wove through tables toward them while munching on a cookie.

She elbowed Bernadette. "Here comes your hubby."

Dave's warm brown eyes, round face, and sweet smile provided a perfect exterior for a minister, his appearance merely the icing to a much deeper soul, one which never failed to connect with their entire congregation.

"Don't you love this smell?" He brushed a crumb from his lip.

"One of my favorites." Sophie nodded and tucked a long strand of hair behind her ear.

He studied her face. "Doing okay?"

Dave had a sixth sense for honing in on quiet distress, one of his strengths, and his concern made her tense shoulders relax. "Better than ever."

He popped the last bite of cookie into his mouth. "Your nana's shortbread recipe adds pounds to my waistline every Christmas."

"Those are for dessert. Your position here doesn't give you special eating privileges."

"Says *you*." He arched a brow then moved to Bernadette, wrapping a loving arm around her waist. "Nice work, sweetie."

The first time she and Mike had double-dated with Bernadette and Dave, early in their relationship, the transition from "Reverend Dave" to "Person Dave" made Sophie feel awkward. Especially when he'd shown up to dinner in jeans and a sweater, like he wore this afternoon.

At the restaurant, Dave had ordered a glass of red wine.

"Pastors are allowed to drink?" The words had popped out of Sophie's mouth before she could stop them.

He'd chuckled softly. "Now we can. John Wesley's dictate for an alcohol-free church goes back to the seventeen hundreds. But 'the times they are a-changing.'" He'd sung the Dylan tune. "Seriously, though, nowadays responsible drinking is a personal choice amongst Methodist clergy."

"Interesting." She'd nodded. "I half expected to see you wearing your clerical robe and preaching stole tonight."

His face had transformed with the same sly grin he displayed whenever eliciting a laugh from the congregation during a sermon. "I would've, but they're in the cleaners."

The moment defined the close friendship they now shared.

Bernadette snipped a strand of red ribbon and offered Dave the branch clippers. "Want to help?"

Dave reached for them but stopped as Lucy Tanner-Scott floated by their table. The former Miss Connecticut top-ten finalist kept her lovely locks as bright as sunshine and her family income registered in the top one percent wealthiest year-round residents on Blue Moon Lake.

Lucy headed a short list of single, divorced females in Sophie's age group in Northbridge, adding to an already awkward rivalry. In eleventh grade, Mike had dumped the beauty then asked Sophie to the junior prom. Tension between their rival groups heightened. Sophie learned payback really was a bitch when four years later, Mike cheated on her with the bedazzling blonde. A one-shot deal, but a sign Sophie should have viewed as a clear warning about her life with Mike.

Lucy's sweet voice crooned, "Good sermon this morning, Reverend, but it got a bit long." She flashed a toothy beam, highlighting orthodontic-perfect teeth.

She wore snug jeans and as she paused near their table, several men standing close by discreetly glanced over. Sophie and Bernadette had shamefully admitted to each other they often found themselves checking her out too. By comparison, today they both wore faded Levis and Christmas-themed sweatshirts, kind of a homespun hotness, for men into that sort of thing.

"Thanks for your input, Lucy. Always appreciate advice. I once heard someone say a good sermon should be like a woman's skirt—long enough to cover the essentials and short enough to keep you interested."

Lucy arched a perfectly waxed eyebrow, giggled and continued to cross the room.

Bernadette tipped her head at her husband. "Seriously, Dave?"

"What? It's a joke." He shrugged, but Bernadette's disapproving gaze didn't budge. "Okay, wrong audience, I suppose."

Sophie patted Dave on the shoulder. "The joke was funny, though."

He sent a grateful nod her way. He reached for the clippers, but stopped and waved toward the entrance. "Oh good. I hoped he'd come."

Duncan stood at the doorway and skimmed the activity in the large room filled with tables, pine branches, and busy workers. His son, who Sophie had met after the school concert earlier in the week, stood at his side. Duncan spotted Dave and waved. His gaze cornered Sophie, making the pace of her heart surpass its regular trot.

The pair strolled in their direction, Duncan's gait purposeful and confident. Overly confident people left Sophie curious about their Achilles' heel. Everyone had one. What was his?

He wore a thick wool sweater and jeans, different than at the office yet appealing in a whole new way. He nodded at a few people but each time he refocused on their small group, his gaze landed right on her.

A sharp pain jabbed her hand and she released the vise-tight grip she held on a pine branch. In the court of being honest with herself, she'd be committing perjury if she said Duncan hadn't been on her mind. When in town running errands this week, she kept scanning the area for him, like a schoolgirl hoping to catch her crush in the hallway. A crazy act, considering her latest pastime involved snooping around in his past to sabotage his offer.

"What's *he* doing here?" Bernadette's low voice reeked of judgment.

"I invited him when we ran into each other at the grocery store." Dave leaned close to Bernadette. "Need I repeat my mantra about God *not* being involved in politics?"

"I think you just did." Bernadette plastered a store-bought smile on her face, not her natural pleased expression. "I'm on my best behavior, dear."

Dave glanced up to the heavens, clasped his hands in prayer, and mouthed *thank you*.

"Hi, Reverend Felton." Duncan carried a string-closed box from Crumbs, a local bakery. "Thanks for asking us today."

"Call me Dave. This is my wife, Bernadette."

"Nice to meet you." Duncan did a double-take, probably remembering her antics at the public hearing. "Hi, Sophie." His voice softened. "Does every path in Northbridge lead to you or only the ones I follow?"

A burn inched up her cheeks. One she tried to ignore. "It probably won't be the last time. It's a small town." Her peripheral vision caught Bernadette's delighted glow, but she focused on the newcomers. "Glad you could join us today. You too, Patrick."

Matt barged into the circle, going straight to Patrick. "Dude, two days in a row? What are you doing here?"

"Reverend Felton invited us."

Sophie eyed Matt. "Two days in a row?"

"Pat and his dad came into the shop yesterday. Boy, I heard all kinds of stories about you, Mom. Oh, I forgot...." Matt's peppy outlook downshifted and he bit his lower lip, reminding her so much of his father when he'd screwed something up. "Mr. J. said to tell you hello."

"Mr. J.?" She looked at Duncan. He grinned and shrugged.

"Come on, Pat." Matt tipped his head. "I'll introduce you around."

Sophie waited until they were out of earshot. "It would take an act of God for me to get any messages from him. Care to work on that, Dave?"

He threw up flattened palms as if a gun were pointed in his direction. "There's only so much I can do."

Sophie returned to the crystal shine of Duncan's eyes, a reminder of why she couldn't get him out of her head. "You visited Dad's shop yesterday?"

He nodded. "Patrick's getting fishing gear for Christmas. I figured we'd practice casting in the yard before opening day."

Dave motioned across the room. "Let's hang up your coat and I'll introduce you to the others."

"Sure."

He lifted the Crumbs box, but before he could say anything, Sophie extended her arm. "I'll take those."

"Thanks." Their hands brushed during the trade-off, the power of the light sweep holding some major voltage. He stared at her several seconds longer than necessary then turned and followed Dave.

Bernadette leaned close and whispered, "You're blushing, you know."

"Uh-huh."

"If Cliff saw you at this moment, he'd take you off the RGI story. Don't you think?"

Sophie didn't answer right away but instead watched Dave introduce Duncan to the church organist. The white-haired, thin-faced grump never smiled at anybody but played a mean "A Mighty Fortress is Our God" on the old church organ. Duncan's charismatic beam even forced the corners of her mouth to bow upward.

She turned to Bernadette. "Then it's a good thing Cliff isn't around."

* * * *

Sophie had been hiding in the kitchen for the past fifteen minutes, where she'd escaped under the guise of warming dishes for their potluck supper, but really needed to be alone to reapply her game face.

Since Mike left five years earlier, her dating life had been as meager as the line of men waiting for a pedicure. It wasn't non-existent, simply short. Of four encounters, only Sam, a doctor living two towns over, had lasted four months. The downfall to their relationship turned out to be Sam's confirmed bachelorhood. A strong reminder why the type of love she'd craved her entire life still mattered a great deal.

The old industrial oven preheated and she threw in as many dishes as would fit. She placed a china platter on a center island dividing the large kitchen then settled at the avocado-green countertop. After she unwrapped Duncan's treats from Crumbs, she placed them on the plate.

A pattern emerged every single time she found herself near this guy. The patter of her heart switched tempo from its normal steady waltz to a Caribbean beat. Her confidence dropped a few degrees. Her radar honed in on his manly aura. Did he make all women he met this unsteady?

Footsteps approached. "Thanks for taking care of those."

Duncan's sexy smile made her game face smudge.

"No problem." She focused on the transfer of a napoleon to the plate with surgeon-like precision to avoid his gaze.

"I'm glad to run into you today."

Sophie glanced up, taking serious note of the way his navy pullover magnified the color of his eyes. "Yeah, me too."

"Dave's invite seemed like a fun way to get to know people."

"Stick with Dave. You'll meet the entire town."

She reached for a cannoli. Some icing from an éclair caught her forearm. Duncan swiped a napkin from the nearby dispenser, took her arm, then gently wiped the frosting. He handled her as if she were a fragile item requiring delicate care, his eyes never leaving her face, his touch making her burn in womanly places.

"Thanks. This thing where you help me is getting to be a habit. Do I seem needy or are you just always ready to lend a hand?"

His brows furrowed for a split second then he laughed. "Oh, right. The kayaks. You don't strike me as needy at all."

"Then helpful it is." She quickly resumed her task with the pastry arrangement, yet could still feel his touch on her skin. A few self-conscious seconds of silence passed.

"I'm curious. Wasn't Dave's wife the one heading up the committee against my development?"

"The one and only."

"Interesting."

"She can be. Bernadette and I have been best friends since we were kids. She carries a big stick but deep down she's a softy. Dave provides a guiding hand. Besides, those are her views, not her husband's."

"I've found most people in town, regardless of how they feel about the resort, have treated me cordially." Duncan's tone softened. "Like you."

Sophie's vision drifted from the platter and his penetrating gaze swept her away, its magic as endless as a clear blue sky.

Psychic abilities at this moment would come in handy. Chances were fifty-fifty his motives were really about her role on the paper. She hoped he didn't sense how his comment or the way he looked at her unraveled her insides.

"Did you meet my brother Jay yesterday?"

"Briefly."

"How'd it go?"

"Not as well as when I've met some others around town." He stuck his finger into stray icing on the box lid, took a little, then licked it off.

The gesture drew her focus to his full lower lip, followed by several R-rated notions involving icing, her mouth, and his.

"Your dad was great, though. Sold me a book on fly-tying. I figured Pat and I would learn together."

She pictured Duncan and his son tackling the intricate task, the resort developer who'd upset her world suddenly a warm and loving father. "Nice. My dad taught me. Sometimes they have classes at the shop, usually in the summer. You should go."

"So you know how to make them?"

"Sure. Bet you didn't know that one of the first significant books on fly-tying was written by a woman."

"Who? You?" He grinned and plunked down on a stool across from where she stood. Resting his elbows on the countertop, he leaned closer.

Sophie laughed. "No. Wanda Orvis Marbury, around eighteen seventy. She's who inspired me to make my own for a while."

"Why'd you stop?"

"No time. Kids, family obligations."

"I know what you mean. My daughter's in college now. Kind of strange only worrying about one kid day-to-day. Nice, though."

"I'll bet. Where does she go to school?"

"Vassar. In upstate New York."

She nodded but didn't share how Henry had applied to a school in Albany, his loss a path she didn't care to go down today. Especially with Duncan. Instead, she paired two cannolis tight on the plate and squeezed a third next to them, an easier task than discussing her loss. The less he learned about her personal life, the better. It crossed her mind to bring up the gunshot at Buzz's, to see how he'd react, but should she mix business and pleasure?

Before she could, Duncan blurted out, "I am sorry I outbid you on the land."

Sophie's response stalled. The property mattered to her. His bid ruined her plans. As she waded in a pool of mixed emotion, a thread of hair dangled near her eye. Her hands gooey, she pushed out her lower lip and tried to blow it away. It moved then plopped back to the same place.

Sharon Struth

Duncan reached over and brushed the strand aside, the light graze of his fingertip skimming her forehead. "It hasn't already come between us, has it?"

His simple touch left her knees wobbly as Jell-O, leaving her terrified by how easily he swayed her from sensible thought.

"I'm talking to you, right?" She attempted a light tone. "Besides, the land isn't yours yet." She walked over to the sink then glanced back. "Unless those zoning changes are a shoo-in and there's something else you'd like to tell me?"

"No. Of course not."

She soaped and rinsed her hands, sensing he watched her from behind. She looked over her shoulder. "So what were you guys saying about me yesterday? Should I be concerned?"

The corner of his lip twitched, as if she'd bumped him. "I told Matt I remembered you back in the days my family visited here."

After drying off with a paper towel, she returned to the island. "What year were you here?" She had to be careful not to slip and mention anything her research had uncovered.

"Around nineteen eighty."

"Ah, middle school, early high school. I drove Dad nuts at that age." She grabbed some wrap to cover the plate of treats. "I hear the environmental studies were completed."

He jerked his head back, surprise obvious. "How do you know?"

"After you left Buzz's office, I asked Adli. He said they'll vote Tuesday night about a possible delay on the zoning changes."

"Did he give you details about the reports?" An amused expression softened the slight creases in the corners of his eyes.

♦   "I'm not *that* good at getting information." She leaned her arms on the island, moving closer to him and softening her gaze. The ease of conversation roused a flirty side, one she didn't easily share. Her voice shifted, silky and soft. "Unless, sir, you'd care to tell me?"

"You're one persistent woman." His voice dropped, huskier than usual. "Is this an official interview?"

"Not at all. I'm curious if the findings will change the outcome of the project. Off the record, of course."

"Of course," he murmured. "Well, it's yet to be determined."

She pushed the island barrier to its limits and inched closer. "Hmm. Guess I'd better work on my persuasive skills."

"Trust me." He grinned wickedly and lowered his voice. "They were adequate."

Sophie's mouth went dry. What was she doing? He was her story. She moved back, stood straight, and dragged a nearby stool so she could sit across from him.

She mimicked his pose with her elbows on the counter and chin tucked in a palm. "Did you think much about our last conversation in your office?"

"Plenty." His words floated out as if sandwiched between two meanings. Had he found his emotional state in the same muddled mess as hers after their talk?

"Then you remember the pyramids?"

"How could I forget? Despite your analogy, I still believe my business can have a good presence here."

She shook her head. "Once a Scotsman..."

Broad delight spread across his face. They sat close enough for her to take in the flecks of light hair brushing his muscular freckled forearm. His large hand cradled the rise in his cheek.

"Something tells me you're the one around here who's going to keep me on my toes." His butter-smooth tone flowed through her. "Not the activists."

"You know what they say around these parts."

"What?"

"Never underestimate a woman who knows how to tie flies."

"I'm not sure who *they* are, but I'm learning never to underestimate you."

The provocative way he sampled the icing earlier replayed like an erotic ad for Duncan Hines. She'd like his sweet kiss to be the next thing she tasted.

"There you are!" Lucy Tanner-Scott's piercing voice sounded as shrill as an air raid siren. "I've been looking all over for you, Duncan."

They both jumped upright on their stools. Lucy sidled close to his side. Duncan's face brightened too sweetly for Sophie's liking. Her heart thumped on the floor. She remembered the church organist's response to him. Perhaps all women were special to this guy.

"There's someone I want you to meet." Lucy spoke in a soft drawl and rested her perfectly manicured hand on the forearm Sophie had been admiring a minute earlier.

"Uh, sure. Can you give me a sec?"

"No problem."

Lucy inspected Sophie with a subzero stare before she turned on a heel and headed for the door. "I'll be out here."

Duncan's gaze settled on Lucy's swaying hips as she exited, his reaction like a knife to Sophie's gut. In a matter of seconds, she transformed into the unruly-haired girl from high school, desperately in search of her confidence and beauty. A lifetime of contempt spewed below her skin.

"Can we talk more later?" Duncan raised his brows, a sincere expression of hope but one she doubted was true.

"Sure." She hoped her faux-smile hid her petty anger at Lucy, who monitored them from outside the doorway.

He turned and went to Lucy. Did he plan to play all the ladies of Northbridge? Especially the single ones?

Lucy slipped her arm through his and led him away. Sophie's ego boost from Duncan's attention numbed.

She lifted the plastic and stole a miniature cannoli from a tray then bit into the sugary center. If Duncan pursued Lucy, he'd be in for a surprise. She was exactly like the decadent pastry, for all appearances sweet and tasty. Too much of her, though, would weigh you down, not making her worth the indulgence. Nope. Sophie wasn't about to start worrying about his weight.

Still, she couldn't deny one fact—Duncan Jamieson tugged at her like a pair of overpriced, sexy shoes in a storefront window. Even though his resort plans shifted her goals and they circled in completely different orbits, she still had a crush on him. The way things went, though, he'd most likely end up landing some rich babe from a Hartford Country club. Or someone like Lucy.

Her bubble now completely deflated, she accepted this disappointment as a sign: time to do her job for the paper and figure out who left her that mysterious note.

Chapter 13

Sophie entered the meeting room three minutes late for the seven o'clock Tuesday zoning board meeting. She scooted down the last row to an empty chair near Bart, where an agenda had been placed on the seat.

"Did I miss anything?" she whispered and waited while he adjusted his video camera.

He glanced over and shook his head. "They're starting late. Just for you." He arched a bushy brow.

She resisted making a retort, especially because he'd gotten her an agenda and saved her a seat.

The metal chair creaked as she got settled and a few heads turned, the sound rather loud in the small meeting space. This room, like many in the dated municipal building, needed the advice of a feng shui expert. Fluorescent lights bounced off ice-white walls and created an atmosphere as sterile as a gauze strip.

The radiator hissed out heat making the room warmer than usual. Sophie shimmied out of her coat, pushed up the sleeves on her knitted top, and took inventory of the dais. The five-member zoning board and three-member board of selectman sat at the long table exchanging stares with the anxious crowd, who talked quietly amongst themselves.

Bernadette and her S.O.L.E. brethren occupied the second row. The Northbridge Anti-tax Group, who supported the added tax revenue from RGI's investment, filled the same spot on the opposite side of the aisle. The members of this group could beat an issue into pulp, with the single goal of paying little or no taxes. Many residents in opposition to their zero-tax policies mocked them behind their backs, calling them by their group's acronym, N.A.G.

Marion Harris, Buzz's wife, sat a few rows behind the N.A.G. members. Three years ago, Marion had stopped the pretense of coloring her hair and let her shoulder-length locks bloom with shades of gray. She glanced over her shoulder and locked eyes with Sophie. The tense lines of her face and worried stare were odd, a contrast from her usual relaxed attitude. Sophie nodded, but Marion pressed her lips tight and turned away.

Against the nearby wall, separate from the spectator seating, sat Duncan and his lawyer. Both men wore heavy gold Rolexes and dark suits of Brooks Brother quality. However, the attorney's appeared two sizes larger than Duncan's around the waistline. Compared to many of the board members, who wore simple sports jackets and button-down shirts, the outsiders dressed like kings.

Duncan looked up from his reading and caught her watching. His expression melted into a smile so slight it could rival the Mona Lisa's. An unexpected tide of affection rippled inside her chest.

Lucy's interruption at church hadn't ended their time together two nights ago. Duncan had later joined Sophie at a table with Dave, Bernadette, and some other friends while they ate their potluck supper. Throughout the meal, he'd possessed the charismatic skills of a diplomat, including a smooth rapport and an "A" for listening to others. The outing proved to her Duncan had a real need for others to like him, especially women.

His tactics worked, though. By the time the meal ended, Sophie found herself caught in a tangled web over him. One side snagged with desire, the other stuck on the harsh reality he'd taken land she wanted, and a third side leery of his real motives for being so charming to her. None of this inner turmoil stopped the imaginary battle raging inside her with Lucy Tanner for his attention. Knowing she'd see Duncan tonight, she'd dispensed with her church country-bumpkin apparel and selected slimming black slacks and a curve-accentuating top. Nobody would ever call Sophie a quitter.

Anxiety blanketed the air. Buzz's three cronies on the zoning board, who were rumored to support the resort project, sat huddled separate from the other two, the trio reminding Sophie of buzzards on a branch. Two of them held their usual scowl, but the frequent twitch of Joe Dougherty's mouth seemed odd for a man who typically possessed the calm of a windless day. His carrot-orange hair must've recently undergone a fresh coloring, much brighter than last time she'd seen him.

Only two zoning board members remained unattached to the strings of Buzz's manipulation: a thirty-something newcomer to town—still considered new even after living in Northbridge ten years—and Adli, a reasonable man by any person's standards. They could vote either way.

The meeting started and she scanned the agenda. Under the last topic, new business, was the discussion of RGI's environmental impact report.

Good. Just as Adli had promised at Buzz's office the other day.

Fifteen minutes passed. The heat in the room, plus a salty dinner, left her as mouth dry as sandpaper. She shimmied down the row of filled chairs and slipped out into the hallway. Adli's voice faded as she rounded the corner and made her way to the water fountain. She pressed the button and leaned over to take a sip.

"Sophie?"

The water stream gurgled as she turned to the voice. Marion Harris scurried toward her, hand clenched to the strap of her handbag and heavy furrowed lines on her forehead.

She released the button and straightened up. "Hi, Marion. You okay?"

"Danny told me you came by his office." She never called Buzz by his nickname. "He said you had an article. One about..." She averted her gaze to the carpeted floor for a split second then continued with an uneasy tone, "About an incident at our home, many years ago."

The strange stare earlier gained clarity. "Yes, I did."

"Can you please drop it?" A watery glaze pooled above her lower lids, magnifying her pale pupils. "There's nothing worth digging up." A tear spilled down her cheek.

"Don't cry. Someone anonymously delivered the article to the *Gazette* offices. I'm only trying to figure out why, what it might mean."

"Well, it shouldn't matter anymore."

"All right." Sophie paused, but her iron-clad curiosity refused to let go. "I don't need the details, but I have one question. Does this involve the Jamiesons?"

Crimson blasted Marion's face. "Can't you leave well enough alone?"

A sound made them both turn. Duncan stood at the end of the hallway and stared back.

Marion's fingers splayed across her parted lips. She gripped Sophie's arm. "Please. No more questions about what happened. It's personal. Just drop it!"

Marion let go then hurried down the hallway, in the opposite direction from Duncan. She barged through the doors leading to the back parking lot. Sophie glanced at Duncan, whose eyebrows squished together while he watched Marion rush out the door. Sophie ran after her.

Several minutes later, Sophie returned and found Duncan waiting for her in the hallway. She bombarded him with questions about Marion's reaction to him. "Mommy 101" had taught her how to spot a lie or even an omission of facts and Duncan acted in textbook liar fashion while answering them.

"I don't understand. Do you or don't you know Marion?"

"Not really." He averted his gaze to a display case of military uniforms to honor the town's veterans.

God, his reaction rivaled B-movie acting. "You either know someone or you don't, Duncan."

"Buzz introduced me to her once."

She'd asked Marion the same question outside and got an equally vague answer. Why would a story about a mistaken gunshot in their house upset her this way?

She turned and headed for the water fountain, unsure what to say next. He followed. Instinct hinted that a story lingered right out of reach. She leaned over and took a drink.

Duncan stood at her side. "Is Marion upset about something?"

She finished, wiped a spot of water from her chin, and stood up. "Well, as a matter of fact, yes."

"What?"

"It's personal. Why'd you come out here?"

"To talk to you. Away from the crowd." The muscles of his face relaxed, a return to the confident, warm man he'd been at the church.

Sophie refused to allow his suaveness to lure her so easily and returned for another sip. In the background of the gurgling fountain, his voice rambled. She finished and stood upright. "What?"

"I enjoyed seeing you on Sunday. Spending some time together." Eagerness prevailed in his words, so unlike the manner he carried himself with when conducting business.

"Yes, me too." She meant it and wished he were anybody but the confusing, guarded man standing before her.

"We keep running into each other." His blue eyes danced with hers and his tone softened, a simple shift in his demeanor that wrapped around her heart and threatened any reason she possessed. "Ever since the kayaks, I keep thinking my return to Northbridge isn't a coincidence."

A part of her didn't either, but a voice way in the back of her head screamed a reminder of Ryan Malarkey and how she couldn't let her reporting be swayed twice by a charming man.

"Pssst." Bart stuck his head around the corner and motioned for them to return.

They slipped back in amongst the stares of many. Buzz watched her, his glare so frosty it sent a chill along the back of her neck.

The discussion about RGI's environmental study had started. Over the next half hour, Buzz's cronies' comments were political, ruthless, and lacking in consideration to problems that could be created by such significant changes to their lakefront.

Joe Dougherty, however, sat quietly, staring at the tabletop, far less vocal than usual. He'd concurred with a remark or two but spent most of the time running his fingers through his carrot-colored hair and fiddling with the end of his mustache. Joe's signature had been on the visitor log the day she interviewed Duncan. A thin thread, but a thread nonetheless. Who had he been there to see?

When the board had discussed every strand of argument related to the pros and cons of a delay, Adli looked to his left. "Mr. Jamieson, do you care to address the board on this matter?"

He stood and buttoned his jacket. "Thank you, Mr. Zimmerman."

"Many of you know I now live in town." He scanned the audience then hovered on Sophie. "It's been pointed out to me how much the lake means to the people who've spent their lives enjoying these surroundings."

She tried to remain still, certain everyone else looked at her too.

"My reasons for being here are not only about profit." Duncan paced, certain and confident, the way a teacher commanded a classroom. "I want this done in a manner that best serves the community." He stopped suddenly and faced the dais, his arms open to gather them into his next statement. "I would ask the board to take the extra time to carefully consider the results of this study. Don't push through the requested zoning changes unless you are ab-so-lute-ly certain there will be no repercussions to this community. Please do what's best to preserve the things people love about this town."

Bernadette's group stood and clapped. Buzz's expression dropped so quickly it nearly clunked on the tabletop.

Adli quieted the room. "I'd like to make a motion to delay the zoning decision and revisit it at our January meeting after we've had a chance to review these additional studies further."

The youngest and newest member of the board seconded a vote on the motion. Adli called on him to vote first and he chirped a loud "yea" to delay a decision tonight. He received the loud approval of the S.O.L.E. attendees. The other two lifetime members of the Buzz fan club voted next, both with a predictable "nay."

Joe Dougherty, who'd been listening with a bent head toward the tabletop, was next. With two nay votes tossed in the bag, Sophie expected Joe to throw in the third, cinching the downfall of the motion, ensuring they had enough votes tonight to pass the new ordinance. Tate Farms would belong to RGI. Sophie's breath stalled, her fate sealed by his vote.

Joe looked up, licked his lips, then quietly said, "Yea."

The entire room let out a collective gasp followed by applause from the S.O.L.E. members. Buzz's nostrils flared like an angry bull, one step away from pawing the ground and charging. Beneath the table, his leg jiggled.

Sophie crossed her fingers. Two in favor of the motion and two against. Any delay meant she remained in the game. All attention centered on Adli, the deciding vote, whose face carried the trepidation of a man holding a lit bomb in his hands a moment before explosion.

* * * *

The next morning, Cliff came over to Sophie's desk carrying the mug she'd given him five years ago at his 65th birthday party with the quote, "Caffeine isn't a drug—it's a vitamin." He stopped at her side and lingered in her blind spot, like an annoying driver.

"Hi." Sophie's fingers continued their march on the keyboard, pounding out the final paragraphs recapping last night's zoning board meeting. "I came in early—super early—to get this story done. Not to give you something to do."

"Yeah, yeah. These Internet deadlines seem even more pressing than the print ones. An old guy like me doesn't need this."

"Neither does a middle-aged gal like me, but deadlines are deadlines." She stopped and looked at him. "Maybe you've had enough of them."

He frowned. "Just because you and my wife think I should retire doesn't mean I'll do it. I was born a newsman and plan to die one."

She'd heard him say this before and flipped through her notes until locating the quote she needed for the story. "Give me ten minutes or less to finish."

He shuffled off in the direction of the kitchen. "What would I do without you?"

"You'd manage."

He disappeared through the doorway and she enjoyed the moment of feeling needed by her employer.

Five minutes later, Sophie proofread the completed article. A teaser headline shouted, "Chairman Tips Scale on Lakefront Vote." Bart had snapped a perfect photo for the story—one of Duncan and Attorney Smith watching Adli cast the tie-breaking ballot to delay a decision on lakefront laws until further review. Buzz sat next to Adli, his dropped jaw and bugged-out eyeballs looking like an advertisement for the word "shocked."

Afterward, the audience had gone wild. S.O.L.E. attendees had jumped from their seats, giving Adli a standing ovation. Buzz had narrowed his glare on Joe Dougherty, who'd uncomfortably stacked some papers, shoved back his chair, and huffed out of the conference room.

Sophie's after-meeting interview with Adli had provided his quote, "If this development is meant to happen, further scrutiny of the environmental report won't stop it."

Her phone rang. "*Blue Moon Gazette*. Sophie speaking."

"It's me. I'm at work." Meg's low tone had a mysterious quality, reminiscent of calls Sophie got during their elementary school sleuth days. "Only got a minute. Remember after exercise class when I said I'd ask Mr. Wilson if he recalled the Jamieson's house sale?"

"Uh-huh. Is he finally home from his daughter's in New Hampshire?"

"Yup. He stopped in unannounced first thing this morning. Parked himself at the reception desk until someone offered to take him to Sunny Side Up for a cup of coffee."

Cliff returned and she handed him the printed story.

"So? Did he know anything?"

"You bet your boots. Not only did he remember it, but when I mentioned the gunshot at Buzz's house, his jaw plunked to his lap."

"Did he tell you anything?"

"Come on. He lives for moments like this. He remembered when Duncan's father contacted the real estate office to list the house. Everyone thought it was odd. I mean, the place had been in the Jamieson family for several generations. But get this." She paused and lowered her voice. "Mr. Wilson remembered a rumor from the summer before. A rumor that involved their family."

"Which was...?"

"At first, he wouldn't tell me because he didn't want to seem like a gossip."

Sophie snorted.

"But I said he shouldn't bait people that way and he reminded me of the boy who cried woof."

Meg's enthusiasm for her story kept Sophie from pointing out that she meant the boy who cried wolf.

"Well, my threat worked and he spilled the beans. The rumor a year earlier was that the gunshot at Buzz Harris's house had to do with the Jamiesons. And, get this. A sizable donation made to the Northbridge police department kept the real details from ever being recorded in the stations records."

"A donation? From who?"

"Are you sitting?"

"Meg!"

"I'll take that as a yes. The donation came from Frank Jamieson, Duncan's father."

Some small part of her, the part that craved Duncan, wanted his family to have a squeaky-clean slate. All her hope deflated.

"Did Mr. Wilson say who took the first call and what really happened over there? I mean, wouldn't the dispatcher know the truth?"

"Good point. Problem is, Mr. Wilson got all close-lipped and didn't utter another peep. Honestly, it's old news. Why be so secretive?"

Sophie grabbed a pad and scribbled some notes. Buzz's nervous response to her questions and his wife's disturbing reaction to Duncan in the hallway were consistent with Mr. Wilson's gossip.

"Great work, Meg. Guess you've uncovered another case of rich folks buying their way out of a problem."

"Well, they say money talks."

"No kidding. I'm wondering if the same family's money that talked back then is talking again. Rumors always start for a reason."

Chapter 14

Two young college-aged gals wearing light-up reindeer antlers swayed their hips on stage to an off-tune version of "Santa, Baby." Gone were the days when Sophie attended karaoke night at Griswold's and got on stage to perform with such fanfare, especially the week before Christmas, where a holiday theme ensured some unusual performances.

Sophie and her small posse had all decided to wear red shirts and holiday-themed earnings tonight. Bernadette leaned across the rustic wood tabletop and her candy cane earrings wobbled. "I wish Meg could've come. I'd buy her a drink for what she uncovered from Mr. Wilson. Can you confirm his story? I mean, he's such a gossip."

Veronica lifted her wineglass toward her lips but stopped short of drinking. "Give the dude a bell and he'd be our town crier."

"You got that right." Sophie glanced over her shoulder as their waitress dropped a platter of nachos in the center of the old pine table. As soon as she disappeared, Sophie leaned in. "Cliff's going to ask some friends. See if anybody's heard the same rumor."

Bernadette brushed aside her long bangs. "Does this change anything between you and your new special friend?"

"What special friend?"

"Really?" She tilted her head. "Look me straight in the eye and tell me Duncan didn't come one step away from charming the pants off you Sunday at church. Probably only stopped because we were in a sacred religious structure."

"Wow, that statement bothers me on so many levels."

Veronica snagged a nacho. "That's it. St. Mary's has lost my patronage. I'm coming to your church."

Sophie chuckled but Bernadette's stare demanded an answer. "Well?"

"Yes, he charmed me. However, he gives me an equal number of reasons to keep my pants on. At the hearing, for example—" Determined footsteps clunked on the old wood floors of the hundred-year-old building and stopped her from telling Marion's reaction to Duncan in the hallway at this past week's meeting.

Arch-rival Lucy's BFF, Teresa Barnes, pranced within inches of their table, squeezed into tight black jeans and a bright red semi see-through blouse which picked up the crimson highlights in her auburn hair. Her perky nose held high, she breezed by their group in silence.

"What a bitch." Veronica's "stage whisper" came out louder than expected and she covered her mouth. "She could say hello."

Teresa disappeared inside the ladies' room.

Bernadette shook her head. "Just like she used to snub us in high school. I'd always hoped this petty stuff would disappear when we grew up." She waved a hand. "Forget her. Finish your story."

The idea of full disclosure about Duncan's problems, even to her best buddies, suddenly bordered on gossip as she recalled Marion's tears. "Not much else to tell, but this is sure amounting into something."

"Something real." Veronica tucked one side of her short hair behind her ear, exposing wreath earrings that didn't match at all with her pearl necklace. "Versus the days the Northbridge Nancys imagined problems?"

Bernadette sipped her wine while nodding. "Hey, it helped pass summer vacation." She looked at Sophie. "What else have you found?"

"Just the note left at my office suggesting the Jamiesons couldn't be trusted. I'd say it relates directly to the incident at Buzz's house. Especially after what Meg found out."

"Makes sense. You wouldn't trust a briber, right?" Veronica raised her brows. "How'd they keep something that scandalous under wraps in this town?"

Bernadette drummed her chin with her fingertips. "Because major bucks were involved. Frank Jamieson is loaded. His law firm is huge... like international huge."

"How does this all fit together?" Sophie glanced back and forth between her two friends. "Why the bribery rumors? Why on earth would Joe vote against Buzz?"

Bernadette's gaze shifted behind Sophie. "Watch this." Bernadette's chin lifted and her full cheeks puffed as she launched a Dentyne-gum smile at Teresa.

Teresa continued on her way past their table.

"Hi, Teresa." Bernadette yelled, loud enough for a few other heads to turn.

Teresa's perfectly-plucked brows arched in unison. "Hello, ladies. Enjoy the karaoke."

"You, too," they all chimed.

"Wonder where Lucy is tonight." Sophie seethed, remembering the church kitchen, and how she swooped in and swiped Duncan from her grip. "I thought they traveled in a pair."

"Like us." Bernadette cracked a grin.

"Sort of. But we're nicer."

"Speaking of Lucy…" Veronica's words trailed.

Sophie reached for a nacho but stopped an inch from the plate and followed Veronica's gaze. Lucy sashayed to Teresa's table, Duncan in tow. While Teresa introduced Duncan to another couple, Lucy brushed against his arm, close, the way an animal staked their territory. She'd dressed to kill in a short denim skirt, knee high black stiletto-heeled boots, and a tight T-shirt that read "What Happens Under the Mistletoe, Stays Under the Mistletoe."

Duncan shook hands with the others. Dressed in his pressed khakis and a light pink and white striped oxford, he was approachable, gorgeous, and desirable. Sophie squirmed in her seat. Yes, they made a lovely couple.

Sophie's hunger disappeared, both for the nacho and Duncan. A lump settled in her throat, one she hoped nobody noticed but felt so large she was certain everyone did. She'd been an idiot. The truth bruised. Duncan viewed her only as a reporter.

In a hushed voice, Bernadette said, "What a phony bastard. He was all—"

Sophie rested her hand on Bernadette's arm. "At least we know. I won't have to endure the embarrassment of what that lying lawyer did to me."

Rage swelled, replacing the ache in her chest. She'd been a passive participant in the fight for her land up until now. One card she hadn't played always seemed wrong: telling Duncan about Henry's death on the land he wanted. Maybe the time had come to put the card in play.

From across the room she studied the man who kept stealing little pieces of her soul. He laughed at something Lucy said to the entire table. The lump in her throat forced itself down and crushed her heart.

She wanted Duncan to feel like a schmuck and knew exactly what she needed to do.

Chapter 15

Half Moon: The moon's angle between the sun and earth leaves it bathed half in darkness and half in light.

January

The pre-New Year's Eve hysteria at Bellantoni's Market a few days ago seemed like a relic from the past. Sophie pushed her half-filled cart along the aisle. With three hours to cook until the basketball team arrived for a pasta supper, she hurried down the aisles, tossing in boxes of ziti, bags of chips, cookie packages, and jarred sauce.

Petula Clark's circa 1960s hit, "Downtown" added a lilt to her step as she tossed in a container of parmesan cheese. The store's Muzak seemed geared for a crowd who wore saddle shoes or those who used "groovy" as part of their vocabulary, but she always enjoy the old tunes.

January had come at her fast. Always did. It hit with the exhausting weight of the last lap of a marathon. The holidays were over, yet Henry's shadow still followed in her everyday thoughts. Soon she'd have to deal with the day he'd have turned twenty-five. Alone.

The appointment with Dr. Keller two weeks ago had given her perspective, as he'd done after the divorce. Even he agreed her being alone on a significant day could be difficult, yet he'd also remarked how the decision to discuss the matter showed a healthy attitude.

Sophie rounded a corner, half considering Petula's advice to forget all her troubles and head downtown, when the front end of a cart almost slammed into hers. She froze. One of her troubles stared back.

Val Hoffman blinked. Her small mouth dropped open. "Oh. Sophie." She pushed out an uncomfortable smile. "It's been a while."

"Yes. It has." She tried to act casual, but Val's presence wreaked havoc on her mental well-being.

Val looked perfect, as she always did. Not one stitch of her bang-less cut fell out of place, the flip at her shoulders flawless. Her suede jacket and scarf matched perfectly.

In the months following Henry's death, Sophie had avoided places around town whenever possible. Pitiful looks from others settled like acid on her fragile soul. She'd grocery shopped in New Scotland for close to two years to circumvent moments like this, because a collision with Val brought forth emotions capable of smothering Sophie.

She reached deep to return a pleasant greeting, so deep she thought she'd gag. "How are you?"

"I'm good. We're all good." The slight hesitation in her voice belied the words. "Matt graduates this year, doesn't he?"

She nodded. "We're working on one more college application due this week."

"Where's he looking?"

"He likes the big university setting. Most of the same colleges we took Henry and Doug to see."

Discomfort spread across Val's long face as Sophie dared to raise the curtain on their past. Pasts neither of them wanted to mention.

Sophie swallowed to help ease the next words but instead, her throat burned like she'd consumed splintered glass. "How's Doug?"

Henry's best friend. The friend Henry had picked up on the fateful winter night to go to a party.

"Good. He just started working at Suisse Bank in Stamford as a quantitative analyst." Her vision shifted, her guilt misplaced on the rows of yogurt.

Val's unspoken thoughts showed in her hiding eyes, her dropped chest, and her muscles twitching beneath her skin. Regret. Blame. Disgrace.

"Great." Sophie forced an enthusiastic lift to her tone even though her heart writhed with pain. "Sounds like a step up from his last job."

"Yes. He's a hard worker." Val shifted her weight away from Sophie.

The details about what had happened on that January night seven years ago would forever haunt Sophie. Five boys left for a party, got bored, and instead decided to hang out at Putticaw Rock. Before leaving home, one of them had confiscated a six-pack of beer from his dad's supply. How the rest of the night evolved still dismayed her. Kids who grew up around the lake were taught about water and ice safety: not to skate in shallow water areas, to listen for cracking sounds when stepping on untested ice. They were even taught what to do if someone fell through the ice: call 9-1-1.

The clearest of minds could forget the rules in a panic, or even from the slight buzz of a few beers split between five boys. She'd never know what thoughts went through Henry's head when he made the choice to ignore the rules. Guess when your best friend is drowning, you try to save him. The sacrifice? Henry's life.

For the rest of her life, she'd never accept her part in allowing him to go out that night. Every maternal instinct she possessed had clanged with the alarm of caution, warning her to make him stay home. The kid throwing the party in the next town and his parents were strangers. The boys driving home on the dark, narrow roads late at night. She'd told Mike she planned to suggest a game night in their family room, where she'd get pizza and soda. Something they'd done a year earlier, before the boys all got their drivers' licenses.

Mike had insisted she back off, annoyed by what he called neurotic mothering. She'd caved to Mike and Henry left. She'd silently watched him leave, the way a mama bird allowed a baby bird teetering on the nest to spread its wings and fly. Never had she dreamed they'd go drink at the lake. Never had she dreamed they'd walk on the ice. Never had she dreamed it would end with such tragedy.

The weight of Henry's decision now rested on her, Val, and Doug each day of their lives. For years, its ache consumed her every waking moment. The weight worsened whenever she bumped into Val.

Val cleared her throat. "I heard the deal with the Tates fell through. I'm sorry."

"Thanks. My hope is the zoning board doesn't approve the changes and RGI removes their bid." She chewed her lip for a second. "You know, never give up."

"No." Val's mouth crumpled. "Don't ever give up."

Sophie had discovered this new mantra after years of soul searching and praying. Henry never got to live his dreams. In a way, neither had she, yet she still had the chance to do so. Memories of Henry would never disappear, but she'd finally been shaken awake from her grief, determined to live her life in a way that would make her lost son proud.

She locked on Val's distant stare, suddenly sorrier for Val than for herself. On cue, Petula reminded them again how a simple trip downtown would alleviate all their problems.

Sophie opened her arms and they embraced with a tight squeeze, as if they were both still clinging onto a past they could never change.

Valerie went in the opposite direction and Sophie headed down the canned good aisle, toward the register, eager to get out of the store.

Sophie considered her lost bid on Tate Farm. She hadn't given up, but she wasn't being active either. Christmas and New Year's had kept her busy. She'd neglected loose ends, like reminding Jay to call his cop friend or mentioning to Duncan about the memorial gardens planted there in her son's honor, and the reason why.

Duncan wasn't an unreasonable guy. He might have questionable taste in women, as evidenced by the way he'd swaggered in with Lucy at Griswold's on karaoke night. Still, the possibility existed if she mentioned Henry's death, it might appeal to his human side and make him reconsider his bid.

Or did he already know and not really care? Certainly someone in this town might have told him.

There was only one way to find out.

* * * *

Duncan hurried down the hallway past darkened offices. Once at his office suite, he grabbed a butterscotch hard candy from a glass bowl on his assistant's desk. Unraveling the wrapper, he popped the sweet, creamy treat into his mouth and enjoyed the way it soothed his anxious nerves.

Trent should be here any minute. Duncan stacked three reports to read at home and stuffed them into his briefcase. He thumbed through some mail, but edginess inside his gut over the planned talk with his brother continued to peck away. He lowered the mail, now unsure if a day's worth of worry had to do with his brother or the fact he'd volunteered to pick up Patrick from Sophie's after the pasta supper.

He'd jumped at the chance to get his son when Helen complained about driving the country roads in the dark. It would be a perfect opportunity to smooth over the fiasco at Griswold's. Awkward barely scratched the surface of how he'd felt when he spotted Sophie in the crowd. He'd gone over to say hello and, while she was polite enough, her tone lacked its previous warmth.

The invite from his neighbor, Teresa, had come as a surprise. He'd arrived home from work to find her chatting with Helen. They'd both insisted he enjoy a night out. Reluctantly, he'd agreed. Teresa's husband seemed like good company the few times they'd talked. An hour before leaving, though, Teresa had called, asking if he could pick up Lucy, due to car problems. He again said yes to be polite, yet the idea he'd been the victim of a conspiracy theory involving the three women held a high probability.

Sophie's presence at Griswold's added another layer to his torment. He was desperate for her approval. Based on the look on her face, he'd lost any gains made in recent weeks, pushing him back in time to become the distraught thirteen-year-old of yesteryear who had so deeply craved her attention.

"You wanted to see me?" Trent strolled into the office and the thoughts of Sophie disappeared.

Trent was giving off his usual rock star vibe, especially today dressed in a dark suit worn with snazzy dress boots and a classic vest, unbuttoned. Duncan could pull off a corporate look in his sleep but sometimes wished to carry cool with his brother's ease.

"Come on in." Duncan bit into the remains of the sweet candy and figured some small talk might ease them into the tough subject at hand. "How was the trip?"

"Fantastic. Man, I think our St. Thomas resort is my favorite location."

"Lola?"

"It didn't hurt." He grinned, highlighting his chin dimple.

Duncan never understood how Trent managed to woo a woman in every port.

"I talked to Mom when I got back." Trent wandered to the window and shoved his hands in his pant pockets, his preoccupied gaze reflecting in the dark glass.

"Oh?" Duncan stifled a quick stab of jealousy. The close bond between Trent and their mother always rubbed a sore spot.

"She said you and Patrick are settled up in the boondocks. Both Mom and Dad wish you'd stayed near the city."

"The new house is starting to feel like home. I made the right choice." He softened his defensive tone. "Patrick likes school. Even joined the basketball team. Thanks to his Uncle Trent's tutelage."

Trent nodded and faced Duncan. "Good. I'll visit when he has a game."

"He'd like that. He sometimes goes by Pat these days. Elizabeth wouldn't be happy."

Trent walked toward the desk. "Yeah, she hated when I called him that. Mom said you went to the old tackle shop. Is the place still owned by the same guy?"

"Yup. Alan Moore. I'm surprised you remember."

"Jesus, you pined over the guy's daughter for two summers."

"What?" He chortled, the comment leaving him embarrassed. "You knew?"

"Dude, everyone in the family knew." Trent chuckled and they joined in a rare moment of genuine laughter. "Why do you think Dad hung out there so much and talked to the owner?"

"I thought he liked fly fishing."

"He did, but Mom told me he hoped you'd ask that girl out."

"I had no idea. I must wear blinders." He cringed at the word "blinders." He'd lost count of how many times his wife used those exact words. Had he worn them his entire life? "Jesus, why wouldn't Dad have the old father son talk or something?"

"Dad?" Trent tipped his head. "Did we grow up in the same household?" He plopped into a visitor chair facing Duncan's desk.

"Yeah, he'd put all the hints in front of us, step back and hope we'd piece together the puzzle. When we didn't..." Duncan shook his head. "Well, he didn't hide his disappointment, did he?"

Trent nodded his agreement but a dark shadow crossed his face. "I always disappointed Dad. Back to your old girlfriend, if I recall, she was pretty hot. She still in town?"

"Yup. She's a reporter for the local paper." A jolt of jealousy went through Duncan at his brother's interest. It'd be just like Trent to come to town and the Northbridge women would all fall at his feet. "Interviewed me about the project. In fact, Patrick's become friendly with her son."

Trent gave a slow, assessing nod. "Married?"

"Divorced."

Trent's brow rose, innuendo way too obvious. "Still hot?"

"In my humble opinion, yes."

"*Carpe diem*, buddy. You're not thirteen anymore. Besides, other than the buyer from Lord and Taylor, your dating life has been pathetic since Eliz—" His gaze fell to his lap for a split second then he looked up. "Sorry. I know it's been tough."

"No. You're right. I should get out more."

Trent lifted his chin and stilled, similar to an animal sensing impending danger. "So, what's up?"

"A few things."

"Shoot." Trent leaned back in the chair, rested his crossed feet on the desk, and jiggled his foot.

"Are you really on board with the project in Northbridge? I mean, I get a sense you've lost interest."

"Jesus, Duncan. I've been traveling. For the firm. When have I had time?"

"I know." Duncan hesitated. "But you've been distant. Now's the time to speak up."

Trent rested an elbow on the chair arm and rubbed his finger across his lower lip while he thought. "Since you've asked, before we finalize this, I'd like to meet with my mother. My real mother."

"Sure. Anything wrong?"

Dark circles under Trent's eyes seemed more pronounced, as if the subject wore him down. "Stepping into my past is tough. Let me deal with this my way," he sniped.

Duncan overlooked his nasty tone. "I only asked because the Moore family was the other bidder on the property. Sophie, her dad, and her brother."

"Does it matter?"

"To them. They're interested in restarting the farm's wine production. Plus Alan Moore told me the land belonged to his family for several centuries before some great uncle lost everything in a poker bet."

"Centuries, huh?" Trent paused for a second then waved a dismissive hand. "They'll find another place to produce wine."

"Maybe." Duncan shifted in his chair. "Listen, besides the obvious, can you think of any reason why Marion Harris would be upset about our return?"

Trent's foot stopped moving. "Nope." He swung his legs off the desk and sat upright, his lips pressed tight. "If that's all, can we discuss this later? I'm pretty beat and want to get home."

Duncan remembered Marion's odd reaction in the hallway during the zoning meeting.

"This is important to me, Trent." Duncan's voice rose with his anger. "Besides what Mom already shared, is there anything I should know about our family ties in Northbridge?"

"I said no." His eye contact seemed forced. "Are we done?"

"No." Duncan rubbed the back of his neck, searching for a gentle way to raise his next concern. "A rumor going around Northbridge suggests officials are being bribed over the zoning changes we need."

Trent's tanned hue turned crimson. "What? You think… Spit it out, Duncan. What are you saying?"

Built up anger pulsed through Duncan's veins. Trent never made things easy. "Cut me some slack. You know why I'm asking. Is this Lake Simcoe all over again?"

Fury blazed from Trent's narrowed eyes, yet it masked a thin layer of pain. Duncan hated to bring up the incident in question, which had nearly cost Trent his job at RGI, but saw no other choice.

"I don't need this." Trent stood and shoved back his chair. "You're exactly like Dad. You never see the good in anybody."

The comment jabbed at Duncan's tender Achilles' heel. "Sit down. I don't want this to turn into a fight."

"Then you shouldn't have asked. Who warned you the time Dad tried to stick his nose into your first project when you started this business? Me!" Trent jabbed his chest with his index finger. "That's who. Maybe Dad's up to no good again."

Duncan's checks tingled and he dropped his chin to his chest. How had he forgotten Trent's loyalty to him? Years ago, if Trent hadn't overheard their father on the phone trying to convince one of Duncan's competitors to start a bidding war over his first hot property, RGI might never have gotten off the ground. Trent had come to Duncan right away. Frank Jamieson reluctantly admitted what he'd done, hoping the failure would be enough for Duncan to reconsider his career goals and maybe study law.

Duncan suddenly hated himself. The incident at Lake Simcoe had happened during the worst of Trent's substance abuse, no longer an issue. "I'm sorry. I've never forgotten you helped me."

Trent averted his gaze to the Newport racing photos, the one love the two men shared. "You hired me when Dad wanted nothing to do with me. Plus, you kept me…even after what I did to you at Lake Simcoe. I understand why you'd ask the question, but I swear I'm a changed man. All I can ask you to do is believe me." He met Duncan's stare and, for once, Trent's watery eyes showed true remorse for his past mistakes.

"I believe you," Duncan said quietly. If the bribery rumor wasn't Trent's doing, then how'd it ever get started?

Chapter 16

Matt and Patrick sat next to each other on a bench seat of the pine table, one that had been sitting in the eating area of Sophie's great room ever since she and Mike purchased this house. Their heads huddled together, the boys pored over a basketball magazine.

Sophie threw another log on the low-burning fire in the stone fireplace and settled into the oversized sofa with a glass of wine and a book. Every so often, she glanced at the boys, noting how much Patrick looked like his dad.

Helen's lateness worried Sophie. The older woman, who seemed to love her work at Duncan's home, usually showed up at practice before many of the other parents. They'd spoken several times at pick-up and Sophie once considered prying about Duncan's interests. Now that Duncan seemed to be involved with Lucy, she was glad she hadn't shown Helen her interest in the man. The less people who knew about her middle-aged lady crush gone haywire, the better.

She looked up again as Patrick reached for a brownie.

"Great dinner, Mrs. Shaw."

"Thanks. Ziti is pretty simple."

"Maybe you can give my dad the recipe." Patrick glanced at Matt, who fought a smile.

"Does he like to cook?" She lowered her book onto her lap.

"Not really." A small brownie crumb stuck to his lower lip while he chewed. "When Helen goes home on Friday's we do a lot of takeout until she comes back on Monday." He took a napkin and wiped his mouth. "Oh, I forgot. Dad sent me a text half an hour ago. He's on his way."

The bruise to her ego after what happened at Griswold's had almost vanished. The idea of facing him, especially after her episodes of blatant flirting, made the area throb again. Part of her wanted to crawl under the sofa and hide. On the other hand, a minute alone with him might give her a chance to bring up Henry's death. She'd learn pretty fast if Duncan possessed a human side or only the cold, corporate robot concerned with his own needs. Boy, if he already knew and had never mentioned it, it would speak to his integrity.

"Mrs. Shaw, do you remember when my dad visited here as a kid?"

"No. I'm afraid I don't. Summer visitors come and go."

A flash of the devil's smile took over Patrick's boyish face. "So you really didn't know he had a big crush on you when he was a kid?"

"He did?"

The two boys exchanged a knowing glance. She worked hard to contain her shock and again scanned the fading tickler file of her memory, coming up short on a miniature Duncan clone.

"Uh-huh." Patrick grinned. "He said you didn't notice him, though."

Matt snickered. "Now he's busted."

"Not exactly, Matt." Sophie tried to sound mature. "That happened a long time ago, anyway."

He shut the magazine. "Can we play X-box 'til Pat's dad gets here?"

"Sure. First, take those last few plates into the kitchen."

They all but knocked over their chairs to deliver the dishes then ran downstairs.

She soaked in the knowledge Duncan had had a boyhood crush on her, news that filled her with schoolgirl delight. It lasted mere seconds. Big whoop. A puberty-driven crush meant nothing. An image of Lucy in her sexy outfit the other night made a sick pit churn in Sophie's stomach. She couldn't compete with Lucy. Anyway, why should she? Duncan had manipulated Sophie with his charm simply for good press. Still…what if she was wrong?

Five minutes later, headlights flickered in the driveway outside the front windows. She swallowed a reality dose. She and Duncan were simply two grown-ups whose kids hung out. End of story.

Bella barked. Seconds later, a knock sent Sophie to the door with the terrier-mix prancing at her heels.

"Sorry I'm late." Duncan stood bundled in his wool coat, hands shoved in the pockets. He broke into a warm smile.

"No problem." She instinctively melted a little and smiled back, wishing she had more control. "Come on in."

Bella sniffed at Duncan's kneecaps as if they were coated with beef juices.

He crouched down and scratched under her chin. "Who's this?"

"Bella. Our guard dog. JFK airport should have such tight security."

He chuckled and stroked her wiry back. "The boys around?"

"Down in the family room playing X-box. Have you eaten?" The words flew out without much thought, although it might give her a chance to tell him about Henry even though the idea of such a conversation left a hard pit in her stomach. Too late to take the invite back, she added, "We have leftovers."

He hesitated. "I don't want to put you out."

"I just handled twelve teenage boys. Feeding one grown man is easy." She held out a hand. "Let me take your coat."

During the hand-off, Duncan's eyes never left hers. She could have sworn his expression carried an undercurrent of longing, as evocative as a schoolboy crush. Or was it just wishful thinking?

* * * *

When the door opened, Sophie's eye-sparkling smile made all Duncan's uneasiness disappear. Being near her seemed comfortable and right.

He sat on a tall stool next to the granite-topped peninsula while she got them drinks. A large stone fireplace lent a gentle smoky aroma, buried underneath the garlicky scent of sauce. He admired the rustic pine-beamed tresses supporting the cathedral ceiling of the living room and overstuffed furniture. Cozy and homey, a far cry from his wife's contemporary preferences or his mother's formal style. A plaque on the kitchen wall, in the shape of a chocolate bar, read "I'd give up chocolate—but I'm not a quitter." He smiled. Somehow, he was certain it referred to Sophie.

She removed a container of ziti from the refrigerator and transferred some into a pasta bowl. Her back to him, he took in details not politely acquired face-to-face. Soft curls of midnight brown hair rested between her shoulders. Gentle curves graced her worn jeans and clingy top. She turned sideways to study the contents in a lattice wine rack built into kitchen cabinets and tucked her hair behind her ear. A turquoise earring dangled against creamy skin.

"How long have you lived here?" He loosened his tie and undid the top button of his dress shirt, at ease in the comfortable setting.

"About twenty-five years. We bought this house from my grandmother right after getting married." She removed a bottle and twisted the traditional wine steward's opener into the cork. "Nana had just gone into the nursing home. Two falls in the driveway trying to get the mail meant the time had come."

"You were lucky to keep this place in the family."

"We're not waterfront property, but from this hill, the views are a plus. I know it's mostly trees, but the two-acre lot gives us lots of privacy."

She seemed preoccupied as she tugged out the cork. "Did you have fun at Griswold's singing karaoke?"

"It was fun." His heart skipped a beat at the mention of the awkward encounter.

Sophie pursed her lips. "I've known Lucy my entire life. Watch your back around her."

All his worry had been well-spent. "Teresa Barnes invited me. She's my neighbor. I only gave Lucy a ride."

She avoided looking at him and poured the wine. "You don't owe me an explanation."

"Sophie?"

She lowered the bottle and her gaze lifted to meet his.

"We weren't on a date."

The tenseness in her mouth relaxed. She finished filling their glasses with dark red wine. "I realize what you do is none of my business, but she brings back every bad memory from high school."

"It's okay. I'm glad you told me."

She handed him a glass and the brush of her hand carried the weight of a slow caress. Her eyes, like pools of melted chocolate, latched onto his. He wandered in their dreamy richness.

"So, you're the wine expert. Care to give me a lesson on how to appreciate this one?"

She grinned and her softened eyes twisted around his heart. "Are you sure?"

"Absolutely."

"Okay. Oh, hold on. Forgot to warm your food." She rushed to the counter and popped the pasta dish into the microwave, pushed a few buttons and returned to the kitchen island. "Ready for your crash course?"

He lowered his tone and did his best sly flirtatious grin, one he hoped would brush away any remnants of the Lucy incident. "I'm ready but always seem to be in for a surprise around you."

Her lips parted and she blushed. "Okay, Mr. Ready. To start, the proper enjoyment of wine involves all the senses."

Sophie tilted the large globed stemware toward the recessed lights above. "This is a shiraz. Hold your glass up to the light. The grapes used for this have a longer growing season and the thick skins leave a bold, dark color." Her delicate hand slipped behind the goblet and disappeared. "See how dark this is? My hand isn't visible on the other side. Other reds, like merlot or pinot noirs, have thinner skins and give a more transparent red hue."

He mimicked her movements and his hand vanished behind the dark wine.

"Now, gently swirl the wine." A slight twist of her wrist rotated the glass.

Duncan copied her moves, realizing she made the gesture fluid, easier than his attempts.

"This gives the molecules a little nudge to entertain us. I mean, who doesn't like to be entertained." She waved a playful brow. "Once you get them moving, stick your nose up close and take a whiff."

Sophie brought her straight nose close to the rim. Her lids dropped, as if prepared to receive a scent from heaven. She inhaled. Passion-filled concentration dominated her expression, leaving him mesmerized, unable to stop watching even as he lifted his own glass. He copied her movements, contemplating the aroma in a way he'd never done before.

When he opened his eyes, she'd been watching. "Anything stand out?"

He took a second, shorter whiff. "Pepper, I think."

Her mouth turned into a half-surprised, half-pleased smile. "Very good."

A sensation fluttered in his gut, her approval an unexpected joy.

"I smelled some kind of berry too. Now take a decent taste. Let the liquid coat your entire mouth. It'll feel different on your tongue versus the roof of your mouth or the inside of your cheeks. There are all kinds of hidden flavors. Some bold, others more subtle."

She brought the glass to her lips then stopped, leaned across the counter, and placed her soft palm over the hand where he held the glass. A sweet floral scent drifted from her hair. She dropped her voice, now low and sexy. "A ready guy like you should take your time with this one." She cocked a loaded brow. "Really work hard and you'll detect the wine's secrets."

Heat crept up his neck again.

The microwave buzzer sounded but she kept her gaze on him as she tipped back her goblet. Her full lips brushed the rim with the delicate touch of a first kiss. Intense lines creased her forehead as she savored the sample then swallowed.

She squinted. "Blackberry. A little plum. That's what I love about wine. Depending on the soil and climate, the same grape can take on a different flavor. A surprise every time." She lifted her glass in a toast. "Well, cheers."

He raised his and took a sip, but it tasted blank. In one short wine-tasting lesson, Sophie had disclosed the love and passion steering her winery dreams. Dreams stopped by his last-minute bid.

Duncan lowered the drink, now bitter to his palate and carrying the flavor of regret.

Never had he surrendered anything he wanted for the sake of someone else. Sacrifice sounded more like losing to him. The reason he wanted to purchase the land, one only known by a select few, crashed head-on with someone else's goals.

For the first time in his life, giving up what he desired for another person came with its own set of rewards.

* * * *

"Here you go." Sophie slid the bowl and fork toward Duncan. They'd been traveling a delicious path of flirtation when a dark front of doubt crossed his face. Did it matter? This all sidetracked her from her real mission.

He rolled up the sleeves on his pinstriped dress shirt. "Looks delicious. Thanks."

Sophie sat down on a stool next to him, leaned an elbow on the counter, and buried her cheek in her palm, watching his profile while he ate. Should she just blurt out about Henry? The words to start such an awkward conversation garbled in her head.

Duncan swallowed. "I loved the wine lesson. Your passion is obvious." He motioned to his bowl. "Excellent pasta, too."

"Thanks. I'm curious about something." She'd work her way into the uncomfortable topic later, when he finished eating. "Back in the day when you visited Dad's shop, did we talk?"

He lifted another bite and made her wait. "Briefly. A couple of times."

"Remember any specifics?"

He grinned. "One time you were loading the refrigerator and I came over. You teased me about not having the skills to catch some fish over by the bridge. Merciless, if I recall."

"Oh my. I was a brat." She took a slow sip of her wine. "Any other times?"

"A passing hello. You were interested in your friends." He lowered his fork and pushed the plate to the side. "If you promise to be nice to me, I'll fill you in on a little-known secret." He cocked his head and grinned, his teasing manner unexpected.

"First off, Carter"—she raised her brows—"other than the day you lied to me about your name, I'm usually nice. Second, are you already indulging in Northbridge gossip?"

"Not gossip. Old news." He turned on the stool to face her. With his index finger, he motioned for her to move closer.

She inched sideways and their knees touched. The grainy stubble of his five-o'clock shadow piqued her curiosity, making her want to feel the texture against her cheek.

"Back then I had a crush on you."

Coming straight from him, the admission made her flush. "A crush? On me?" His gaze blazed through her, following the same path the wine lit down her core.

"You're blushing," he said tenderly. "Wish I'd had that effect on you in those days. I should be blushing." Duncan fingered his glass stem. "A little embarrassing to admit my first crush didn't even know I existed."

"I'm sorry." She touched his forearm and he stilled.

"Don't be. I was thirteen." He shrugged it off, but she could tell some residual awkwardness remained. "A part of growing up. Right?"

"I guess." She let her hand slide away, unsure what to say next.

The only sound in the otherwise silent house came from downstairs, where the boys yelled in the throes of their game.

"Sophie, I can't get past the idea you were the other interested party in the Tates' land."

"Would that have mattered?"

"Maybe." He blew out a breath. "It's complicated."

"Didn't you wonder who you outbid? I mean, this is a small town."

Duncan's broad shoulders dropped and his usual confident chin lowered to his chest. "No." A pause. "Not once."

Remorse didn't strike her as something a man like him showed often, yet she found herself at a loss for words.

He looked up. "My decision to bid was personal. Not only for my firm."

"You mean because your family used to own here?"

"Yes and no." Duncan rested an elbow on the counter, covered his mouth with his palm. He dragged the hand slowly down to his chin. "It does involve my family. I'm afraid telling you would break a confidence, though. I want to, but…" He shrugged.

She averted her gaze to the counter. The strange notes. The payoff to the Northbridge police by Frank Jamieson and the gunshot at Buzz's house. How did that fit in with all this? That his bid might be personal had never entered her mind. A discussion about Henry right now seemed wrong. Very wrong.

She nearly jumped when he tenderly took her hands his. He raised his brows and the shine in his eyes showed hope.

"If I'd known you the way I do now.... Well, I'm not sure my other reasons would have mattered." He studied her, as intense as a seer trying to read her mind. "That day I went to help with the kayaks and found you after all these years...." He shook his head lightly and a smile pulled on the corners of his mouth. "I couldn't believe it. You looked at me like..." His voice softened. "Like you felt it too."

His gaze pinned her in place, demanded an answer. Every emotion from that day returned, how his hand in hers had seemed so right, how the encounter seemed like their destiny. "Yes. I felt it too."

Duncan cupped her cheek in his large palm. His thumb moved in a slow caress and she stared into his kind, loving gaze.

"Are you sure there's nothing between you and Lucy?"

He softened his eyes. "You're the one I can't get out of my head."

He leaned in and brushed his lips against hers. Reaching up, he spread his fingers through her hair and pulled her closer, Duncan's heady gaze made her cheeks flush then his warm mouth covered hers and parted her lips. His cheek rubbed against hers and the soft shadowed grain tickled her skin. Awareness of his faded cologne collided with the sweet flavor of wine on his tongue while he sampled her lips with a soft and certain caress. She ran her hand up his solid shoulder, along his strong neck. He sighed against her mouth as she raked the soft, thick waves of his hair with her fingertips.

Heavy footsteps pounded the stairs from the lower level family room. They slowly pulled apart, breathless. His gaze stayed locked on hers, his lusty thoughts quite readable.

Sophie cleared her throat, but it did little to clear her swimming head. "Should I reheat your food?"

The kids hit the top landing.

"Nah. Things in this room are hot enough. I'm pretty sure it's still good." Duncan grinned, kind of goofy and she tingled inside.

She grinned back, but the spectacular kiss made her question her decision to investigate his family behind his back. Earlier today, Cliff had suggested they meet with Les Wilson to learn more about what he'd told Meg. Les might know exactly what the Northbridge PD had buried years ago for the Jamiesons. She reached up and touched her lips, still tender from his kiss. Was this a sign she should step away from the story?

Sophie stood at a crossroad but had no idea which way to turn.

Chapter 17

"I'm gonna see if Daddy's in the lobby and say hi then go sit with Megan and Danielle." Tia popped up from her seat and skipped down the high school gym's bleacher steps.

Sophie cringed, picturing her daughter falling if she tripped. "Tell Daddy I need to talk with him." Mike's promise to come to Matt's basketball game also meant he could no longer ignore her.

"Okay." Tia continued without looking back.

Duncan passed Tia on his way up the bleachers. His long strides made the trip seem effortless. Single digit January evening temperatures had left his cheeks scarlet, although the rest of him looked warm, bundled in a tan tartan scarf and dark wool coat buttoned to the top of his chest. A bit like the way she'd bundled the kids when they were little. These temperatures even had her fully wrapped in winter gear.

"Thanks for saving me a seat." Duncan surveyed the gym while he undid the scarf. "Quite a crowd."

"Last year's district championship win has left the Northbridge natives restless for more glory." Sophie scooted closer to Dad and filled the space where Tia had been. She patted the place next to her. "For you. If you're hungry, they sell hot dogs and pizza out in the lobby."

"Helen said she'll have something for me when I get home." He removed his coat. "Hello, Alan."

Dad glanced up from his paper. "Duncan. Good to see you. Want to join us?"

In any venue with background noise, her father's hearing worsened, nothing like the super-power abilities she remembered growing up. In those days, he could hear a mocking facial gesture made behind his back.

"I'd love to." Duncan gave her a between-us grin, put the coat on the bleacher, and settled next her as Dad continued to read.

Duncan lowered his voice. "By the way, thanks for the wine-tasting tips. Maybe next time we can tackle a white?" Hope reigned on his face, as if he'd practiced that line all day.

"Sounds like fun. Sure you can handle it?"

A thin grin veiled his lips. "Do I seem like a man who backs down from a challenge?"

"No. I'd never say that about you."

"Bet you don't either." He tipped his head a bit analytically. "You probably go about it in a whole different way."

"Think you know me, huh?"

He stretched his long legs onto the bleacher in front of them. "Think I'm starting to." He undid the knot in his tie and studied her for a reaction.

The remark, coupled with the allure of his loosened tie-look, pushed her into a zone so deep she might lose air. "Yes," she softly replied. "You're starting to know me."

Duncan's stare captured hers long enough for her to gauge his satisfaction.

"Bet you could teach me a thing or two about sailing. Those racing pictures in your office were impressive."

"Do you sail?"

"Yeah, with a boat the size of your dinghy. We have a Sunfish and used to own a small sixteen footer."

He nodded. "Maybe someday you can join me on my boat."

"Sure. Why'd you name it *True Love*?"

His cheeks turned a light shade of pink and a strange expression settled on his face. "Let's just say I really love my boat."

She didn't prod, yet one thing remained clear: she still had a lot to learn about this man.

The teams ran into the gym from the locker rooms and the large crowd roared. She scanned the court for Matt but instead, at the doorway beneath the large hand-painted eagle mascot, Mike stood watching her with a military-like stance and crossed arms.

The years had changed the dirty blond-haired boy Sophie had given her virginity to, both inside and out. Now trimmed sideburns accompanied a neat semi-buzzed cut. His long, rugged face showed even more forehead due to the dip of a receding hairline and his blue-green eyes never revealed anything he wanted to hide. He'd aged pretty well, considering he didn't agonize at the Estee Lauder counter for products to delay the process like Sophie did. Her son said he'd joined a gym in Stamford, where he now lived, and he looked in better shape than ever.

Sophie thinned her gaze at Mike, who quickly turned away and headed to a seat in the first section of bleachers. What a coward!

When it came between fight or flight, Mike always ran. A fact evidenced repeatedly during their marital problems and the way he'd handled the loss of their son. The e-mail she'd sent him demanding to know why he'd undermined her decision about Matt's concert and how he'd discussed her handling of Henry's death with them, had gone unanswered.

"Friend of yours?" Duncan stared in Mike's direction.

"My ex."

"Did you want to sit with him?"

She chortled and shook her head. "Mike's here for Matt. I'm quite happy with the current company."

Duncan's eyes sparkled, leaving her as winded as if they'd twirled to a rapid salsa and he'd dipped her into a tango finale. Close together, their shoulders touched and arms flowed in tandem down their sides. His hand moved in the space between them, as if searching for something. The movement stopped when he wrapped Sophie's hand in his warm fingers, gave them a gentle squeeze, then rested them so they were hidden from view. He stared straight ahead, attention on the game but smoothed the top of her hand with his thumb.

* * * *

Almost an hour and a half later, the final score flashed on the scoreboard. The eight point lead was a close win for Northbridge, but a win nonetheless.

Dad leaned around Sophie. "A helluva game, don't you think, Duncan?"

"Absolutely. Not sure if I can take an entire season of this stress, though."

Before they could leave their seats, a few folks from town approached him with amiable energy, probably supporters of his resort. Dad mumbled something about getting a candy bar at the concession stand. She motioned to let Duncan know she'd be helping her father down the stairs and left him with a small audience.

They reached the bottom step. Mike stood near the doors with a guy who'd coached Tia's soccer team in second grade. "Dad, I need to see Mike."

He nodded and walked off.

Mike's back was to Sophie. She reveled in the element of surprise and picked up her pace before he made an escape. "Hey, Mike?"

He turned with a smile then it vanished. "Oh. Sophie. What's up?"

"Got a minute?"

"Um, sure. Give me sec."

"Meet me outside the front doors."

"Outside?" He glanced at the crowd around them. "Okay."

She made her way through the entry foyer then pushed open the glass doors. Her thin cardigan, worn over a long-sleeved shirt, was no match for the frigid air. About a minute later, Mike came out.

"New boyfriend?" He shoved his hands in his jean pockets and avoided looking directly at her.

"I didn't ask you out here to discuss my love life." Sophie crossed her arms. Why did every conversation between them have to be so difficult?

He sneered. "Yeah, I figured. Look, I answered your e-mail about Florida. What more do you want me to say?"

"If I recall, your response was 'got it.'" She dropped her voice. "You didn't even address the remarks you made to the kids about how I'm handling Henry."

The upper floodlight bounced off the tense lines of his jaw. "Listen, that's how I feel. Did you forget why we're not married anymore?" He dropped his chin and stared at the concrete sidewalk, as hard as the wedge they'd formed during their marriage. "It's been seven years since we lost him. You need to move on."

An icy snowflake grazed Sophie's warm cheek, the start of predicted overnight snow. "I have moved on." The onset of tears sent a prickle through Sophie's cheekbones. "You make me sick. This isn't about a bad test grade or a lost baseball game. That's our child you're talking about."

"You know what I meant."

"No. I don't."

He slowly lifted his chin, studied her with a glare frosty as the surrounding air. "I think the only reason you bid on the Tates' land is because of what happened there. You're stuck in the past."

"Oh come on, Mike. You know what it means to my dad? My family has always wanted that land back. How many times did you hear Jay and I discuss how much we hoped to run that vineyard someday? God, what's wrong with you?"

"I'm just saying you'd better be sure this property fight is for the right reasons. I don't think it is." The hard, cold stare of disgust, from a man she had once loved, sent a shiver along her spine. "Maybe this company taking it away from you is a blessing in disguise."

"Everything okay?" Duncan stepped from the shadows holding her coat. "Tia said she saw you go outside. I figured you might need this."

* * * *

Duncan threw on flannel pajama bottoms and a T-shirt then crawled between the cool covers of his bed with a book. After reading the same sentence multiple times, he tossed the paperback aside. The tail end of the conversation between Sophie and her ex-husband played over and over in his head. He'd sensed she was hiding something about why she wanted the vineyard property. Based on her ex-husband's remark, she was. But what? He should've asked, yet somehow prying didn't seem right.

He kicked off the covers and headed to the bathroom for two aspirin. Most of his life, he'd managed to keep relationships emotion-free. Exactly the way he liked them. Yet now, a force ran wild, leaving him all wrapped up in Sophie. Holding her hand tonight made his heart ache with a longing he hadn't craved since high school. Since Carolyn.

The first official girlfriend in his life. So many years had passed since he'd uttered the heart-revealing confession of love to her. When the transfer student from Massachusetts moved to the village of Briar Cliff Manor in their senior year and registered at Greenbrier Academy, he'd been smitten immediately.

She'd stood apart from the other girls at school. Most wore their hair in headbands or low-tying ponytails, but Carolyn's straight, brown locks swung like Cher's and hung to the middle of her back. Her funky pendant necklaces and multiple bracelets, a far cry from the delicate jewelry on most girls, were a permissible assault to the school's strict navy blazer and pleated skirt policy. Duncan couldn't get enough of her. Soon they'd begun to date.

One rainy spring afternoon, Duncan's baseball practice had been canceled. Carolyn had come to his room when classes ended. With his roommate in the library working on a paper, they'd kicked off their shoes and fell onto the bed in each other's arms. Carolyn had loosened Duncan's tie and unbuttoned his shirt, the hunger and urgency unlike other times they'd made out. His developing feelings for her were validated by the physical need.

The trail of kisses she placed between his throat and naval had driven him wild. In a fit of passion, he'd blurted out, "I love you, Carolyn."

She'd looked up, a bit surprised. "You're special, too, Duncan."

The wallop to his ego had more than embarrassed him. An icy pain had settled around his heart. One he hadn't fully understood. A month later, when he and Trent returned home for Thanksgiving, his mother had doted on Trent and he'd again recognized the same hurt. His mother's subtle neglect toward Duncan, one he'd witnessed his entire life, rubbed at his need for attention, a need still raw from Carolyn's lack of love.

Once in college, all the power and confidence he'd applied to his schoolwork was put to use in his dealings with women. Women, he learned, liked confident men. The less interested he acted, the more they wanted him. Dating was easy and the minute anybody got too serious, he controlled the direction by ending things.

Earlier tonight, sitting on those bleachers, though, Sophie's nearness had made his blood rush and his knees unstable. He stared at his reflection in the medicine cabinet mirror. Pitiful. Where had the grown man with charm and enough aloofness to preserve his heart gone?

That moment on the bleachers, when he'd clutched her hand and it melted into his, everything he'd pushed away drifted toward him. The axis of his relationship with Sophie had tilted. Which was why her ex-husband's comment outside left him wanting to know more about her past.

Chapter 18

The familiar scrape of Jay's truck pushing snow off Sophie's driveway stirred her from a deep sleep. She peeked through half-opened lids at her nightstand clock. 6:10. Reaching for the TV's remote, she switched on the news and pushed herself up on both elbows.

The quirky weatherman, an energetic and amusing guy who did things no other person on the morning news dared, reported the forecast in black derby, plaid vest, and a pipe hanging out of his mouth, a la Burl Ives as the snowman in *Rudolph the Red Nosed Reindeer*. A map of the state showed northwestern Connecticut had received eight inches of the fluffy white stuff, enough to close school.

Sophie plopped her head back on the pillow and Bella pounced up onto the bed, tail wagging with metronome efficiency. "Hey, girl."

She nestled next to Sophie, who rubbed underneath the dog's furry chin and tried to ignore her doggy breath, instead reliving the excitement after the basketball team's victory last night. She'd had a personal victory too. Duncan's presence filled a cavernous space inside her, a space reserved for deep desire, a space vacant for too many years. Every part of her soul believed he was the real deal, yet the newfound recognition wrestled with her conscience. Her lies to Cliff meshed with her strong feelings for Duncan, the weight of both a lot to bear.

Bella poked Sophie with her cold, wet nose.

"So what if I don't tell Cliff. Right, Bella?"

The dog's ears pricked.

"I mean, my reporting on this story has been more than fair."

Bella's head tilted, a sure sign of agreement.

"Bet you want to go out."

The wiry terrier's chestnut eyes beamed as if to scream "Yes!" then she pounced off the bed onto the hardwood floor and waited by the door.

Sophie threw on thick sweatpants and a fleece pullover then peeked out the mini-blinds. Dwindling flurries and the gray sky hid the dim glow of the sun. Jay's ten-year-old red Dodge Dakota, nicknamed Trusty Rusty, revved then descended down the long, freshly plowed driveway.

Downstairs, Sophie opened the front door. Cold crisp air hit her face just as the *Hartford Courant* fell from where Jay must've wedged it near the knob. She lifted the paper from the snowy stoop, shook off the light flakes, and inhaled the bleach-clean sensation of fresh snowfall.

A minute later, the dog scampered inside. Sophie settled at the kitchen island with the newspaper and coffee. After reading a few stories, she reached the end of the first section and refolded the paper. A headline she'd only glanced at made her pause and she reopened the paper. "Blue Moon Lake Citizens' Group pulls strings to roadblock RGI Project." Sophie quickly scanned the article. In the last paragraph, her hand flew to her mouth. "What the…"

All her suspicions about Duncan Jamieson being a two-faced political machine were re-launched with rocket force.

* * * *

Bernadette and Dave's village Victorian, built in 1890, was walking distance to the church and situated along Main Street amidst other historic homes built around that same time. A place they all gathered each year to view the town's Fourth of July parade. Sophie turned into the driveway and hopped out of the car.

Dave stopped the snowblower and approached. "Thanks for coming over. Let's hope you can calm her down."

Glare from the all-white landscape made her squint. "When she mentioned the new reporter, I had a bad feeling."

"She's threatening to drive over to the Jamieson's house. Even though the paper said unnamed sources at RGI gave them the statement, she's certain he's behind it. What do you think?"

Sophie wavered. "Close to a hundred people work at the headquarters, but the fact is none of us are really close enough to Duncan to trust him."

Dave frowned. "God knows I want to like the guy."

"Mmm." She didn't offer too much, afraid she'd give away her conflicted emotions.

"If Duncan's not involved, perhaps he can fix what's been said." Dave's usually calm face showed a new kind of worry. "I like to think the best of people."

"Me too." Sophie headed to the porch. "I'll call Marcus, my friend who works at the paper."

She entered the front foyer. Bernadette, already on her way down the wooden staircase, glanced at Sophie and frowned.

"I'm glad you're here." One hand rested on the home's oak banister, in the other she carried her pumps, and a newspaper had been secured under her armpit.

Sophie unzipped her boots. "Since you're wearing a skirt, can I assume you're going to work and not to the Jamieson house to pick a fight?"

"I can fight in a skirt." Her dark grimace suggested her mood hadn't improved. "You won't believe who called me."

"Duncan?" Sophie slipped off the furry boots, which Cliff said made her look like Big Foot's sister.

"Yes." She growled and landed in the foyer, her last step an angry stomp. She continued through the dining room, the yellowed floral wallpaper in this area a relic from the home's past.

"He claims to have no idea who from his office might have spoken to the *Courant* reporter. I know you like the guy, but what's your honest take on this?"

They stopped in the kitchen. "I don't know, Bern. I'm trying to keep my feelings out of it. Can I see the paper again?"

Bernadette handed over the one she'd just carried down.

Sophie reread the statement in question.

A source at Resort Group International suggests Save Our Lake's Environment's President and founder, Bernadette Felton, an attorney at Kramer, Paine, and Anderson, may have influenced the recent Department of Environmental Conservation decision against RGI. Three years ago, Felton represented the DEC in a case against Petrusky Pesticides, accused of violating environmental and consumer safety laws. The source suggests that Felton used her ties at the DEC in order to ensure RGI's preliminary study be deemed insufficient to proceed with the project due to environmental concerns. When asked, Felton denied the allegation.

Vague enough to cultivate the planted seed: S.O.L.E. shouldn't be trusted. Sophie's disgust for media abuse exploded. "These days, all someone has to do is suggest you've done something wrong and kazaam... you're guilty."

"That damn reporter was sneaky, too." Bernadette paced the kitchen. "He discussed the case at Petrusky like it wasn't a big deal. He asked if I might think the past relationship influenced the decision and I said no.

I told him I hoped this didn't go in his story since it had no bearing. He promised it wouldn't. Do you know this guy? Barry Thomas."

"No." Sophie took out her phone. "Let me call Marcus." There was a missed call on her phone, but she didn't recognize the number.

Bernadette poured two cups of coffee, handed one to Sophie, and continued pacing, the way she always thought through problems. Sophie sipped the hot drink and Marcus answered on the fourth ring.

"It's Sophie. Did you read what your replacement wrote about Bernadette?"

Marcus' anger rivaled her own, both firm believers in ethical reporting. After a few minutes, she thanked Marcus and hung up.

"Barry Thomas is a recent hire from the *Stamford Advocate*." Sophie leaned against the counter near the sink with her back to the window. "The reporter has a reputation. Likes to stir the pot with barely creditable accusations. Somehow he gets away with this crap every time."

Bernadette stopped. "How does that happen?"

"Wish I knew. Reporters like him give us all a bad rap. Marcus said his boss hinted the assignment change came directly from someone high up at the paper." She considered Duncan's relationship to Will Steiner and the possibility he had contacts at other papers, too.

Bernadette's gaze drifted toward the open pantry door, where she stared in deep thought for several seconds. "Do you think Buzz has anything to do with it? He seemed pretty mad at me during the hearing." She huffed a sarcastic snort. "What else is new?"

"Anything's possible."

"Did Marcus mention Duncan?"

"Not directly. He's certain someone from the firm is sticking their nose into the newspaper's business. Who, though, remains a mystery."

Dave called to Bernadette from the front door, so she excused herself.

Sophie turned and watched out the window. A threatening blue jay flew to a snow-covered branch near two cardinals, who twittered with the nervous energy of Bernadette. The blue jay's beautiful sapphire hues settled in a mosaic pattern along his backside and rendered him a handsome creature of nature. The idea he presented danger seemed almost impossible.

Looks could be deceiving. After this, she'd have no problem cornering Duncan at next week's interview during *Northbridge in Focus*. This little bit of revenge, however, did nothing to massage her stung ego. How could this guy hold her hand at the game and give her that tender kiss at her house then pull a stunt like this?

Never before had she felt such a kinship with the word naïve.

* * * *

Bart snapped a few last photos as a menagerie of wooden sleds, ski boards, and snow tubes flew past them like rush hour on the interstate.

"I'm all set." Sophie brushed some snow off her jeans. "I got the names for the pictures and even took a run down on a borrowed tube."

"I know. I'll e-mail you the photo when we get back to the paper." Bart tucked his camera back into the bag slung over his shoulder and adjusted the knit cap keeping his nearly bald scalp warm.

Her stomach growled, earlier than its usual time. "Want to stop at Sunny Side Up? I'm starving."

"Sure. Let me toss the camera in your car." Bart held out his hand and she gave him her keys. "Go grab us a booth."

She rounded the corner onto Main Street and a windy gust of powdered snow sent her scurrying inside.

A minute later, the restaurant door swung open. Duncan headed straight for her booth, an underlying question mark forming his expression.

"Hi. I was across the street when you came in. Didn't you hear me yell your name?"

"No."

"I tried to call you a little while ago. Cliff gave me your cell number."

"Oh?" She sat back and crossed her arms. She'd have a long talk with Cliff about loyalty when she returned to the office. "What do you want?"

"Something wrong?" His hands pressed deep into the pockets of his field coat.

"Why don't you tell me?"

"You mean the article in the paper?"

"Gee, ya think?" Several people in nearby booths turned, so she motioned to the bench seat opposite her. He slid in. She leaned forward, lowered her voice, and pointed until her index finger fell one step short of poking the center of his chest. "We're not having a very good day."

"Sophie, I have no idea how the story got in the—" He stopped and clasped her finger in his warm palm. He grinned. "Finger pointing isn't very polite."

"You're right." She jerked her hand away and he twitched as if he'd been slapped. "Neither is planting lies to ruin someone's reputation?"

"You think I planted that lie?" His jaw flexed.

"If the shoe fits."

Momentary annoyance shadowed his eyes, and then he moved closer and dropped his voice. "Sophie. There's one thing I want more than anything." His gaze pleaded. "Your trust. Please. Tell me how I can earn it."

She floundered for a response, his request for trust the last thing she'd expected him to say. "Well, I just assumed when the paper said RGI...."

His mouth bowed into a frown. "You assumed it was me?"

"It's your company."

He folded his hands on the tabletop. "I've been trying all morning to find out who's behind this. I'm coming up dry." He tilted his head. "You really thought I'd do something like this?" His pained stare rested on her for several seconds, then he looked away, toward the counter and row of old red leather stools. His jaw tightened then he sighed and turned back to her. "I'm aware how this looks, but weren't we—I mean, last night I thought we were getting closer."

She had, too. The kiss they'd shared in her kitchen had kept her awake the past two nights and the sweet way he'd taken her hand during the game made her heart swell.

"Hey." Bart arrived while unzipping his ski jacket. His head swiveled between the two of them and a slow realization settled over his face. "Um, back in a sec. I'm heading for the men's room."

Duncan studied his hands while tense lines dominated his face. Not the face of a manipulator, but someone experiencing hurt. It was possible someone else in his company was behind the story. Had Ryan Malarkey left her so overly suspicious that she couldn't tell genuine caring from manipulation? Duncan's overtures toward her were too intense not to be heartfelt.

"Duncan?"

He looked up.

"I'm sorry. Really."

"It's fine." She deserved his crisp tone, but it still hurt.

"Listen." Sophie sighed. "Once I had a man use me. Take advantage of my role on the paper. He showed an interest in me and fed me lies. Guess I'm gun-shy."

His forehead crumpled and he nodded. "I'm glad you told me, but that's not what I'm doing to you." He paused. "Like I said, I only want your trust."

She blew out a breath. "I'll try." She wanted to reach out, take his warm hand, and make everything better. The lunch crowd made her resist. "Any idea who at your firm might have pushed that angle to the paper about Bernadette? She's really upset."

"No. Wish I did. I called her this morning. I knew she'd be upset." He took a sugar packet and his fingers fiddled with it for a few seconds. "Dave and Bernadette have been very kind to me. I'd never have condoned the statement."

Every part of Sophie wanted to believe him. She spoke softly, "Can you narrow it down to a short list of people?"

He nodded. "There are only two I can think of. Since the main roads are clear, I'm going to Hartford to try to get to the bottom of this. I hoped you could help me."

"How?"

"By clearing Bernadette's name. At least locally. Can you can get something in the *Gazette* right away saying the *Courant* accusation isn't true?"

"You're asking me to plant a story for you?"

"Well, yes." He paused. "I don't want people to think RGI would be involved in spreading rumors. I also don't want Bernadette's reputation hurt."

Duncan's hopeful gaze worked overtime to convince her manipulating the press to repair her best friend's reputation had merit. He clearly had no problem pulling her across a journalistic line. His expectant stare turned into something more sincere and almost awkward.

He reached across the table and threaded his fingers through hers. "Please, Sophie. I wouldn't ask if it didn't matter so much."

Her resistance wilted. Letting go of his hand would be the right thing to do, but his touch felt so secure and right. Quietly she replied, "I'll discuss it with Cliff."

He studied her for a long moment then his face softened. "Thank you."

She hoped nobody in the restaurant watched them, but a lifetime of living in Northbridge told her they all were.

Chapter 19

Stan Polanski cracked an egg and it sizzled on the hot grill. His back to Sophie and Cliff, he kept talking. "Yep, Farmer's Almanac says this winter will be tough. Last Friday's storm may be the first of many."

Cliff's voice rose over the hissing grill while he removed his wallet. "Seems like when we were kids, every winter had tons of snow." As Sophie reached for hers, he put out a hand to stop her. "My treat, kiddo."

It had been at least twenty years since Sophie entered Polanski's Grocery. Third generation owner of the business, Stan Polanski, looked a little plumper and grayer than years ago but, according to Cliff, he still made the best damn cheesy egg sandwiches in town.

Every Wednesday, Cliff met here for breakfast with other members of the Northbridge High School class of '55, or thereabouts. She figured the older crowd found nostalgic comfort in the yellowed linoleum floor and the old metal-rimmed Formica countertop.

Cliff invited Sophie to join him this morning, part of a well-thought out plan to pry more information out of gossipmonger extraordinaire, Les Wilson. Since he'd clammed up on Meg a few weeks ago at the real estate office, refusing to give full disclosure on Frank Jamieson's bribe to the town Police Department, Cliff seemed hell-bent on finding out the rest of the story. Nobody else he'd spoken to remembered a thing.

A part of Sophie wanted to stop their hunt on the Jamiesons' past. What if they learned something even worse than bribery about Duncan's father? How would she tell Duncan, who remained oblivious to her research?

Of course, the only way to suggest this to Cliff would be to ante up with her indiscretions. Something she wouldn't do. In her current position, she could protect Duncan from any scathing news that came out about his father. She ignored the tug at her conscience, screaming something about a journalist's ethics. There was always a chance today's venture wouldn't even tie into Duncan's land purchase. If so, she'd insist Cliff put the story to rest.

Protectiveness over Duncan now guided many decisions, a severe shift in her loyalty compared to a few short weeks ago. Well-hidden shame filled her every move and yet she couldn't seem to stop herself.

Five days had passed since the storm and their major handholding PDA—her daughter's acronym for public displays of affection—at Sunny Side Up. Sophie was shocked it hadn't shown up in one of the newspaper's "Eye Around Town" entries. If Cliff knew, he hadn't said a word. His silence offered her a false sense of security, though. Cliff always gave matters their due consideration. However, if he wasn't talking, neither was she.

The short store-owner stretched on his toes and removed a bag of napkins from one of the ancient steel cabinets lining the wall then flipped the eggs. "Leave the money on the counter. Make it an even seven. I'll bring this to you."

"Thanks." Cliff dropped the bills near the register and they picked up their coffees.

She followed him down an aisle of canned goods toward the back of the store. Adli's familiar gentle chortle came from the direction they headed. They rounded a corner. Les Wilson had taken some time away from bothering the folks in Meg's real estate office. He sat with Adli at an old round veneer table with folding chairs.

"Morning." Cliff motioned for Sophie to take a seat with the men.

Adli's face lit up. "Here he is. The only working man over seventy in town. Time to retire, don't you think? Maybe run for office, like me."

"I only turned seventy six months ago." Cliff removed his VFW cap and put it on the table.

Adli nodded at Sophie. "To what do we owe the honor?" The bright morning sun peeked through a nearby window and glinted off the lens of his wire-framed glasses.

"Cliff tells me Stan makes the best breakfast sandwich in New England. Figured it was about time I tried one."

"A true statement if I've ever heard one." Les scratched the side of his balding scalp, the only hair remaining a bit like a baby chick's fuzz. "What's the good word down at the paper? Seems there's plenty going on to keep you two busy."

Cliff poured a packet of sugar into his Styrofoam cup and stirred. "Yup. It's been one of our busier months."

"I watched the last zoning meeting on the local cable channel the other night." Les chuckled. The shake of his curved belly moved underneath his tight turtleneck and the tall neckline bumped the jowl of his chin. "Better than those new reality TV shows. Jamieson worked the room like Donald Trump."

"Well, he is a big-time New Yawk City based developer." Adli's knock-off Bronx accent surprised Sophie, a bit out of place for his usual serious demeanor. He dusted a little confectioners' sugar off the chest of his sweater vest, residue from the powered donut near his cup. "Probably even has lunch now and then with 'the Donald.' I can't figure out what the hell he's doing in Northbridge."

Cliff added his sugar and stirred. "What do you think of him, Adli? You've worked with him more than anybody else in town."

Adli rubbed the gray stubble on his long chin with his fingertips. "If you'd asked me when he first made the offer, I'd have told you he was up to no good. He's surprised me. This guy is used to getting what he wants, but he's not unreasonable. Seems to appreciate the things we offer as a small town. Doesn't buck the system."

Adli's assessment left Sophie relieved. Her instinct to believe Duncan suddenly stood on more steady footing.

"Buzz is really cranky over this project." Sophie broached the next question with caution, as Cliff had coached. "You think he's behind the bribery rumor going around town related to RGI's project?"

Adli's willowy fingers slid along the rim of his cup. "Buzz has never been considered a moderate politician. Just because he wants this, doesn't mean he'd do anything illegal. Although, I'd swear he thrives on the drama." A guilty look spread across Adli's face, the gossipy statement not his usual style.

The loud clearing of Les' throat couldn't be missed. "Speaking of drama…" He waited until everyone looked in his direction. "Seems Buzz has a bit going on behind the scenes." He turned to Sophie. "Your pal Meg McNeil asked some strange questions about Buzz the other day. About something that happened in town a long time ago."

Les had taken the bait, as they'd hoped. She worked extra hard to keep every muscle neutral.

"Hmm." Cliff acted uninterested, his poker face bar-none. "Soph, could you pass me a napkin?"

She did as asked but furrowed her brows and glanced at Les. "Are you sure? Why would Meg stick her nose into Buzz's business? Maybe you misunderstood."

"Well, she did." Les sounded annoyed and his wobbly chin and cheeks quivered. "Asked me if I remembered when the Jamiesons sold the house they'd owned for close to seventy-five years on the upper eastside." He sneered. "How could I forget? The gossip mill worked harder than a butter churn as those rumors started flying about a problem at Buzz's house."

"Rumors?" Cliff probed. "I don't remember any rumors."

Sophie peeked at Adli, who stared into his coffee, his lips pressed tight.

Les looked over his right shoulder with the paranoia of a covert agent ready to swap a military secret. He leaned into the tabletop. "Don't you remember the time—" He clamped his mouth closed when Stan rounded the corner.

"Here you go." Stan put down Sophie's and Cliff's egg sandwiches then plunked an issue of the *Hartford Courant* next to Cliff's arm. "Paper's on the house."

Les waited until Stan moved far enough away and lowered his voice. "Before the Jamiesons listed the house, the year before, someone reported a gunshot at Buzz's place to the police. The paper said he'd been cleaning the gun and it went off by accident." He sat back and rested his hands on his stomach. "Word around town claims that's false. Seems the original police report told the real story, but those records were changed." His vision bounced between them. "Someone made a generous offer for the amended version."

"Les, don't go any further." Cliff held up his hand like a cop stopping traffic. "May I remind you what Mark Twain used to say?"

Les squinted. "Mark Twain?"

"Yup. He said 'Better to be thought a fool than to open your mouth and remove all doubt.' I can't believe someone would—"

"Now you hold on!" Les slapped a palm on the tabletop. "I'm no fool. This came from a reliable source."

Cliff bit into his egg sandwich and chewed.

Les glared at him while Cliff slowly swallowed.

"Okay. What'd you hear?"

"The offer was from none other than Frank Jamieson himself. Duncan's father." A satisfied smugness settled on his face. "I can't say who told me."

Cliff chortled. "No offense but how would you alone be privy to such news?"

Les puffed his thick chest. "I have my sources."

Cliff shrugged, offered a doubting shake of his head. "I'm simply saying that's quite an accusation. Without knowing where the story originated, I'm not sure I buy it."

Adli now watched Les with interest.

Les leaned close and folded his forearms on the table. A lethal mixture of guilt and anticipation shined in his eyes. Bait taken. Cliff was right. Sophie got the same rush she got when a trout grabbed hold of her line.

"Well," Les paused. "I shouldn't repeat this, but it happened so long ago nobody will care."

* * * *

Sophie yanked up the sleeves of her thick wool sweater and scrolled on her computer to the latest remark from a reader. Three days after Cliff had given her the go-ahead to write a rebuttal to the *Hartford Courant's* slanderous comments about Bernadette, people were still posting to the *Gazette's* online conversation.

Many readers' complained Sophie's piece had shown favoritism toward Bernadette and her lake-saving political action committee. Thank God others believed the Hartford paper had overstepped their boundaries and came to her rescue. The negative remarks, however, played to every concern she'd had about Duncan's request. Today's single comment spoke in her favor.

She reread her after-meetings notes from this morning's breakfast at Polanski's, which had been a great use of time. Les' face had glowed with tall-tale teller's glee when he recounted a tale of gossip over thirty years old.

All his information came from Jack Carney, the dispatcher in those days for the Northbridge Police Department, and Les' next door neighbor. During an afternoon break from their yard work, Les had mentioned his office had received a few nibbles on the newly listed Jamieson property. Jack, who possessed a cynical attitude on a good day, had been all too happy to trash the police chief and flat-out said the house sale had to be because of what happened the previous summer. When Les had asked, "What happened last summer?" Jack hesitated then blurted out, "Money talks and BS walks. Jamieson forked over some cash and next thing I know, the chief is making me revise my paperwork like certain things never happened." He'd then clammed up, despite Les' best efforts for more details.

As they'd driven back to the paper, Sophie considered asking Cliff if they could drop the matter, even though it would sound suspicious. Before she could, Cliff had glanced at her from the driver's seat. "Looks like Jack Carney is our key to finding out what happened at Buzz's house."

"Yeah. I'm not sure what we've learned is enough to warrant continued digging. I mean, it doesn't look like Duncan or RGI has done anything here."

Cliff's lips had pursed while he stared ahead at the road. "Something's strange, though. That new reporter slandering Bernadette didn't just happen. Why would someone go through all the trouble to leave you those notes without having a damn good reason? How 'bout we try to talk to Jack Carney. If it's another dead end and RGI is in the clear, we'll drop the hunt."

"Sounds good." She'd studied Cliff's profile and he hadn't shown any signs that indicated he knew about how close she'd gotten to Duncan, much to her relief.

The phone on her desk rang and she answered.

"You won't believe this," Veronica murmured into the mouthpiece.

"Try me."

"Remember over a month ago when Mrs. Payne couldn't recall who asked for the microfiche?"

"Sure. Our only clue, lost in the recall of a senior citizen."

"This morning she walked in with the answer."

"Better late than never. So? Who'd she see?"

"Jane Dougherty. Her husband's on the zoning board, right?"

"Yes, ma'am. Joe." His nervousness at the last zoning board meeting took on new life. "Interesting. Did Mrs. Payne say anything else?"

"Yeah. Want to know about her sister's cataract surgery?"

"No. Thanks for the other information."

She hung up and pounced up the stairs to Cliff's office. "Got a minute? I found another puzzle piece for our mystery." The strong aroma of fish blasted her senses.

Cliff held half a tuna sandwich in one hand and the latest issue of *American Angler* in the other. His chin motioned to the empty seat across from him. "Sure. Have a seat."

She divulged the details Veronica provided à la Mrs. Payne. "Joe has never done anything to defy Buzz. Yet, at the last zoning board meeting he voted against Buzz. I've never seen Buzz so ticked. Do you think Jane's involvement is a coincidence?"

"Not one bit." He popped the last of his sandwich into his mouth.

"Buzz and Joe are registered in the same political party. Jane sits on the town committee for the party. Her handing me dirt on Buzz makes no sense."

He finished chewing and dabbed his lips with a napkin. "Maybe this isn't about Buzz. After what Les told us at Polanski's this morning, something weird happened here years ago and it involves the Jamiesons. For once, I think one of Les' yarns holds the key. Told you I know what makes him tick."

"Sometimes you scare me. Glad you're on my side."

The corner of his mouth lifted as he tossed the napkin into his wastebasket and made the shot. "Two people from Northbridge know the real story. Jack Carney and—"

"Buzz," Sophie finished for him.

Did Duncan know?

"Buzz isn't talking. I think Jack's in the Southbridge Nursing Home. I've already left a message with his son to give me a call. We used to bowl on a league at Lenny's Lanes in New Scotland. Want to join me if I get can him to set up a meeting?"

"Yeah." Sophie's fingers drummed the chair arm. "Do you really trust Duncan Jamieson?"

Cliff shrugged. "For some reason, we all seem to trust the guy."

Sophie teetered on the edge of telling Cliff how her path with Duncan now wove an intricate line between business and personal and threatened to hamper her usually spot-on radar. He'd probably yank her from this story so fast she'd get whiplash. It wouldn't matter, except now she wanted to stay on it for one reason: to act as guardian to this rumor, in case what they turned up had nothing to do with the land deal.

Disgust with her silence to both Cliff and Duncan settled like bile in the back of her throat. At the start of the assignment, her stake in the land had threatened her as a reporter. Everything had changed. She'd officially become the kind of journalist she despised.

Chapter 20

John Lennon's opening scream in "Revolution" blared in Sophie's iPod earbuds during her morning run at the exact moment a shiny, red Audi TT with New York plates whizzed past, in clear violation of the thirty-five mph speed limit.

The brake lights flashed and the car stopped, performed a three-point-turn and returned toward her. It slowed as she approached. The driver's darkened window rolled down and she stared at a man with black disheveled hair. His lips moved, but all she heard were the Beatles, letting her know things would be all right.

She removed her earbuds but kept a safe distance. "May I help you?"

He wore sunglasses, the reflective kind. Always a little creepy. An image of her, wearing a knitted cap and knockoff Ray Bans, stared back from his lenses.

"I'm looking for Clear Brook Lane." Crabbiness oozed from his tone. "Things aren't marked very well around here."

The street he wanted was near the expensive homes in Northbridge, not surprising given the snazzy vehicle.

"Another runner a few miles back said to turn at the red school building. All I see are houses." He lifted his glasses and grazed her from wool cap to running shoes.

"That's because the school is white."

"White? Jesus. Why'd he say red?" His unzipped black leather jacket, plain dark T-shirt and snug leather driving gloves that gripped the steering wheel satisfied his hip theme. "Don't they teach the color wheel around here?"

She was tempted to give this jerk another set of wrong directions. "The structure is a single-room school house, like the kind they used back in the olden days. Not a large building. It used to be red."

His eyes flowed into an exaggerated roll.

Any interest she had in being polite to the outsider disappeared. Sophie lifted her sunglasses to the top of her head. "You can afford a car like this but no GPS?"

He flinched, visibly shot down a notch from the direct statement. "I lost satellite." His lips pressed tight and he studied her for several seconds. "Sorry. I'm just frustrated."

Something was familiar about his face, but she couldn't figure out what. Guess she'd cut him some slack. Anybody could have an off day.

Sophie pointed down the road. "Head back this way. The schoolhouse will be on your left. A small wood-framed building, not a modern day school. There's a little glass and wood display near the entrance, the honor roll for the last graduating class."

"How quaint." His brows huddled and he studied her more closely. "You're Sophie, right?"

"Have we met?"

"Trent Jamieson. Duncan's brother. My dad used to take us to your family's tackle shop." He threw the car in park, lifted a large super-sized Starbucks cup from his console, and sipped. "A long, long time ago. You have an older brother, right? I used to talk to him."

"Yes. Jay." His remark jarred a new memory. The summer before ninth grade, Meg had developed a serious crush on a visitor, a brooding high school sophomore who came in with his father and brother then ignored them while they shopped and he talked to Jay. Meg had noticed him instantly. In contrast to her positive perkiness over life, Meg's sonar often veered toward difficult men.

Suddenly, the entire Jamieson family crystallized in her mind. Even in those days, Trent's miserable attitude glowed as if dotted in neon lights. He hadn't changed much.

"I remember you." She also now had a distant visual on young Duncan, short with freckles and bright copper hair, like Patrick's.

"Duncan tells me your dad hasn't retired and Jay still works at the shop. Doesn't anybody ever want to leave this place?"

His comment pinched, as if someone had clamped the sensitive skin near Sophie's upper arm. "This is a great place to live. Why do you keep knocking it?"

"I just prefer the city." Trent's jaw hardened. He crossed his arms and rubbed his biceps, "Jesus. Is it always this cold here?"

"Not in the summer."

"Ha. Ha." His lip curled upward as he reconsidered her.

Veronica's comment on ladies' night suddenly carried more weight. Had one of the Jamieson sons caused them to sell the house? Duncan didn't act like a troublemaker, but Trent sure had the attitude for one. Had he caused enough trouble that their father felt a need to bribe police to clean up the records?

She crossed her arms to stay warm. "Being back in town must be interesting. Have you caught up with anybody you knew back then?"

Trent frowned. "No. We really weren't close to anybody."

"Hmm. Well, your project has a lot of support from some people in high places. Our Selectman, Buzz Harris, can't stop extolling its virtues for our area."

Trent shifted in his seat then wrapped a gloved hand around the steering wheel. He stared past her in the direction of Sunnydale Dairy Farm, his thoughts unreadable. "Yes. Seems like a decent place for a resort." He looked at her. "Guess I'd better get going. Thanks for the directions." He revved the engine and pulled out.

The car disappeared over the picket-fenced ridge near the farm. She turned to head back toward home. Time to do a little research on Trent Jamieson.

* * * *

Matt shuffled into the kitchen, rubbing one eye with a rounded fist, clad in a wrinkled AC/DC T-shirt with navy sweatpants. He stumbled on Sophie's running sneakers, left near the sink when she downed a glass of water after her run. There were days she was no better than her kids.

"Mom? On Sunday afternoon—"

She held up her index finger and pointed to the phone handset next to her ear. The loosely followed rule in their house was that unless the place caught on fire or the zombie apocalypse had actually started, they were not to interrupt while she was on the phone. The odds were about fifty-fifty they remembered. Matt left the room.

Since coming back from her run, she'd scanned Google for any character-revealing fact she could find on Trent Jamieson. She'd learned he had worked at Jamieson, McDonald & O'Reilly as an attorney for several years, the father's firm in Manhattan. There was no reason given for his leaving, but he now showed up on the web pages of RGI as a senior project manager. The lawyer angle had prompted her call to Marcus, whose brother-in-law was a big shot lawyer in Manhattan. The chance he knew Trent was slim, but worth asking.

On the second ring, a wave of guilt walloped Sophie. This call to her friend defied Duncan's request to trust him.

Ring Three.

This could be classified as grade-A snooping.

Ring four.

Going behind Duncan's back showed a lack of faith in his ability to investigate any manipulation at his firm, like he said he was doing.

On the fifth ring, she had convinced herself to hang up but Marcus answered. "Hey, Soph. What's up?" Voices filled the background.

"Catch you at a bad time?"

"Yeah. I'm at work, but I've got a quick second for you. Hope you're not calling about another slanderous article by my employer."

"No, well, uh, I called because..." With a swift calculation of her dilemma, she concluded Duncan would never know she'd spoken to the other reporter. "I ran into Trent Jamieson this morning." She gave him the details. "After meeting him, he made it to my list of suspicious characters at RGI. This is a long shot, but do you think your brother-in-law, the lawyer, might have any scoop on him?"

"There's a chance. He's been at the same firm for a long time. I'll give him a call."

Matt came in again and glanced in Sophie's direction. He skulked to the refrigerator and stared inside, as if waiting for his choice to jump into his hands.

"Thanks. I owe you one. I'll do more digging too." She hung up.

"What's up, Matt?"

He finally selected the orange juice, reached into the cabinet for a tall glass then poured. "Tomorrow afternoon, after church, can we go bowling at Sal's Lanes?"

"Sure. You can go."

"No. I mean all of us. Tia wants to bring two of her friends and I want to bring some of mine. Since the stupid law says I can't drive with them until I've had my license a full year, you need to take us."

"Oh. *We* really means *me* driving you there?"

He tipped back the large glass and nodded.

"Sure, but I can only fit five in my car."

He wiped his mouth with the back of his hand. "We've got another driver. You can take me, Tia, Katie, and Alyssa."

"Okay. Any time after one-thirty is good." She hopped off the stool to take a shower. "Who else is going?"

"Trevor Trafford and Pat. Mr. J's driving them."

Duncan. Guilt over the call to Marcus swarmed her conscience, but she swatted the horrible feeling aside. "Has Patrick ever been duck pin bowling before?"

"Nope." Matt downed the juice remains. "Neither has Pat's dad." Leaving the glass on the counter, he headed toward the hallway. "Maybe you can play a few games with Mr. J."

"Sure."

She should've talked to Duncan more about Trent, not called Marcus. "Matt?"

He stopped and looked back.

"Glass in the dishwasher, mister."

* * * *

"Then this guy tells me to turn at a red school." Trent threw up his hands and leaned into the kitchen table, moving closer to Duncan, nearly bumping his coffee. "I drive and drive. No red school building. Turns out he meant a teeny white schoolhouse, like they used a hundred years ago."

Duncan hoped he calmed down by the time Buzz and Marion arrived. After all, this get-together was at his request. Trent's edginess probably had to do with meeting Marion for the first time. It couldn't be easy meeting his birthmother.

Trent's adoption into the Jamieson family had never been a secret, but the details never interested Duncan. In late high school, Trent told Duncan he'd known for many years his real parents were from Northbridge, the town where they'd vacationed a few summers back. When his mother pushed for them to pursue the Tates' property, Trent met Elmer Tate, who never showed any signs of discomfort with their history. Trent didn't ask about Marion, only Duncan happened to meet her when he dropped by Buzz's office in early December. When she learned who he was, her calm smile had vanished and she'd nervously said, "Nice to meet you," then hurried out. Similar to how she'd acted the night he'd seen her talking to Sophie in the hallway at the zoning meeting. How would she act today while meeting her son?

Duncan sipped from his mug. "Buzz told me the historical society decided to restore the schoolhouse to its original color."

"Whatever. Good thing I ran into your friend, Sophie. Her directions got me here."

A jolt traveled up Duncan's spine, not from caffeine. "Where'd you see her?"

"She was jogging. We had a nice conversation."

Nice, by Trent's definition, didn't make him feel better.

Trent snorted a laugh. "You look worried. I didn't tell her about your teenage crush."

Duncan clenched his jaw. "Jesus, could you drop it? She knows, anyway. I was picking up Patrick at her house and we had a glass of wine. I told her."

Trent's brows raised then he shook his head. "Man, little brother. Didn't any of my finely honed skills with women rub off on you?"

Duncan shrugged. "Look. You do what works for you. I like being honest."

"Hey, she asked this strange question. Had we caught up with anybody we knew years ago? Did you say anything about why we're really here?"

"No. Did she say anything else?"

"Only that Buzz really supported RGI's plans."

The questions made him wonder if Sophie was being completely honest with him. The harsh sound of his cell phone vibrating against the marble countertop distracted him. He got up from the kitchen table and glanced at the caller ID. "Hey, Buzz. Running late?"

"Sorry to call last minute. You know, I got up with good intentions of getting over there for breakfast, but nothing's going right today." A long explanation ensued, with several reasons why he couldn't get there, all sounding made up. Was he uncomfortable, or maybe Marion? Trent would be disappointed.

While Buzz rambled on, Duncan snuck away from the kitchen and went to his office. Since the basketball game a week earlier, one question had bugged him.

He shut the office door. "We'll reschedule. I need your help with something else, though. Has anything unusual ever happened on the Tates' land? Anything that would concern Sophie?"

"Define unusual."

Duncan almost laughed into the phone. Buzz's caution sounded as pitiful as Bill Clinton's request during a grand jury hearing, when he'd asked for clarification of "what 'is' is." He understood why Clinton had stalled, but this reaction from Buzz, on a run-of-the-mill question, raised a red flag.

"Anything out of the ordinary." A pause hung in the air and Duncan waited it out.

Buzz cleared his throat. "The Moore family settled the land a long time ago. They lost the property in a bet with Otis and Elmer's father. Alan Moore's always yapping about how he wants that deed back in his family's name. That's all I can think of."

He couldn't pinpoint why, but he didn't believe him.

Chapter 21

"It's the building with the big yellow duck, Mr. Jamieson."

Duncan glanced in the rearview mirror at Patrick's new friend, the bulky point guard on the school's basketball team. For a big kid, he really moved on the court.

Duncan pulled into a near-empty lot. A large colorful sign read "Sal's Duckpin Lanes...All That It's Quacked Up To Be." The flat-roofed, brick and mortar building had a plain façade, except for the bright yellow picture of a duck wearing a red bowtie on the front doors.

The three got out and Duncan went over to Patrick. "You sure you want me hanging out? I don't mind taking a drive around Southbridge. We don't get over here much."

Patrick sighed. "Well, I didn't say so before, but Matt said his mom is staying and likes to bowl. He figured you guys could play."

"Oh?" The news lifted him. "Guess our bowling won't infringe on your time."

Patrick's sheepish shrug suggested matchmaking wasn't his thing and he ran to catch up with his friend.

Duncan had never even heard of duckpin bowling until his son mentioned the need for a ride today. Once inside, the greasy aroma of a concession stand made him crave a fry. "Rock Around the Clock" crooned through hidden speakers, a true complement to the dated interior. He half expected the Fonz to greet them. A thud, followed by a thunderous roll, resulted in the shattering of pins.

For all appearances, this seemed like any other bowling alley he'd ever visited, not that there were many. Upon closer look, however, the softball-sized balls and miniaturized pins told him it wasn't.

"Hey, Pat!" Matt yelled and motioned from the far end of the lanes.

Sophie stood near her son and handed her daughter a pair of bowling shoes. A gentle panic settled in his chest. God only knows what Trent had said to her yesterday.

She glanced his way then cast a sweet smile. He caught his breath, only then realizing he'd held it in, and returned the greeting.

The boys got their shoes and rushed over to the lower pit area where the other kids were gathered. Duncan went straight to Sophie, who stood next to a small round table, searching through her handbag.

"Aaaay…" She looked up and he flipped an Arthur Fonzarelli thumbs-up. "Is this place all its quacked up to be?"

Sophie grinned. "Nobody told me Fonzie would be here today."

Snug Levi's and a simple black fitted turtleneck showed off the natural beauty she possessed. He resisted the urge to take her in his arms, kiss her as he had the other night.

"Your friends Potsie and Ralph coming too?"

"Nope. I'm flying solo today. If you're not too tired from running around in my mind all day, we could bowl a few games."

Her brow arched. "Wow, last time I got fed a line that corny, I had heartburn for days."

"Ouch."

"Aw, come on." She laughed. "All part of the act. The Duncan Jamieson I've seen in action has thicker skin."

"So…that's a yes?"

"Absolutely." She motioned to the reception desk and they headed over.

Sophie hinted to the man who worked the register that they wanted a lane away from the kids. He gave a knowing nod and assigned one at the opposite end of the building, where they went and changed into their shoes.

"Ever been duckpin bowling before?" She slipped off short black boots.

"Nope."

"Only a handful of lanes exist in the country, mostly on the East Coast. I think the game originated in Massachusetts. Although my grandmother told me she once read Maryland claims the same thing."

"I've learned something new every day since moving here. Speaking of family, you met my brother yesterday morning?"

"As a matter of fact, I did." She stopped tying her shoe and thought for a second. "He's different than you."

"True." Duncan tied his laces and adjusted the cuff of his jeans. "So your conversation with him went okay?"

"Sure. It was fine." The slight twist of her nose suggested their talk wasn't perfect. "He's a little edgy." She chuckled, tied off the other shoe, and stood.

"What's so funny?"

"Oh, nothing really. Just thinking about my grandmother and what she'd say about him."

"Why would she say anything about Trent?"

Sophie's mouth turned upward into a coy simper, as if she held in a private joke. "Nana believed a person's name really spoke to some part of their character."

He stood and stomped down his pant leg. "Really? What's your name mean?"

Her perfect lips twisted. "Wisdom. That's what she said. I'm not saying it's true."

"Any idea what my name means?"

Her cheeks turned soft pink. She quickly leaned over to tuck her boots beneath the seat. "No."

He laughed. "Did you check mine?"

She headed to the score desk. "It's silly."

He followed her. "I'm relentless, you know? My business didn't happen by pure luck. Maybe Duncan means relentless."

She sighed and faced him. "Your name means dark prince. I don't put much stock in these name things, though. At least not like my nana did."

His humor deflated. There were times in his life when that meaning defined him. All those years he'd ignored the needs of his wife and kids, his focus on his work despite their protests for his attention. To outsiders, their life hid the darkness he'd kept inside, at least before Elizabeth jarred him to reality.

Sophie frowned. "Hey, it doesn't mean anything. Sorry. Sometimes I'm too honest." She shook her head, disappointment in herself obvious.

"I'm not upset. I'd rather someone spoke their mind. My wife didn't."

Sophie stepped over to the ball return and removed one. She frowned and stared at the ball for several seconds before looking up at him. "I'm sure you miss her."

"Yes. I wish I'd been a better husband."

"Why would you say that?"

"I buried myself in work for our entire marriage." His mouth went dry, the admission out loud a tough one.

Sophie studied him without judgment.

"When we discovered Elizabeth's illness, she'd reached the terminal stage. I guess fear of not being around for the kids made her pummel me with a dose of reality. Like how I should be a more visible father. You know, what you said about my name has some truth." The honesty brought him some relief, as if he'd finally come out of hiding. "At least it did then. I'm glad to have found out before I lost all chances to make amends with the kids. Family matters."

"Yes." Sophie cupped the ball into her hands, staring down as if she detained a precious butterfly in her palms. "Family does matter."

Her eyes lifted and the tail-end of pain vanished, but he'd seen the ache before. He wanted to ask why, even ask about her husband's remark the night of the basketball game, yet pushing too hard might backfire.

She stepped closer. "We can't change the past. Only learn something."

"I'm trying. I moved here to bridge the gap with my son. Hopefully my daughter too."

"Then I think you will. Here." Sophie placed the ball in his palms, closed them together, then wrapped her soft hands around his. She moved closer, near enough for him to catch the aroma of her floral scent. "Don't let this go to your head, but I believe you have some good prince tendencies."

A stampede of footsteps startled them both and Sophie pulled her hands from his.

"Mom?" Tia's chest heaved as she took several deep breaths, winded due to her sprint across the building with her friend. "Can I have money for food?"

"Sure, honey." She went to her purse.

While he waited, he relished the moment of opening up about himself. It felt damn good, even created a closeness he never expected. The things he'd been keeping from her, though, stared him in the face.

* * * *

Sophie studied Duncan as he positioned himself at the lane. The two brothers were both nice-looking men, but opposite as sunrise and sunset. Duncan's charisma shined bright whereas Trent's snarky scorn brought her down. Duncan's oval face, framed by soft cinnamon hair, had a touchable quality. Trent's more slender profile and shaggy dark strands were aloof and sharp. Duncan's broad chest balanced his comfortable midsection, the welcoming frame of a middle-aged man who enjoyed a good meal and exercised enough to stay healthy. In contrast, Trent's lean physique and long arms had a moody rock-star vibe.

His ball rumbled down the wooden path and knocked over the two final pins. "All right!" He approached her with a hand stretched to receive a high-five. "Now we're talking."

She slapped his palm. "Nice."

He stood behind her chair and rested his hands on the back edge to read over her shoulder. "Guess there's no way this'll be a three hundred game for me?"

She looked up to where he hovered. "You're doing quite well. This isn't as easy as it looks. I suggest you lower your expectations. You can't walk before you crawl."

"My dear, RGI never would have achieved success if I'd lowered my expectations. Besides, who just threw a spare?" He bent down, right next to her face, to read the score sheet.

The sweet blend of sandalwood and soap drifted close. She tried to calculate the third ball into the frame, but his presence had the same effect on her brain as a lobotomy. Besides his closeness, he'd shown her a new side of him. Until now, she'd believed his quest for the Tates' land and his relocation to Northbridge had been driven by simple success and less noble motives. She'd been wrong. Plus, his comment about connecting with his kids seemed sincere.

After a third attempt at adding, Sophie finally got a number. "With two frames left in this game, you're at sixty-three. Not bad."

He frowned. "Not good either."

"Those two gutter balls threw off your score. You'll do better next game."

"Better be careful." The corner of his eyes softened and his voice dipped, smooth as melted chocolate. "I find optimism in a woman sexy. Your turn."

She stood and his palm slid to her mid-back, guiding her upright. He stared into her eyes while the heat of his touch radiated on her back and she wiggled into the warmth.

"Why don't you show me how it's done?" His tender pitch caressed her, spoken as such an enticing offer that he could've won a Grammy for best erotic tone used in a sentence.

She quietly whispered, "We're still talking about bowling, right?"

"Maybe." Duncan's lip curled into a seductive grin. He motioned for her to step up to the lane, and then he took her vacated seat.

Through hidden speakers, Johnny Cash crooned with a reminder to keep a close watch on your heart. She stopped and turned to look at Duncan, whose gaze rested on her. His handsome face, playful and relaxed, made her heart flutter. She willed it to land in his hands. Calm settled over his face. He winked and a slow heat crept through her entire body, her knees nearly melting.

He cleared his throat. "If you don't go soon, this really won't be about bowling."

"That wouldn't be so bad." Desire shadowed his expression and she winked right back at him then turned to face the pins with a confident flip of her hair. Yesterday's call to Marcus popped into her head, and with it a heaping dose of guilt over not having trusted Duncan. Wasn't her trust all he'd asked for?

Stepping forward, she released the ball. It banged then rolled to the left and dropped into the gutter inches from the pin.

Forty minutes later, they'd finished their second game. Duncan rounded Sophie's chair and sat beside her, in the seat meant for the unused lane next to them.

"Final score?"

"I got one forty-three. You got one ten."

He reached over her arm and found his row, following each box with the tip of his finger. "Maybe I should double check your math. Seems you were having trouble adding before." The corners of his lips struggled to stay serious.

"Thanks to you." She placed her hands over his and trapped them with her palms. "Duckpin bowling rule number one...trust the scorekeeper."

Their hands remained snuggled together in a heap on the tabletop. The atmosphere shifted, but she still couldn't shake the idea Duncan had asked for her to have faith in him and she'd gone elsewhere.

"Well, Ms. Shaw, do you plan to distract me this way when you interview me tomorrow night for *Northbridge in Focus?*"

His thumb stroked the top of her hand. Talk about distracting. "Nope. I play fair. Since you brought up the interview, could I ask an awkward question?"

"Okay. Shoot."

"Have you considered who on your staff might have talked to the press about Bernadette?"

"Yes."

"Did your brother make the list?"

The grooves in his forehead crumpled. "Yesterday I talked to Trent about the story from the *Courant*. So, yes. He made my list. He also denied being involved, and I believe him."

"Any other ideas?"

"I wish I knew." He paused and stopped caressing her hand. "I think you should know something. I hope you won't share what I'm about to tell you."

Sophie's inner Benedict Arnold tried to ignore the faith he showed in her. "I won't say a word."

Duncan drew in a deep breath. "Trent's adopted."

"So?"

His hands slipped off hers and he fiddled with the black leather band of his watch. "His birth father is from Northbridge."

"Oh. I had no idea. Mind if I ask who?"

He studied her with great consideration before answering. "Elmer Tate. It's the reason we're interested in the property."

Sophie digested the relationship. "Wait. Elmer doesn't have any other children. So Trent's kind of the heir to the Tates' land?"

Duncan slowly nodded while her mind raced with a dizzying array of questions. She grabbed the first one making any sense.

"Who's Trent's mother?"

"Nobody you'd know." He glanced away for a quick second.

He was hiding something, but she kept quiet, still overwhelmed by the news about Elmer. He'd lived here his whole life. Not that she was privy to all his business, but she never pictured him leaving town and meeting a woman. He and Otis belonged to the local VFW hall, so perhaps in the military he'd met someone.

"If he wanted his real son to have the land, why'd they put it up for sale? Why let me get my hopes up?"

"The men disagreed. Elmer wanted an owner from inside the lake community, but Otis didn't care who they sold the place to." He stopped playing with his watch. "In fact, we didn't realize there was another bidder until we had already shown an interest in the land."

She now hated Otis more than ever. "I knew Otis was behind this. Did he contact you?"

He hesitated for a moment. "Not me, my mother. She saw this as an opportunity for Trent." Duncan averted his gaze down the alley. "He's got a history of problems. Drug related ones. He's been substance free for a few years, but she thought a little piece of his past might give him some incentive to stay sober. He once outright told me being in our family made him feel like a charity case."

Trent's off-putting demeanor reminded her how life's circumstances played a huge role in our adult behavior. "What about Buzz? Why'd he get involved?"

"When Trent came up with the idea for the resort, it changed everything. Otis called us two days later and said Buzz was behind the project." He rubbed the back of his neck. "You know the rest."

She factored in her reasons for wanting the property.

He took her hand and squeezed. "I can see how much the land means to you, but I had reasons too. Not only about my firm and profit." He blew out a huge breath. "It's such a relief telling you this. I've been so conflicted, like I've been lying to you."

Lying? Sophie's emotions tangled in a nasty web. Duncan felt so right, something she didn't want to lose. Now, though, the lines of idealism she'd lived by for years, so orderly and clear, were blurred.

"You're not a liar," she spoke softly. "You're trying to do a good thing for your brother."

Sophie stared up into her own mountain of lies: the call to Marcus, the anonymous note about the Jamiesons, even keeping Henry's death a secret.

"Hey." He tipped up her chin with a finger. "Something wrong? I heard your family used to own the land. Sounds like you all have many reasons to want the land. I still feel so bad about barging in and taking it away—"

"Nothing's wrong. Let's forget about my past."

Duncan's kindness for his brother struck the soft spot in her heart. He'd handed her a huge piece of himself today.

The pack of lies she'd stored now made their way to the tip of her tongue. "I think it's time I—"

The continued caress of his thumb left a fluttering in her stomach and made her reconsider the outcome of dumping this pile of truth. The truth about Henry would put him in an awkward position, having to decide whose past mattered more to him—Trent's or Sophie's.

She reached out and smoothed a hand over his bristly cheek. "I want you to know you've officially earned my trust."

His whole face softened then he leaned in and softly kissed her lips. He paused and searched her face for approval.

"Don't stop," she whispered.

His mouth covered hers, coaxed her lips apart. Warm breath mingled with hers then he cupped her cheeks, pulled her closer, and deepened the kiss. A kiss she didn't want to end, however, she slowly pulled away knowing the kids bowled nearby.

Duncan smoothed his palm slowly along her shoulder and stared into her eyes with heavy lids, the desire in his gaze making her burn for more. The tender touch of his lips still imprinted on hers served as a reminder to call Marcus and call off the hunt on Trent. Duncan had put his trust in her, trust she didn't deserve.

The time had also come to remove herself from both tomorrow's interview on *Northbridge in Focus* and her role on the paper. No story was worth ruining what she'd just found.

Chapter 22

Duncan's car slowed in the rush hour traffic and he admired the winter sun setting in the west, leaving a pattern of salmon-colored clouds against a darkening sky. Even the beautiful scene didn't remove the edge he'd carried all day. His appearance tonight on *Northbridge in Focus*, on behalf of a project he no longer believed in, was a charade.

How had his well-intentioned act for Mom and Trent taken a wrong turn?

Sophie's interest in the land turned him upside down and inside out. Either path he took, he'd wind up seeing himself as disloyal as Judas. Who mattered more, the woman whose kiss pounded his heart and soul into tender meat or his brother? Loyalty ripped down his center.

After he left the bowling alley, he'd tried to remember if he'd experienced the same euphoria when he first began to date Elizabeth.

Their first meeting, in a small town near Florence, Italy, seemed like a lifetime ago. There to check out a site, he'd headed out alone for dinner. He'd stumbled upon a place for locals, the type of place he usually gravitated to, but had some trouble ordering with a waiter who spoke only Italian. As he'd struggled with his small pocket translator book, a woman at a nearby table interrupted.

"*Mi scusi. Egli vuole lo spezzatino di cinghiale con Pappardelle. Grazie.*" The waiter had nodded and left. She'd turned to Duncan and said in perfect, non-accented English, "It sounded like you wanted the wild boar stew with Pappardelle. Good choice. An area specialty."

Duncan had smiled. "I did, but I'll bet no matter what he brought out, it would be great. You're American?"

He'd joined their small group and met Elizabeth Cole, his unofficial translator She'd moved to Tuscany from New York City two years earlier to work as a buyer for a family friend who owned an import business. In the scheme of small-world stories, she'd grown up in Scarsdale, not far from Duncan's hometown of Bronxville, both towns on the high end of expensive Westchester County communities. Their interests had been similar, their families had money, and in the States their lifestyles had paralleled.

Upon her return to the States a year later, they'd dated. He'd enjoyed her beauty, charm, and stories of travel, not exactly love at first sight but she'd fit into his world. Many of his friends had married. He'd pondered the idea of settling down, considering the timing with Elizabeth just right.

Elizabeth's arrival in the Jamieson household had brought his father to life. The old man's pride tugged at the seams with the notion Duncan had brought forth a serious daughter-in-law prospect, one whose family name provided a fitting pair next to theirs. Duncan's refusal to become a lawyer had changed their relationship years earlier, so regaining his father's accolades brought some unexpected relief. After Duncan made a hasty marriage proposal to Elizabeth, Dad's approval had completely returned.

Eventually his feelings for Elizabeth were laced with something he'd believed to be love. He'd never admit to anybody she hadn't received his full heart, though.

Yesterday proved one thing. A deeper force propelled his desire for Sophie. A force which enticed and terrified him at the same time.

* * * *

Sophie scurried through the dimly lit parking lot to the back entrance of the local cable station. The stiletto-heeled boots Bernadette had convinced her to buy made walking in a lot camouflaged in patches of ice like crossing a minefield.

Northbridge in Focus always began at seven thirty sharp. She was running behind schedule for the pre-meeting.

Before they could even leave the bowling alley yesterday, she'd realized there was no easy way to dump her role on the show or paper without causing great suspicion about what she'd been doing. She'd asked Duncan if they could keep their relationship private, at least until the zoning board made a final decision on the matter, mainly due to work. He'd understood. The other reason, one she couldn't tell him, were her concerns about her brother's reaction to them dating. He hated Duncan. She'd ease Jay into the idea.

The chime of her cell announced a text message. She ignored the sound and entered the brick building where all local cable access shows around the lake were filmed.

"Sorry I'm late."

"No problem." Ken's easy grin always relaxed her. "There's some pizza over there. I've arranged the seating on stage already."

She glanced at the makeshift stage, a foot-high elevated platform serving as the show's set. Not nearly as elaborate as *Good Morning America*, but the place suited their needs. The beige curtain backdrop and a few large potted ficus trees weren't much, but they didn't have a big budget.

She sat at a small conference table across from Alex Fitch, her co-host, and lifted the pizza box lid. The aroma of every pizzeria she'd ever visited escaped. "I'm starving. I gave the kids leftovers and ran out without eating."

"Let's work and eat." Alex poked his fork into a salad and grilled chicken.

A huge kid, health issues had forced him to address his weight problem. There were days now she still thought he seemed too thin.

He slid a paper in front of her. "I combined the questions you e-mailed with my own."

Sophie plunked her large canvas bag on the tabletop and fished for her cell phone. The text sent a few minutes ago had been from Marcus. She'd called last night and told him to cancel the hunt on Trent Jamieson but only got his voice mail. The text read, *Got your message. Need 2 talk. Call me.* She threw the phone back in her bag and hung up her coat.

On her way back to the table, she studied Alex, who wore his standard TV garb: camel-colored slacks, white oxford shirt, and tweed jacket, all of which suited his short hair and neat part on the side. At their first show, three years ago, Alex had arrived at the studio in black slacks and a black button-down shirt. Sophie could still recall the dismayed sarcasm of Ken's voice when he asked Alex if the other ninjas would arrive soon.

Tonight she'd selected a gray herringbone skirt and a plum, ribbed turtleneck since the outfit matched the Scottish thistle necklace she'd wanted to wear this evening.

Nana had given her the piece of jewelry, one she'd received from Sophie's granddad when they first married. While they'd packed to move Nana to the nursing home, she sat Sophie down on the bed and pressed the round, brushed silver pendant dangling from a chain into her hand. "It's a thistle pendent, Sophie." Nana's thick brogue always sounded soft and familiar to Sophie's ears. "The Scottish symbol for bravery, courage, and loyalty." She could still hear the way Nana rolled her r's.

Interviewing Duncan tonight wouldn't be easy, so she wore the necklace for luck. Her role as host crashed head on with his kiss yesterday, as well as the future kisses she expected to get during their Saturday night date at a restaurant in Hartford, far from Northbridge. She reached down and lifted the special jewelry. A purple stone in the center sparkled from the overhead lights. Around the gem were protruding swirled pointed ends, a decorative representation of the thistle, a thorny flower which some might think a weed. Nana's words again gave her a boost of encouragement... bravery, courage, and loyalty.

She could handle this interview. His unforgettable kiss stayed fresh on her lips yet wouldn't interfere with her professionalism.

For a half hour, the three of them poured over questions, fine-tuned their notes, and decided who'd ask what. The back entrance door creaked open and Bart's loud voice echoed down the hallway, a conversation with someone about his new camera lens purchase.

He entered the room. "Guess who I found." Marcus stood at his side.

After a chorus of hellos, Sophie said, "Just got your text. I planned to call you later."

"The paper sent me one town over to cover a story." He yanked off a tight wool cap and his short black hair jumped up from static electricity. "I hoped to catch you before the show aired. This can't wait."

A rock hard pit developed in Sophie's stomach.

Marcus cut a glance between Ken and Alex. "I figured you guys would be interested in this too." He dropped his canvas satchel on the table. "Sophie and I have been working together on some RGI research." He dug through his messy bag then stopped and looked at her. "What I found this afternoon confirms your gut read on Trent."

The pit grew in size. Duncan trusted his brother. Had Marcus uncovered evidence to the contrary?

Marcus glanced at her as he removed a piece of paper. "Remember how you said rumors always start for a reason?"

She nodded, calm on the exterior, but inside the winds of conflict rushed at hurricane force. What had she done?

"Check this out." He handed her the paper.

As the others waited in silence, she read the contents and passed the information to Ken, resisting the urge to crinkle the paper into a ball and toss it in the trash. Marcus shifted his feet. There was no mistaking his excitement. A short, heated discussion ensued over whether they should drop this bomb tonight. Marcus and Ken voted yes, but Alex and Sophie wanted more research on the find. The arrival of the first guest put an end to the conversation. Ken's final word on the matter was, "Let's do it." The walls around Sophie shrunk, leaving her as cornered as a mouse trapped in a shoebox.

Twenty minutes flew by. Every guest had arrived except Duncan. Ten minutes before show time, he entered the studio. He seemed more frazzled than usual.

Ken rushed to greet him, anxious over his late arrival. The other guests, Adli, Bernadette, and Tony Renzo, a member of the Goshen, Massachusetts Zoning Board, stood in a huddle chatting.

Ken cornered Duncan. She waited for an opening to nab him alone, where she might at least try to give him a heads-up about their coming on-air ambush. Her real problem suddenly smacked her in the face. The minute she told him, he'd also learn she had been the one to pull the starter rope on the research about Trent.

Normally, a curveball like this would be tossed at a guest with the pride of the Yankees. Not this time. No other guest had wrapped his large hands around hers, touched her with his tender lips, or confided intimate details about his family. Professional right versus wrong yanked her from side to side

Ken talked and Duncan glanced her way. She moved her head in the universal "come here" tip. He refocused on Ken. The next time Duncan's eyes shifted toward her, she mouthed, "We need to talk." The corner of his lip flickered and a subtle softening of his gaze suggested they shared a secret, which they did, but he again ignored her.

Bernadette sidled close and whispered near Sophie's ear, "What's up with you two?"

She nearly jumped "Jeesh, weren't you just with Adli? I think you move at vampire speed."

Bernadette chuckled. "I have no idea what you mean, but I once again thank you for taking my daughter when you and Tia went to see *Twilight*." She cocked her head and gave Sophie a don't-try-to-pull-a-fast-one-on-me pose. "Well? What's going on?"

"You mean with Duncan?"

Both Bernadette's newly waxed brows rose. "Uh-huh."

"I need to talk to him before the show starts. That's all."

"Talk? The way he's been ogling you, talking seems to be the last thing on his mind."

Sophie sighed.

Bernadette tapped Sophie's toe with hers. "Nice boots."

"What can I say? There are days your footwear inspires me. Any suggestions on how to walk fast in these? Or run."

"Yeah. Don't." She returned to her posturing. "Sooo? What's really going on?"

Ken stepped away and Duncan approached Sophie.

"Bern," she whispered. "Give us a minute alone."

She nodded and disappeared.

He moved close enough to be appropriate and quietly said, "I had fun yesterday."

"Me too."

"I have to catch a flight tonight after we're done here. I'll be on the West Coast for business until Friday, but we're still on for Saturday, right?"

"Of course. I can't wait." She'd already decided Saturday she'd tell him about losing Henry, especially since that was the day her son would have turned twenty-five and spending the anniversary with Duncan meant a great deal. "Listen, some—"

"Duncan," Ken interrupted. "I'd like you to meet Alex Fitch, Sophie's co-host."

Argh! Sophie nearly screamed. The clock ticked. She'd thought men didn't like to chat, but when Alex said he'd seen Duncan leave the tackle store one afternoon, they cackled more than two hens in a pen. Her nerve endings stung with impatience.

"Two minutes 'til airtime." Bart positioned his camera toward the stage. "Let's get seated, everyone."

Sophie's window of opportunity to warn Duncan slammed shut.

Alex and she sat side-by-side, at a slight angle to view the panel of guests to their left. Sophie concentrated on her host duties, hoping Ken forgot about the recent discovery.

While the guests got settled, Ken faced his hosts with his back to the others. He lowered his voice. "Sophie, delicately raise the issue Marcus brought us. Wait until the end, though, in case the question backfires."

Delicately? Even if she asked with the delicacy of a surgeon removing a vital organ, there was no diplomatic way to phrase the issue. Her relationship with Duncan had ventured into new territory yesterday. This would surely cause a war.

Sophie crossed her legs and started to jiggle her foot. Bart gave the "we're on" sign. She didn't dare glance at Duncan, afraid a combination of craving and culpability would create some odd on-camera facial twitch.

The first fifty minutes flew. She liked the panel, who all handled themselves with polite discourse when taking opposing viewpoints. Even Bernadette, who owned stronger opinions behind the façade, controlled herself. Duncan answered each question with confidence. He outlined his explanations with squared hands and the pointed fingers of a politician, listened as if statements were a test question, and threw in an occasional line of good humor. He also publically apologized to Bernadette for the *Courant's* damaging article, noting he'd been trying to find out who in his firm was behind the false allegation.

Alex asked Tony Renzo a question. Sophie glanced toward the camera. Ken stood behind Bart and offered her a subtle lift of his brow, his sign to toss the zinger. The stout, bushy-browed Massachusetts board member answered Alex's question, but she didn't hear a word. Her mind scrambled for ways to phrase the pending accusation, hoping the right words might lessen the blow. No matter how she phrased it, though, every single word made her a traitor.

Tony finished. Instead of following Ken's instructions, she asked the Goshen Zoning Board member an unnecessary follow-up question. Ken's stare burned through her. Tony chattered away. There was no place left to hide, unless she pretended to faint or stood up and screamed fire. For a fleeting second, both received serious consideration.

Tony wrapped up his answer so she caught her breath and turned to Duncan. "Mr. Jamieson, at the public hearing in November, the subject of bribery allegations related to this project surfaced."

He nodded calmly which meant he couldn't hear the stampede of her heartbeat as she formed the next comments. "Our local officials denied any such deals are taking place. However, we recently discovered information about a past project your firm worked on."

Duncan tilted his head and raised his brows as if interested in the question, but she perceived a slight dip in his usual confident posture.

"We've found information suggesting someone at RGI was accused of bribing Ontario public officials on a controversial project on Lake Simcoe." She left out that the employee was Trent and caught Ken's scowl.

Her air supply stalled, cut off by the glimpse of a dark front moving across Duncan's face. He folded his hands and stared at them, maybe to stop from strangling her.

Sophie swallowed hard. "The records also show all charges were later dropped. Would you care to comment?"

Duncan finally looked up, every facial muscle stoic and controlled. "Certainly. An employee acted in a manner not condoned by the company. The matter has been dealt with and the charges were dropped by the parties involved. There is no bribery taking place from RGI here in Northbridge." His icy stare sent a chill along Sophie's neck.

"Thank you." Sick over what she'd done, she did her best to wrap up.

As soon as the cameras were off, the guests stood and removed their microphones. Tony Renzo cornered her with a question. Before she finished her answer, Duncan said good-bye to Ken. For a nanosecond, his eyes cut over to her, and then he grabbed his coat from the rack and stormed out.

The weight of the pendant pressed to her chest, a reminder of the flower's symbolic meaning. Yes, tonight she'd exhibited bravery and courage. When it came to loyalty, however, she'd failed miserably.

* * * *

As he left the studio building, a gust of cold night air hit Duncan's face, the frosty nip as hurtful as the blow Sophie had just delivered.

He threw his briefcase into the backseat of his car, got in, and turned on the engine, revving it louder than necessary. Had she known this yesterday?

Thanks to his mother, he'd learned early on any expectations of warmth could lead to hurt. A safe emotional distance from women allowed him to avoid pain, a prescription that had worked, at least until now. He'd been played for a fool. An ache settled in the dead center of his chest, more painful than he'd have ever dreamed.

Tap, tap, tap. Sophie stood at the window. One side of her face glowed from a tall parking lot light, but a dark shadow rested on the other cheek, like a mask with two faces.

"Duncan, can we talk?" The glass barrier muffled her voice. "Please."

He lowered the window. "What?"

"You have every right to be mad."

"Yes, I do. Please step away so I can leave. Besides, you're not wearing a coat. It's cold. Go inside."

"Give me one minute to explain."

"One minute?" The mental wound he'd nurtured for years throbbed. "That's all the time you needed to warn me."

"I tried."

"We spent the day together yesterday! You had all afternoon."

"I only found out minutes before the show."

He threw the car into park and crossed his arms. "Listen, I can handle being ambushed on an interview. You're not the first and won't be the last reporter to do that to me. But never, *never,* would I have dreamed

someone I've opened up to about my personal life…someone I trusted….
would take advantage of me."

"You can trust me."

He grunted, his disagreement clear.

Sophie's lips parted, but no words came out.

He grabbed the gearshift. "I need to leave. Now."

She wrapped her fingers around his forearm. "Duncan. Please let me
explain."

The weight of her hand dissipated his anger and stopped him as if she
possessed the energy of a shaman, capable of healing his deep emotional
wounds. He studied the determined tenseness in her lips, ready to launch
into an explanation, and the way her worried expression begged for his
forgiveness.

"Go ahead." He didn't care if he sounded pointed and cold. It didn't
come close to the torture inside his chest. "Explain."

"This Lake Simcoe thing landed on my lap right before the show
was about to start." Her hand slipped off his arm and rested on the open
window. "Ken wanted me to ask you, but I wanted to wait."

"How does something like that sail in and land on your lap on its own?"

Her chin dropped and she stared at the ground. "A friend of mine who
works at the *Hartford Courant* uncovered the story."

"Why would he bring this to you?"

She slowly lifted her chin and exhaled. Her arm fell to her side as she
stood upright, brave as if she faced a firing squad. "After I met Trent…
before you and I talked about his problems… I thought he might have
something to do with the leak in your firm. I called Marcus, from the
Courant, to help find information about Trent."

"*You* initiated the search?" He clenched his jaw and gripped the
steering wheel so tight the laces holding the leather cover in place cut into
his fingers. "Why?"

Sophie paused for several long seconds. "It's my job, Duncan."

For a split second, he got lost in her beautiful chestnut eyes, which
yesterday had toppled the wall guarding his heart. Her last comment,
however, quickly resurrected his barrier. He'd not simply opened himself
up to a woman he liked but exposed himself to a reporter who could take
him down with a single paragraph. The red lights of caution flashed in his
mind. He'd been a complete idiot!

She chewed her lower lip and studied him. "I'd never abuse the things
we discussed yesterday. This is different. Marcus found the story late this

afternoon. He happened to be nearby doing an interview so he stopped at the studio. If I'd heard the news alone, I'd have spoken to you first."

A part of him wanted to believe her, yet he struggled in a match with his old cynical self. "Couldn't you have told them to wait until you confirmed the find with me?"

"Oh, right. That wouldn't look suspicious? While I was at it, I could tell them how you left me enchanted yesterday and my emotions blinded me from doing my job." She shook her head. "Don't you see? If it wasn't you, I'd have been thrilled when Marcus brought the information to me. I would *not* have hesitated to throw the question at our guest." Shame crossed her face.

"Well, it was me," he said softly.

"Give me some credit. I left out Trent's name."

"Thanks for nothing."

She shifted, showing the first signs of impatience, but he hurt too much to care. "Do you think I should let a personal bias interfere with my job?"

"Not if work matters that much. Hey, I understand. I'm devoted to my job too."

Another dose of hurt made the ache in his chest swell. Her work mattered more than him. Poetic justice. Payback for all the times he'd ignored his wife's needs.

He pushed aside his past mistakes. "I shared some deep parts of myself with you. I should've kept my mouth shut."

Her voice rose. "Do you have any idea how much I agonized over this?"

"No. Oh, and for the record, Trent did commit the bribery on the Canadian project. Six months after I hired him. His addiction problem contributed to what went down."

He kept to himself how Trent's salary at RGI couldn't pay for his cocaine habit. How a manipulative contractor promised Trent plenty of the drug if he convinced the board to use their firm for the RGI project. Or how Trent had railroaded money from RGI's accounting department to bribe the official.

"Your brother's drug problem. Of course." Her voice sounded weak, as if subdued by the truth. "I didn't know."

"You didn't ask." Disappointment nestled into the space he'd opened in his heart.

"No, I didn't." Her gaze fell to the ground. "Ken insisted I deal with this tonight."

"So you've said." Duncan glanced at his dashboard clock. "I need to go."

Sophie moved her face nearer, so near he caught the floral scent he'd enjoyed during yesterday's kiss. Overhead lights in the lot reflected the glistening in her eyes, the start of tears. She touched his arm again, but immunity from old bruises of his childhood kicked in and prevented him from reacting to the power of her contact.

"Please, Duncan. I'm so sorry." Her voice begged for understanding.

An awareness of the steady beat of his pulse drew him to the place inside himself capable of heartless actions. "I need some space right now."

Sadness veiled her face and almost crumbled his emotional barriers, but his anguish won out. She finally took a step back. Duncan rolled up his window and drove away.

Chapter 23

Sophie tossed a second suitcase from the attic and it thumped on the floor. "Kids!" She climbed down the steps. "Come get your luggage."

Tia came out of her room and grabbed one. "Thanks, Mom."

She hit the bottom rung. "Where's your brother?"

"I think he's on the computer." Tia ducked into her bedroom and shut the door. Always a closed door these days.

Sophie double-checked Matt's room. Next to his unmade bed hung a new picture of some super model in a bikini pinned near a towering poster of a Patriot quarterback. Not one stitch of clothing had been laid out for packing. His dad would arrive at six a.m. to catch their Thursday morning flight out of Bradley Airport. There'd be no time that early for Matt's usual puttering.

She marched to the downstairs family room, already edgy over what happened two days ago with Duncan, certain their upcoming Saturday night date was a goner. Matt had picked the wrong day to mess with her. She stomped past the large sectional and stepped over the game controls, toward her son, who hunched over the computer. Facebook stared back from the monitor.

"Get off there, please. Start packing."

He didn't even glance back. "Jeesh, relax. It won't take me long."

"Packing takes longer than you think. Come on. I asked you to do this after school. Your father blames me when you're not ready."

"No, he doesn't." Matt looked over his shoulder and cast a subtle eye-roll in her direction then returned to the screen and started to type.

Matt's dismissal, coupled with some wrongful insights into his father's behavior, zapped the remains of her patience. "Get. Off. The. Damn. Computer."

Matt shut off the machine and shot up from his seat. "You're always so grouchy this time of year." He stormed past her toward the stairs

"What does that mean?"

"Never mind."

"Stop!"

He turned around.

"What do you mean?"

His fair skin took on the tint of beets. "You're always bitchy near Henry's birthday. The day he died too."

His honesty stunned her like an unexpected slap. Bitchy? Sad, maybe, but had her mourning come out in other ways? She wanted to reprimand him for talking back and for swearing, but her dropped jaw failed to operate.

"Dad won't tell you, but he picked this week to leave on purpose." Matt's toxic tone seared her skin. "He said this trip is to celebrate life, not dwell on the past. He thinks Henry would have loved a trip to Disney on his birthday. Instead of us sitting around while you make us all sad, he'll be with us in spirit."

Her throat grew thick, as if a clamp bottlenecked all her pain in that one spot. The idea that every year she'd caused Tia and Matt pain loomed above her like a dark shadow. How many times had she hurt them while the despair of losing Henry owned her soul?

Matt studied her closely. She wanted to grab him, hug him, and say sorry a thousand times, however, sadness numbed her body.

The angry clamp of his jaw relaxed and he frowned. "I know you're sad, Mom. We all miss him."

Matt's faced blurred behind Sophie's tears.

He moved close and, taller than her now, wrapped his long arms around her shoulders in a hug. "I'm sorry," he whispered.

She tightened her arms around his waist. "Don't be sorry. I needed to hear that. I'm sorry too." She sniffled. "I never wanted to hurt you. Or Tia."

"I don't think Henry would want you this upset, Mom."

She leaned back, brushed away some tears, and looked at her son. A glossy sheen in his eyes betrayed his tough stance. When had he become so wise?

"You could be right." She tousled his hair. "The teacher learns from the student, huh?"

"What?" Matt scrunched his face, returning to his norm.

"Nothing. Thank you for your honesty."

"Sure." He gave her his trademark grin, the one she had no doubt would get him far in life. "I'll go pack now."

* * * *

After two days in a quiet house, with Bella her only companion, chatter now bounced off the cathedral ceilings of Sophie's great room as the monthly ladies' night gathering met at her long pine table.

"I thought you sounded nice when you asked Duncan that question." Meg's voice raised an octave with disbelief. "I'm not sure what he got so mad about. I mean, you guys kissed at the bowling alley. He must still like you."

Sophie lowered a plate of grilled chicken to the center of her dining room table and sighed. Meg's selective listening often tested Sophie's patience. Twice already she'd explained to her why Duncan got angry. "It wasn't about how I asked," she tried to say nicely. "Rather I didn't warn him the question was out there."

"Ooh." Meg nodded, as if she'd really listened this time.

Tonight's gathering, dubbed "Rom-Com Night," was a perfect distraction from her problems. They'd selected the romantic comedy *When Harry Met Sally* for their entertainment. Sally's fussy meal ordering at the diner set the tone for their food selections, a make-your-own chef's salad spread, heated apple pie with the ice cream—on the side—and real whipped cream, nothing out of the can.

"So wait," Veronica stopped loading mixed greens on her plate and looked at Sophie. "Even after you explained everything, he drove off?"

"He had a plane to catch." She speared a grilled chicken breast from the platter and laid it on top of a bowl of shredded lettuce. "Plus, he said he needed his space, or something along those lines."

Meg took the handed-off platter. "Did you try to call him?"

"He asked me to leave him alone. I am. Wednesday night, though, the phone rang while I was taking a bath. Naturally neither of the kids picked up, but when I got out, caller ID showed his name. He didn't leave a message." The disappointment she'd felt then struck again. "Probably to say let's call it quits before we ever really started. At least he had the decency not to leave that in a message."

"I'd have called him back." Veronica's deliberately raised eyebrows came across as smug.

"Easy to say when you're not the one being dumped."

"I doubt he'll dump you." Bernadette pushed aside her bangs and pursed her lips. "I caught the way he checked you out when he got to the studio. He's hurt. Give him space."

"Hurt is mild. Try crushed. Betrayed. Devastated."

"Come on, Soph." Bernadette shook her head. "You're exaggerating. Sometimes men need to get over things."

Meg waved her hand. "Ooh, on another note, tell us about Trent. Is he still cute?"

"Jeesh, Meg. You're a married woman." Veronica's voice filled with disapproval.

Meg tipped her head to the unmarried librarian. "Not everyone thinks life is a romance novel like you. Marriage doesn't come with blinders." Meg turned to Sophie. "Well? Still cute?"

"You wouldn't have been disappointed. He still has the slight bad-boy thing and he's aged well."

Bernadette snorted. "He always acted too cool for us, hanging around with Jay and the older kids."

Meg's face brightened as if she hadn't heard a negative word. "Do you think he'd remember me?"

Veronica patted Meg's arm. "Honey, you had the crush. Not him."

"Yeah, but I saw him around town and he noticed me."

"Probably because you were ogling him," Bernadette mumbled.

"Very funny." Meg recapped a bottle of salad dressing and returned it to the lazy Susan. "Remember the time at Sunny Side Up he said hello?"

They all shook their heads.

Meg tapped her chin as she thought. "Oh, maybe I was with my parents. It doesn't matter." She swiped a dismissive hand and smacked right into her wineglass. White wine rushed across the pine tabletop, cascading over the sides like a Chardonnay waterfall and landing on Veronica.

Meg lifted the glass to stop the rest from creating more damage. "I'm so sorry!"

"Accidents happen." Veronica pressed a napkin against the edge to dam the liquid, already spilled on her white sweatshirt with a Crickle Creek Orchards emblem near the shoulder. "This belonged to an old boyfriend. No biggie."

Sophie ran into the kitchen and grabbed two dishtowels. "Here." She tossed them to Meg.

"At least it's white wine. On Italian night, this would've been disastrous." Meg dabbed at the small puddle on the tabletop. "Sometimes I think I was born without disposable thumbs."

Sophie was two steps from the counter and reaching for more paper towels, but stopped and turned around to the group while digesting Meg's remark. The others stared at Meg, too.

Bernadette finally said, "What?"

"You know." Meg wiggled her thumbs. "How our thumbs help us hold things…. And I spill a lot."

Veronica stifled a grin. "I think you mean opposable."

Meg's brow furrowed. "Opposable?" Then she laughed. "Oh, right! Nobody has disposable body parts."

"Only Mr. Potato Head." Veronica continued to dab the spilled wine.

Sophie went to the kitchen and ripped off a long strand of paper towels just as the phone rang. The caller's name, *Jamieson, D.* flashed.

She reached for the handset and then reconsidered. Ever since she'd made the shift from neutral reporter to reporter with an interest in her subject, she'd been more conflicted than a juggler without opposable thumbs. Was she trying to pull off an impossible act?

He was either calling to dump her or to make amends but, either way, maybe the time had come for her to sit in the driver's seat of her life. Tomorrow she'd face Henry's birthday, alone and not afraid. The idea gave her a boost of encouragement, a real sign she'd stepped into the final stages of grief. Then she'd finish the job Cliff had assigned her on the paper, without the distractions she'd faced since the start.

She bunched up the paper towels and headed back to the table, ignoring the phone's ring.

Meg took the paper towels. "Aren't you going to answer? Maybe it's Duncan."

"Nope. Just a telemarketer."

Sophie resisted the urge to run into the kitchen and answer. All her reasons to avoid him seemed reasonable, but was reason always the best choice?

Chapter 24

Duncan shifted in the king-size bed to a cool spot between the sheets and hoped to fall back to sleep. Still on California time, he'd suffered a restless night, mostly thinking about Sophie. He opened his eyes and squinted at the daylight breaking through the window, now realizing he'd left the heavy gold-striped curtains open when he'd gone to bed at midnight.

He should have left her a message during the midweek call, but his tongue twisted into a knot while the answering machine gave instructions and he'd quickly hung up. Apologies in messages were awkward. He'd hoped to catch her home last night when he called. Was she avoiding him? He pictured her staring at the caller ID and sneering at the phone. After his unreasonable exit after the show, he couldn't blame her.

Visions of their bowling alley kiss provoked him. Why hadn't he accepted her explanation for what happened? How many times with Elizabeth had he refused to listen to reason?

He rolled onto his back and stared at the high ceiling. Was he incapable of truly loving a woman? Jesus, even his boat's name had been a joke. What did he know about true love? Sailing had captured his heart. Swept away by the breezes, put in the hands of nature, yet with tools to control the outcome. Love with another person, though, couldn't be controlled. Yet when Sophie entered a room, his pulse raced out of control. Funny thing, though. He didn't care.

He rolled on his side and checked the clock. 8:16. He got out of bed and took a quick shower. After tossing on jeans and a sweatshirt, he went downstairs.

"Morning." He stuck his head in the family room where Patrick and a few friends who'd stayed for a sleepover sat on their sleeping bags and played a video game. "You guys want breakfast?"

Patrick paused the game and gave Duncan a funny look. "Since when do you cook?"

"I learned some skills in my single days. Right now, I figured I'd run into town for donuts."

"Helen's about to make us chocolate chip pancakes. But thanks." Patrick returned to his task.

Duncan patted his pants pocket and realized he'd left his cell phone in the bedroom. Persistence always paid off and he wasn't done trying to reach Sophie. He sprinted back up the stairs and grabbed the phone and his wallet off a dark-stained highboy dresser.

"Dad. Got a sec?" Patrick stood at the doorway, worry lines creasing his dimly freckled face.

"Sure. What's up?"

"Um, Matt told me something the other day. I figured you should know. Maybe you already do."

"What?"

"Did you know he used to have an older brother?"

"No." An uncomfortable sensation twirled in his gut. Perhaps he didn't know as much as he thought about Sophie. "Used to?"

Patrick blinked a few times then nodded. "He died."

He paused, trying to recall if she'd ever once alluded to such a horrible loss. No, she definitely hadn't. "How old was he?"

"I think around eighteen."

He steadied himself against the despair every parent thinks of when they hear such horrible news, a step shy of imagining it had happened to their child. "Do you know when?"

Patrick shook his head. "Matt said he was in elementary school when it happened."

"That's so sad. Did Matt say how?"

"He drowned. In the lake." Patrick almost whispered. His shoulders drooped and his eyes dulled with the same look Duncan had seen so many times as his wife's condition worsened.

Pieces suddenly fell into place. Little comments Sophie had made here and there. The wave of sadness so obvious after certain subjects came up.

How could he have been so insensitive?

He wanted to grab his son and hold him tight but respected the teenage space Patrick had requested as of late.

A roar of laughter downstairs made Patrick glance out the door. "One other thing. Matt told me how his mom would be alone this weekend and kind of sad. Guess today's his brother's birthday. Well, the day he would've had one." Patrick chewed his lower lip. "Their family usually visits the place he died on days like this, some garden in his memory. I feel bad for them."

Duncan put a hand on Patrick's shoulder and squeezed. "Thanks for telling me. You okay?"

"Uh-huh." Patrick started to turn away then stopped. "Oh, yeah, the garden for Matt's brother is on the land you're buying."

The words crashed in his ears like shattering glass. "Are you sure?"

Patrick nodded and the copper curls of his messy hair bobbed. "The land you want is near that big rock, right?"

Putticaw Rock sat on an easement through the Tates' land, but Duncan had never really checked that area of the property. "Yes. The memorial must only be near the land. I'm sure the sellers would've told me otherwise."

"Matt said it's there." His son shrugged and headed out of the room.

"Pat."

He looked over his shoulder.

"Sometimes Dads need a hug from their sons."

Duncan stepped close and wrapped the tall boy in his arms. Tears pooled along his lids. Tears for Sophie. Tears for missing his own kids growing up. Tears over the pain of loss. After a minute, he gave him an extra squeeze then let go.

"Thanks for letting me know. I'll call Matt's mom."

Duncan returned to his room and shut the door. He tried Sophie's house. Again, no answer.

How had this slipped past his radar? He clenched his fist. Never had he felt so manipulated by a seller. He had one stop to make before he tried to find Sophie.

* * * *

Snow crunched beneath Sophie's tires as she parked in the familiar wooded clearing off Lake Shore Road and stepped from the car. This morning's air carried the raw, crisp bite of a fresh picked apple. A small rotting sign, announcing "Putticaw Rock," plunked securely into the ground, had been there for as long as she could remember.

Her emotions right now were as tender as a baby lamb, but nothing would keep her from this visit.

A car flew past her on the well-traveled road and sent a chilly gust her way. She zipped the black fleece jacket to her chin, grabbed a pashmina scarf from the front seat, and draped it over her head, crisscrossing the long ends over each shoulder like a Russian babushka. A search for gloves revealed nothing. She must've left them at home.

A faded arrow pointed to a snow-trodden path toward the historic rock. She walked along the trail surrounded by lifeless shrubbery and trees. Like every other corner of this small town, each season revealed a different brushstroke of its beauty and the winter nakedness revealed secrets hidden when everything was in bloom.

The night Henry died the boys had come through here. His car had been parked in the same lot she'd used today. The memory rolled onto her chest like a boulder. She ignored the pressure and kept walking to the clearing, where the view opened to a gray ceiling of gentle clouds.

Whenever she reached this spot, the panoramic view of Blue Moon Lake always jumped up and stole her breath. She stood still and took in the view. Peaked hills surrounding the lake were neutral and brown with patches of bright white snow everywhere else, including the frozen water.

In her younger days, Sophie often stood in this spot and pretended to be a queen overlooking her kingdom. A kingdom lost in battle, not a poker game. Dreams that a fictional army would retrieve her father's land sometimes kept her entertained. Some days her fantasy included a horse carrying a handsome knight to aid her struggle.

What an ironic twist. The one thing close to a handsome knight turned out to be the force keeping her from the land.

At the ridge of the hillside in front of her was the sloping span of land leading to Henry's garden. Her mind said, "move" but her feet stayed put. This birthday trip would have been easier with Tia and Matt by her side. Her last visit here was in early October, when she added a plaque to the memorial. She didn't tell anybody about the visit, for fear they'd think she couldn't cope. She could cope, but wanted to leave a message. She closed her eyes, pictured the black zinc square with silver lettering, now buried beneath the snow.

"Yours is the light by which my spirit's born: – you are my sun, my moon, and all my stars."— E.E. Cummings.

A familiar weight bore down on Sophie's chest, but she opened her eyes and took a deep breath, then slowly exhaled. Another visitor had already left footsteps imprinted in the snow, leading right to the ridge. Time to move forward and face the gardens alone.

* * * *

Duncan stood in the Tates' foyer with Otis and bit the inside of his cheek to check his anger. Only once before in the course of buying properties had Duncan been misled. A property in Jamaica where he'd learned, a day before the closing, there had been a history of fires related to an old land dispute going back centuries. He'd immediately backed out of the deal.

Otis raised his brows. "What can I do for you, Mr. Jamieson?"

"I need to talk to you and your brother."

Otis yelled for Elmer. "I'm surprised to see you so early. Must be important."

Elmer shuffled down the hallway from the kitchen.

"Yes, it is." Duncan nodded at Elmer. "I've learned some facts about your property. Facts you neglected to disclose when we negotiated the purchase."

Elmer glanced at his brother, but Otis only massaged the tip of his long beard and stared at Duncan with the energy of a stone wall.

"Did Sophie Shaw's son die on this land?"

"Yeah." Behind Otis' bearded jawline a muscle flexed. "So?"

"So? Is that all you have to say?" Duncan harnessed his struggling anger. He'd dealt with ruthless businessmen in his day, but this guy should work on Wall Street. "There's a memorial garden for him on this property?"

"Yes." Otis shrugged. "Look, if you end up buying the land, you're under no obligation to keep—"

"Otis!" Elmer snapped, sharper than Duncan had ever heard from the quieter of the two brothers. His long face drooped and the whites of his eyes glistened. "The entire town mourned Sophie's loss. Her son worked at our farm several summers. A nice boy. I agreed to let the community put up the memorial and wanted her family to come and go as they pleased. If things work in your favor on this purchase, I hope you'll do the same."

"Why wasn't I told about this when we first talked?"

"I wanted to." Elmer glanced at his brother.

Otis snarled. "I always said that garden was a mistake." He glared at his brother. "See. Now Mr. Jamieson's having second thoughts." His angry glower focused on Duncan. "Her loss has nothing to do with this purchase."

Duncan leaned close, and spoke through the tightness of a clenched jaw. "This is about dealing with people in good faith. Something you didn't do."

Otis jutted his chin. "What about Trent? I thought you wanted this property for him."

"You still don't get it, do you?" Duncan turned to Elmer. "I heard she visits the garden on her son's birthday?"

Elmer spoke with a slight crack to his voice. "She'll be there today."

"How can I get there?"

Elmer gave Duncan directions. One step from leaving, he paused and stared at Otis, who had listened to the last part of the conversation in silence, wearing a bitter scowl. "I'm on the fence with this deal, Otis. Is there anything else you're not telling me?"

He cleared his throat. "Not a thing."

Duncan glanced at Elmer, who pressed his lips into a thin line and stared at the wood floor.

Duncan suspected both men weren't telling him something, but right now the urgency to speak with Sophie made him reach for the knob and leave. At the bottom step, he turned around to ask one more question. Elmer's worried gaze stared back at him as Otis slammed shut the door with the thud of a gavel.

* * * *

Sophie stared at the beautiful memorial gardens planted for Henry, located to the right of the large boulder and on the cusp of the Tates' land. First started by friends from church, others in the community later joined and assisted in planting the assorted shrubbery, flowers, and trees circling the place where the EMS crew found Henry's body that horrible night.

When planting first began, Sophie refused to visit. Their gesture unearthed more than the dirt. It unearthed her pain. Pain she'd struggled with every waking second. A few months later, though, she'd agreed to see what they'd done.

Bernadette had shown her around the gardens with a caring arm slung around Sophie's shoulders. She'd shared how the circular design came from the Native American belief that circles represented the sun, the moon, the seasons, and the cycle of life from death to rebirth. She'd pointed to the yews, planted to give year-round green and tulips and daffodils to represent the spirit reborn and give some spring color. Summer would bring black-eyed Susans, planted for their colors of gold and black, the high school colors and a reminder to visitors that Henry loved his school, a place he'd shared friendships and a love of music. Today a black-capped chickadee, frightened by a fat squirrel, disappeared into a simple wooden birdhouse on a pole in the center of the garden. On sterile winter days like today, she was happy for the signs of life. A reminder that even in the bleakest of times, life still went on.

A cold breeze stirred the powdery snow. She shivered and dug her naked hands deeper into the fleece pockets.

Visiting here often brought back memories of the night he died. Especially the midnight phone call, the one every parent hoped they never received. Every detail felt close enough to reach out and touch, even all these years later. She'd gone to bed with half an ear tuned to the downstairs door, waiting to hear the click of it unlocking, assuring her he'd returned home safely. Instead, an hour later, the shrill, unexpected ring of the phone made her heart thump against her ribs.

"Sophie. It's Officer Boland." The clock had read one o'clock and the foyer light in the hallway told her Henry had missed his curfew. Panic had simmered.

"What's wrong?"

He hadn't answered right away. The short second of silence had screamed with the clang of an alarm. "I'm in your driveway. Can I talk to you and Mike?"

"What's wrong?"

Outside their bedroom window, flashing red lights from the police cruiser had bounced off the blind slats. Mike had already jumped out of bed and slipped on sweatpants over his boxers.

"I'd like to talk," the officer had said quietly. Too quietly.

"We'll be downstairs in a second." She'd hung up.

"Is Henry okay?" Mike had asked over his shoulder as he headed for the bedroom door.

"I don't know." Their eyes had met and a hard pit formed in Sophie's gut. She'd thrown on clothes and raced out behind him.

The next minute had changed Sophie's life. Forever.

Officer Boland's statement hit with the force of an unpredicted tidal wave, the crash leaving only the echoes of words: *Accident. Henry. Ice. EMS. No pulse. No heartbeat.* The pit in Sophie's gut had grown and threatened to explode. Her muscles had wobbled and refused to support her frame. Numbness had seized her tongue, the ability to ask for answers not within her control.

The real terror of parenthood pounced on her and smothered her without warning. The terror she'd imagined from the time they were babies. Every time they were left in another person's care, went to the mall alone, drove to a party where there might be alcohol, or hung out with friends, who really knew what they were doing? The same voice she sometimes ignored when logic intruded and reminded her kids needed space to grow up too.

Sophie's father had stayed with Matt and Tia that night. Jay had driven them to the hospital, where EMS had taken Henry's body. The entire ride, Sophie had sat in the back seat stunned, sobbing, and wishing someone would shake her awake from this nightmare. After a lifetime of careful moves, she'd made a call so bad she truly had no say in the outcome.

Her unfixable mistake.

A flurry landed on her cheek, leaving a tiny spark, removing her from the dreadful night. When a second one fell, she realized the snow had mixed with her tears. Using her fingertip, she wiped the wetness and sniffled.

The enormity of Sophie's life sat before her right now, then a notion she'd never entertained hit with great force. Circumstances had always kept her in Northbridge, but maybe here was exactly where she should be. The circle of her life followed a path around Blue Moon Lake. Family. Friends. Lovers. Even losses.

Small specs of fluffy white flurries danced in the sky, like angels forming a blanket of silence in the air. After Henry died, she'd learned appreciation could come as much from understanding pain as it did joy. Without one, the other would be empty.

Please, Henry. If you're okay, send me a sign.

Another flake fell on her cheek. She left it alone, in case this was the sign from her son.

Footsteps crunched in the snow behind her.

Sophie turned. Bernadette must have seen her car in the lot and stopped. Instead, Duncan stood there, hands shoved deep into the pockets of a navy barn jacket, wearing a herringbone wool cap. He stayed motionless, as if he'd intruded on some holy ritual, but his pained, watery gaze suggested he'd found out about Henry.

Every part of her wished Duncan knew she wasn't upset with him, however, the surrounding memories made it impossible to push out a smile. She looked away.

His footsteps crunched through the snow. He came up from behind and cocooned her in his arms. His hold weakened the tough stance on which she'd arrived.

He pressed his lips gently against her cheek, their warm touch to her cold skin soothing a deep ache in her soul. "I'm so sorry," he whispered. "Why didn't you tell me?"

The reasoning she'd used over the past several weeks replayed. She didn't share the worst moment of her life with people she didn't know well. Guilt seemed like a petty way to get him to give up the land. Or how she'd begun to question if her reason for wanting the land was rooted in a loss, a fact that suddenly seemed all wrong.

She twisted around, buried her face against his chest and the dam of her tears exploded. His arms tightened and he stilled, only moving once to nestle her head more securely to his chest. Silence soaked up her grief yet, without any words, his nearness gave her support.

She finally looked up. Duncan's watery eyes mirrored her pain.

He cleared his throat. "I'm sorry I left the studio mad. I've been trying to call you. Figured you were done with me since you didn't answer any of my calls."

Sophie sniffled. "I thought you were making the 'let's end this now' call."

The soft edges of his lips turned into a shy smile, one lifting her heart into a fluttering mess.

Was Duncan her sign to move on?

"How'd you find out about... About my son."

"Matt told Patrick. Then he told me. Elmer Tate filled in the blanks. God, Sophie." He bowed his head toward the ground for a brief second. "I had no idea. I know so little about you. Why wouldn't you tell me?"

"It's not a good conversation starter."

Duncan frowned.

She took a deep breath and slowly exhaled. "The truth? I thought about telling you the first time we met in your office. When I barely knew you. Back then, I figured the truth would shame you out of town."

He raised a brow.

"Now I don't want you to go away."

"I'm not going any place." He leaned over and brushed his lips tenderly against hers. "Will you forgive me for driving off angry?"

"Of course." She slipped her arms around his neck. "I'm sorry about the ambush at the studio too. I was backed into a corner professionally and personally."

"Once my anger settled down, I realized that." He shook his head. "I must be going through some middle-aged man thing."

"What do you mean?"

"My emotions have been worse than a teenage girl lately." He shook his head. "Opening up about myself has never been easy, but I can with you."

She planted a soft kiss on his cheek and breathed in the clean soap scent on his skin.

"You're a brave woman, Ms. Shaw."

"Brave? Hardly." Pain lodged in her throat. "Fear rules my world. I worry every day I'll lose another child."

"You're standing here, facing your fears. You were willing to buy this land, to face memories some would run from."

The size of her heart swelled in multiples for Duncan, who hardly knew her, yet gave her more credit than she'd ever given herself. "I wish you could have met him."

Duncan nodded, a watery glaze recoating his eyes. "Me too."

"When he was born, I felt like I'd been given new life. A chance to share new adventures, share my favorite books and movies, maybe see him live the life I'd wanted to have, away from Northbridge." Duncan's sad gaze made her drop her chin to her chest and stare at the snowy ground instead.

She looked up and caught Duncan blinking back a few tears. "My wife's last days were painful for her, but I was at her side when she died and..." He swallowed. "She seemed at peace wherever her soul went."

"I always wonder about that. Once Bernadette and Dave came here with me. I was a wreck that day. Dave talked about what happens after someone dies and he told me Henry was in a good place, with people who loved him like my Mom and Nana. He also said Henry would want me to stop punishing myself." She softly chuckled. "I asked Dave if he planned to leave the church to practice as a medium."

"Always a little sarcasm, huh?" Duncan curved his lips into a sad smile.

She nodded. "Dave said 'No, but both require strong belief.' Then he said, 'Henry died once, here. Don't make him die every day where his soul now lives because of your sadness.' It struck a chord."

"Dave's a pretty insightful guy." Duncan pulled her close, wrapped her in his arms, and whispered, "I'd give up everything I own to change what happened to you."

They stood quietly for several minutes, but the honest moment about her past felt right, even necessary. Duncan was no longer a passing ship in her life.

He loosened his hold and looked at her. "Does your ex-husband think wanting this land is wrong because of losing your son here?"

"You heard him at the basketball game?"

He nodded.

"I'm beginning to wonder if he's right. Letting go of everything about this place could be my bravest move of all."

"But I took this from you."

She shrugged. "Or maybe I need to let go."

He winced, shook his head. "No. I feel horrible. My bid took this—"

She covered his mouth with her palm. "Stop. Everything happens for a reason."

He removed her hand and kissed her fingertips with the softness of a single flake. "You're cold."

"I kind of like the chilly weather. You, on the other hand…"

He glanced down at her faux fur, calf-high boots. "Did you steal those from Chewbacca?"

"Good guess." She pointed to his Timberland Docksiders. "Did you miss the turnoff for the yacht?"

He chuckled, quiet and throaty. "No. I didn't plan on hiking through the woods this morning." He tipped his head toward the garden. "Is that for…for your son?"

"Yes. Henry. The place is beautiful in the spring."

"Will you bring me to visit here then?" He surveyed her face.

Duncan's offer bathed her in the golden light of a generous gift: his support and caring. The gesture to visit together was one Mike had stopped offering by the third year.

She smoothed his cheek with her palm. "Bringing you here would mean everything to me."

His irises darkened and he covered her mouth with his, a warm and tender kiss that made her light and airy as the flurries surrounding them.

When they stopped, she brushed a few snowflakes off his shoulder.

"Want to join me at home for some pancakes? Filled with chocolates chips. We'd have the company of Patrick and his buddies too."

"You made chocolate chip pancakes?"

He chuckled softly. "No. Helen."

"Sure. I'd love to come over. Let's go."

They headed back toward the parking lot and Duncan's fingers slipped through hers. He tightened their grip with a gentle squeeze, as if he'd captured something and was afraid it might slip through his fingers. She glanced over. He considered her with such deep longing that the heat of a blush rushed her cheeks.

Yes. This was her sign.

Chapter 25

Full Moon: The earth, moon, and sun are in alignment, just as the new moon, but the moon now sits on the opposite side of the earth with the sunlit part completely facing us, the shadowed portion hidden from view.

February

Duncan didn't consider himself a man who took the word "no" lightly, so he'd give this one more try. Maybe the third time would be a charm.

He watched Sophie at the top of the snow-covered hill he'd just sled down.

She waved to him from the hill's crest and cupped her mouth. "Be down in a sec. Hurry up, Tia!"

Tia slowly dragged a snow tube behind her up the hill.

In the two weeks since Duncan had learned about Henry's death on the Tates' land, he'd twice offered to take his firm's bid off the table. He no longer cared about his original goals and, quite simply, believed she deserved a future on the land.

Both times, she'd shaken her head with an adamant no. "I can't let you ignore the reasons that sent you here in the first place. It's his real father's land."

He didn't want to say this to her, but his trust level with the two elderly brothers had dipped to below zero. Elmer's strange expression as Duncan left their house last time they talked made him wonder what else they were keeping from him.

He moved to warm his feet. Standing in one place made him chilly. According to the news, the blizzard of '96 was the last time this much snow had covered the ground in Northbridge. Yesterday's storm left twenty-three more inches of the fluffy white granules in one fell swoop, mounting on top of their second week of steady snowfall.

A car pulled out of the entrance to Crickle Creek Orchards, across from the large hill near Duncan's house. He waved to the orchard owner, who had downplayed the uncontrollable weather with a sign in the cab of a vintage truck displayed at the orchard's entrance reading "FREE SNOW."

"Here I come." Sophie dropped the tube onto the ground and plopped into it, adjusting her seating.

She pressed her hands in the snow and pushed to start, gaining speed on her way down, and veering in his direction. "Fore!"

He jumped aside and she flew past then spilled off the tube. He ran over, his feet slowed by the heavy boots and deep snow. He stuck out his hand and pulled her upright.

She brushed snow off her pants. "Thanks." Her fair cheeks and the tip of her nose were bright red. "Want another turn?"

"Maybe. Come here." He pulled her close and pressed his lips to hers. "Damn, your lips are chilly. This is fun, but I like the part where we go inside to warm up."

"Me too."

He kept hold of her mitten-wrapped hands. "Listen, now that I've got you here, I think we have some unfinished business."

"Careful, Sparky, the kids are over there." She arched a suggestive brow.

"Not that. But I always like a woman with a dirty mind. Seriously, though. Hear me out before you say no to this."

Her lips pressed firm, as if she knew what came next.

"I have this weird feeling something else is going on with the Tates. My gut says I should step away. I don't want to remove my bid and have someone else buy the place. It belongs to you, your family."

Her mouth dropped open. "God, you're stubborn."

He chuckled. "Funny, I had the same thought about you."

She stared at him for a few long seconds. "In truth, the money end had me stressed from the start. My dad and Jay too. We'd have to sell at least two of our homes, take out a pretty hefty mortgage, and… Frankly, it was a financial stretch. Besides, I don't want the guilt of taking the land from your brother. Can you understand that?"

"You shouldn't feel guilty. Trent's interest is for a good reason, but yours is equally as valid. Probably more so."

She crossed her arms and bit her lower lip. "Yes, mine is valid. Here's the thing, I don't know what our future holds, but I'd never want you to look back on this decision and regret what you gave up for Trent. Please let fate decide. After all, fate brought you back here." Her eyes softened. "To me."

His heart fluttered, the way it had when he'd found himself around her at the age of thirteen. "Okay. If you want me to wait, I will."

* * * *

Sophie devoured the aroma of fresh bread in Bellantoni's Market's bakery then tossed a warm paper-wrapped loaf into her basket. The mouthwatering aroma did little to make her forget the question bugging her all day. Why hadn't she just said yes to Duncan's last request she reconsider buying the land?

In part, every major decision she'd made in her life had factored in the happiness of others. So did some minor ones. Duncan tripped her up, a paradoxical catch-22. Someone ended up unhappy no matter what choice she made.

What did *she* really want?

One thing was certain. Duncan's willingness to give up the land so easily confirmed he had nothing to do with the alleged bribery, a fact that created a vat full of remorse over tonight's after-dinner trip with Cliff to Southbridge.

Cliff had called early this morning and said he'd made arrangements with his friend Sean Carney to go to his father at a nearby nursing home. In a way, Sophie hoped Jack Carney didn't remember anything from his old job as dispatcher at the station. She'd almost asked Cliff to call the meeting off. The request, however, might draw attention to the thing she'd kept from Cliff, her relationship with Duncan.

The extent of her dishonesty these days sent a ripple of nausea to her stomach. After how upset Duncan got at the studio when he'd learned about the call to Marcus, there was no way she'd open another gooey can of worms by telling him about the anonymous note she'd hidden from him. With any luck, tonight's visit to the nursing home would reveal nothing and Duncan would be none the wiser.

Turning down an aisle, she spotted Duncan halfway down, still dressed in his work clothes and holding two spray bottles of bathroom cleaner. His brows dipped together and he studied the back of the bottle with more care than she'd give to medication. Glancing around and seeing the aisle empty, she inched closer, then abandoned her cart nearby, tingling with a rush of excitement over his unexpected presence.

She stretched on tiptoes and grazed his cheek with a kiss. "Hey, handsome."

He looked her way and his eyes softened with the onset of a quick smile. "Thank God it's you. I get kissed all the time when I'm in here. What's with this town?"

"Really?"

"Sure." His voice dropped, now low and husky. "You're very distracting."

"If you're that easily distracted, I don't know if you'll be able to handle tomorrow night."

"I won't be trying to purchase bathroom cleaner tomorrow night."

Anticipation over their upcoming adult-only date had teased her thoughts all day. A good roll in the hay with him—or any surface—was overdue. Mike's weekend with the kids had come at a perfect time.

"Cute coat." He fingered one of the large gold buttons on her square-shouldered navy coat. "Sophie Pepper's Lonely Hearts Club Band?"

The consignment shop purchase screamed the seventies but, worn with a below-the-knee wool skirt and leather riding-style boots, Sophie thought the garb looked trendy. "We gals call this vintage."

He inspected her more closely. "You look cute."

"Thank you. Any aches and pains from Sunday?"

He groaned. "Only several thousand. You omitted the side effects when you arm-twisted me into going."

"Come on. You had fun."

"I did. The best part was getting warm with you on the sofa afterward." His lids hooded and his voice took on a low purr. "You're almost making me like winter."

"If you play your cards right, I might even give you a massage tomorrow for those sore muscles." Her fingers itched to reach inside his unbuttoned wool coat and take a path on the strong muscles of his back.

Duncan's gaze softened and he studied her with such deep longing she drew a breath. Regret over tonight's interview about his family knotted her stomach, but evaporated the second he leaned close and parted his lips.

Sophie tilted her head upward but her peripheral vision caught a cart coming around the corner and she took a step back.

Jay plodded down the aisle, coming right at them. Heat rushed up her neck, and she hoped her expression didn't scream the guilt she held inside.

"Hey, fancy running into you." Sophie forced herself to relax and hoped he hadn't seen anything.

Jay glanced back and forth, his silent stare filled with accusation.

"Nice to see you again, Jay." Duncan placed the bathroom cleaner in the seat of his cart and extended his hand.

Jay put out his, too, but his jaw flexed while they shook. An awkward silence surrounded the group.

Duncan lifted two containers of cleaner. "Sophie was just about to give me some advice on these bathroom cleaners. Bleach or the regular."

"Bleach," Sophie piped in quickly, thankful for the diversion.

He tossed the can in the cart and shelved the other. "Bleach it is. I'd better run. Thanks for the help. See you soon, Jay."

Jay's stiff nod didn't even make Duncan flinch. As he went past Sophie, he winked then whistled all the way to the end until he disappeared around the corner.

Jay reached for some dishwasher detergent and dropped the box into the cart with a bang. "Did you hear the zoning board has rescheduled the vote?"

"No. To when?"

"Next Thursday night." His neck muscle flexed. "I'm getting tired of waiting for their decision."

"Me too."

"You and Jamieson seemed pretty chummy." He crossed the aisle and picked up a can of Pledge. It clanged against the metal cart with his toss.

She lowered her voice. "Jay, Duncan's son is a friend of Matt's. They play basketball together. They live here too. Jeez, if he ends up building the resort, will you snarl every time you pass him in town?"

"No." Jay gripped the shopping cart handle so tight his knuckles went white. "I'm still disappointed. Aren't you?"

"If things are meant to be, they'll happen." She gave his arm a friendly tap even though shame over withholding Duncan's offer from her brother tapped at her.

They hugged good-bye and Sophie continued to shop. A distant tune played through the store's speakers, but did little to drown out the word "liar," which now played in a constant loop inside her head.

She'd hid Duncan's offer from Jay.

She was hiding their dating relationship too.

As a cherry to the sundae, she'd hid from Duncan the documents about his family. A foreboding wave rippled through her. A perfect storm of lies stood in her path, but she pushed her cart toward the registers and ignored the warning.

Chapter 26

I love you.

Duncan turned the words around in his mind as he pushed a hard butterscotch candy with his tongue. The idea of uttering them to any woman had always carried a greater risk factor for him than opening a resort along the Gaza Strip.

The Four Corners traffic light, close to the southern tip of Southbridge, switched to red. Blinding snow and daydreaming almost made him glide right through, but he tapped his brakes to slow down.

Should he slow down with Sophie too?

No. Their physical needs demanded time together. Duncan glanced at the bouquet of red and white long-stemmed roses on the passenger seat. When he'd asked the florist for roses, she'd said if they were for someone special, the color combination represented unity. He'd bought them without hesitation. Now the overt symbolism forced him to consider how fast things were moving emotionally between them. The car behind him beeped. He glanced up. The light had turned green.

As he accelerated, a tight clench strangled his gut, worse than the stage fright he used to have before project presentations at the start of his business. Admitting his heart's desire for her was one of the scariest things he'd faced in a long time.

Fifteen minutes later, he turned into a combined gas station/convenience mart for a cup of coffee. While he stood at the counter to pay, a row of red, plastic heart key chains with smiley faces under a sign reading "Squeeze me" caught his attention. He squeezed one and the cheap object glowed. He tossed it on the counter along with some gum.

Once back in the car, he called Sophie.

After one ring, she answered. "Hey. Have you left the office yet?"

"On my way."

"Are the roads bad?" She sounded worried. "Mike picked up the kids an hour ago and said they were getting slippery. At least he's driving south to get home."

"I'll be fine. My car's been handling them pretty well." Duncan's old BMW never could've handled this snow. His recent switch to a Mercedes SUV had been a smart move.

"What's your ETA?"

"Are you in charge of Northbridge ground traffic control now?"

"One of my many hats."

He almost heard the smile. "I'm about fifteen miles outside of Northbridge. With this snow, I'd say at least a half hour, maybe forty-five minutes."

"Okay." Her voice softened. "I'm so glad we'll be together tonight."

"Me too. Be there soon." He hung up, strapped his seat belt on, and took a left out of the parking lot.

I'm so glad we'll be together tonight. Her words floated in his mind and left him aroused for her touch.

From the first time he held her slender fingers at the kayak hut, he'd devoured their softness and played with thoughts of them on his body. He sometimes drifted off in work meetings, thinking of the times she'd taken his hand and rubbed the back of it against her soft cheek, like he was some kind of security blanket. Or her carefully placed kisses behind his earlobe, a spot that always made him moan and heightened his desire.

He neared Northbridge in good time. On the steep curve heading into town Duncan's car swayed momentarily, but his trusty vehicle dug deep and kept him steady. He passed the street leading to Alan Moore's tackle shop and was reminded of Jay's lukewarm greeting at the store last night, only a slight improvement from the cold chill of their first introduction. If Jay was aware of Duncan's offer and still carried that much hostility, then he'd prove to be the hardest nut to crack in this town.

A few minutes later, he reached Sophie's street. He again glanced at the roses. Could he give himself completely to a woman without letting fear block him this time?

* * * *

Sophie's lies had finally reached their toppling point, leaving her with one question: how should she handle what she'd learned last night at the nursing home?

With patience and a lot of questions, Jack Carney revealed that none other than Trent Jamieson had been at Buzz's house when the gunshot was fired. The elderly man drifted off and lost focus on the "whys" behind the visit, however what he shared connected the lone gunshot to the Jamiesons. To her relief, the facts showed no bearing to Duncan, RGI, or any kind of corruption as it related to the purchase of the Tates' land.

Last evening also offered some relief from the aching work-related guilt of the past weeks. After thanking Sean and saying good-bye in the nursing home parking lot, Sophie had turned to Cliff. "We need to talk."

"Oh?" He'd raised his eyebrows.

"Duncan found out about Henry's connection to the property. He's offered to remove his bid. I asked him not to, though."

Cliff had nodded, his expression neutral.

"My point is I believe a man who'd hand over the land isn't bribing anybody. What we learned tonight is weird, but doesn't justify us poking around in old family business."

"Anything else?" He'd cornered her with his fatherly eyes.

She'd been busted. "How long have you known I've been seeing Duncan?"

"Since the day you two were holding hands at Sunny Side Up. Two people called me." Cliff's soft smile had surprised her.

"This isn't like what happened with that lawyer, you know."

"I know. I never trusted that Malarkey guy, but I can tell Duncan's different. Besides, I figured something pretty special is going on, given how quiet you've kept it."

Her throat had grown thick and she'd avoided his eyes by staring at the side of a parked car. "I'm ashamed, Cliff. So many times, I wanted to tell you." She'd looked up. "Are you mad?"

He'd shook his head. "Even if I was, how could I stay mad at my star reporter? I'm still curious about what happened back then, but you're right. Let's drop this search. I'll have Gabby cover next week's zoning board meeting."

Cliff's understanding meant everything. She could only hope Duncan would be so accepting if she told him what she'd learned about his family. Did he know Trent and his father had some history in Northbridge?

She went to the sliding glass doors looking out to the woods surrounding her house. The dark sky shook loose heavy snow that cleansed the ground's imperfections, leaving a clean white covering everywhere. A part of her wanted to thoroughly cleanse her soul, admit to Duncan every little thing she'd hidden from him. He'd stormed from the studio when he learned she'd contacted Marcus, didn't even listen to her explanation. What if he reacted like that again? Her aching libido politely suggested she keep her mouth shut.

Sharon Struth

After turning on several lights, she lit some candles and started a fire in the living room fireplace. At the mirror near the door, she fluffed her hair so it bounced nicely at her shoulders. A long silver necklace hung perfectly over the scooped neck of a simple black knitted dress and she adjusted her black tights. The aroma of roasting Cornish hens reminded her to baste them.

Ten minutes later, Bella barked. Sophie placed foil over the finished green beans and peeked out the kitchen window. Duncan's silver SUV chugged forward and stopped beside the shed. She opened the front door and Bella ran outside, straight to Duncan's car.

He stepped out, patted the dog's head, and smiled at Sophie. Holding up a canvas overnight bag, he said. "Is it too presumptuous for me to bring my bag in?"

"Not at all. We've discussed this."

The upper half of his body disappeared inside the car again. This time, he removed a bouquet of white and red roses.

"For you." He walked inside and handed her the flowers. Bella shot in behind him.

Fast falling snowflakes had covered the arrangement like powdered sugar on a cake. "Beautiful. Red and white?" She buried her nose inside the flowers and inhaled the sweet fragrance. "Did you know these colors mean unity? I once read it in an article."

He placed his bag to the side and shrugged. "I didn't. I thought they're pretty. Like you."

Sophie stretched on tiptoes and pressed her lips gently to his. "Thank you. They're lovely."

Before she could ask for his coat, he pulled her into his arms, covering her mouth with a hungry, soul-melting kiss.

When he stopped, he murmured, "I've thought about kissing you for the last hour."

"That's all?" She neatened the collar of his soft, button-down shirt. "I've thought the same thing all day."

He chuckled and removed his coat and snow-covered boots. They strolled into the kitchen, holding hands. "What smells so good?"

Sophie discussed the menu while she arranged the flowers. "Want a drink? I have some chardonnay chilling."

"Sure."

"Make yourself at home." She pulled a bottle from the refrigerator. Duncan wandered into the living room area, still visible from the peninsula where she poured their drinks. She watched him study objects on the thick oak mantel over the stone fireplace.

He passed hand-painted candlesticks and a group of ceramic animal figurines. At a framed picture of all three of Sophie's children, he stopped. She knew the special photo well. Christmas morning, surrounding by ripped piles of wrapping paper, tenth grader Henry sat cross-legged on the floor and held up the flight simulator game he'd literally begged for. Matt, a mere seven, stood behind him and proudly clutched a transformer robot above his head. Four-year-old Tia sat nestled in Henry's lap and hugged an American Girl doll.

In the mirror above the mantel, Sophie caught the downward turn of Duncan's lips while he took in the details.

She picked up their drinks and went to his side, just as he lifted a snow globe Bernadette had given her, one she always kept next to the photo. He studied the midnight blue base, dotted with antique gold stars and a large sun, similar in color to the stars and surrounded by snaking rays. He shook the globe. Sparkling white crystals danced like a blizzard around a brushed-gold crescent moon, where a single star dangled from the uppermost point.

"I used to love these when I was a kid. This looks like an antique."

"It is. Bernadette gave me that one." She took a second to remember the sad day. "For Christmas one year."

He checked the bottom and motioned to a turnkey. "What song?"

"'When you wish upon a star.'"

"May I?"

"Sure."

About to turn the key, he paused and studied the bottom. "I like to think the moon is there, even if I'm not looking at it. Love, Bernadette."

"That's an Albert Einstein quote."

"What's it mean?"

"Back when we were in elementary school, we learned how the moon always hangs in the sky but during the day we sometimes don't see it." Her gaze shifted to the mantel, to Henry and the maturing face of the boy she loved so much that, even now, her heart wilted against her ribs. "On the first Christmas after Henry died, Bernadette gave me the globe as a gift." She swallowed the wedge in the back of her throat and added quietly, "She said the quote was a reminder how Henry is still always with us."

He nodded with a pensive stare then cranked the turnkey until it stopped. The hopeful song about wishes plucked in simple chimes, filling the quiet room. After replacing the snow globe on the mantel, he took the wineglasses out of her hands and left them up there too. He reached for her hand, kissed the top, then tucked their folded hands close to his heart. The gesture helped massage the ache in her chest, stirred by memories of her son. Their warm cheeks pressed together as they moved to the music and she allowed herself to melt against his chest, feel his support.

He tipped his head back to see her. "You're a lucky woman."

"Me?" Sophie's hand stroked his strong neck. The fire crackled and a spark popped. "You grew up with so much. Your business is a huge success and you've traveled all over the world. You're lucky too."

"Those are all very little compared to what you have here. Family and friends. The love."

Duncan almost sounded sad. Maybe with all his money and success, his life wasn't so great. The negative things she'd been uncovering might explain that some old wounds ran deep through his veins.

The music slowed then ended, leaving only silence. Sophie nestled in the crevice near his shoulder, lost in the peppery scent of cologne dusting his neck. She tenderly kissed a spot close to his Adam's apple and continued to his sturdy jaw. By the time she reached his lips, he eagerly took over, covering her mouth with his. His lips caressed hers, a slow and deliberate dance, stirring fierce passion in her belly.

Duncan slid his large hands along her backside and a blast of heat shot straight to her core. He moaned into her mouth then cupped her face as they kissed. Hot, demanding kisses. Her hands wandered down the muscles of his back, slipped beneath his shirt, and caressed his warm skin. The piercing beep of the stove's buzzer sounded, ignored by them both at first, but then Duncan pulled back.

"You'd better get it." His breathy voice matched the hunger pouring from his gaze. "We don't want the Northbridge Fire Department out here tonight. Might turn into front page news."

She kept her hands on his skin, dizzy with her own desire. "Even my connections couldn't stop that." She slowly removed her hands and headed into the kitchen, shut off the oven, and took out the dinner.

Duncan came up from behind and circled her in his arms. He nibbled tenderly behind her ear. "Looks good."

Heat surged through Sophie's body. He pressed against her while his lips stroked her neck with tender kisses. The soft touch of his palm smoothed along her shoulder then took a slow path along her side until he reached her hip.

Duncan moaned and his warm breath bathed the base of her neck. "You're in my head from the minute I wake up until I go to bed." His low, husky voice made her clench between her thighs. A throaty gasp escaped from her mouth and he twirled her around.

A playful leer shadowed his face. "Care to work up an appetite?"

"I thought you'd never ask." Sophie took his hand and led him to her bedroom.

* * * *

A noise woke Duncan. He stared up at an unfamiliar ceiling fan, confused for half a second before he realized he wasn't home. He rolled to his side. Sophie lay sleeping, her pink lips slightly parted and the pattern of her breathing steady. Dark, tangled hair cascaded over the pillow and her fair skin seemed even lighter against the rich navy comforter resting partway over her shoulder. The soft, pale mounds of her chest tempted him and, like Pavlov's dog, his arousal stirred, but he didn't reach for her as he'd done more than once during the night.

Quietly slipping from beneath the covers, he retrieved the clothes he'd tossed on the floor at bedtime and slipped them on. Bella lifted her head off the dog bed in the corner and followed him out. Downstairs, he scoured the kitchen for a coffeemaker and coffee. Maybe he'd make breakfast too. He located a can of Folgers just as the front door handle rattled then unlocked. He froze.

Were the kids back already?

Bella barked and ran to the door as Jay hurried in, followed by a dusting of snow caused by a wind gust.

He stomped the snow from his boots then leaned over and scratched the dog's head. "Hey, girl." He looked up and his jaw unhinged.

He scanned Duncan from top to bottom then his forehead crinkled. "What the... Is my sister sleeping with you?" Unshaven, with dark circles under his lower lids, Jay carried a thermos tucked under his armpit.

Duncan's tongue twisted in a knot, it was a little too early in the day to be caught off guard. "You should talk to Sophie about this." He cringed at his unmanly response. "Do you always walk right in? I don't think she's expecting you."

"Obviously." His gaze seared Duncan. "I was about to plow the driveway. I came in because of the strange car in the driveway. Figured I'd refill my thermos and make sure my sister's okay." He walked in and clunked the thermos on the counter. "I figured something was up when I saw you two at Bellantoni's. How long has this been going on?"

"Let's not blow this out of proportion. Sophie's a grown woman."

"I know she can date. *You're* my issue." Jay's voice boomed. "We couldn't compete with the ridiculous price you offered the Tates. We were counting pennies to get the deal to work from the start. Don't you understand how much this land means to her?"

"Of course I do. That's why I offered it to her."

Jay's lower lip dropped. "You did? When?"

"Stop!" Sophie stood halfway down the steps in a white terry cloth robe, arms pretzel-folded tight against her chest, with flushed pink cheeks. "Is this true? The property is ours?"

She proceeded down the stairs, biting her lip. The taut lines of her face reminded Duncan of the same unmistakable fury he'd seen the night after the public hearing, when he'd lied about his identity.

"Why'd you tell him about your offer?" Her words were quiet, the kind of quiet almost scarier than yelling.

"You never told me not to. Why did you hide this from him?"

Her face went blank and she looked away.

Jay stepped toward Sophie. "I can't believe you kept this from me."

"I had my reasons."

"Are you crazy?" Jay's jaw tightened. His angry stare cut a path between her and Duncan. "RGI has more properties than they know what to do with. Give me one good reason."

She glanced at Duncan, a clear plea for assistance. He considered telling Jay about Trent's real relationship to Elmer but wasn't sure he could trust him, at least not in this state of mind. "Listen, Jay. You're crossing a line. Back off."

Jay glared at Sophie. "You're going to let him talk to me that way?"

She stared at Duncan with a downturned mouth then sighed.

She finally looked at her brother. "You and I don't think alike. We never have. He offered the land to me. I've made the decision to wait and see what the town decides."

"Jesus, Sophie. Do something for yourself for a change." Jay jabbed a finger in her direction. "You're not gaining points with anybody by giving up this chance for our family. Especially not with him." He pointed at Duncan.

Jay swiped his thermos off the counter. "Don't come crying to me when you wish you'd said yes. It'll be like you complaining about how you didn't go away to college. Or married Mike. An old story, Sis, and getting overplayed. Take a chance on yourself for once."

"I resent that. I don't complain about my choices."

"Not directly, but it comes up. How you've missed out in life. Do you know the guilt I've lived with because you stayed here to help Mom?"

"You shouldn't. You came back for Dad later."

"Whatever." He swiped his hand through the air. "You seemed so excited over the Tates' land. More excited than you've been in a long time." His tone went flat, lifeless. "Especially since losing Henry."

A tear escaped and she quickly brushed the wetness aside.

Jay turned to Duncan. "Are you two dating or did I walk in on"—he pressed his lips tight—"a casual night together?"

Duncan wanted to jump to her defense, admit his strong feelings, but Sophie cut him off before he could.

"I don't owe you an explanation on how I spend my spare time," she snapped before he could answer.

Not the answer Duncan wanted to hear. Was he reading her signals wrong?

Jay cheeks reddened and he stayed silent.

"Thank you for doing the driveway." Sophie's voice was monotone. "I appreciate what you do for me.

Jay stormed toward the door. "I know." He slammed it shut.

* * * *

Jay's comments left Sophie stripped bare of a disguise she'd worn for a good portion of her life, naked for Duncan to judge. She walked into the kitchen to make coffee and deal with her humiliation in private.

Duncan came up behind her. "I'm sorry. Jay was so angry. I wasn't sure I could trust him if I told him about Trent and Elmer's relationship."

"I understand."

"I probably shouldn't have even told you, but trusted you'd keep things quiet."

She nodded but cringed at his use of the word trust.

"Why didn't you tell your brother about my offer?"

"He would've insisted we take it."

"So?" He slipped his arms around her waist. "Would that be so horrible?"

"No. What about Trent? Doesn't he matter?"

Pity filled his sad smile. "You matter, too." The sharp buzz of his cell phone echoed from the pocket of his overcoat, strewn over the coatrack. "I'd better get that."

She started some coffee then shuffled to the window. Outside the fresh snowfall gleamed clean, no blemishes, unlike her. Duncan's disappointed expression reminded Sophie of the day Bernadette called her a people-pleaser. The summer after sophomore year of college, they'd been tanning themselves at the town beach. Hot sun had warmed Sophie's skin, putting her seconds away from sleep when Bernadette blurted out, "You should take this *Cosmo* quiz."

Sophie had lifted her head from the reclined, low-lying beach chair. "On what?"

"The title is 'Are you a people pleaser or a selfish Sarah?'" Bernadette had been lying on her stomach on an aqua towel, elbows propped in the sand and a folded magazine in front of her.

"I'm not selfish."

"No. I'm pretty sure you have the opposite issue. First question. Your boyfriend wants to go to see a movie but it's nothing you'd like. You, A, stay home and watch TV instead. B, go to the movie to keep him happy. Or C, find another movie which both of you could enjoy." She chewed the pen cap and lifted her eyes over the magazine, waiting for an answer.

"C, I guess."

Bernadette had lowered the pen and dipped her chin. "Really?"

"No, wait. B. I'd go to the movie. There'll be other chances to see something I'd like."

Bernadette gave a judgmental grunt. "Question two, your coworker spends too much time on the phone with friends. When the boss comes down on her over a deadline you A, point out how she shouldn't take personal calls at work. B, ask if there's anything you can do to help. Or C, tell the boss she'll never get the job done because she can't manage time."

"Hmm…" Sophie had hesitated. "If the work needs to be done for the good of the office, what's the point of A or C? I mean, of course, I'd help."

Bernadette had covered three more questions, all with the same result. "People pleaser," she'd laughed. "I got you pegged."

It wasn't the first time her friend had made this point. "Your honesty isn't always your best quality, Bern." Sophie had leaned back in the chair and closed her eyes.

Bernadette had swatted her arm. "Don't get mad. You know you're my best bud. You just need to lay off always accommodating people, especially Mike. You give in to him on everything."

Bernadette had offered the same look of pity Duncan had just handed her. Neither was wrong. If Sophie had given more credence to the stupid quiz, her life might have been different.

She'd spent her life accommodating others. Those acts proved an easy way to please Mom and Dad, especially because Jay always gave them so much to worry over. The habit continued. Small things here and there. Bigger things followed.

Even with her unplanned pregnancy. Heck, a simple "no" to Mike's amorous advances the weekend she'd visited his university, and the life she currently lived would've been erased from the map. But she hadn't said no that day. She'd said yes because of what had happened two months earlier, on his weekend home in Northbridge. As she'd worked at the tasting room of the Tate Vineyards, Mike had fooled around with Lucy Tanner at Putticaw Park. If Meg and her boyfriend hadn't ventured there for a picnic, Sophie would have been none the wiser.

When confronted, Mike had apologized like a politician caught taking a bribe, but he'd cited several incidents where Sophie acted standoffish about sex when he'd asked. Lucy, he'd admitted, was a mistake and he'd begged her not to breakup. On that visit with Mike, they'd had sex, her motive not love for Mike but simply her pure hatred for Lucy.

A stupid move if she'd ever made one.

When her period hadn't arrived, resentment toward Mike's pushiness flourished. After they'd lost Henry, she blamed Mike even more.

Duncan slipped his hands along her hips and startled her from the past. He dropped his chin on her shoulder. "Sorry."

"Everything okay?"

"Uh-huh. I was thinking, maybe Jay has a point."

"About?"

He lifted his head and turned her around to face him. "I'm not judging you. I've been pretty blinded by my own goals most of my life. There has to be something more balanced than what either of us is doing. There's nothing wrong with wanting things for yourself in life, you know?"

She laced her fingers around the back of his neck. "How about I reconsider your offer? This isn't a yes, but I'll think about it. I want to make sure I'm doing this for me, not you."

The corner of his eyes wrinkled with a slight smile. He pulled her close and kissed her deeply. Sophie rested her palms against his chest, enjoying the muscular tenseness beneath his thin T-shirt. He pulled back and they gazed at each other while he eased his hands under her robe. With slow movements, he explored her backside then he pulled her close, his arousal obvious. He traced the panty line along her thigh then slipped his fingers under the fabric between her legs, making her inhale a quick breath. She whimpered a cry of pleasure and combed her fingers through his thick hair. Desire snared his expression and his gaze wandered her exposed chest through heavy-lidded eyes.

They hurried to the bedroom where Duncan removed her robe with one swift movement and slipped off her panties. He undressed and pressed her to the bed, holding her hands above her head. His strong frame hovered over her, possessed her, and made her squirm with need. Using his knee, he guided her legs apart. They joined as one, moved in tandem, speaking the silent language of love through touch. Without a single word, Duncan Jamieson seized every part of her. Mind, body and soul.

Half an hour later, she snuggled in a secure space near Duncan's chest and twirled her index finger in his curly chest hair as he ran a smooth hand along her shoulder.

He took her hand in his. "Before all that commotion, I planned to start breakfast. How do you want them? Over-easy or scrambled?"

"Scrambled, please."

"Your wish is my command." He kissed her forehead and hopped out of bed.

As he hunted the floor for his clothes, she studied his long muscular legs. Moments ago, she'd been trapped beneath them while the sandy-colored stubble on his cheeks teased her skin. He caught her watching and paused, the desirous, eye-softening expression she'd seen multiple times before they'd made love spreading across his face and making her heart swell.

Duncan located his sweatpants and watched her as he slipped a Nike T-shirt over his head. "A penny for your thoughts." He leaned over, grabbed her robe off the floor, and tossed it in her direction.

She caught the corner and sat up, gripping the robe to her chest and searching for the courage to say the next words.

His grin disintegrated. "You okay?"

"Yeah." She slipped on the robe and held the sides closed with her hand. "I want you to know these past weeks with you... They've been unbelievable. You've really swept me away. In a way that's never happened before."

He came close and sat on the edge of the bed. His eyes shifted downward and a pensive expression overtook his face. Taking her hand in his, he leaned in and gave her a short kiss. "I've really had a great time too. Really great." An awkward aura filled the air as if he wanted to say something else but couldn't. "How about I get those eggs started?"

"Sure." She forced a smile.

He headed for the door, tossing a wink her way just before disappearing into the hallway. What was that about? The moment highlighted how much she had to learn about him. Guess he had a lot to learn about her too.

She rolled out of bed and headed toward the bathroom for a quick shower. Hopefully all this research she'd done on his family could now disappear. She never wanted him to know. He'd run off once because of it and even though hiding the details was dishonest, she never wanted to risk losing him over a past she really didn't care about.

Chapter 27

Dad came into Jay's kitchen and refilled his mug with coffee while Sophie loaded the dishwasher with their brunch dishes. "Want some?" Dad held the carafe in her direction.

"Sure." She pushed down her sweater sleeves and picked up her near-empty cup so he could pour.

A cheer sounded from the living room, where Matt and Jay watched the Patriot's game while her sister-in-law, nephew, and Tia played Scrabble in the dining room.

"You and Jay okay?" Dad lifted his thick white brows. Today he'd worn his navy Patriot's jersey, which made his broad chest seem even wider. "You both seemed quiet."

"Just a small issue. Everything is fine now."

She'd phoned Jay right after Duncan left yesterday. He'd apologized right away. Apologies were his kryptonite, so one offered quickly had to be sincere.

He stirred sugar into his coffee. "Nothing like one of Jay's brunches, huh? Thank God someone paid attention to Mom's cooking tips."

"No chance that was going to be me." She paused. "Mind if I ask you a personal question?"

"I suppose." He poured a dollop of half-and-half then offered her some.

She took the container. "Remember when Mom used to share the story of how you two met?"

His mouth crumpled. "Of course I do."

"How come you were so quiet whenever she brought it up?"

He shrugged. "What more could I add?" His gaze averted to the avocado refrigerator in Jay's dated kitchen, where a few years back he'd spent a small windfall on a used twenty-year-old gas-powered Viking stove but ignored his wife's request they replace the other appliances first. "Guys don't talk about that stuff, honey."

She poured and put down the container. "You felt the same way as her, right?"

"I sure did. The first time I saw your mother, she took my breath away." Tenderness radiated from his voice. "Whenever she shared the story about those bells ringing, I liked to tease that she needed to get her hearing checked."

Sophie warmed. Her mother would act annoyed over the remarks but had never seemed to be too upset.

Dad took a slow sip of coffee. "I never told her, but I swore I heard them too."

She reached out and squeezed his forearm. Over twenty years had passed since Sophie's mother died, but his deep love for her stood strong.

He stared into his mug. "I suppose I should've said something. Guess I did, in my own way." He looked up. "Men are different. Words don't come easy to us."

"What?" She blurted a laugh. "When I was a kid, you had plenty to say to me. Jeesh, seemed like Ann Landers raised me some days."

"Then how'd I raise such a smart-alec?" He grinned. "You know what I mean. We show *how* we feel. Gifts or small gestures."

Friday night, Duncan had arrived with those beautiful flowers. Saturday morning, she'd come downstairs to a set breakfast table. At her napkin, a little smiling heart key chain had been propped against the plate, which lit bright when squeezed. A tender smile had crossed his lips as she attached the token to her keys right away.

She sighed. "All right. That helps, I think."

Dad's light brows lifted. "Who's the lucky guy?"

"Duncan Jamieson."

Dad gave a noncommittal head-bob. "He's a nice man, honey. Even though Jay has his knickers in a bundle over the land issue, you're more sensible than your brother. Go with your heart. You deserve to this time."

Jay walked in wearing the long-sleeved T-shirt his wife had given him this past Christmas with a chubby, mustached cartoon chef and the words *Never Trust a Skinny Chef* above his head.

"Dad, you missed a great play." He looked between them. "What's going on?"

"We're discussing how lucky we are Mom taught you to cook." He cast Sophie a conspiratorial grin on his way out and patted Jay on the shoulder. "Great brunch, Son. Back to the game."

Sophie returned to the dishwasher task, adding a few more glasses to the top.

Jay plunked his mug in the sink she'd cleared. "What were you really discussing?"

Sophie pointed to the mug then cast Jay the same disbelieving look she'd have given her kids as she motioned to the dishwasher.

"Oops. Sorry." He stuck the mug in the top rack. "So, the real topic?"

"Love."

He wrinkled his nose, opened the refrigerator, and removed the bowl of fruit she'd just put away. "Then he knew about you and Duncan?"

"He does now."

Jay put the bowl on the counter and removed the plastic wrap. "Are you guys that serious?"

"Maybe."

Jay's lips pulled into a thin line. "Hmm."

"Hey." She tossed a dishtowel at him. "We okay?"

Jay reacted fast and caught it with one hand. "Yeah. Eileen told me I made a big deal out of nothing and you had your reasons for not telling me about the offer. I'd stopped in yesterday morning to tell you something else, though." He plopped the towel near the sink and dropped his voice. "Remember when I said I'd contact my high school buddy Andy Murray? He used to work at the Northbridge police station?"

"Yeah." Dread wormed through her. She'd hoped he'd forgotten the request.

He took a cereal-sized bowl from the cabinet. "Andy is living in and working outside of Hartford. Anyway, we met for lunch Friday. I asked if he remembered anything about the gunshot at Buzz's house. Turns out your instincts are right. The incident involved the Jamiesons. Did you know Duncan has a brother named Trent who's adopted?"

"Uh-huh."

"How'd you—" He waved a hand. "Never mind. So you probably know there might be another reason the Jamiesons have returned to Northbridge."

Even though Duncan had told her plenty, years of interviews had taught her to wait to hear what others said first, sometimes not what she expected. "What'd you find out?"

"The gunshot in the article happened when Trent Jamieson paid a visit to Buzz and Marion's house. Andy told me a neighbor reported she saw Trent running from Buzz's house right after a gun went off. She called the cops. A little later, they found Trent downtown hanging out with some kids and took him into the station."

This confirmed the old dispatcher's story. "Did Andy know why Trent showed up there?"

"He said the guy wanted to find out the truth about his birth parents."

"So he went to them?"

"Have I out-scooped the 'queen of the scoop'?" Jay smirked with too much glee.

"Come on! Don't torment me."

His grin disappeared. "Get this... Marion Harris is Trent's real mother."

Marion's strong reaction when Sophie had uncovered the newspaper story and spoken to Buzz took on new meaning. In the hallway at the December zoning board meeting, she'd had that strange, almost fearful, reaction to Duncan, too. An uncomfortable wave rushed at Sophie. At the bowling alley, when he'd mentioned Trent was adopted, her question about Trent's birth mother had been quickly glossed over.

She leaned against the counter and crossed her arms. "Are you positive?"

"You want me to do blood work? No, I'm not. I'm repeating what Andy said."

"Sure explains a lot."

Jay's eyes opened wide. "Like what?"

"Between us, okay?" Sophie raised a warning finger. "I've never been more serious."

He nodded.

"Duncan's purchase of the Tates' land wasn't only for the resort. Elmer Tate is Trent's birth father. So he's kind of the *de facto* heir to the land."

Jay's lips pursed. "Did Duncan tell you that?"

"Of course."

"I'm not sure it's true."

"Why?"

"Andy said Trent went there to ask Marion the identity of his father."

"So what? Maybe he didn't know Elmer was his dad in those days."

"At the station, Trent confessed he believed Marion had lied about his real father. Claimed the birth certificate wasn't true. He refused to leave their house until Marion told him the truth. When Buzz got home, he pulled the gun to make him leave." Jay shook his head and his short ponytail bobbed. "Freaking Buzz is crazy. Anyway, Trent went to grab the gun and a shot fired. Luckily, nobody got hurt."

"Did Andy say who else Trent might have believed to be his dad?"

"That's the real rub. You won't like this."

A sick feeling settled in Sophie's stomach. The problem with snooping was sometimes she got answers.

Chapter 28

Ice pellets bombarded Sophie's windshield on her way to Duncan's house. She'd spent the entire afternoon mulling over Jay's find. Had Duncan kept this crucial part of his family's past from her or would this be news to him?

She followed the town sander truck as it threw a dusting of salt and sand on the slick roads. The truck went straight when she turned toward Duncan's place. The tail end of her car swerved. Sophie regained control of the vehicle and continued along the road as the Subaru wipers batted away hard pellets hitting the windshield, like bullets warning her to stay back.

Sophie played out the possible scenarios that might unfold tonight, none great. This news tested her trust in Duncan, gave him every reason not to trust her, and, if true, would deliver a walloping punch to his reality.

What the hell was she doing?

Maybe the Jamieson brood preferred their dirty business kept tucked away in the vaults of history. Who wouldn't? A tidal wave of caution knocked her over, the kind where you second guess an idea that seemed perfect only seconds earlier.

She approached his house. Bright headlights peeked out from his driveway. A car pulled out and headed her way. She immediately recognized the extended front end and barred grill of the 1998 Buick Park Avenue. As it passed, she caught a shadowed glimpse of the driver, Buzz Harris, behind the wheel. A silhouette in the passenger seat looked like Marion. Sophie's palms tingled, the way they always did when a lead on a story dragged her under its tow. Any other day, she'd have thought Buzz's visit might be about the resort or zoning matters.

This wasn't any other day.

At the end of his long driveway, she parked next to an Audi she recognized as Trent's car. She hurried from the car to the walkway, covered by a salt-sand mixture. The sleet assaulted her as she took careful steps. She pressed the doorbell and made every effort to ignore the panicked voice inside her head urging her to flee before it was too late.

Duncan opened the door. Right away, his face broke into a smile. "Hey. What a nice surprise." He led her inside, planted a quick peck on her lips, then stole a glance toward the driveway.

"They're gone."

"Oh, you passed the Harris' on their way out?"

"You can't miss him in that big sedan." The welcoming aroma of a baking pie or cake with coffee reminded Sophie he had guests. "Sorry to barge in unannounced. I didn't realize you had company."

"Just my brother. I was going to call you later." He gently cupped Sophie's cheeks and gave her a tender kiss. "Should you be driving in this ice? They left because of the weather."

"I won't stay long. Are you social friends with Buzz and Marion?"

"Not really. They stopped by to say hello to Trent." The words came out fast. "They met during our summer visits."

"Oh."

The strange facts from Jay stood on more solid footing. Trent's deep voice carried from another room, followed by Patrick's laughter.

"Can we talk in private?"

"Sure." He pressed his hand to her lower back. "Let's go to my office."

He led her from the spacious foyer, down a hallway and into his study. Oversized, like most rooms in the McMansions in this part of town, oak panels against light cream-colored walls created a cozier than expected space. This trip served as a reminder they lived in different worlds, her house quite small by comparison.

He shut the door partway and drew her close. "Listen, I was going to call you. Yesterday morning, you said something very personal to me. About how you felt when we're together." Worry lines creased his face.

"Sorry I came on so strong."

"No. I'm glad you did. You bring out feelings in me, too, but they're not easy for me to share." Duncan tapped his chest near his heart. "They're in here, though. Please don't give up on me."

"I'll never give up on us." She meant every word.

His shoulders relaxed. "Buzz wasn't here about zoning, you know."

"I didn't think so." She stepped away from his embrace but still felt trapped by circumstances.

"There are some things you should know about my family situation here."

Tension in her body, present since she'd left her house, disappeared. Duncan's offer to share the details Jay found meant she wouldn't be the bearer of sordid family news.

He lowered his voice. "Marion Harris is Trent's birth mother. That's why they came here tonight. Trent wanted to talk to her, now that I've returned to town."

She studied Duncan's face for any signs he might have more, but he only stared back and seemed to wait for her reaction. Did he really *not* know what happened with the gunshot or his father's possible involvement?

"Anything else?"

Duncan tipped his head. "What do you mean?"

Sophie went to his desk and dropped her bag on top. She removed the two pieces of paper that had started her chase. "Before you moved here—before we got close—someone left this for me at the newspaper."

He went to her side and picked up reading glasses off his desk. Slipping them on, he studied the first note. "The Jamiesons are corrupt. Both now and in the past. Question the gunshot." His forehead crumpled in deep lines. "What gunshot? Why would anybody...?" His eyes narrowed. "Who gave this to you?"

"It was left anonymously at the *Gazette* office. For me. Cliff suggested I do some research on why." His brows rose, but she didn't stop. "The same person also left me this." She handed him the news story with the police report.

Duncan's jaw muscle flexed as he read. He looked up. "So? What does a story about a gunshot at Buzz's house have to do with anything?" He glanced at the paper again. "This happened in nineteen eighty-one. I wasn't even—" He paused and stared at a spot on the wall behind her. "Eighty-one. The summer before I started high school." His voice dropped. "We were here. Our last summer before Dad put the house on the market."

"So you don't know anything about that story?"

"No, I don't." His tone strong and unshaken, Duncan narrowed his gaze. "Why haven't you mentioned this before? We've been together enough."

"Until today, this really had no meaning."

"Oh?" The tight press of his lips offered a deadly pause. "You've been researching me again?"

"No! I started this before we... Before I had feelings for you."

He lowered the paper then wandered to the window, crossing his arms and staring into the black night.

She went to his side and touched his forearm, which tensed under her hand. "I learned the answer today. This time, I came right to you."

Duncan's neck corded tight and he kept his gaze fixed on the darkness. "What'd you find now?"

"Hey! Cut me some slack. I'm trying to be honest."

He faced her and his facial muscles softened. "You're right. So, what's this about?"

"The incident here is related to Trent's real father."

"Elmer? How?" He tilted his head.

Either Duncan was a phenomenal actor or he hadn't heard the tidbit Jay had told her. "It's a long story." Every muscle in Sophie's body tensed as it prepared for impact. "The article is about Trent. He was there when the gunshot in the police report was fired."

Duncan returned to his desk and again studied the short news clipping. "I don't see his name here."

"I've been told the story in the paper isn't what really happened."

His pupils turned to dark pools and his voice rose. "Let's stop playing games. What's going on?"

A creak from the door opening made them both turn. Trent stood in the doorway, somber and less confident than the first time she'd crossed his path.

He stepped inside. "Hello, Sophie. Looks like you've uncovered the very thing I'd hoped had disappeared for good."

* * * *

Duncan's head throbbed. How had he missed all this?

Trent paced in front of the desk, hands jittery with wild animation as he divulged details Duncan couldn't believe happened right in front of him their last summer here. Yes, his parents had acted strangely when he'd been told their vacation would end early. He hadn't even tried to guess why. They never shared their behind-closed-door issues with the two kids.

He leaned his elbows on the desk and pinched the bridge of his nose. The inside of his head felt like a pane of shattered glass. He digested Trent's explanation about how he'd gone over to see Marion one day, to get answers to questions only she could answer. Duncan was about to ask what kind of question only Marion could answer when Trent continued with his story.

"Buzz came home early and all hell broke loose. I didn't know a neighbor saw me leave or she'd even called the police until they found me downtown and took me in. I was scared, so I told them the truth."

The idea his entire family had kept the story from him pounded Duncan's ego worse than a hard kick to the groin. "Why would you all keep this from me? This is why we sold the lake house?"

A thin layer of humiliation lined Trent's face, one Duncan witnessed every single time Trent screwed something up. "Yes. It's why Dad insisted we sell it. He didn't give Mom any say in the matter. It's also why he bribed the police."

"Bribed the police? Why on earth would he have to do that?" Duncan glared at his brother, but before he could answer, he shifted his attention to Sophie. "I can't believe you kept the note from me."

An end table lamp cast a light on her face and he caught a glint of moisture in her eyes. "They came to me anonymously. I wouldn't ever—"

He held up a hand. "Don't."

She dropped her chin. Her silence about those notes over the past weeks burned his wounded soul. Could he ever trust her?

His focus returned to Trent. "Why did Dad need to bribe the police?"

"To change the records." Trent lifted his head. "He didn't want the details I shared with the cops anywhere in writing."

"I know I'll be sorry I asked, but what did you tell the police that Dad wanted erased from the records?"

"That I went to Buzz's house to learn who was really my birth father."

Duncan slammed his palms onto the desk and the bang resonated off the walls. "I'm only buying this land because Elmer—I'd been told—was your real father! Now you're telling me he may not be?"

The muscles of Trent's jaw clenched and his cold, hard stare bore through Duncan. "Yes. Look Duncan, there was no easy way to tell Mom what I suspected without upsetting her. This whole deal with the Tates happened so fast."

Duncan squirmed, Trent's unusual calm during a crisis leaving him uneasy. "Why would she be upset if Elmer wasn't your real father?"

"Because..." Trent pulled in then slowly released a deep breath. "It might be Dad."

"Our dad?"

Trent nodded.

"Where would you get that crazy idea?"

Trent plopped into an oversized chair. "I found some letters."

Sophie stood and took the straps of her purse, left on the desk.

"Stop." Duncan's voice rose louder than he intended.

She released her hand and looked at him with her mouth downcast, her usual glow gone.

"You started this, you might as well stay." The request came out nasty, nastier than he planned. "Please. Take a seat."

She returned to the sofa, not far from Trent. Duncan massaged the edges of his mouth between his finger and thumb, staring at his brother and the woman he believed he loved.

A woman who kept digging up the past about his family.

Her gaze locked with his, its sadness wielding a power over him. He forced himself to detach, not sure he wanted her to sink into his soul any deeper.

"Let's hear it, Trent. The truth. For once, give me the truth."

Trent folded his hands in his lap, his gaze focused on the area rug. "About two months before we were to come up to the lake for the second summer, I'd been in the attic trying to find my old baseball trophies. Remember the year I set up a display on my bedroom wall?"

Duncan recalled his brother's sports success in high school and the endless trophies and write-ups in the local paper. He nodded.

"I found a box marked 'Frank's college papers.' Dad acted like such a pain in the ass about my schoolwork. I got nosey about his performance. Halfway down the box some letters were bundled with a rubber band. They were addressed to Dad at his office. The words 'personal and confidential' were on the outside." Trent shifted in his seat. "I read them."

Trent described the details of letters spanning several years about a secret romance between Frank Jamieson, then twenty-three, and an eighteen-year-old housekeeper at their family summer home. Marion Price.

"He dated Mom at the time, too." Trent raised a judgment-filled brow. "When they got engaged, Dad ended the affair with Marion. One of the last letters showed how, a few years into the marriage, Dad resumed his affair during a summer visit." He met Duncan's eyes. "When I was conceived."

Duncan considered the flimsy evidence. "A letter doesn't prove anything. Maybe she'd been with some other man besides Dad."

Trent shrugged. "I don't think so. The letters suggested Dad asked Marion to get an abortion. Marion's last note was dated the end of October and explained everything. Seems Mom came to Northbridge by herself, to close up the place for the winter. She hired some of the local help to give her a hand, including Marion, who was two months pregnant at the time. Mom caught her crying. You know Mom…everyone's savior."

Duncan motioned with his hand for Trent to continue.

"Marion told Mom she got pregnant by a married man who left her on her own. Mom jumped to the rescue. Seems she and Dad were having some difficulty conceiving so she offered to adopt the baby and help out with expenses during the pregnancy. Of course, she got pregnant with you shortly after adopting me."

He recoiled at the notion his father had cheated on his mother and had also abandoned a pregnant woman. "Mom never knew about his affair?"

"If she did, she didn't tell me."

Duncan's throat tightened, the story lodging there and making him want to choke. He gulped hard and tried to push the facts through his system. He peeked in Sophie's direction. She looked at the window.

He turned to Trent. "What happened at Buzz's house?"

"Sometimes I act first, think later." Trent shrugged it off, his usual attitude when he screwed up. "Since we were here for vacation, I decided to go to the one person who knew the truth. I showed her the letter and demanded answers. She insisted the birth records were accurate, but I didn't believe her. She asked me to leave." His mouth crumpled into a frown. "But I stayed and kept asking."

Duncan choked back the urge to scream at his brother. Instead, his fingers dug into the leather arm of his chair and waited for him to finish.

"Buzz came home from work. Things got out of control and he took out a pistol from a kitchen drawer. When I tried to grab it, the trigger went off." He studied his hands. "The rest you know. Dad talked to the police, worked everything out with them, and got rid of the records."

"He didn't work things out." Sophie snapped. "He bribed them." Her contempt-filled glare swung toward Duncan.

Embarrassed over his father's actions, he cleared his throat. "My father has a way of getting what he needs from people. I'm not proud of him, but he'll never change." He turned away, but his father's actions filled him with unbearable shame.

"That's the reason I wanted you to arrange for a get-together with them. I figured I could talk to Marion privately. When Marion and I talked alone in the kitchen tonight, I vowed never to bring up the past again. With your return to town, I figured she'd be worried."

Duncan leaned forward. "Why didn't she just tell Buzz to back off encouraging us to come here?"

"I asked her that. Buzz doesn't know about Dad. It would kill him to learn she'd lied about the father for so many years. He understood his wife had some problems in the past, but she never told him the real reason I showed up that day. Only said I wanted to know why she didn't want me." Disappointment shadowed his expression. "If the affair with Dad is true, bringing it up now would only hurt everybody."

After a lifetime of watching his father distance himself from their family, especially Trent, Duncan saw the possibility this story could be true. An ache settled in his chest, pity for his brother who'd had to spend all these years living with the knowledge his parentage came with lies.

He looked at Sophie, who stared at her lap. "Sophie, at the January board meeting, when you and I spoke in the hallway, did you know about the gunshot story?"

She looked up. "Yes, but I didn't understand it. In fact, I had showed Buzz the article. He claimed it was true, but he's a terrible liar. Now I see he did it to protect his wife. Guess this explains why Marion got so upset when you came over to us."

He didn't reply, only silently stared in her direction wondering why she hadn't told him sooner. She lowered her eyes.

Trent rested his elbows on his knees. "Duncan, you're the last person I wanted affected by this. I understand how much a fresh start meant to you after Elizabeth's death." His attention shifted to Sophie. "Someone's been spoon feeding this stuff to you. Probably hoping this would come out. The question is why?"

"There's only one person I can think of." Duncan sounded glum and sorry to have to make the admission.

"Dad?" Trent asked.

Duncan nodded. He glanced at Sophie and the ache in his chest pounded from where he'd once again given his heart to her and she'd left him battered and bruised.

Was this what love did?

"Sophie?"

She looked up, hope reigning in her expression.

He worked extra hard to keep his skepticism about her actions from thawing. "I assume none of this will make the paper."

Tears pooled. In an instant, he regretted the comment and wanted to take her in his arms. She stood and approached his desk, meeting his eyes directly for the first time since this conversation had started. "I'd never do that to you. You mean everything to me."

The power of her gaze held the same control over him as the soft skin of her touch. She lifted her purse off the desktop and left the room. Her footsteps sounded down the hallway and the front door opened then closed.

Duncan considered running after her, begging for mercy, but his wounded pride kept him stuck in his seat.

"Man." Trent stroked his throat and sent a judgment-filled grimace in Duncan's direction. "You're an idiot."

Chapter 29

A half hour later, Duncan and Trent stood on the icy front stoop of the Tates' 1800s farmhouse. Elmer opened the door, his shoulders hunched over and with an initial look of wrinkled confusion, one quickly replaced with a wary smile.

"Oh. Trent, Duncan. Come on in. It's cold out." He buttoned up his tattered gray cardigan as they stepped inside. "What can I do for you?"

"Sorry to show up unannounced." Duncan caught a whiff of sweet pipe tobacco. "Hope it's not too late."

"Not for me. Otis is upstairs, though. Did you want me to call him down?"

"No. We came to see you." Duncan undid a few buttons on his heavy winter coat, the house warmer than he kept his. He wiped his feet on the floor mat.

"Come have a seat in the parlor. I need to sit." Elmer started a slow, stiff walk into the next room. He lowered himself onto a rocking chair positioned near a small table holding an opened book turned upside down, antique lamp, and a mahogany colored pipe resting in an ashtray.

The old boxed television built into a faded wood console and dated furniture were relics of decades gone by, reminding Duncan of an organized estate sale.

He settled into a clean but worn sofa across from Elmer, close to the brick fireplace. Trent paced the room, acting interested in the knickknacks.

"So, what brings you here?" Elmer's long face, usually clean-shaven, held a prickly late-day shadow. He ran a hand through his thin white hair and glanced at Trent.

Duncan waited to see if Trent would speak, but he seemed to have taken an interest in a Presidents of the U.S. dinner plate hanging on the wall with an image of Richard Nixon dead center. The former President's disgraceful departure seemed fitting given the scandal bringing them here tonight.

Duncan cleared his throat. "We hoped you might help us set the record straight."

"I'll help if I can." The old man cast a nervous glimpse at the staircase.

A few times over the past weeks, Duncan had sensed Elmer had something to tell him, however, Otis kept a tight leash on every conversation.

Trent swung around. "Elmer, I'm not sure you're my father."

Elmer's shoulders sagged and he sighed. "I can't keep up with this lie anymore."

"It's true?" Trent blinked several times.

He nodded, slow and resigned. "Who told you?"

"I found letters Marion wrote. Years ago. Why… I mean how could you…?" Trent's eyes bulged. "Why'd you let me believe you were?"

He sighed. "For Marion. She didn't want me to tell you the truth. She doesn't want anybody to know how she got involved with a married man."

Trent's face paled, his voice a notch above a whisper. "Dad really *is* my father."

Duncan walked over and rested a gentle hand on Trent's shoulder. "Come sit down." He led him back to the sofa where Trent hunched forward and buried his face in his hands.

"Elmer, how'd you get involved?" Duncan grappled with the fact Sophie had uncovered something true and shameful about his family.

"Our families go way back. We were close, like an older brother and sister. When the offer for adoption came through from your mother, Marion asked if I knew a place where she could go and have the baby. I contacted a buddy from the service, from upstate New York. He and his wife had a cottage on their land. Said she was welcome until she had the baby. I visited her sometimes."

Longing in the old man's distant gaze made Duncan speculate he owned stronger feelings for Marion. Another stab of regret at the way he'd treated Sophie struck hard and fast, just like the ones that pummeled him on the drive here.

"As the delivery date neared, she worried the father's name on the birth certificate would be blank. She asked if she could use my name." His lower lip puffed. "She was so ashamed. How could I say no?"

Trent lifted his head. "How could you lie to me?" He spoke slow, his tone thick and throaty.

"I'm sorry." Elmer stared at the floor for a long moment, his shoulders lifting up with a deep sigh. "Does Marion realize you've discovered the truth?"

"Yes, she didn't flat out admit it but didn't deny it either." Trent shrugged. "I promised her I'd never share her past with anyone."

Duncan admired Trent's loyalty to his birth mother and wished he possessed the same devotion to his own.

Elmer's body melted into the chair, suddenly looking tired and even older than when they first arrived. "Marion always felt you were where you belonged. With your real father."

He pointed a crooked finger at Duncan and straightened up in his seat. "Now you listen to me. Sophie Shaw and her family are the ones who should have our property. I never wanted to involve outsiders. Otis and Buzz saw dollar signs."

Footsteps banged on the stairs. Otis appeared in the arched opening to the room. "I figured you'd blow this."

Elmer scowled at his brother. "Otis, I think you were born without a heart." Tears welled and one escaped down his wrinkled cheek. "I refuse to watch this property sold under the guise of a lie. This land means so much to Sophie. All the Moore family."

"Why?" Trent's brows knitted.

Elmer shared details of Sophie's son's death and the memorial. Pain over hurting her earlier crippled Duncan. Would she ever trust him again?

Trent looked at Duncan. "Were you aware of this, about her son?"

"Yes. I wanted to pull the firm's bid, but she wouldn't let me."

Otis muttered a few barely discernible words of disgust and shuffled toward the staircase.

"Wait a second," Duncan said sharply.

Otis turned around.

"Why'd you do this? Why'd you contact my mother?"

Otis sneered. "I didn't. Years ago, she contacted me. Said since Elmer was her son's birth father, she wanted us to call her if the land ever went up for sale."

Duncan's mother had lied. The day she asked Duncan to help with the land, she'd claimed they hunted her down, flat out lied to him to benefit Trent.

Duncan clenched his fists, but it barely bottled his anger. "So you pushed this, even though you knew Elmer wasn't really Trent's father?"

A fleeting moment of indignity crossed the old man's face. "Nobody knew the truth except me, my brother, and Marion."

Duncan shook his head. "You misled Buzz."

"I wasn't about to tell him. I needed his help with the board to get through the zoning changes." He looked between Duncan and Trent.

Disgrace for his family's lies and his father's history made Duncan want to change everything, to do the right thing, for once.

"Elmer, Otis... We could still have a deal. But this time, we're going to work on my terms."

* * * *

Sophie lowered the volume on the TV, thinking she heard a noise outside. Bella, who rested at her side curled in a tight ball, lifted her head and uttered a low growl. "Shh. The kids are sleeping."

When she didn't hear the sound again, she turned up the volume, but had lost interest in the program. She closed her tired, sore eyes and tipped her head back on the sofa.

She'd cried most of the way home from Duncan's. The tears finally slowed, replaced by irritation over his righteous attitude. His reaction surpassed upset.

The sandy dog's head cocked just as Sophie heard the faint sound of a car door shutting. Bella barked, hopped to the floor, and raced to the door.

"Quiet!" Sophie headed to the window.

The dog gave one last final yip.

Nobody who knew her would visit after ten. An insistent knock at the door made her consider her tartan plaid flannels and Mike's old sweatshirt. She peeked out the window. Duncan's car sat in the middle of the driveway, headlights on and still running.

What'd he want, another chance to bash her with his harsh judgments and make a quick get away? Swallowing the little bit of pride she had left, she opened the door.

Duncan stood with his hands shoved in his jacket pockets and stared back with the remorseful, terrified face of a man who'd just made the worst mistake of his life.

"I'm sorry, Sophie." Duncan's unexpected words rushed her. "Please tell me I haven't lost you."

Sophie's heart had flat-lined on the way home. Twice circumstances got in their way and twice Duncan didn't even give her a fighting chance.

"Say something." An urgent puff of condensation filled the night air, and he reached for her hand. "We just left Elmer Tate's. I didn't want to wait to apologize. What I said... I've made a horrible mistake." His voice lost some power. "Will you forgive me?"

Sophie pulled away from his warm grip. "Forgive you?" She shook her head. "I've made some mistakes, but you shut me out the second things don't go as planned. Same way you did that night at the studio. This is no way to start a relationship." His sad eyes threatened her resolve so she looked past his shoulder. Trent sat in the passenger seat.

"You're right."

She shifted her gaze back to him as he scrubbed his hand over his cheek.

"I was shocked about my father. Truly shocked. I know you were just the messenger, but hearing my family kept this secret, well, it seemed surreal. It hurt."

"That didn't make right to hurt me."

He frowned. "No. It didn't. Please accept my apology."

The wheels of logic churned and she tried to stand in his shoes. She'd dumped many things on him tonight. Things she'd known about for a long time.

She blew out a breath. "Duncan, I expected you to be upset. I just hoped you wouldn't push me away so..." She swallowed. "So coldly. God, don't you understand how I feel about you?"

He took her hands again and this time she didn't pull away. "I guess things hurt more when they come from people we care about. I admit I overreacted."

Rock music filled the air and they both glanced toward the car as the window lowered.

Trent waved. "Hey there, Sophie. Look, I know my brother can be a little hotheaded, but I still love him. He gave me a second chance when nobody else would. He deserves one too."

Duncan's jaw unhinged. "I swear I didn't ask him to say that."

Trent's comment reminded her how Duncan cared about others, how he worked hard to change the way he'd handled his life in the past.

The tense pull in her shoulders relaxed. "An un-coerced endorsement like that can't be ignored." She offered a slight smile. "I know I've made mistakes too, but so help me God, Duncan, next time we have a problem, you'd better count to ten and be willing to work on it with me. In return, I'll tell you every little thing from now on. So much so you'll be begging me to stop."

His face softened. "I promise. If ten doesn't work, I'll count to twenty. And about what you said on your way out..." He inhaled deeply. "You mean everything to me too."

The ache in her chest lifted. She threaded her hands around his strong neck and he wrapped her in his arms, pulling her close. He kissed her, so tender and filled with affection that it would be impossible to stay mad at him.

Trent applauded from the car. Maybe Sophie had misjudged him.

They stopped kissing. Duncan grinned and his eyes sparkled. "Now, if I can come in for a minute, I want to talk about the Tates' land. I'm done with it, but you're not and I've got an offer you won't be able to refuse."

She asked him to come inside. Once they got settled on the sofa, he drew in a nervous breath. "I withdrew my offer on the land." He studied her, his expectation obvious. "It's all yours."

"I guess that's great, but owning the land carries other stresses. I've told you. Mostly financial."

Duncan curled the corner of his lip upward, one of those cat-who-ate-the-canary grins. "What if that wasn't the case?"

"Why?"

"After I removed my offer, I asked the brothers if they'd agree to accept the previously agreed upon price with your family."

"But the money is still—"

"Please. May I finish?" He waited and she nodded. "I'd like to offer to buy a percentage of the business. Not RGI." He tapped his chest with his finger. "Me. As a silent partner."

All the times she'd watched Duncan in any setting, he'd never been silent.

He frowned. "What?"

"The offer is generous. Amazing, in fact." She touched his forearm. "If I were to be honest, I can tell you're a take-charge kind of guy. I don't want your presence to overpower the rest of us, no matter how well intended."

Duncan's chin buckled as he thought. "Okay. Thanks for being honest, but I still think this can work." He took her hands. "Things are busy at RGI right now, so I won't get involved with much of anything. Maybe you guys can tap into my expertise with the business end. Or marketing." He cocked a confident grin, one as sure as a poker player who'd just laid down the winning hand.

"I suppose we could use some help. Having another owner would sure boost our financial situation. We'll have to talk to Dad and Jay."

Sophie sifted through a list of pros and cons, one large con stood in the forefront.

He studied her closely. "Now what?"

"I hate to be Debbie Downer, but what if something happens between us?"

"I thought about that, but the way I feel with you, I only plan on us getting closer. A lot closer. Don't you feel that way?"

The story of her life had just turned a page and her entire existence on Blue Moon Lake suddenly fell into place. "You bet I do."

Chapter 30

Sophie's stomach growled. The aroma of coffee and grease cut through the air in the old-fashioned diner, located outside of Bloomfield, Connecticut. She glanced around the busy eatery, hoping to spot the waitress with her omelet. Skipping breakfast before work hadn't been her smartest move. She never dreamed the interview would take until almost lunchtime.

This morning's trip to a Bloomfield farm was due to another collapsed barn roof. The state's farmers were used to harsh winters, but this year soared to a new level. Repeated snowfalls had caused over a hundred buckled roofs on barns, greenhouses, and sheds statewide. Today's interview brought tears to her eyes as she spoke with a farmer whose barn roof caved in from the weight of the snow, killing a baby calf. This year, she'd welcome spring with open arms and a martini.

The busboy filled her water glass. She traced the loop of her silver hoop earring with her finger and held on to the last tidbits of her reconciliation with Duncan last night. Her heart softened as she remembered how eager he'd been when he came inside to tell her his idea, showing how much this whole thing meant to him.

Another customer shimmying into the booth behind her jarred her back to the diner. She glanced at her watch. By now he'd reached Bronxville, to speak with his father. Frank Jamieson had every reason to keep his family away from Northbridge, even toss Sophie clues to scare Duncan into reconsidering any move to Northbridge.

The waitress, a matronly woman wearing a gray uniform a little snug along the bust line, arrived with Sophie's egg-white and veggie omelet. "Want a coffee refill, hon?"

"No thanks."

She closed her notebook and ate with half an eye out the window. The sunny day promised to be snow-free, a relief since the sides of the roads and edges of parking lots were filled to capacity with mountains of white.

Two men left together and headed to the parked cars outside Sophie's window. They stopped at a white Range Rover and faced each other. Sophie lowered her fork, and did a double take at the man with carrot-orange hair tucked under his wool hat. Only one person she knew had such a distinct hair color: Joe Dougherty. When he turned sideways, her suspicions were confirmed.

The other person had his back to her and talked as the Northbridge Zoning Board member peered nervously around the lot. Joe's position on the board was an unpaid, elected service to his community. He'd been out of work for the past year and recently got a new job in medical sales. Maybe this was a sales call.

She studied his cohort, a classy dresser. At an angle, with his scarf bundled around his neck, dark fedora, and black dress coat buttoned to his chin, only his eyes and nose were visible. The stranger removed keys, aimed at a Range Rover and the taillights flickered.

The car had New York plates. Sophie squinted at the dealer insignia. "Land Rover Manhattan." Joe still seemed stiff and uncomfortable. Not a good quality for a salesman.

She slowly nibbled at her omelet and watched. After a minute, they shook hands and Joe went to his car. The other man got inside the SUV and shut his door. He seemed familiar, although she couldn't place why. Through his rear window, she caught movements as he removed his hat and scarf. The car backed up and the driver's side window faced her view. She caught the driver's profile.

A gentle shock raced through her. Yes, she not only knew him, but these two men together just might be the missing piece of a puzzle she'd been trying to solve. She dialed Duncan's number and hoped to catch him before he spoke to his father. She got his voice mail. "It's Sophie. Call me as soon as you can."

* * * *

Entering Bronxville, NY, Duncan zipped through the Pondfield Road underpass and admired the Spanish style of the nearby train station, unusual architecture for the area. As he passed a bright yellow awning of a local florist, he made a mental note to stop there on his way out to get Sophie flowers.

A minute later, he turned onto the street of his childhood home. Nervous pings ricocheted in his gut. Dad was never easy to talk to, but today Duncan would demand honesty, for once in their lives.

He pulled into the driveway of the white-brushed brick house, a few minutes early for their lunch. Trent had driven his own car from Hartford and hadn't arrived yet. Towering leafless maples and beech trees surrounded their lot. The place he grew up suddenly seemed naked, exposed to him in a way he'd never noticed before.

At the front door, he pulled out his cell and saw Sophie had left a message. He'd call her later. With a quick knock on the door, Duncan walked inside. "Dad?" He entered the foyer.

"In here." Frank Jamieson's tired voice came from the kitchen.

Duncan threw his coat over the usual chair, pushed up the sleeves on his sweater, and went in. His father sat at a cherry, rectangular table, looking lost amidst the high-end, stainless steel cooking equipment and made-to-order cabinetry. He glanced from the *Wall Street Journal* and then closed the paper.

"Hi, Duncan." He hoisted himself from the seat, giving a slight grunt, and headed toward the counter. "Mom ordered us these sandwiches from the deli I like."

"Good." Duncan went to the refrigerator. "Want a beer or soda?"

"Beer sounds good."

He grabbed two and handed one to his dad then sat at the opposite end of the rectangular table. "Trent must be running a little late."

Frank put the sandwiches on the table's center. "I'm starving. He won't care if we start." They twisted the caps off their drinks and started lunch in silence.

"So, you said on the phone you'd removed your bid on that farmland." Frank avoided eye contact with Duncan as he opened the paper wrapper on his sandwich "Any chance you'll come to your senses and move back here too?"

"Not a chance in hell."

The old man looked up, his hard stare the same as always, but now full-blown bags hung beneath his lids. He pursed his lips and didn't respond.

Duncan wrapped his hand around the cold bottle. "In fact, I'm hoping you can explain to me why my purchases there matter so much to you."

"My son's well-being matters to me."

Duncan snorted. "Even Trent's?"

"What the hell is that supposed to mean?"

Duncan's heart thumped against his ribcage. "Care to talk about what happened with Marion Harris? Or I believe you knew her as Marion Price."

The color drained from his dad's face. "What are you talking about?"

"I know all about you two and the results of your affair."

Frank shut his lids and his posture sagged. He slowly opened his eyes, now glistening from tears.

"Why'd you have to go back there?" Frank put down the beer bottle with a bang.

"So it's true?" Duncan couldn't believe he'd given in so easily to his bluff, didn't even try to fight when caught in the lie of his life.

"I'm getting too old to play games anymore. Why do you think I didn't want you to move there?"

"Jesus Christ, Dad. How could you do that to Mom? Or to Marion?"

Frank dropped his chin to his chest and didn't answer.

"Why'd you take us there those summers?"

"Your mother insisted." His weary voice struggled and he looked up.

"You should've sold the house after what you did to Marion."

"Your mother wouldn't let me," he grumbled. "She reminded me how the place belonged to my granddad. How we'd spent some lovely summers there." He dropped a shame-filled gaze to the tabletop. "I proposed to her there." He covered his mouth with his hand, highlighting his agony-filled eyes. His hand slid down and clunked on the table. "She has no idea Trent's mine."

"Why the affair? Did you and Mom have problems?"

"Not at first. The fertility problem left us stressed." He studied his hands. "Things were so relaxed with Marion." He paused, as if reliving some memories, then met Duncan's stare. "The pregnancy gave me a reality dose. I offered her money for an abortion, but she refused."

Duncan recoiled, not even bothering to hide his disgust.

His father glared. "Don't judge me. You weren't a model husband either. Besides, I never dreamed her child would end up in my household." He frowned and shifted his focus to the tabletop. "Your mother would have left me if I'd told her the truth. Damned if I did the right thing by coming clean. Damned every day having to be near a child I'd had by another woman. I took the second. But Trent served as a reminder every single day of my infidelity."

"Is that what I am?" Trent stood in the doorway. He held his head high, but his cheeks flamed red. "I'm just your damned mistake!"

Frank Jamieson's mouth fell open and he blinked as if he'd seen a ghost. "Trent, I didn't mean for you to hear that."

"Too late." Trent turned to leave.

"Wait!" Frank blew out a defeated last breath. "I've wanted things between us to be different. Why'd you make it so hard? The drinking, the drugs."

Trent's lips tightened as if he held back a thought, then he turned away and left the room.

Duncan shook his head. "What's wrong with you? Are you behind the recent bribery rumors in Northbridge too?"

The lines of his forehead creased. "What bribery rumors?"

"Rumors going around Northbridge that someone's trying to influence the zoning board's vote." He snorted a laugh. "Jesus, Dad. Don't act like my asking is completely out of line. Someone dug up the story about the gunshot at Buzz's house and left a note about you bribing officials. I figured you were trying to scare me off buying the land."

Tomato red inched up his father's face. "Duncan. I swear to you, it's not me. I've not busied myself in your affairs since last time." His gaze dropped to the floor. "Your mother threatened to leave me if I did."

The news his mother even cared about his happiness surprised Duncan.

Frank toyed with his beer bottle but didn't drink any. "How'd you find out what happened at the Harris' house?"

"Northbridge is small. Things don't ever go away." He didn't want to tell him about Sophie's involvement. Their relationship would involve extended family. Dad liked to hold a grudge.

A tear spilled along Frank's cheek. "Son, deserting Marion fills me with shame. Cheating on your mother fills me with shame. She doesn't know. If you tell her, our lives will be ruined."

Despite what he'd done, Duncan teetered on the edge of sadness for his father, yet his remorse for Trent went deeper. He stood. "The way you treated Trent should fill you with shame too. You two should talk this out. I'm going to find him."

Frank Jamieson's face contorted, more terrified than Duncan had ever witnessed, then he bowed his head into his hands, for once, a defeated man.

* * * *

Sophie carried the bouquet of wildflowers Duncan had just handed her into the kitchen while he tossed his coat on the coatrack. Placing them on the counter, she stretched up to get a vase. Duncan slipped his hands around her waist and she turned into his embrace. He brushed his warm lips to hers while the heady aroma of soap and sandalwood wooed her like a scented aphrodisiac.

She nestled her nose near his neck, closed her lids, and inhaled a deep breath. "Yankee Candle should sell your scent." She sensed his smile.

"Oh? What would they call it?"

"Hmm? Good question." She tipped her head back and caught his grin, happy to see him so relaxed after talking with his dad. "They could call your candle something like 'Seduct her.' A play on seductor."

"I think I should help the winery naming the wines, especially after hearing that one."

"Quit while you're ahead." She smoothed her palm against the grain of his cheek. "Mmm. I love a little stubble."

"Since you're seducing me, I guess the kids aren't around?"

"Nope. They're with friends. I'm glad we're alone. Before we get too sidetracked, you won't believe what I saw today."

"Sidetracked, huh." He leered, gave her bottom a gentle pat, and released her. "How about we open this and talk?" Duncan picked up a bag and pulled out a bottle of *Cristal* champagne. "To celebrate your new land purchase."

Sophie questioned if the price point on the popular drink spoke to the quality but kept the thought hidden. "Wonderful. Thanks."

He worked at removing the foil-wrapped top. "Is this news why we played phone tag all day?"

"Yup. Too good to leave in a message." She took two champagne flutes from the upper cabinet. "I had breakfast at a diner outside of Bloomfield after covering a story. I spotted Joe Dougherty from our zoning board with your assistant, Carl Hansen."

"Are you sure the man was Carl. Have you two even met?"

"I'm positive. He ushered me to your office the day I interviewed you."

Duncan pursed his lips, unbuttoned the sleeves of his soft flannel shirt, and folded them up his forearm, looking more rural Connecticut than ever. "There's no reason why the two of them would need to speak. Especially today." He paused. "Maybe they've become friends. Carl did have to work with people in Northbridge about the plans."

"Guess anything is possible. But on my first interview with you, when I signed the front desk register, I saw Joe had been at RGI a couple days before me."

"Who'd he visit?"

"I tried to snoop but your receptionist politely removed the book."

He snickered. "Good ol' Sally. Nobody gets anything by her. Can you find the approximate date of your appointment?"

"I think so." Sophie went to her bag and removed her work calendar.

"I'll call our Chief of Security, Earl." Duncan reached into his shirt pocket and took out his phone. "He can check the registers for me right now."

She found the date and Duncan explained to Earl what they needed. While they waited, he slipped an arm around her waist, drew her close, and nestled his nose in her hair. "Thank you for telling me."

She enjoyed his closeness. "There's more."

He let his hand slip. "Oh?"

"A few other things don't add up. Joe always—and I mean *always*—votes with Buzz. On the zoning decision delay in December, he didn't. Remember?"

"I do."

"On top of that, my friend Veronica works at the library. She confirmed the printout with the story about a gunshot at Buzz's came off microfiche requested by Jane Dougherty, Joe's wife. Maybe they were trying to scare Buzz into dropping support for the project. Why, though, I can't figure out."

"My dad claims he had nothing to do with those notes. But Carl? I can't imagine he'd ever—" Duncan held up a finger. "Yes, Earl." He listened, thanked him, then hung up. "Joe visited Carl."

Duncan traced the speckled pattern of the granite countertop with his index finger. "How would Carl know anything about...?" He hit a few buttons on the phone. "Time to talk to my brother."

Chapter 31

"Can I offer you a cup of coffee?" Jane Dougherty reached out and took Duncan's and Adli's coats.

The two men glanced at each other then Duncan said, "No thank you. I'm sorry we didn't call first."

While his wife hung the coats in a small closet near the front door, Joe stood in the foyer and watched in silence. He blinked and slowly rubbed the back of his neck, more uncomfortable than Duncan had ever seen him.

"Well, then, why don't you join us in the kitchen," Joe finally said then turned and walked down a short hallway.

As they followed, Duncan marveled at how luck had stepped over to his side when Sophie spotted Carl at the diner yesterday. His call to Trent had filled in the missing pieces. Trent readily admitted how, back when he first came to RGI, he'd gone to a bar with Carl and shared the story of what happened at Buzz's house decades earlier. Tequila shots could be quite revealing.

By noon the next day, Duncan had uncovered phone records showing multiple calls made from Carl's line to Joe over the course of the project. Alone, they proved nothing. Sophie had suggested that, as chairman of the zoning board, Adli be pulled into the loop. He'd come up with the idea for tonight's surprise visit.

Joe motioned with a hand flip to the kitchen table and they sat down.

Adli wasted no time. "Joe, we have some concerns about foul play on the board with regard to RGI's proposal."

Jane neatened a pile of opened mail at the counter, but Duncan caught her nervous glances at her husband.

Joe ran a fingertip around the curved edge of the rounded table then shrugged. "Yeah, I remember the rumor."

Adli reached into his breast pocket and removed the documents Sophie had acquired back in November and unfolded them. "Any idea what this is about?" He handed them to Joe, whose mustache twitched as he took them.

While he read, Jane loaded some dishes from the sink into the dishwasher, but kept glancing over her shoulder and smoothing her hair.

Duncan hadn't forgotten Sophie's suspicions about the woman's possible involvement. "Jane?"

The plump woman fumbled the plate she'd been about to put in the dishwasher but regained control, slipped it in the slot and looked his way. "Yes?"

"Come take a look." He motioned to the pages Joe held. "Do these mean anything to you?"

Jane stepped over, peeked at the papers. She shook her head, a jumpy gesture making her reddish-brown curls bounce.

Adli glanced at Duncan then turned to Joe. "Back at our December meeting, I found your 'no' vote a surprise. You and Buzz having problems?"

Joe's lips locked zipper-tight, but a peep escaped from Jane.

"This is ridiculous," she finally blurted out. "They know, Joe. Let's not drag this out." Her lower lip quivered as she fought tears. "I left those notes about the Jamiesons at the *Gazette*."

Joe's jaw dropped then his shoulders wilted. "I can't live like this anymore. Yes, I know what's behind those notes."

Joe's voice choked with tears as he unveiled a plan set in motion by Duncan's assistant, Carl, to hire Joe to manipulate things behind the scenes in Northbridge. Carl's plan stemmed from his knowledge of the Jamiesons' Achilles' heel in Northbridge and Trent's prior bribery accusations at RGI. Joe had planted a rumor about bribery, easily exaggerated with the gossip mongers around town. Carl had hoped Trent would be under suspicion because of his past with Lake Simcoe and get fired.

"How could you, Joe?" Adli spoke softly, reminding Duncan how these men had known each other a lifetime.

The zoning board member stared at his folded hands. "Look, I didn't want the project either so I figured Buzz might back off his interest in RGI's investment out of fear his wife's past would rise to the surface. Sophie was a perfect middleman. The press probing into this wouldn't raise suspicions."

Adli slowly shook his head. "You never should have taken that man's money."

A tear slipped down Joe's cheek. "I'd lost my job. We almost lost the house. Those damn credit cards were easy cash, but then we had so much debt. More than a man should have at my age." He slowly lowered his head, his shame obvious. "This was a way out. I'm sorry."

Duncan felt bad for the guy, the circumstances enough to make anybody take desperate measures. Carl, on the other hand, had no good excuse and would pay for this.

* * * *

"Thanks, Derrick. Everything's set. You guys did a great job." Duncan hung up.

Hiring Derrick Martin's private investigation firm had proven to be worth every cent. In the past, he'd used them when he suspected anything seedy about someone he had to deal with on a new property. Today's dealing with the PI firm crossed a line between work and personal.

He'd asked Carl to come to his office when the workday ended. Duncan's nerves pulsed, jittery with aggravation that an employee he'd trusted had worked against him. He suppressed an urge to punch the traitor right in the jaw.

He flipped through the mail to keep busy and a few minutes later, Carl swaggered in. "Hey, Boss."

"Have a seat." Duncan put the mail aside and pulled in front of him the neatened pile of damning evidence.

Carl plunked into his usual chair, comfortable and confident. "What's up?"

Duncan handed off the small stack of phone records. "These highlighted calls should help answer your question."

Carl looked at the data, but his face remained unreadable. He looked up.

"Recognize the number?" Duncan spoke firm, in his no-nonsense voice.

Carl blinked several times and shifted uncomfortably in his seat. "One of the guys from Northbridge. Joe, I think. He had some questions about the project.

Duncan pushed a manila folder across the desk to Carl. "Why don't you tell me what this is then?"

Carl hesitantly opened the folder, the way someone would if they expected a hornet to fly out. One by one, he turned each page of the contents. His skin paled from healthy beige to pasty white.

The photos, taken this morning by the PI firm, showed Carl and Joe in their booth at the same diner where Sophie had spotted them. According to Joe, his final payment from Carl would come when RGI formally withdrew from the project, which Duncan had already done. Joe, as part of the agreement to avoid charges against him, set the wheels in motion to meet with Carl for the payoff, done under surveillance.

"Why, Carl?" Duncan's ire rose. "What'd you stand to gain from this?"

Carl's posture shrunk and his gaze dimmed. "I left my other job because I wanted to run this place someday. The day you brought Trent into the firm, it changed everything. I wanted him fired."

It occurred to Duncan how close Carl came to getting his wish when Duncan had a brief loss of faith in his brother. In hindsight, after Trent was handed more responsibility, Carl occasionally grumbled over the way Trent had handled certain work matters. Never would Duncan have dreamed, though, Carl's hatred for Trent ran so deep.

Duncan recalled the one loose end. "One thing. How'd you get the *Courant* to write a damning report about Bernadette Felton?"

Carl looked out the window. "My buddy is the reporter who wrote the article. He'd just been hired by them, so I called the paper's owner on your behalf. Said you wanted the guy to interview her and dig up anything he could to discredit the group."

Duncan's jaw clenched tight. Betrayal of this kind would not be tolerated. He lifted the phone handset and dialed. "Earl, you can come in now." He hung up. "Security is on their way to escort you after you clean your office. It goes without saying you're fired. I hired an auditor who's been working with accounting. I know the cash you gave Joe came from our bank account. Expect to hear from the police. Now, get the hell out."

Chapter 32

April

The sound of bells woke Sophie. She squinted at her nightstand clock. A few minutes before eight. The chimes signaled the early service at St. John's Lutheran Church, or as Pastor Dave jokingly called them, "the competition."

Some productive birds chirped outside the window and sun peeked through the tab curtains, leaving the bedroom bright and sunny. Winter had finally left Northbridge. A season change was never more welcomed. The record snowfalls through February were now considered a once in a blue moon event. She rolled over and snuggled closer to Duncan and found him wide awake.

"Morning, sleepyhead." He pushed a few stray hairs away from her face. "Did the bells wake you?"

"Mmm-hmm." She stretched her arms above her head and yawned.

Duncan slipped a hand beneath the oversized Patriot's T-shirt she'd thrown on to sleep in, resting his palm on the dip of her waist.

"You know, my mother said the bells of love chimed when she met Dad." Sophie rubbed her sleepy eyes. "That's how she knew it was the real deal."

"I thought those were for the church service."

She laughed. "I'm simply reporting the facts, funny guy. Not analyzing them. What time are we meeting your parents at your uncle's house?"

"One. Guess we should get up soon." He showed no signs of leaving the bed. He smoothed his palm along a slow trail from her waist to her lower back. "Mike's expecting us to pick up the kids in Stamford at twelve thirty. Right?"

"Yup." Her heart elevated, swept into the tidal wave of longing in his gaze.

In a few short months, her life had taken a hard turn. At the age of forty-four, she finally stood on solid footing with both love and life, all on the same grounds where she'd lived a lifetime of happiness and tragedy. Grounds which held her future too. Plans were well underway with the vineyard. Jay had already checked the current irrigation system, done some soil testing, and ordered some dormant vines to add to the existing lot.

Duncan eyed her with longing. "Uncle Stan's house in Westport is about twenty minutes away from Mike's. My parents are punctual."

She pressed her hands to his chest. "Are you implying I'm not?"

"Yes." He grinned. "We don't want you to be late the first time you meet them." Duncan's relaxed face slipped into concern.

"What's wrong?"

"I haven't seen Dad since Trent and I had our long talk at lunch almost two months ago."

She shifted closer, his soft caress of her backside driving her wild. "It'll be fine. The worst is over."

"I hope so. Trent called me yesterday when he and Patrick got into the city. He's taking today's gathering in stride. My uncle's place is good neutral territory for us to get together." He pressed Sophie's torso against his and warmth flooded her core. "One of the benefits of our time alone is Pat loves hanging out with his uncle on these weekends. He told me the other day 'Uncle Trent is so cool.' How come he doesn't see me that way?"

"Because, Fonzie, Trent would never use a word like cool." Sophie massaged his shoulders. "I think you're pretty cool."

He dipped his head and kissed her throat.

"Speaking of nerves." She twirled her fingertips in the curls of his sandy chest hair. "Do you think meeting your family is easy for me? The tackle shop owner's daughter isn't exactly serious dating material for the son of a prominent New York City lawyer. Plus, your uncle's a U.S. senator."

"First off, my uncle is a down-to-earth, great guy. As far as my parents go, who I'm with is my concern. Besides, they'd be crazy to not love you."

"Says you." Sophie had her doubts.

"We're getting sidetracked." Duncan slid his gaze from her eyes to her mouth then he gave her a quick kiss. "I've got a proposition for you."

She snickered. "I'd have said yes without the really bad come-on line."

He smirked and wrapped his solid leg over hers in a playful lock position. "I'm serious."

"Okay. Shoot." She tried to pull her leg from his pin, but he held her firm and fought a smile.

"I've wanted to cut down my office hours and spend more time in Northbridge. The new guy I've hired to replace Carl is great. Plus, I've been doing some reading on vineyards."

Sophie stopped her futile struggle.

"With Jay busy planting, I could spread myself between the tackle shop and the vineyard. Now before you get your knickers in a bundle, I don't intend to take over. I'm asking as someone who can learn from you guys. I'll work behind the scenes."

She considered his proposal. The idea of spending more time together sounded wonderful.

"Look at it like this. I'll be working for you." He tugged at the bottom of her T-shirt. "Aren't you getting warm with this on?"

She playfully swatted his hand away. "Now who's not being serious?"

"So? What about my proposal?"

"Jay is warming up to you these days. Plus, I'd love for us to see more of you." She paused. "I can't promise great pay."

"We'll negotiate." The lines of his face relaxed. "Bartering can be a very useful tool."

"It can be." Sophie slid her fingers through the curls of his messy hair. "Maybe Jay can give you fishing lessons in exchange for your help."

"That wasn't what I had in mind," he replied, the husky tone igniting her arousal even further.

"You should take it. I drive a harder bargain than my brother."

His grin disappeared behind the look she now knew spoke to his love. A clear sign the path she'd followed in life kept her in Northbridge for a good reason.

Meet the Author

Sharon Struth is an award-winning author who believes it's never too late for a second chance in love or life. When she's not writing, she and her husband happily sip their way through the scenic towns of the Connecticut Wine Trail. Sharon writes from the small town of Bethel, Connecticut, the friendliest place she's ever lived. For more information, including where to find her other novels and published essays, please visit www.sharonstruth.com.

Keep reading for a special sneak peek of Sharon Struth's new Blue Moon Lake novella:

TWELVE NIGHTS

True love waits forever…

For Erik Lindholm, it's been a long climb to the top of his company. Now, as president he has the power to bring his vision to life and speed his company in bold new directions. If that means a complete staff overhaul, so be it. If that means firing the woman who left his heart in tatters fifteen years earlier, it's a business decision, not personal…

Beryl Foster is highly competent and respected by everyone at the office. But rumors of a big shake-up are rampant and—surprisingly, scarily—Beryl's job as CFO is on the line. Fifteen years ago she made a decision to put her career before everything else. It was also the last time she and Erik shared a life together. Every Christmas is a reminder. This one could be a second chance…

A Lyrical e-book on sale November 2015.

Learn more about Sharon at
http://www.kensingtonbooks.com/author.aspx/31604

Chapter 1

On the first day of Christmas, my true love gave to me—
A necklace with a heart key.

"If you value your reputation, you'll get moving."

Darcy's clear and calm voice jarred Beryl. Before she could respond, Darcy looped her arm through Beryl's and pulled her from the doorway into the crowded room.

"Didn't you see that mistletoe overhead?" Darcy raised her classically thick eyebrows, darker versions of the ones that made Brooke Shields famous years ago. "Chase was on his way over and he had his sights set on you."

Together, they neared Chase Stockard, VP of Communications for Global Business Solutions. His charisma had landed him the prime role dealing with the firm's media issues, plus the attention of most women in the office.

His Ken-doll smile turned into a frown. "Aw, ladies." He arched an eyebrow. "Catch you next time around?"

"Or save the mistletoe moves for outside the office," Darcy said, her tone stern, her brows lifted. "All due respect."

Chase laughed it off, and headed for a gaggle of females not far away.

"He really ticks me off." Darcy tossed back her hair, dark as onyx and always worn to the shoulder with a little flip. "I'm beginning to wonder if anybody listened to me at last summer's sexual harassment workshop."

Darcy took her job as director of human resources seriously. She once claimed to view corporate policy with the reverence of the Ten Commandments. Beryl was especially glad her best friend had stopped Chase. A mistletoe kiss might not be a big deal for some women, but in Beryl's position with the firm, others would talk.

They blended into a sea of formalwear, mostly black mixed with every imaginable shade of red. Beryl gazed at the Temple of Dendur, just ahead as they moved through her favorite room at the Metropolitan Museum of Art. Amber spotlights illuminated the sandstone structure. Around it were tables covered with crisp linens and bowl candle centerpieces, gleaming balls of gold light befitting the royal display. As a backdrop to the temple, a floor-to-ceiling projection screen played a continuous hypnotic loop of cascading snowflakes falling against a dark sky.

Darcy leaned close to Beryl's ear. "Did you hear the rumor he's dating a new copywriter?"

"He who?"

"Chase. She's a subordinate, works in his own department. That's pretty much the mother of all inter-office dating rule violations."

"Thank goodness men like that are a rare breed." Beryl didn't want to discuss gossip. She had her own worries tonight. "Ready for another drink?"

"Lead the way." Darcy grabbed a bite-sized quiche from a server passing by them with a tray, and popped it into her mouth.

Beryl moved slower than usual in the satin dress covered by a black lace overlay, a nice change from her usual corporate attire. Leaving her arms bare, the gown showed a peek of skin beneath the satin near the scooped neckline. A fitted silhouette followed the curve of her hip, and gently flared from the knee down. Though most of her immediate peers were men, she refused to dress like one.

"Any idea why they've thrown the Christmas party so early this year?" Darcy dodged a waiter holding a tray of fluted champagne glasses. "Thanksgiving was only last weekend."

"Saul's choice. I'm pretty sure it's so he can announce his replacement tonight."

"And you really don't know who it is?"

"One, if I did, I wouldn't tell you standing in this crowd of our coworkers. Second, this is the best kept secret since what was hidden inside Al Capone's vault."

Darcy laughed. "Probably will end up being as anticlimactic as the vault unveiling, too. Word around the office is that Rob Peterson is a shoo-in."

Beryl shrugged. As chief financial officer, she ranked high enough on the scale to be considered as Saul's replacement, too. Most expected someone with a sales or marketing background and many would argue that at the age of thirty-nine, she wasn't experienced enough to oversee the company.

Beryl glanced both ways and dropped her voice. "I hope he chooses someone from inside Global. An outsider will surely bring in some of his or her own upper level staff. I may get tossed out on the street with a pink slip."

A sick pit settled in her gut. She'd been with this company her whole career and had given up everything else to achieve success. Losing the job by being fired would be more than humiliating. It would leave her empty-handed in life.

Darcy hoisted up the neckline of her strapless dress, her willowy frame without the meat to hold up the attire. "You shouldn't worry. Anybody would be out of their mind to get rid of you."

"The entire executive board is worried. Saul promoted us to these jobs and was our boss. If his replacement comes from outside the company, nobody is safe." Beryl tipped her head to the bar. "Come on. Let's get those drinks."

As they walked, she kept an eye open for the firm president, Saul Weinstein. Mentor. Friend. Ten years ago, he'd transferred her from the Boston office to be part of his management team. They were so much alike when it came to their work ethics and beliefs, they could nearly read each other's minds with a glance across the boardroom table. The faith he put in her abilities from the start had given her the incentive to work long, hard hours.

They ordered two glasses of Moscato and joined Darcy's husband, Will, who stood talking to a few people from Darcy's department. Saul appeared at the entrance, his full head of white hair like a beacon in any crowded room. He turned halfway, his mouth moving as he spoke with someone still outside the doorway. Beryl's heartbeat quickened, this anticipation more nerve-racking than she realized.

She elbowed Darcy. "Saul's here."

Their group went silent, all eyes on the firm president. He turned around and came into the room, someone directly behind him. At the same time, a small group came through the other set of double doors, swallowing both Saul and the person she suspected was her new boss into the crowd.

"Did you see who he's with?" Beryl whispered to Darcy, who stood several inches taller.

She shook her head.

Saul appeared at a podium set up at the temple's front facade. The hum of voices subsided and people started to clap. Beryl put down her drink to join the applause.

Saul cleared his throat into the microphone. "Welcome to this year's Christmas gala. I hope the food and wine makes up for such humble surroundings." Chuckles rumbled through the crowd. "Rather than torture you all with further guessing, I do plan to announce my successor tonight." He scanned the room, a subdued expression appearing on his age-lined face. "I almost can't believe the company I started forty years ago has grown to such heights. So many memories. The day we went public. The day we hit four thousand employees, operating in twenty countries across the globe." He raised a brow and motioned with his hand to his wife, who Beryl knew quite well. "And yet, my wife informs me that it's time I moved on. In three days, she's putting me on a plane to take that grand European trip I never had time for."

The crowd laughed. Beryl perched on the tips of her sling-back pumps and tried to catch an early glimpse of whoever had followed Saul inside. Nothing stood out but familiar faces. She returned to her normal stance as a knot twisted tight in her stomach.

"In selecting my replacement, I asked myself one question. Who could take the top-notch crew I have here now and guide Global to great heights in the future? Although we possess huge talent within our fine organization, I wanted a fresh take on the business and decided to search outside of our four walls."

Disappointment rushed through Beryl. Time to update her resume, just in case.

"So, without further ado, I'd like you to welcome the new president of Global Business Solutions—believe it or not a former employee of our firm—Erik Lindholm."

Beryl's body numbed. Loud applause faded in the background as his name pounded inside her skull. It couldn't be. It wasn't possible.

Erik stepped up to the platform and shook Saul's hand. Beryl blinked, thinking this might be a bad dream, a hallucination, or one too many trips to the bar.

Darcy touched Beryl's arm, ruling out the first two. "A former employee?"

Beryl was too stunned to speak or even nod. Erik's dirty-blond hair was still parted on the side and worn short, with thick wisps sweeping his high forehead. He smiled, making the dimpled cleft in his chin deepen and softening the rugged angles of his sculpted face. Old emotions bubbled to the surface. Love. Happiness. Anger.

Erik shook hands with employees seated near the podium, his smile still as confident as it had been years ago. Last she'd heard, Erik worked in Chicago and teetered at the top of the corporate ladder with The Holder Group, a competitor of Global's who could never quite beat her firm's status as number one in the industry. The same firm Erik had gone to after they split up nearly fourteen years ago.

"Did you ever hear of this guy before?" Darcy whispered in Beryl's ear.

Beryl nodded, her gaze stuck on the man she'd almost married.

* * * *

"Good to see you, Samir. You look great. Haven't changed a bit since college." Erik embraced the hand of Global's senior VP and general counsel. Only once since college had they spoken. Erik had needed advice on a company visit to Pakistan, the country where Samir's parents were born.

Samir's black eyebrows lifted and quickly dropped with a grin. "Ah, my friend. I see you're still well versed in the fine art of flattery. If I recall, it served you well around campus."

"Let's not go there in front of Saul." Erik tipped his head to the outgoing firm president. "He hired me based on my resume, but I'm not sure my college antics would've impressed him."

Saul laughed. "I may be a old man, but I was once young at heart."

Samir introduced his wife and a conversation ensued about Saul's retirement plans. Erik listened, but the chatter belied the enormity of his big night. He'd reached the pinnacle of his career.

Fifteen years ago, Erik had let Global management know his frustrations that they weren't moving him up the corporate ranks quickly enough. They had done nothing. After an interview with The Holder Group, he'd received an offer from their London office. The competitor of Global had loved his ambition and offered Erik a step up in his career. He'd grabbed the opportunity.

He studied the Egyptian monument. The temple, built by Emperor Augustus around 15 B.C., was a perfect symbolic location to make this announcement, especially given Erik's desire to return to Manhattan and rule the empire created by Saul. Running Global had always been his hope.

Saul rested a hand on Erik's shoulder. "I'd like you to meet Beryl Foster. She's one of the best CFO's out there."

Beryl. Erik's gut knotted. "Great. Is she around?"

"She couldn't have gone far. We'll be sitting for dinner soon and I believe she's at our table."

Quick. Shrewd. Understated beauty. He'd never seen anybody recite a tax law with such ease, juggle figures in her head with rapid-fire results, or confidently list the pros and cons for any argument without batting an eye. The way she'd done the day he'd been offered a job with The Holder Group. The day their wedding date hung on the brink.

Erik looked at Saul. "Can you excuse me a minute?"

"Sure."

Erik wove his way to the men's room, wading through the employees watching his every move. Good. Let them watch. Saul's were big shoes to fill. Their faces registered curiosity, doubt, maybe a little excitement. At the moment, there was only one face Erik was actually interested in seeing, and by the time he reached the men's room door, he hadn't.

They'd be sitting together at dinner, according to Saul. He had hoped for an air-clearing moment before then. Erik's chest tightened, the way it had after getting Saul's offer. Beryl had been the first thing he thought about when he got the call, but he'd accepted, afraid he might say no if he saw she was still there. Seeing her face on the firm website afterward had caught him off guard. Poised and beautiful, she'd stared back at him like a challenge, reminded him of their last, ill-fated conversation.

As he came out of the men's room, the ladies' room door beside it whooshed open.

"Have a great trip. I want details when you get back."

Pleasant, certain, her voice was just as he remembered. His heart pumped faster.

"Hello, Beryl."

She looked up. Their gazes collided, the sparkling green of her eyes as instantly familiar as the sound of her voice.

"Oh. Erik." Her creamy cheeks blushed pink. Dark chestnut waves caressed her slender neck. She still possessed a pureness that one might easily mistake for naiveté, yet he knew she could hold her own against anyone.

She pushed the bangs from her forehead as she approached, extending her hand like the professional businesswoman she had become. "Congratulations are in order."

"Thank you." He shook her hand. Cool as her approach, impersonal, but fitting after everything they'd once shared. "I was surprised to see you're still with the firm, but happy you've gotten everything you set out to achieve."

"I did." Beryl straightened her shoulders. Behind her eyes, thoughts ran deep.

He shifted his weight, but it did little to balance his skewed confidence. "Your dad and sister, they're well?"

"My sister moved down south." The composure of her expression withered. "Pop passed away last year."

"Oh, God. I'm so sorry." Chet Foster, a great guy. Beryl had adored him, called him her rock since losing her mom as a teenager. Erik fought the urge to hug her, inappropriate not only in his new role, but also after how things had ended. "Was he sick?"

"Cancer." Beryl's stoic frame sagged. "I spent his last week with him, up at the lake."

She'd soon suffer another blow. Erik's changes for the company included a few replacements of top management. One person he planned to steal from The Holder Group was Matthew Quinn, the current chief financial officer and VP of finance. He'd all but promised Matt the job, a promise made before he'd realized Beryl currently held the position. Only at this moment, he was almost sorry he—

"Erik?"

He snapped his attention to the sound of her voice. "I'm sorry. What?"

"How's your family?"

"Everyone is fine." He couldn't tell her how annoyed they'd been with him all those years ago, when he took the job over a life with Beryl. "Thank you for asking."

"Please tell them I said hello. Especially your mom."

Sadness in her tone reminded him how she'd once said being with his mother was like having hers back. "I will. They'll be glad to know you're doing so well."

She blinked, pressed her lips tight. "If you'll excuse me, I need to get back inside. Congratulations again. I look forward to working together." She started to leave, but stopped. "Do me a favor. I'm pretty sure nobody here knows about us. I'd like to keep our old relationship under wraps, if at all possible. I reached this position by working hard, without screwing a single man in power to get here. I'd hate to have rumors start flying now."

The unexpected comment caught him by surprise. After a moment, he snapped out of his stupor. "Sure. I understand."

"Good." She walked away, leaving him slightly tussled on the inside.

He held his head high but couldn't move, his feet suddenly heavy as cinder blocks. Nothing about being near her again was going to be easy.

Keep reading for a special sneak peek of the second Blue Moon Lake novel:

HARVEST MOON

Getting past the librarian's guard...

Trent Jamieson isn't one for virtual romance, but there's something about the intriguing woman he meets on the Internet he can't resist. Then the small town bachelor discovers the mystery woman who shares her secrets with him online is the laced-up librarian in his self-defense class! Veronica Sussingham may just be his toughest student yet. Because how can he show the vulnerable beauty that some men are worth letting your guard down for?

Veronica returned to her hometown seeking shelter for her shattered spirit. The last thing she needs is a blue-eyed charmer who wants to show her how to live—and love—again. Then she discovers Trent is not just another admirer, but a man who knows her deepest secrets. Now Veronica must choose between running from her past—or finding future happiness with the kind of man she swore she'd never fall for....

A Lyrical e-book on sale December 2015.

Learn more about Sharon at
http://www.kensingtonbooks.com/author.aspx/31604

Chapter 1

Three things shine before the world and cannot be hidden. They are the moon, the sun, and the truth...-Buddha

If Veronica Sussingham believed in signs—which she didn't—this was the second one today suggesting she crawl back under the covers and avoid the world. She stood at the doorway and stared at the bed, too stunned to speak.

She drew in a calming breath. "Come on, Boomer. Can't you ever give me a break?"

The two-year-old Newfoundland lifted his eyes while his full tail swished against the patterned quilt. He continued to chew the near-shredded tag dangling off Veronica's brand new silk blouse. The expensive fabric bunched like a ball in his large black paws, and the same slobbery drool resting on his neck also soaked the blouse. Last week's half-eaten electric bill and torn-to-shreds Sunday news was proof the dog had a paper fetish. But a clothing tag?

She marched closer, attempting a stern expression.

Chomp. Chomp. Chomp. He avoided her gaze. If she didn't know better, she'd swear she spotted a grin on his snout.

"Drop it."

Boomer released the tattered tag, and it fell on her bed. At least the training they'd taken last year wasn't a total waste. He hopped down with a thud and headed for the door, the nails of his large paws clicking on the hardwood floors.

She tossed the filthy shirt near the hamper, washed the slobber off her hands in the bathroom sink, then went to her closet to pick a new outfit. It would take more than an early morning broken hot water heater and ruined blouse to keep her from the annual librarian luncheon in Hartford.

She flipped through dresses, shirts, and slacks lined up in neatly separated groups, then arranged by color. A pretty red wraparound dress with capped sleeves caught her eye, one she hadn't worn since the spring. She shrugged off her terrycloth robe, slipped the garment over her head, and tied the side. Stepping to her dresser, she twirled her necklace carousel to her five strands of pearls, in varying gem size and length. Since receiving her first pearl necklace as a gift on her eighteenth birthday, a strand always draped her neck.

She lifted the graduated arrangement and slipped it on. The smooth beads rested against her collarbone, their touch in the familiar place always a source of comfort. She took a brush to her loose curls, dotted on some soft pink lipstick, and slipped into her black, open-toed pumps.

With some time until she needed to head into Hartford, she went into the living room, settled in front of her roll top desk, and logged into her computer. A quick perusal of e-mail showed mostly retailers, which she bypassed, in search of a reply from Ry. Nothing. She swept aside her disappointment and deleted the unwanted spam, but stopped when she hit an online invitation from PartyTime.com, a service she'd used last time she hosted a Christmas gathering at her place.

The subject read, "Gail and Eli's End of Summer Bash." Last year's party had been fun, the annual event one of the few times she'd see her graduate school friends. She opened the invite, double-checked the date on her calendar, then responded yes. Fond memories of her friends brought a smile to her face. A section listed all invited guests, so Veronica figured she'd see who else might be coming.

Sometimes Veronica missed a good old-fashioned paper invite, but the Internet had changed the world. Her friendship with Ry was living proof.

Combing through the list, she noted how half the guests had profiles set up with personalized photographs, including hers—a photo holding Boomer when she first got him. Her gaze swept the faces and names, looking for her closest friends. She skipped past an unfamiliar couple, but then backtracked to take a closer peek. The man in the photo stared back. Panic rushed through her limbs.

For twenty years, Veronica hadn't seen Gary Tishman's face, but his image still haunted her. The clang of a silent alarm screamed inside her head, begged her to close the computer. Only she couldn't move or figure out why he was on the invited guest list.

She scrutinized the face of the man who'd changed her life. Twenty years had added a few pounds, his handsome face slightly fuller. A soft sparkle rested in his eyes, set off by a warm smile. Veronica grimaced, recalling how it was the same bait he'd used to lure her to his side, a mask worn to hide the real monster lurking inside.

The woman at his side was her old friend Carin Cummings, who now wore her honey blond hair in a blunt cut, but otherwise still looked the same. Next to the photo, the name read "Carin Cummings-Tishman." After grad school, Carin had moved west and rarely kept in touch with their posse of friends. She was now married to Gary? It didn't make sense. They hadn't mixed in similar circles back in college, so how did they meet?

Their response to the invitation remained unanswered. Still, sickness twirled in Veronica's stomach as a cold reality hit. If she'd seen him on this online invitation, had he seen her? Did he remember her?

A slow chill tickled the hairs on her arms when a movement fluttered in her peripheral. She quickly jerked around, catching the flurries of her sheer curtains moved by the breeze from an oscillating fan. Taking a calming breath, she stood and went to the fan to shut it off. Outside the window, thick woods surrounded her small house, always giving her privacy and the illusion she lived in a protected fortress. The way her picture randomly appeared on the same website as Gary's, however, told her otherwise.

Gail might be at the librarian luncheon today and could explain how Gary suddenly stepped into Carin's life.

Enthusiasm for today's event withered. Instead, horrible memories of the moment Veronica's life and goals had changed shattered her well-being. For half a second, she considered changing her reply to "no," only a voice inside her head whispered a challenge. *Hasn't the past haunted you long enough?*

Despite the warm breeze drifting through the window, she shivered again. First the broken hot water heater. Then her ruined blouse. Now Gary Tishman's return into her world. Going back to bed and starting the day over wasn't a bad idea.

Instead, she grabbed her purse and went out the door, glad bad things were said to only come in threes. Nothing else could possibly go wrong today.

* * * *

Forty-five minutes after leaving the quiet country roads of Northbridge, Veronica spotted the jagged Hartford skyline. She'd nearly forgotten her one errand before the luncheon and now ran a few minutes behind schedule. The GPS directed her straight to the corporate offices of Resorts Group International.

She pulled into the underground garage and parked. The envelope she'd promised her friend Sophie she'd take to Duncan—Sophie's fiancé—sat on the passenger seat. She slid the package containing his cell phone and signed contracts into the side pocket of her large purse. Lucky for Duncan, Veronica had planned to come into the city today and could make the drop off. Sophie had said he'd woken up so anxious about today's meeting to finalize the sale of his firm he'd forgotten to put on his socks, a surprise to Veronica because the successful executive always seemed to have a handle on all matters.

Fifteen minutes until the luncheon started. She hurried from the car and hoped she wouldn't miss the opening address by one of her favorite Connecticut authors. At the elevator, she tapped the "up" button and waited, jittery with anticipation of getting to her real destination. Bright orange cones placed near a used pile of yellow and black caution tape sat on the concrete floor several feet away from the elevator. She leaned forward to read a sign wedged between the cones. Please Use Stairs.

The loud screech of tires echoed against the walls. She snapped her head around to spot a red Audi TT navigate the corner. The vehicle zipped into a nearby reserved spot, close to the elevator. A rock beat rumbled from the car.

Veronica tapped "up" a few more times. Her peripheral vision caught a tall man with dark hair exiting the Audi. He leaned over and disappeared into the back seat. She gave the button another impatient swipe.

Ding. The doors parted. She hurried inside and scanned the panel until she spotted "RGI Reception-8." She tapped the button and pressed her back to the far wall as the doors glided together.

Bang! An arm covered by a white dress shirt poked between the nearly closed doors, and they popped back open. The guy who'd just pulled into the lot stepped inside, now wearing a fedora, à la Justin Timberlake, and humming a song.

Their eyes met and his humming faded. She quickly looked to the safe spot right above the doors, annoyed she couldn't enjoy her ride alone. He pressed his floor and leaned against the side wall. The doors slammed shut, and the metal box lurched upward.

Veronica peeked at her fellow passenger. His slightly wrinkled shirt hung outside the waist of black jeans and the top three buttons were opened, revealing a small patch of dark chest hair. Proper corporate attire didn't seem to be his thing, surprising in this office building filled with company headquarters.

He cleared his throat, glanced her way. For a nanosecond, she couldn't tear her gaze from his chiseled chin, but when his steel blue eyes softened, heat brushed her cheeks. She forced herself to look at the hardwood elevator floor.

His humming resumed. She again covertly peeked his way. He spread his thick fingers across his thigh and patted out a beat, his head moving with a slight sway to the music. She recognized it. "Oye Como Va," by Santana. The only thing corporate about this guy was his leather attaché and prime parking spot in the garage. Other than that, he belonged in a nightclub or an opening act for JT.

His gaze slowly drifted toward her, his dark lashes flickering as he studied her from head to toe. "You've got something on your dress." He spoke with a delicate, smoky tone, then motioned with his hand to her chest.

She dipped her chin. A dollop of dried toothpaste perched atop the mound of her left breast.

"Damn it," she mumbled. "Thanks."

She frantically rubbed the chalky mess, but the silence in the elevator made her glance his way. He watched her with interest, a little too much interest. Instead of finishing, she folded her arms to hide the mess. She'd deal with this later, without an audience.

His demeanor switched as deep lines burrowed along his forehead. "Oh, shit." He patted his pant pockets on both sides, front and back, and took two long steps to the panel. He hit "G" several times with his thumb.

Once was all he needed, and she'd been about to let him know, but her own impatient behavior earlier in the garage made her stop.

An exaggerated groan thundered from gears overhead. *Thump! Boom! Clunk!* The steel box vibrated. Veronica swayed. *Thud!* The elevator stopped with a jerk. Veronica's arms flailed. Her feet lifted from the floor. Her purse slipped off her arm. No control, she slammed into the other passenger, sending his hat flying. He wrapped his arms around her waist, but the force of her body propelled them both into the wall. They slid to the floor. Veronica sat posed on his lap, like a ventriloquist's dummy.

"Jesus. You okay?" His blue eyes widened and blinked a few times as they stared into hers.

Move. Move. Move.

She inhaled, filled her lungs with air, but couldn't ignore the protective way he still held onto her. "Yes. I'm fine."

She wiggled to get off and he released her. She shimmied away and pushed herself to the opposite wall, where she sat on the floor and tried to regroup.

"Sorry I knocked you over." She glanced up and followed the direction of his eyes, right to the spot where her skirt had lifted to the tippy-top of one thigh. Grabbing the hem of her dress, she tugged it down to her knees and glared at him.

He looked up without an ounce of guilt and ran his hand through his black hair, setting the strands askew. "Don't worry about it."

Concern etched the corners of his eyes as his gazed skipped over her. He stood and extended his arm. "Let me help you up."

She shook her head and pressed her hand to the floor. "I'm fine."

Once up, she smoothed her skirt, adjusted the sash at her waist, and swiped at the caked on toothpaste, loosening a few crumbs. "Next time you decide to change floors mid-ride, you could just hit the button once."

He raised a brow but said nothing and walked over to retrieve his hat. Replacing it on his head, he went to the panel, pressed emergency several times, and started pounding on the steel doors. "Hey! Anybody out there? We're stuck in the elevator!"

She stared, silently willing him to stop yelling. Hysteria never solved anything.

"Help! Anybody?" He waited a few seconds and turned to her. "I can't believe this. I've spent the past ten hours at airports, left my cell phone in the car, unless I mistakenly left it back at the United Airlines lounge at O'Hare. And now...now this."

He turned around and made a fist, one step from giving the door another pounding. Veronica searched the recesses of her memory for the details from an article she'd read online about elevator safety.

"You should relax. Once you push the emergency button, there's not much more we can do."

He glanced back and chuffed a disagreeable sound, right before hitting the door several times. After a moment, he gave up and paced in the small space.

She fiddled with the smooth beads of her pearl necklace, but they didn't bring their usual sense of calm. The stranger continued his random patrol, his thoughts his own.

Veronica recalled the article details. She stepped to the door and peeked through the crack. "There's light up there." She glanced up to see where they had gotten stuck and returned to the crack, hoping to gauge how close they were to signs of life. "We're close to the fifth floor. Someone should be here soon."

He moved behind her, too close for her comfort. In the space above her head, he pressed his eye to the crack.

She gritted her teeth and stepped aside. "I'd be happy to move."

He didn't respond, only banged on the door again and yelled, "Can anybody hear us?"

She sighed, loudly, hoping to make a point. He continued banging. When he stopped, she cleared her throat.

He turned, raised his brows. "Yes?"

"Relaxing in a crisis lets you think clearly. You might want to give it a try."

His mouth slackened and eyebrows rose, as if nobody had ever asked him to chill. Looking up, he studied the ceiling. "I'll bet that panel pops out. I could help you shimmy up there." His gaze dropped to the lower half of her dress, and he wrestled with a smile. "Or you help me up."

"I'm not doing either. Want to know the first rule of elevator safety?" She tipped her head but didn't wait for his answer. "Stay put. Climbing out is the last thing you should do. So save your energy, Bruce Willis. We could be in here a while."

"Bruce Willis?"

"In *Die Hard*. Wasn't he in an elevator when he fought those terrorist?" She again brushed at the toothpaste remains. "Not that I typically watch his movies."

He chuckled and the frustration evident on his face slipped away as he considered her for a moment. He took a step toward her. "Sorry. I'll calm down. You're ri—"

The elevator lurched. Veronica grabbed his arms at the same time he reached for hers. They steadied themselves for a few seconds, their eyes locked. The elevator smoothed and each let go.

She leaned over and picked her purse up from the floor just as the doors opened at the fourth floor.

He motioned with a sweep of his hand. "Ladies first."

She nodded and hurried out, greeted by a short man wearing maintenance overalls.

"You two okay?" he asked.

She hoisted her purse over her shoulder. "I am, thank you. Which way to the stairs?"

He pointed down the hallway.

"Thanks." She hurried down the hall. If she dropped Duncan's package off fast, she might still catch the keynote speaker's address.

"Hey?"

She stopped and turned at the sound of her fellow passenger's voice.

He studied her with a curious stare, then grinned, kind of sweet, as if they'd become best buddies during their quest for elevator survival. "Bye. Nice to meet you."

"Oh, right. Good-bye." She rushed inside the stairwell, flustered but not really sure why. What else could go wrong today?

* * * *

Trent Jamieson wedged his fingers alongside the passenger seat of his car and breathed a relieved sigh when they brushed against the smooth edges of his cell phone. How it ended up there during his drive to the office from Bradley Airport he'd never know.

He retrieved the device and hit the "on" button, but nothing happened. Well, a phone with a dead battery was better than one sitting at O'Hare. He tucked it in his pocket and got on the elevator, despite what just happened. Even in his crappy life, with all his crappy luck, he didn't think he'd get stuck twice in one day.

Maybe the stalled elevator was a foreshadowing of his future. The powers above hinting he should be glad this was his last day working at RGI. Or maybe the message was he should stay here, in a steel box for the rest of his life, not even try to make a fresh start.

Duncan had pushed for him to leave the company when RGI sold and wanted him to join him at Litchfield Hills Vineyard as VP of Marketing. Having his brother nearly beg him to make the change made him consider it more seriously. Only a few years ago, his brother had almost fired him from RGI, but Trent mended his ways. This new offer was quite generous.

The steel doors parted. He headed down the hallway to his office, the brunette he'd been stuck with making him smile. The cute way she'd played with her pearl necklace was revealing and the honesty of her comments refreshing. A bit uptight, and yet, there was something about her he liked but couldn't pinpoint. The perplexed look she'd given him when he said good-bye made his ego deflate, but if their time together was any longer, he'd have bet he could change her view of him. He loved a challenge. She, on the other hand, didn't seem to want one.

He entered his office, catching a nice view of downtown Hartford from his window. Empty bookcases and cardboard boxes stacked in the corner meant his secretary had done some packing. She'd even cleared the top of his desk, except for a note.

He searched through his briefcase for his phone charger, plugged in the phone, then read the note.

Welcome back. I'm at lunch. You're packed except for some personal items in your lower drawer.
Back by one. T.
P.S. You're very messy.

He opened the drawer. No wonder Tina passed on this one.

One by one, he lifted items from the pile, a potpourri of things he had no other place to store. Notes he'd saved from women he'd met in his travels were tossed into the nearby trash can, along with some paperbacks used to entertain him while flying around the globe. He smiled as he removed a small statue of a hula dancer given to him by the resort manager at their Maui location. Exotic Luanne, who'd taken him to see the sights when they weren't working. He pushed the dancer to the keeper pile.

At the bottom he came across a framed photo of Gemma, one he'd tossed in the drawer the day he'd been served the divorce papers. A gentle ache pressed to his heart, an ache for everything that had gone wrong in their marriage. She'd taken no interest in following him on the road to sobriety. A journey she needed as badly as he had. He'd tried to get her to join him in rehab, but she wouldn't. Her request for a divorce had blown him away. All so she could marry a man Trent had witnessed dabbling in the world of cocaine, the same bad place he'd successfully left several years ago.

One thing he'd learned in rehab was you couldn't help someone who didn't want to help themselves. Sometimes, keeping himself afloat was all he could bear.

"Knock, knock." Duncan stood at the doorway dressed in khakis, his new casual style in the office since he'd announced the sale of his firm. "Tina said you survived an airport nightmare."

"Barely. My first flight was delayed. I missed my connection. They canceled my second connection, and the rest is history. Another reason to be thankful my traveling days are over. When is the big powwow to sign the papers on the sale?"

"Two." Duncan frowned and ran a hand through his sandy curls. "I hope the new owners will stick to their word and keep most of the current staff."

Trent nodded. "Me, too. Hey, be glad you're getting out of this building. The damn elevator got stuck again. Second time this year it's happened to me."

The mahogany eyes of the dark-haired beauty from the elevator teased his thoughts, making it hard for him to let go.

"Damn shame," Trent mumbled.

"What?" His brother laughed, shaking Trent loose from those long, lovely legs.

"What?"

"You're talking to yourself."

"Am I?"

The brothers laughed together now, yet the woman he'd never see again didn't dodge his thoughts. Instead, a part of her settled inside him, in a vulnerable place he rarely visited. His own laughter died down, and he wished he'd introduced himself.

"Penny for your thoughts," Duncan said.

Only then did Trent realize he'd fallen silent again. "A penny won't cut it."

"Okay, a dollar."

"I got stuck in the elevator with a woman. A sexy, rule abiding number." Trent tried to sound cavalier, as if those long legs didn't haunt him.

"Rule abiding, huh? Sounds just like what the doctor ordered for you. Did you get her number?"

"She ran off before I could ask."

"Oh. Well, aren't you seeing...Ruby?"

"I dated her last summer. I'm seeing Angie now."

"Oh."

Duncan looked confused, so Trent changed the subject. "Listen, before I left on this last site visit, did you see I moved myself into the cottage at the farm?"

"I did."

"The place is a far cry from the shack you showed me last spring. I'd never have known it was the same place. Thanks for fixing it up."

"Sophie handled renovations. She did a great job." Duncan's face softened when he said his fiancée's name. "Will you stay up there tonight?"

"Maybe. I have a date later today in Hartford. So I'm not making any promises."

"With Ru... I mean, Angie? So how long have you been dating her?"

Trent turned in the chair, pressed the cell phone "on" switch, and the phone came to life. "Guess it's been about a month now."

"I can't keep up. You need to settle down."

Trent only laughed. Settling down again didn't seem in his cards these days, only he couldn't quite get a pulse on what left him so unsatisfied with the women he dated.

"Oh, don't forget, at four the staff is having a going away party for us."

"I didn't." Trent searched for his contact list for Angie's number.

"One other thing."

He looked up, met Duncan's stare, more serious than a moment ago.

"I'm really glad you're joining me on the vineyard. Having some family with me as I get this new business off the ground means a lot."

Trent's heart filled with a love he found hard to express. He and Duncan hadn't been close while growing up. A long and winding trail of bad choices made by Trent had left everyone else in his family with the notion he was a screw up. But not Duncan.

"Thanks. I'll do everything in my power to help make the vineyard a success."

Duncan studied his feet for a few seconds before looking back up. "Sometimes you've got to shake up your life a bit to find the gold. I know this will be different for you, but Northbridge is a special place."

Trent nodded, even though he worried about how he'd be received in the close-knit community. "Part of the reason I said yes."

"Bring Angie to Sophie's party on Saturday night, so I can meet her."

"I'll see."

Trent returned to his search for Angie's number but couldn't ignore the nervous tug at his gut, rocking the confidence it took to make a move to the small Connecticut town. Confidence easily shaken by the stupid things he'd done there many years ago, acts capable of threatening his chance for a fresh start.

CPSIA information can be obtained
at www.ICGtesting.com
Printed in the USA
FFOW04n1553141015
17722FF